AMBUSH
LONDON N...

Candy stopped at the second of the doors opposite the stairs and produced a key from her purse. She opened the door, stepped inside, and held it open with her elbow for Fallon to go ahead of her. He noted the name DR. F. VELKER inscribed on a piece of card held in a metal frame on the door. As he moved into the doorway, his hand came up instinctively to finger the Browning Hi-Power automatic in the armpit of his jacket. He had barely begun taking in the drably furnished, somewhat antiquated sitting room inside, when everything happened at once.

Beyond an open door across the room was a black man with a gun aimed straight at him. At the same instant as the sight registered, George shouted, "WATCH YERSELF, BERN!" Fallon knew he was too slow as he recoiled back from the doorway, but a shove delivered with the power of a swiping grizzly bear helped him on his way just as the sound of two shots cracked. . . .

**PRAISE FOR JAMES P. HOGAN'S
THE PROTEUS OPERATION**

Books by James P. Hogan

THE INFINITY GAMBIT

James P. Hogan

BANTAM BOOKS
NEW YORK · TORONTO · LONDON · SYDNEY · AUCKLAND

THE INFINITY GAMBIT
A Bantam Falcon Book / April 1991

FALCON *and the portrayal of a boxed "f" are trademarks of Bantam Books, a*
division of Bantam Doubleday Dell Publishing Group, Inc.

ISBN 0-553-28918-7

Published simultaneously in the United States and Canada

Bantam Books are published by Bantam Books, a division of Bantam Doubleday
Dell Publishing Group, Inc. Its trademark, consisting of the words "Bantam
Books" and the portrayal of a rooster, is Registered in U.S. Patent and
Trademark Office and in other countries. Marca Registrada. Bantam Books,
666 Fifth Avenue, New York, New York 10103.

PRINTED IN THE UNITED STATES OF AMERICA

RAD   0 9 8 7 6 5 4 3 2 1

To:
Cathy
Sue
Tracy
Evie
Juanita

THE
INFINITY
GAMBIT

Prologue

THE BABY WAS EMACIATED AND COVERED WITH flies. Its eyes looked glazed, and its breathing came fitfully. Jomar had seen the signs before and knew that it was dying. His wife, Neraya, knew it too. They hadn't said so to Miralee, but pretended instead that they shared her hope. There was no need for her to know yet.

Word was that a truck would be coming to Jaquesville from the capital today. The foreigners would be handing out food. Jomar watched sullenly from his chair as the woman and the girl got ready to leave. The chair was a tubular steel frame with a roughly woven mat of hemp fiber covering the space where the seat had been. Some boxes and a broken stool, a plywood packing crate serving as a table, a doorless refrigerator used as a closet, some grubby mattresses, and a scrap of oily canvas on the floor completed the furnishings of the single-room shanty that they called a home. Jomar was sullen because the way his family had to live was a blow to his pride as a man. . . . And because his daughter's child was dying, and there was nothing he could do.

"There will be many soldiers in the town," he said. "You know that always means trouble. Stay away from the soldiers."

Miralee picked up the piece of red cotton printed with white that she used as a scarf against the sun and tied it around her head. It hung bright and pretty against her neck. "But we must go. They say there will be fish and millet grain. Good for making milk, and then Baby will soon get well again."

Neraya caught his eye and smiled quickly with her mouth only. "We will be careful, Jomar," she promised.

Miralee adjusted the sling that she had made from a piece of sacking and lifted the baby carefully into it. It would have been better not to move it, but she was young and didn't know. Besides, it was too late now to make any difference. Jomar watched and said nothing.

The two women left. Jomar sat on his chair and stared at the sunlight streaming in through the doorway. In the narrow alley outside he could see the bare frame of a child's tricycle, an abandoned shoe, empty beer bottles, an upturned rubbish can, its contents scattered by dogs. Mindless music blared from a transistor radio in another shanty nearby.

In the old days, his father had tilled the land and grown food. Hard work, yes, but his family had eaten. He had known pride. Then the socialists had come, promising wealth for all. They had taken the land from the farmers, the money from the merchants, the factories from the foreigners. They distributed transistor radios and told the people that they now owned everything. But all Jomar was aware of owning was what he could see in the room around him.

He wondered where his son, Imo, had disappeared to since daybreak. What would cause an impetuous and angry sixteen-year-old to start acting furtively and stay away sometimes for days at a time? And Imo had been spending long hours talking with Neraya's sister, Annette, who was involved with the rebels and used her position as a medical technician in Kinnube to steal government drugs and medicines for them. In her last visit she had hinted that she would be going overseas for a while. Very probably that had something to do with her underground work too.

Could Imo be getting himself mixed up with the rebels? A faint smile softened Jomar's features for a moment at the thought of it. Now, *that* would be something to feel proud of, he told himself.

Julius Embatto, Director of the Department of State Security, lit one of his personalized gold-monogrammed cigarettes while the tape recorder rewound. He exhaled a stream of smoke, then leaned forward and pressed the "play" button to hear the recording again.

"State Security, hello?" The voice of the desk officer at the main entrance of the headquarters building, taking the call.

"Listen, and listen well, because I will say this only one time." The voice that answered, a man's, was low but firm. There was tension in it, but tempered by a determination to say what had to be said. The slow, even pacing of the words suggested that they were being read from a prepared statement. "I represent the Zugendan Republican Front. We have learned that an attempt will be made to assassinate the chief of police, Denyaka, when he attends the distribution of rations in the marketplace at Jaquesville today. It will be by means of a bomb inside the drainage culvert from the cattle pens, which runs beneath the area where the truck will be parked. Chief of Police Denyaka is no friend of the ZRF, and we have no interest in saving his life. We are telling you this out of concern for the innocent people of Zugenda, and to disprove in advance any claim that this attempted atrocity was the work of the ZRF. End of message."

"Sorry, but we've got a bad connection. I lost you for a while there." The desk officer again, trying to keep the caller on the line. "Can you say again—" He stopped as the line went dead.

Embatto turned off the recorder and sat frowning as he tried to associate the voice with known subversives. He was still staring at the machine when a tap sounded on the door. He looked up. "Who is it?"

"Corporal Utamme from the guardroom. You sent for me, sir."

"Yes. Come in."

The door opened. Utamme entered and saluted awkwardly. Embatto leaned back in the chair and looked him up and down while continuing to draw on his cigarette. Not yet twenty, probably, but with a shirt properly buttoned for a change, and his beret on straight instead of pushed to one side at the usual, supposedly jaunty angle to impress the girls. A cut above the average fresh-from-the-bush cowboy in his first uniform, Embatto concluded.

Embatto gestured at the recorder on his desk. "You were the desk officer who took this?"

"Yes, sir."

"How long ago did the call come in?"

"About fifteen minutes ago."

"You didn't get a trace?"

"He cleared down too quickly, sir."

"Hmm . . ." The eyes had an intelligent depth to them, but at the same time roamed the room nervously, unwilling to meet Embatto's and unsure of where else to settle. It was the face of a man who understood things and who would think about them. Thinkers were dangerous. This could be a problem. Embatto reflected for a few seconds longer, and then looked up again. "Have you told anyone else about this, Corporal?"

"No, sir. I did as you said when I called you and sent the tape straight up."

"Very good." Embatto felt relieved. He sat back and looked up at the corporal inquiringly. "You are aware of the significance of this, I take it?"

"I . . . It's not for me to say, sir."

Embatto opened the center drawer of the desk and took out a numbered, sealed envelope of the kind used for conveying special orders, along with a notepad and a letter-size envelope, both with the same monogram as the cigarettes. "Well, it could be a hoax, but obviously we can't afford to take chances." He took a pen from its holder on the desk and scribbled rapidly. "I want you to take this to Colonel Freyno, who is with the Second Special Action Detachment near Rivusi. This is absolutely confidential, so mention it to no one and go there alone. An escort will meet you at the upper bridge. Tell Colonel Freyno that I will take care of the situation here in the city personally. Is that clear?"

"Yes, sir."

"That's all, Corporal." Embatto handed the envelope across. "Your efficiency is commendable. It won't be overlooked."

"Thank you, sir."

Embatto waited for a few minutes after Utamme had left. Then he picked up his secure phone and called Freyno via radio link. After establishing that the colonel was alone, he instructed him to switch in the frequency scrambler.

"A Corporal Utamme is on his way up to you with sealed orders. I've told him he'll be met at the upper bridge."

"Yes," Freyno acknowledged.

"He is a potential threat to the security of the operation today," Embatto said evenly. "When he gets there, kill him."

Chapter One

IF ANIELLO FRANGINI HAD HAD MORE BRAINS AND refrained from resorting to the kidnapping of children to enforce his political demands, he wouldn't have ended his days prematurely at the age of twenty-four, stretched out on a bed in the Novotel hotel in Paris with two closely spaced .22-caliber holes in the middle of his forehead.

The assortment of violently disposed misfits and malcontents who had nursed their various grievances under his leadership at different times numbered typically between ten and twenty, and had begun as a splinter faction of the Italian Red Brigade. A ragtag affair operating in the fringe world of European political-linked crime, it sought to legitimize a record of kidnappings, murders, and small-time bank holdups through a fairly standard recipe of anticapitalist semantics and leftist ideology. Aniello had seen it as merely a prelude to bigger things to come, which would propel him to glamour and notoriety on the international terrorist scene, another "Carlos." But he hadn't had the connections. So he had kept the funds coming in by subcontracting the group's services to other, longer-established groups in the network. The Japanese Red Army had begun the same way.

And that was how Aniello had agreed to front for the Belgian anti-NATO "Cellules Communistes Combattantes" and provide the snatch squad that had grabbed the ten-year-old daughter of the technical director of a French military electronics supplier, the Compagnie Electronique Spatiale. The arrangement worked well, and the child had been released earlier that day for a quarter-million-dollar ransom. With CCC doing the negotiating while Aniello's people held the hostage, the negotiators had been able to claim that the kidnappers were acting according to set instructions and not under their control. Now, according to the plan, all that should have remained to complete the job was for Aniello and the CCC moneyman to meet at the hotel, and for Aniello to deliver the proceeds, minus his agreed cut. The only problem was, Aniello wouldn't be there.

Bernard Fallon finished transferring twenty-five wads, each of a hundred hundred-dollar bills, into plastic bags and packed the bags into a black Samsonite briefcase. He peeled off the surgical gloves that he had used—the cash would doubtless have been marked by an ultraviolet-fluorescent dye and possibly other devices—sealed the gloves in another plastic bag for disposal later, and snapped shut the lid of the Samsonite. As he stood up from the chair at the room's bureau-cum-vanity, he clicked his tongue at the corpse on the bed and shook his head reproachfully. "Fancy using second-raters for your protection." The two Tunisian bodyguards should have stuck to Aniello like glue all the time the money was in his possession, but Fallon had lured them to the far end of the hotel with a ruse for a few vital minutes. "Which I'm afraid, my old son, makes you a bit of a Berkeley Hunt."

Fallon spoke in the flat, softly cynical tone of the native Londoner. He was thirty-eight, with a lean and supple 180-pound frame which in years gone by the British Special Air Service had shaped into a fine-tuned coordination of reflexes and muscle. He had a dimple-chinned, puckish face with brown, curly hair that he kept comfortably short without a part, though a shade full above the collar and with generous sideburns. His eyes were deep and contemplative most of the time, varying from amber to dark brown depending on the light, and tending to take on a lazily distant look when his mind was at its most active, a look that could be both deceptive and disarming.

He crossed to the door and opened it a fraction to check the corridor, then went down to the lobby and left the hotel. Walking quickly, he went a block and a half back to his own hotel and checked into his room. By then, he estimated, the two Tunisians should have returned to Aniello's suite. He called the Novotel and asked for the room number.

"*Oui?*" The voice that answered sounded fearful and

shaky. Hardly surprising, considering what they had just come back to.

Fallon spoke in accented French, which could have been from the Flemish-speaking parts of Belgium. "Who I am does not matter. You are being set up. The CCC is double-crossing Aniello."

"Who is this?" the voice demanded.

"I said it does not matter. But their hit man is there in the Novotel. He is using the name of Duvalier. I thought that Aniello might like to know."

Fallon hung up. "Duvalier" was in fact the pseudonym that the moneyman coming to meet Aniello would be using. He opened the Samsonite again and put the plastic bags containing the money into a mailing carton already addressed to the board of directors of the Compagnie Electronique Spatiale. He didn't want to touch any of this stuff himself—the agreed twenty-percent commission would be paid in clean money via a regular transfer to London. On top of the wads of bills he placed a piece of notepaper bearing the letters "BF" scrawled with a distinctive flourish, which was his whimsical hallmark—surely only a bloody fool would have chosen to make a living this way. Above the initials he drew a simple design of a fork formed by two elongated, curvy shapes tapering to points, suggesting a pair of ass's ears. It could also, depending on the variation that he chose to emphasize, be read as the indomitable Churchillian "V" sign, or alternatively the ultimate British gesture of derision as conveyed with the fingers reversed. He sealed the carton, which he would mail from the airport, picked up his already packed garment bag, and went downstairs to check out.

In the Novotel farther along the street, meanwhile, a Monsieur Duvalier was paged to the front desk. A minute later, a swarthy, mustached man in a black suit went up to the desk, where one of the clerks handed him a large envelope easily recognizable from a distance. Duvalier moved a short distance away, opened it, and frowned in bemusement as he read the slip of paper inside. The message wasn't important; but now the two Tunisians who had been watching over newspapers from chairs on opposite sides of the lobby knew who he was. They nodded to each other, folded their papers, and rose to follow when he left.

In revenge for losing the money as well as their moneyman, the CCC would take out more of Aniello's operation. And the ensuing internecine exchanges would save European counterterrorist units such as France's GIGN and the Belgian ESI a considerable amount of trouble and expense. And a lot of would-be victims would be spared from other crimes which now wouldn't happen. Everything smooth and without hitches for once, Fallon reflected, as he allowed himself to relax fully for the first time in days and sat back in the taxicab, gazing with satisfaction at scenery along the route to Charles de Gaulle Airport.

Less than an hour later, he took off aboard a British Airways Boeing 757 on his return flight to London.

Chapter Two

THE M4 MOTORWAY IS A SEVENTY-MILE-AN-HOUR traffic jam snaking across southern England from London to the West Country—one of the web of radiating concrete-and-steel trachea through which the sprawling metropolitan organism inhales its morning intake of life-giving vehicular gas, each molecule carrying its quota of people atoms to oxygenate and revivify the cells, and expels it again at the end of the day. The first ten miles of the M4 also form the principal road connection between Heathrow Airport and the western reaches of the city.

Fallon drove the silver-gray Mercedes at an unhurried pace, savoring the slow release of tension that came at the end of a successful job and allowing the last of the evening's home-bound neurotics to work off their pent-up frustrations in the fast lane. Presumably they needed this brief, nightly flurry of verve and exuberance: a fleeting brush with reality on the way from eight make-work hours in an office to four comatose ones in front of a television. Fallon was happy to stay out of it. The last thing that his metabolism needed right now was an adrenaline trip. A big part of living life to the full, he sometimes thought, was to have escaped the necessity of escaping from it.

Past Hammersmith and Earl's Court Road, he turned north off Cromwell Road into the southern fringe of Kensington, where Kelso Close lay concealed in the maze of twisting streets, narrow mews, and cheerful urban anarchy that preceded the orderly rows of stucco Regency cliffs surrounding Queens Gate.

Number four Kelso Close was an architectural oddity, even for London, that shocked tradition and logic, while delighting the imagination. Part of the cellars and some sections of garden wall at the rear went back to a large farm or manor house that had occupied the spot in the

days when Kensington was a village far to the west of the
city. That had burned down and been rebuilt as a Georgian
squire's residence, part of which remained, altered and
modernized, as the kitchen and dining room; later, various
experiments in extension and demolition by successive
waves of Victorians left behind a library, two formal sitting
rooms, and a glazed turret with a spiral staircase leading to
a guest suite on one side. When London finally arrived, it
hid the resulting potpourri of styles behind a wall and
shrubbery at the end of a cul-de-sac as if unsure of what to
do with it, screened it behind imposing frontages all facing
outward in their mild embarrassment, and flowed onward
and around as if hoping that it might go away. Remodeling
exercises since then had seen the introduction of a modern
sunken lounge and living area, along with the creature
comforts to be expected of the twentieth century, and
since Fallon's acquisition of the place, a number of specialized adaptations connected with his work. The house also
boasted that priceless residential asset of crowded central
London: its own basement garage.

He found Julia, his secretary and guardian of the home
front, sorting through papers at the large desk in the
room that functioned as an office, four steps down from
the library and angling off in an odd direction. There was
also a computer terminal and printer on a side table, a
photocopier, several steel filing cabinets, and almost a
whole wall of shelves sagging under untidy loads of books,
boxes, papers, and various items accumulated over years.
It was the kind of office that had evolved into comfortable
surroundings that people liked to work in, not the kind
that was designed by designers to impress clients. A
smaller room opening off the far end contained a console
for an exterior closed-circuit-TV system and other security
devices. Known as the "bridge," it was normally kept
locked when any but a few special visitors were in the house.

Julia was in her late forties he guessed, having honored
tradition despite their years of working together by never
having asked. Originally from somewhere near Boston,
poised and punctilious in the kind of way that goes with
afternoon tea and drawing-room plays, yet with an American stylishness that stopped short of tweed and cameos,
she was New England come in search of the Old; a
fugitive from the final triumph of matter over mind,

returning to the wellspring of Western thought and tradition before its waning trickle ran dry. She had rich, wavy auburn hair curling up at shoulder length, a rounded figure, and deep, dark, ever-inquiring eyes that interrogated everything around her constantly with the curiosity of a cat in a new house. She was wearing a plain green, low-collared dress with a pearl necklace when Fallon sauntered in and tossed his Samsonite down on the desk.

Julia pushed the papers aside and sat back in the chair. "The wanderer returns."

"On the M4 at this time of day? You've got to be joking. You won't get much chance to wander far astray there."

"Was it bad?"

"The usual. It must be the longest, thinnest car park in the country. They've dug it up again at Heston."

"I don't think I've ever seen an English motorway in a continuous piece from one end to the other," Julia agreed.

"I've got a theory about it," Fallon murmured as he ran an eye over the desk. "Once upon a time they dug a hole, you see—"

"For reasons undisclosed?"

"For reasons known only to municipal authorities."

"Ah."

"And after the customary period of contemplation thereof, they filled it in again. But they found they had a pile of dirt left over. So they decided to bury it ten miles farther down the road. However, that left another pile to get rid of, and the hole has been propagating itself round the motorway system ever since, returning periodically to its point of origin like Halley's Comet in its orbit." He cocked a questioning eye at Julia. "What do you think?"

"Ingenious and plausible," she pronounced. "It meets the bureaucratic definition of common sense. The unions would love it too."

Fallon scanned the top sheets from a wad of computer printout text on a shelf by the desk. "What've we got now, then?"

"Oscar has uncovered an urban redevelopment scam. The city officials are in collusion with developers to create depressed areas that can be bought up at bargain-basement prices, then rezoned and rebuilt for selling off later. I got the idea from something I was reading about that's going on in Hollywood."

Oscar was a fictional character. Julia wrote thrillers under the pen name of John Clyde. In fact, John Clyde's was quite a well-known name, conjuring up images in readers' minds of raciness, excitement, and glamour. Julia Clarrel's was not. She had wanted to write, not become a celebrity, and working ostensibly for Fallon suited her temperament and her taste. It was probably better for business, too, since it would no doubt have jaded many enthusiastic fans to learn that the John Clyde books were written by a hardly racy American female edging into later middle age.

"Hmm . . . do you think that might be why the Soviets are being agreeable about scrapping some of their missiles?" Fallon asked, turning another sheet as he read. "They don't need them. Our own urban planners are devastating all our cities for them. We've wiped out more of London since the war than Goering ever dreamed of."

Julia nodded. It was a recurring theme of Fallon's. "And what's more, the victims pay. It's neat." She began scribbling a note in a pad. "I'll have to work that in somewhere."

Fallon sat down in an easychair opposite the desk, crossing his legs in an attitude of exaggerated repose. "Anyway, you haven't asked me how things went with our friends at CES," he said. "Don't you want to know if we got Maurice's daughter out?"

"I already know that you did," Julia replied, still writing and not looking up. "Congratulations."

Fallon stared at her, frowning as he went over in his mind everything he'd said and done since entering the room. "Okay, you've got me," he conceded finally. "How?"

Julia glanced at him and inclined her head to indicate the navy blazer he was wearing. "Just above the pocket. And your nails."

Fallon looked down. There was a faint smudge of fine white powder on his right pocket. He turned over his hands and saw more traces at the base of his cuticles. "Ah," he said, nodding. "The French chalk." He had used it to lubricate the insides of the surgical gloves.

"So presumably you handled the money, which CES wouldn't have parted with unless they had Felice back,"

Julia completed. She put down her pen and looked up. "How did the rest of it go?"

"Aniello's with the *ániellos*. And very probably three-C's bagman is being fitted for his wings, too, by now, so we should be hearing about some brotherly infighting across the water in the near future." Fallon braced his elbows back above the arms of the chair and stretched. "What else is new here? Anything?"

"Yes, as a matter of fact. Perry surfaced again yesterday." Fallon raised his eyebrows. "And how's he?"

"Just fine."

Perry was a former officer in the Rhodesian security forces whom Fallon had known in his SAS days, and who reappeared from time to time. Much of Fallon's new business came through discreet personal referrals.

"What did he want?"

"He's been contacted by some people who are looking for Boris," Julia replied, meaning Boris Fugleman, which was the principal alias that Fallon operated under professionally. "It sounds as if somebody somewhere wants to raise a private army."

Fallon wrinkled his nose. "Mercenaries? Perry knows I'm not in that line."

"He knows. But he said he thought you might want to pick it up if things were a bit slack."

"Oh, really? The old sod. It sounds more to me like something he doesn't want to be bothered with himself."

Julia paused just long enough to convey the right shade of empathy. "Yes, I, ah...did rather get that impression."

"What else did he say about it?"

"Not much."

Fallon grunted and rubbed an eyebrow dubiously with a knuckle. "What do you think?"

"It can't do any harm to find out, I suppose."

"How are things otherwise?"

"Actually, a bit slack."

"Hmm...So what do we have?"

"Just a phone number and a name: Mr. Black. Call him to set up a rendezvous."

"Did you check it out with Martin?" They had a friend in the engineering department of the British Telecommunications Corporation, who could trace telephone numbers.

"Of course," Julia replied. "It's one of several ex-directory numbers assigned to the embassy of the People's Democratic Republic of Zugenda."

Fallon stopped rubbing his eyebrow and looked at her in surprise. Zugenda was one of the problem-plagued countries that had emerged from the confusion of postcolonial Africa. It was a relatively minor state located to the north of the central region and extending into the sub-Saharan belt. "I'm not sure I even know where their embassy is," he said.

"It's in Marylebone, not far from Regents Park," Julia said. "So it doesn't sound as if Boris is being tracked down by somebody with a grudge to settle"—which was always a thing to be wary of in Fallon's chosen line of business.

He pondered for a few moments longer, then nodded. "Okay. I'll see if I can set something up for tomorrow." With that he turned his attention back to the printout. "Is this what I've been busy with this weekend?"

"Yes."

He turned his attention back to the sheets and settled back to read.

For officially it was he and not she who was the author of the books. The same arrangement that afforded Julia the obscurity that she preferred also provided Fallon with his cover. The arrangement worked quite well. But it did mean that Fallon's picture never appeared on any of the books, and that nobody in the world at large knew what John Clyde looked like. His publisher complained despairingly of being saddled with what had to be the most publicity-shy writer in the business.

Chapter Three

FALLON ROSE EARLY THE NEXT MORNING, FEELING recharged and ready to take on whatever the world had in store for him next. The tension of seeing a job through, followed by the release upon completion and a good night's rest generally had that effect. Danger was in many ways similar to sex. Each offered the same kind of euphoria in return for meeting its own kind of challenge, and the ever-renewed lure with both lay in the promise of the unknown and the unexperienced. Survival, reproduction, rivalry, competition. It all linked together, and those who refused to accept it got ill from trying to repress themselves. Or else they wiped themselves out playing substitute games on rush-hour motorways.

For breakfast he made himself a cheese omelet with hot taco sauce, Mexican style, then refilled his coffee cup and settled down to begin reading the file of clippings and notes on Zugenda that Julia had collected and left with him before returning to her flat in Belgravia the previous evening.

Zugenda had been in the public eye for several years as a basket case among emerging postcolonial Third World nations. Shaky at the best of times, its economy was collapsing under the rigidly Marxist policies of the current regime headed by President Aloysius Molokutu, whom a military coup had brought into power almost ten years previously. Its agricultural program was a shambles, foreign-investment capital had either been seized or had fled the country, and the media had been featuring grim documentaries and appeals for aid, along with pictures of grieving parents and potbellied babies. Predictably, the country was also in the throes of civil war between the authorities and a rebel faction called the Zugendan Republican Front, which of course was fighting for nationalism against the nation, and to secure the people's freedom from the people's government. Not surprisingly, there were widespread stories of the systematic use of terror, with each side blaming the other as the prime instigator in the endless cycle of atrocity, reprisal, retaliation, and escalation. Molokutu also accused the ZRF of conducting a campaign of economic sabotage, to which he attributed the country's problems.

From what Fallon could make of it, the whole thing boiled down to another squabble for loot and power between tribal divisions that predated the irrationalities of long-dead European politicians, with the wrong people caught in the middle, as always. His first inclination was thus to view the prospects with something less than enthusiasm; but since he had spent some time in parts of Africa himself in his SAS days and still counted more than a few close friends there, he also felt a degree of curiosity. Deciding that it could do no harm to find out a little more, he called the number that Perry had given to Julia.

"Hello?" A guarded voice answered.

"I'm trying to contact a Mr. Black."

There was a pause. Then: "Did you say Mr. Black?" The voice was quiet but clear, and had a recognizable African quality.

"That's right."

"Who wants him?"

"My name is Fugleman. I got a message that he wants to talk to me."

"I'm going to put you on hold for a minute, okay?"

"One minute. Then I hang up."

It didn't really matter, since Fallon had all day. But one of the rules was never to be edged into an acquiescent role. The phone Fallon had called on wasn't listed to his name or the Kelso Close address. He visualized the man who had answered as a diplomatic clerk, in a soberly black, three-piece suit, possibly with a subdued pinstripe, and crisp white collar and cuffs. Fallon had a habit of composing pictures of people from their voices over the phone. Almost invariably he was wrong.

After half a minute the voice returned. "Mr. Fugleman?"

"Yes."

"Are you free tonight?"

"I could be."

"There is a restaurant and grill called Konstantiou's, off Baker Street on the south side, a short distance behind the Underground station. Mr. Black invites you to join him there at seven. A room will be reserved in his name."

"Fine. Thank him for me and tell him I'll be there."

"Very good."

Fallon replaced the phone and sat staring at it. For some reason he added a pair of heavy-rimmed glasses and a short beard to the image.

Kelso Close lay to the rear of Cornwall Place, a tall, solidly ranked row of Victorian immutability, unwavering and defiant before the onrushing cavalry of twentieth-century change. Number twenty-seven Cornwall Place was outwardly nondescript, with nothing to set it apart from its neighbors—the same four-story frontage of high windows, pillared porticos, and outside basement areas with their own entrances, originally intended as servants' quarters. It had long ago been converted into flats, some of the residents of which were in evidence as they went about their day-to-day affairs.

In the rear flat on the ground floor there lived a man whom the other residents referred to as "006½" because of his perpetually unrevealing appearance and guarded manner. He was seen only when coming or going, which could be at the most unlikely hours; he said little, never anything of consequence, and even that only when he was addressed first; and he baffled the nosy and the curious by consistently giving no hint upon which to base any speculation about him. All in all, he did a pretty good job of trying to be an 007, they agreed among themselves, but he didn't quite measure up to it.

In many ways 006½ was the opposite of the writer Bernard Fallon, who lived in the odd house in the close behind the terrace, whom none of the residents of twenty-seven had ever heard of. Although known by his friends to value his privacy, Fallon remained generally visible and was a familiar figure in many of the pubs and restaurants in the neighborhood; 006½, by contrast, was known to nobody and was never seen in the vicinity after he left his flat. Fallon tended to be outgoing and gregarious enough in his own selective way; the other was wary and uncommunicative. Fallon dressed in a style that indicated an open, receptive personality; 006½ had a penchant for hats and dark glasses, which in conjunction with his subdued, enveloping clothes, suppressed all vestiges of personality.

In height and build, however, they were very similar, which was hardly surprising since the two, in fact, were the same person. The basement garage of number four Kelso Close connected through to the cellar beneath the lowermost rear flat of 27 Cornwall Terrace, where the name beside the bell push for Flat 3 at the top of the front-door steps read in gleefully flaunted impenetrability, "Smith, J." Those with a reason for wanting to find out more about the elusive Boris Fugleman might have succeeded in tracing him back to the misanthropic Smith, J. The further connection from there to the author who lived in the next street, however, was one that they were not supposed to make.

Fallon left the Cornwall Place flat at 6:15 that evening and took the Circle Line tube from Kensington High Street to Baker Street. A short walk brought him to Konstantiou's, which had an appealing wooden frontage of small, whirl-paned windows and hanging plants that gave it a look of pleasant seclusion from the busy sidewalk outside. The interior had something of the feel of an East Side New York restaurant, with a dark bar off to one side of the entrance, where yellow lights buried in the ceiling strove valiantly to infuse some color into black leather upholstery and glass-topped tables. There was a hatcheck counter on the other side of the foyer. Fallon went across to hand over his raincoat.

A couple before him were making a fuss about whether or not to check the woman's bag, and Fallon looked around casually while he waited. Things were warming up for the evening, with businessmen unwinding over a drink or two in the bar and groups of prospective diners studying menus. He idly noted a tall, lean-limbed woman, either African or black American, who was sitting alone at a table a short distance from the door. She had clear, not unattractive features, more coffee-colored than pure Negro, and seemed to be watching the lobby. But when Fallon looked at her, she averted her eyes hurriedly.

Then a girl's voice said, "Sorry to keep you waiting. Did you want to leave your coat?"

Fallon forgot the woman and returned his attention to the hatcheck counter. "Yes. Just the one."

"It'll be in the back. Would you like a drink at the bar before dinner?"

"No, I'm supposed to be meeting some people. Where should I check?"

"With the hostess in the restaurant. Straight through that way."

"Thanks."

Fallon went into the restaurant, where maroon-jacketed waiters hovered over snowy, silvered tables packed a shade too closely together for comfort. The pastel-painted hostess at the desk smiled professionally.

"Hello," Fallon said. "I'm looking for a Mr. Black."

"Ah, yes. We've been expecting you. Mr. Fugleman, is it?"

"Yes."

"You have a private room reserved. The manager will take you up."

The manager had already seen him from the far side of the room and was coming across. As Fallon waited, he cast a routine eye about for the heavies who he knew had to be around somewhere. He spotted them almost immediately: two swarthy men at the nearest table to the door, whose eyes lingered over him for just a moment too long and a fraction too curiously.

The manager arrived, mustachioed, black-jacketed, oiled, and beaming. "Mr. Fugleman?"

"Yes."

"The rest of your party is here. This way, please."

Fallon followed him up deep-carpeted stairs and along a short corridor to a paneled door bearing the sign PRIVATE. The manager tapped lightly, and the door was opened from within by a form which at once impressed itself on Fallon as the Negro race's answer to the Frankenstein monster. He stood six-foot-six at least, solid and unsmiling, with the same angled blockhouse for a head, slab jaw, and shoulders like the Cliffs of Dover—everything but the needlework and the bolt through the temple.

"Mr. Fugleman has arrived," the manager said, gesturing. The ebony Goliath flickered a pair of yellowed eyes suspiciously over Fallon, then nodded curtly. He ushered Fallon in and closed the door behind him.

The table was set for dinner for four, and three partly filled glasses stood among the cutlery and napkins. The two other occupants, who were again both black, rose from their chairs. The older of the two, somewhere in his early to midforties, Fallon judged, had a flattish face and was heavy in build, with spare neck overflowing the collar of a white shirt worn with a conventional Western dark suit. The younger man was lithe and sinewy, with a clean, thrusting chin and alert eyes that danced with a faintly mischievous light—whether signifying innate humor or craftiness was impossible to tell. He, too, was wearing a Western-style suit, blue, and cut more flamboyantly than the older man's. He could have been a salesman, but something about his stance and the professional way he weighed the newcomer up as he entered instantly evoked "policeman" from Fallon's store of filed stereotypes.

Frankenstein turned from a side table behind the door. He was holding a portable metal detector in one hand and motioned with the other for Fallon to raise his arms. Fallon had seen no need to bring a weapon—somebody who had come here to listen to a business proposition from people he didn't know could hardly be looking for trouble. The way the other two were watching him told him it was a test. He brushed the metal rod aside and looked across the room coldly. "When I come as a guest, I expect to be treated like one," he said, and turned back toward the door. As he opened it, he tossed back over his shoulder, "And you won't be needing the two guardian angels downstairs, either. So you might as well give them the night off."

Fallon was already retrieving his raincoat at the hatcheck counter when Frankenstein caught up with him. "Mr. Black says not to be so hasty," he said in a voice like a muted peal of Wagnerian thunder. "He says to forget the stunt upstairs. They want you to come back and have a drink."

It was what Fallon had half expected. But he had made his point. He handed his coat back to the hatcheck girl and turned to go upstairs again.

"We understand that you can assist in the disposal of persons who persist in making themselves troublesome, Mr. Fugleman," the man calling himself Black said across the table. The soup had been served, preliminaries were over, and it was time to get down to business. "That's a type of service that the organization we represent might be interested in."

From the firm, even quality of his speech, Fallon guessed him to be the voice on the phone that morning. At a superficial level his manner still displayed the personableness of the salesman or the public-relations official, but beneath it the detachment of the policeman remained, weighing Fallon up, assessing, and evaluating all the time. Fallon typed him as a manipulator—not the kind who would be in charge, but a good front man for somebody higher, who was remaining out of sight. Black's partner, "Mr. Green," had been content for the most part to observe Fallon's reactions and let the other do the talking. From the cut of his clothes and the few things he had said, Fallon got the impression that he could be American. Frankenstein, who by now had been introduced as "Sullivan," scowled silently from the chair nearest the door.

"That can depend a lot on who's being troublesome to whom, why, and in what kind of way," Fallon replied.

Black tipped his head to one side with a brief downturning of his mouth. "As long as the client can pay, what do you care about the reasons?"

"A lot, as it so happens. I do have my own scruples. We all have to live, sure, and money's nice. But it's not the only factor that comes into it. There's no such thing as the wrong job at the right price."

"How about the right job at the wrong price?"

"I've done worse."

"So how do you decide?" Green asked, making one of his rare interjections.

"Let's just say I'll help people out who are being pushed around and don't deserve it."

"What about their politics or ideology?" Black asked. "Does that matter?"

"Not a lot."

Green leaned forward and rested his elbows on the table. "Would the victims of terrorism qualify, would you say?" he inquired.

Fallon pursed his lips. "Now there's a word that has come to mean a lot of different things to different people these days," he replied. "How would *you* describe it?"

"Deliberate violence against innocent people for political ends," Black offered.

"And how do you decide who's innocent?" Fallon shrugged in a way that said they could pursue that subject all night and get nowhere. "Anyhow, did you ask me here to swap philosophies, or did you have something specific in mind?"

Black continued to stare curiously across the table for a few seconds and then glanced questioningly to the side. Green returned a slight nod. "Allow me to tell you who we represent and why we have approached you, Mr. Fugleman," Black said.

Tiring of the playacting, Fallon said, "No, I'll tell you." There was no reason not to raise his score another notch. "You're with the Zugendan security service, and you're looking for help against the ZRF guerrillas. So let's forget all this Black and Green business and get properly introduced." Fallon raised his eyebrows to look first at one, then at the other, and returned his attention to finishing his soup.

Given that they were from the embassy and that Perry had told Julia they wanted to hire a mercenary force, action against the ZRF was the only viable explanation. It followed that they were most likely security people, which fitted with the general way they were going about things.

The two exchanged glances. Even Sullivan dropped his guard for a second and looked impressed. "My compliments," Black acknowledged. Fallon continued with his soup. "Very well. We'll come to the point. My name is Makon Ngoyba, and as you say, I'm from the Zugendan Department of State Security. This is Mr. Robert Lichuru, who is a consultant to our government." The heavily built man inclined his head.

At that point there was a lull while a waiter appeared to clear the dishes and prepare the table for the next course. The description of Lichuru as a "consultant" seemed deliberately vague, but it was all that Fallon was going to get for now. He noted that Sullivan remained on his feet all the time that the waiter was in the room.

When the door had closed again, Ngoyba resumed, "Two weeks ago, the Zugendan chief of police was killed by a ZRF bomb in a town called Jaquesville. So were twenty-two other people, including three American volunteer workers. Thirty-six were wounded, many of them horribly. The explosion was in the midst of a crowd to whom food was being distributed."

Fallon nodded. "I read about it."

Ngoyba went on, "It was typical of the kind of callousness that we've come to expect from the ZRF. President Molokutu has decided that it's time for a concerted effort to eliminate them permanently." He paused, "but as you probably know, our country is going through a rather troubled period at present. And as you've already guessed, we're looking for outside professional help."

The conversation seemed to be heading in the general direction that Fallon had anticipated. "Mercenaries aren't my line," he said.

Ngoyba raised a hand. "It isn't a mercenary force that we're looking for, Mr. Fugleman."

Lichuru added, "We don't need a mercenary force— and besides, too many circuses in the past have given mercenaries in Africa a bad name. . . . No, what we want is just a small group of professionals. Top men. We're told that you have the right contacts."

Ngoyba chimed in, "We're talking a flat fee of up to fifty thousand each for the right people."

"Pounds?" Fallon queried.

"Dollars. Let's be sensible. It's tax-free."

"How much per head for the recruiting agency?'" Fallon asked, meaning himself.

"Nothing."

"What? *You're* talking to *me* about being sens—"

"Handling matters on a headhunting basis wouldn't be appropriate," Lichuru interrupted. "The numbers would be too small, and it would be asking for second-raters."

Ngoyba explained, "Your terms would be a flat fee also, plus bonus: fifty thousand up front to cover expenses, the same again when the force is dispatched, and another hundred when the ZRF is defeated."

"Negotiable?"

Ngoyba shrugged neutrally. "Anything's possible."

Fallon thought about it. The "circuses" that Lichuru had referred to were no doubt, among other things, the events that had taken place in Angola in the midseventies, when an attempt by one of the anticommunist factions to

use a primarily British mercenary force had turned into a
fiasco. An unstable and undisciplined mix of former criminals, civilian adventurers, and ex-rankers without officer
experience, they had earned notoriety for murder and
atrocities committed against the native population, and
ended up killing more of each other than the enemy had.

"So what, exactly, are we talking about?" he asked at
last. "Training for the Zugendan army? Forming an elite
unit inside it? Something like that?" He didn't really think
so. The pay scale was too high.

"Something more specialized than that." Ngoyba sat
forward in his chair. "You see, we agree with the sentiments that you expressed earlier—that was why we were
interested in your motives. It's always the innocent who
do the dying in these situations. We are humane people
also. We want to avoid the suffering that always goes with
the murderous kind of civil war that this is turning into. So
what we want you to help us do is form a small, specialized, assassination team to infiltrate the ZRF camp and
eliminate its top leadership cadre. It's the kind of organization that attracts various freebooters, cutthroats, and
misguided idealists from all quarters—the kind who always
show up hoping for a piece of any action that's going when
people aren't choosy. Well, our intention is to supply them
with a few 'volunteers' of our own."

Fallon pulled a face. "That's all very well to talk
about. But the leaders of a guerrilla army on a war footing
aren't going to oblige you by sitting out in the middle of
the road somewhere, waiting for anyone who might come
by to bump them off. How is this team of strange faces
supposed to get close enough?"

"Naturally, we have given that some thought, and we
think it can be done, Mr. Fugleman," Ngoyba replied.
"But the first part of your mission would be to assess the
feasibility of the operation from the inside, under a suitable identity which we shall arrange." He spread his hands
briefly. "You will understand that I cannot divulge more at
this stage. To learn more, you would need to come and
meet my superiors in Zugenda."

Fallon sat back and regarded the two Africans through
narrowed eyes while he turned the proposition over in his
mind. The humanitarian angle was a line that he didn't
buy, nor did he especially feel that he was expected to. It

was the kind of rationalization that parties to ugly deals like this usually went through: the motions of pretending to believe that the other one believed, without probing too deeply. It constituted a kind of mutual conscience assuaging. In other words, the Zugendan situation was being offered to him in clear-cut terms that would make his decision easier, and the opportunity was there to accept it on that basis. So far, so good.

But there was another aspect that Fallon still found puzzling. He shifted his position and brought his hands together in front of him. "What makes me curious is, why would a Marxist government want to hire Westerners? There have to be more than enough Soviets, Cubans, Chinese, or whatever, depending on your choice of flavor, who'd be happy to help. Why come to us?"

Lichuru was already nodding, evidently having expected the question. "That's what the ZRF want us to do," he said. "It's what their terrorism is aimed at provoking."

Fallon looked puzzled. This was a new one. "What for?" he asked.

Ngoyba explained, "If they can get the communist bloc officially involved, they'd be able to pose before the world as nationalist liberators. Then they would try to get backing and funds from the Americans, which would lead to precisely the kind of all-out war that we don't want. But we don't intend playing their ballgame."

Fallon stared down at his plate. Embroilment with governments of any kind was something that he tried to steer clear of, although he sometimes accepted deniable assignments through channels that operated unofficially. But this didn't sound like something he'd want to get mixed up in.

Lichuru read his thoughts. "You told us that your fight is against oppression of the undeserving in all its forms, irrespective of ideology," he said as he refilled his wine-glass. "Well, Mr. Fugleman, here is an opportunity to prove it."

Chapter Four

JULIA HAD A WAY OF UNRAVELING LOGICAL TAN-
gles that intrigued and captivated her readers, and which
in her work with Fallon was invaluable. Congenitally
incapable of declining an intellectual challenge, she would
pick and draw at the fibers cocooning a truth until the one
solution stood finally bared which was compatible with
every fact and contradicted by none. She circled and
closed gradually in upon her eventual goal with the
fastidiousness of a queen wasp exploring every niche and
crevice of the prospective territory before selecting a site
for her nest. And having arrived at her conclusion, she
never accorded it greater status than the merely theoreti-
cal, constantly testing it against further information and
always ready to modify or abandon it if the facts so
dictated.

George, by contrast, confined his ruminatory horizons
strictly to the realm of the obvious and inarguable. Tearing
aside the speculative undergrowth of multiple hypotheses
and plausible alternatives, he bore down on decisions with
the directness of a hog plowing through oak-tree roots on
the scent of Périgord truffles.

"If it were oop to me, I'd 'ave noothin' ter bloody do
with it," was his considered verdict in the Kelso Close
house the next morning, when Fallon had given his account of the previous evening's meeting with Ngoyba and
Lichuru.

Originally from the netherest regions of Yorkshire somewhere west of Leeds, he was as solid and steady as the
crags that brood over Ilkley Moor, with a square, hefty
frame, fresh, pinkish complexion, light curly hair cropped
close to his head, Adonis-like, and clear blue, rounded
eyes. He sat at the table in the breakfast area adjoining the
kitchen, cradling a glass of Sam Smith's Tadcaster Ale in

one hand and toying with a toothpick in the other. The biceps squeezed into the rolled sleeve of his shirt rippled as he speared another olive from a dish on the table. Fallon had first met him years ago, as a close-combat instructor in the Parachute Regiment.

"I don't think I'm exactly crazy about it either," Fallon agreed, standing propped in the lounge doorway with a cup of tea in his hand. "Something about Ngoyba gives me creepy feelings in the gut."

"And where does this oother chap fit in, this Lichuru? Did yer find that out?"

Fallon shook his head. "He stayed in the background. But from some of the things he said, I'd say he's got an American connection somewhere."

Julia was sitting across the table from George, erect but with a faraway look on her face. After the silence had persisted for a short while, she said, "This angle of approaching someone in the West to do the job in order to preempt an appeal by the ZRF for U.S. backing is the kind of thing that would get Molokutu's support, isn't it?"

"Well, obviously he'd have to know about it," Fallon agreed.

"No, that's not quite what I meant," Julia said. "It's the kind of line that somebody might use if they needed to get his approval to go ahead."

"Ngoyba and Lichuru?"

"And whoever Ngoyba reports to."

Fallon frowned. "You mean for other reasons of their own. They might be up to something that they're not letting Molokutu in on?"

"Stranger things have happened," Julia replied.

"Want to hazard any guesses?"

"Well," Julia answered, "Molokutu is a Soviet client. The people who run Zugenda's state security are looking for outside help to destroy the ZRF. But they're not looking for it from the Eastern bloc, which is the first place you'd think they'd go." She traced a query mark lightly on the table with a fingertip. "What that suggests to me is that they're planning something that they don't want Moscow to know about."

"Could be . . . Interesting," Fallon murmured, contemplating his cup.

"An even better reason not ter get mixed oop in it,"
George declared.

"Just curious." Fallon downed the last of his tea. "In
fact, that was pretty much the conclusion I'd already come
to last night. . . ." He set the empty cup down on the table,
then reached into the inside pocket of his jacket and took
out a pale green card. It was like a business card but
larger, and printed with a dark script. He passed it to
Julia. "Then I got this."

Julia took it from him and examined it. It was from
Konstantiou's, one of the complimentary publicity cards
that restaurants sometimes display at the cash desk or by
the door. Along the bottom margin in blue ballpoint was
written:

> *M. Fugleman, need to meet you most urgent. Go to
> the pub Calthorpe Arms in Gray's Inn Road, one
> o'clock tomorrow.*

There was no name or initial.

"There's always something to complicate things, isn't
there?" Fallon said. Julia showed the card to George, who
looked at it cursorily, shrugged, and passed it back, while
Fallon explained, "The hatcheck girl gave it to me when I
left. Somebody must have left it for me while we were
eating."

Julia looked at the back of the card, then turned it
over to study the writing again more closely. "Did she give
it to you openly?" she asked. "Without making any secret
of it, or more . . . furtively?"

Fallon gave her an odd look. "Furtively," he answered.
"She slipped it to me when I picked up my coat."

"In such a way that the others wouldn't see—as if
she'd been told it was confidential?"

"Yes."

Julia nodded. "Ah, I see. . . ."

Fallon pulled out a chair and sat down to join the
other two at the table. "What's their plan if you do decide
to go ahead with it?" George asked him. "How do they
think they're goin' to get you an' this team they're talking
about inside the ZRF? Did they say?"

"Last night was just the preliminaries," Fallon answered.

"Ngoyba's only the messenger boy. I get to know the rest when I talk to whoever's at the back of it."

"When's that?"

"That depends on what I say. If we go ahead, they want me to go to Zugenda."

"When?"

"Straightaway."

"They're not wastin' much time, then," George observed.

"So we need to make our minds up." Fallon turned to Julia, who was still turning the card between her fingers and staring at it. "But first, I'm kind of curious about that. Who did it come from, and what do they want?"

Julia thought for a few seconds longer. "Well it's from a woman who's left-handed, and if you'd like a further guess, I'd say she's black, and probably fairly tall. . . ." she offered finally.

"Bloody 'ell," George muttered, shaking his head.

Julia looked up at Fallon. "And she quite possibly wants to kill you."

Fallon stared incredulously. "I saw her!" he exclaimed. "I'm sure I did. At Konstantiou's. She was in the bar when I arrived."

"Very likely."

"How did you work that out?"

Julia exhaled sharply, knotting her eyebrows in mock reproach as if it should have been obvious. "Well, it had to have been somebody who knew that a Mr. Fugleman was due to be there, which means they probably knew why. The fact that they couldn't let their presence be known to the Zugendan security people points to someone from the ZRF."

"And therefore probably Zugendan themselves," Fallon agreed, nodding. "Okay, the handwriting's definitely feminine, I'll buy that. But what made you go for tall?"

Julia turned the card and pointed at it. "See how the message begins: Not 'Mr. Fugleman,' which would be usual, but 'M.' Then there are a couple of peculiarities in the construction. Look there... 'urgent' instead of 'urgently.' And here, 'pub, Calthorpe Arms' is an unnatural inversion. I'd say that English wasn't the first language of whoever wrote this."

"Go on," Fallon said.

"Zugenda was formed from parts of two remnants of the colonial era. It comprises two provinces: Kashinga to the north, which is mainly French-speaking, and Sorindi in the south, which was British. I'd say that this woman spoke French." Julia handed him back the card. "And Zugendans from the northern tribes tend to be slender and tall."

"You've been doing some homework," Fallon complimented.

"But of course."

"And what makes yer think she's out to give 'im the chop?" George asked.

"I only said she might be," Julia replied. "Well, ask yourself this. Why would the ZRF want to meet somebody that they've found out is being approached to organize an assassination plot against them?" She shrugged as if the answer were not worth dwelling on. "Either to try and talk him out of it, or else to get rid of him." She sipped her own tea, which had been getting cold, and looked back at Fallon. "So if you do intend keeping this appointment, Bernard, I'd suggest that you take a gun with you and keep George close at hand as backup."

Chapter Five

IT WAS MIDMORNING BY THE TIME FALLON EMERGED into Kelso Close. The day was unsettled, with indecisive winds stirring the tatters of a ragged, gray sky, and he had put on his raincoat again.

Mainly out of curiosity—but also from a belief that both sides ought to have a hearing in situations like this—he had decided that he would go to the pub in Gray's Inn Road for lunch; all the same, he didn't expect much to come of it. The Zugendan kind of wars tended to be nasty affairs, with each side pressing its case at the court of the public news media for a verdict upon the other of guilt by accusation. And in any case, political assassination wasn't his line, and he had no ambitions of diversifying in that direction.

He stopped at a news agent and tobacconist's around the corner for a copy of the *Times* and refill for the cigarette lighter that he found useful to carry, even though he didn't smoke. Robert, the heftily built, balding proprietor, greeted him with genial familiarity.

"'Allo, Mr. Fallon. 'Aven't seen yer fer a while."

"Hello, Bob. No, I've been away for a few days."

"Looks like we could be in fer a bit o' rain before tonight, if you ask me."

"I wouldn't bet money against it."

"Workin' on a new book at the moment, are yer?"

"Yes . . . er, it's about corruption involving local government and property developers."

"Good timin' too. There's plenty 'o that goin' on, right enough. Here's your paper. Thirty pence, please. Don't let it get you down too much when you read it."

"Oh, that's all right, Bob. I only get it for the crossword. The only thing that I believe is the advertising, anyway."

"Har, that's a good un! Thank you . . . Good day, Mr. Fallon."

"See you, Bob."

A blonde with long hair, smartly turned out in a long, black wintry coat and calf-length suede boots, entered as he turned to leave. He had seen her on a number of occasions around the area, but never had reason to talk. She seemed to recognize him by sight, too, for she smiled coyly for a second as she held the door. Fallon grinned and returned a cheerful nod.

"Ta, love."

" 'Allo, Audrey, yer lookin' fine today. . . ." Robert's voice boomed from behind as the door closed.

Fallon paused outside and scanned quickly over the front page of his paper. Audrey, eh? That could be worth remembering, maybe. . . . But for the time being, he had enough on his plate with tall, lean, mysterious African women. He folded the paper, thrust it under his arm, and went on his way.

Farther along, he came to the corner of Cornwall Place. As he crossed the road, he looked casually along the street and picked them out almost immediately: two men in a nondescript Ford Cortina, parked some distance away from number twenty-seven and on the opposite side, from where they could watch the entrance.

Curious for no particular reason, Fallon stopped at the corner and pretended to search in his wallet while he got a look at them. They were facing the other way and he was out of the viewing angles from the mirrors. He memorized the number of the car, to be noted down later when he was out of sight. The occupants had the look of bored surveillance people everywhere. Just routine, as he'd expected. The Zugendans were keeping an eye on "their" man.

He was about to resume walking when a cultivated, very English voice that stopped short of being an affectation said quietly behind him, "I presume they're waiting for Boris. You'd imagine that they'd at least try to vary the act once in a while, wouldn't you? No imagination, these security types."

Fallon had recognized the voice even before he turned around in astonishment. The figure regarding him was of medium height and leanly proportioned, wearing a camel-hair overcoat with lapel carnation, maroon silk scarf, black bowler hat, and carrying a tightly furled umbrella. His features had an aristocratic quality about them, enhanced somewhat by a ginger mustache, vigorous complexion, and distinctly military bearing. He was staring at Fallon with pale blue eyes which, in spite of their undisguised twinkle, still put Fallon in mind of a porcelain cat.

For several seconds Fallon could only stand and stare, nonplussed. It had been years now. His Zugendan involvement dated precisely since yesterday. . . . And how could anyone outside his own small, select circle have known about Boris Fugleman?

Colonel Marlow continued, "It's hardly necessary to look quite *that* flabbergasted, Bernard. You'll start attracting attention if you're not careful, and I remember you as being always the meticulous professional."

"It's . . . been a long time, sir," was all Fallon could manage, struggling, for once, to maintain some sort of coherence.

"Oh, there's no need for any of that 'sir' business now," Marlow returned breezily. "Let's take a little stroll, shall we? Fresh, gusty weather—good for the constitution."

A ghost of a grin crept into Fallon's face as he regained his composure. "You old sod!"

They began walking back the way Fallon had come, and continued northward in the direction of Kensington Gardens, Fallon with hands thrust into his raincoat pockets, the colonel pacing his stride with even taps of his umbrella on the flagstones.

"Life been treating you well, has it?" the colonel inquired casually.

"Oh, can't grumble . . . Well, you can if you want to, I suppose, but nobody wants to know, do they?"

"Still the same penchant for variety and a touch of excitement, I hear. Finding it sufficiently satisfying and rewarding, are you?"

Fallon shrugged. "It pays the rent. I get by."

"Oh, I've no doubts about your success materially. That's quite a pad you've got just around the corner, as our American friends would say. Not bad at all for a onetime ranker, made captain, who started out from the wrong end of Kensington." The colonel flipped a discarded Coca-Cola can into the gutter with the tip of his umbrella. "I was referring to what might be termed the more 'spiritual' kind of satisfaction. It's nice to be getting something out of life, I agree. But are you really happy that you're putting enough *in*?"

"That's a question you don't get asked too often," Fallon commented.

"Hmm, yes, in these days of me-me-me and I'm-all-right-Jack-so-screw-you, I'm afraid I have to agree," the colonel conceded. "But *you* have a rather different disposition, Bernard, and I more than suspect that you understand exactly what I'm talking about."

"It's not something I've been thinking very much about lately," Fallon said vaguely.

The colonel stopped to admire a gleaming, prewar-model Bentley parked by the side of the road. "My word! Look at the quality of the leather in that. Walnut dashboard, knobs that won't come off. Built like the *Queen Mary* . . . You won't see the likes of that again." They resumed walking, and the colonel picked up again. "It's all a bit small-time, though, isn't it, if you don't mind my saying so? I mean, doing in a few dragons and coming away with the occasional damsel here and there is all very nice, and that kind of thing, but you have to admit that in terms of life being guided by enduring principle and devoted to what really *matters*, it does leave a certain something to be desired, wouldn't you agree?"

"That depends what you mean by 'matters.'"

They came to a main road and waited for the traffic lights to change. The colonel didn't speak again until they had reached the other side. "I take it that the Zugendan government has made you a proposition." So, suddenly they were down to specifics. After the little he had heard already, Fallon was past being surprised.

"They want me to go there and talk about one, anyway," he said.

"And has the Republican Front contacted you yet?"

"I'm supposed to be meeting one of them for lunch today."

"Were you planning on going?"

"I didn't see why not."

"Just curious?"

"Maybe."

"But you don't think you'll take the job." It was a

question phrased as a statement for form's sake. Marlow's insight was even keener than he had given him credit for, Fallon realized. Memories of old times were beginning to come back.

Fallon shook his head. "I wasn't going to, no. Third World domestic squabbles aren't really my cup of tea." He looked at the colonel again, now making no attempt to hide his curiosity over where this was leading.

"We'd like you to take it," the colonel said. "The Zugendan business is something that we're extremely interested in, and having somebody on the inside and in a position to evaluate the situation firsthand would be invaluable. There's no specific brief at this stage. Just use your eyes, your ears, and your brain, and we'll see where it leads later. You don't have to give me an answer here and now. But if you do accept the invitation to Zugenda, I'll assume that your action speaks for itself. How does that sound?"

The whole thing was so outrageously presumptuous that Fallon stopped in his tracks, gesticulating in mute protest. "Look . . . Colonel Marlow, this may come as something of a surprise, but I'm not with the department anymore. I haven't seen you for years. I don't—"

"Oh, this has nothing to do with *them*," Marlow scoffed. "I'm not with the old firm these days. Haven't been for some time now."

"Who's 'we' then?" Fallon asked.

The colonel abandoned his easygoing air, and all of a sudden the piercing blue eyes were deadly serious. Then he seemed to go off on a suddenly different tack.

"Can I ask you something? Why did you quit the service?" Marlow was referring not only to Fallon's time with the SAS, but also to the various covert intelligence operations that he had graduated to during his latter years. Fallon didn't answer immediately. The colonel turned away, and they resumed walking.

Exactly what Fallon's reasons had been, he still had difficulty putting into words. Some of it had to do with having his thinking done for him by distant, faceless people who didn't always seem to understand the business; another part had been an indefinable discomfort at having to function as an obedient instrument of political forces that he wasn't always sure he was in sympathy with. . . . And then, of course, there was the question of what his neck was worth to him, as opposed to the value put upon it by those who answered to the overseers of Her Majesty's exchequer. But he'd found that the action and the promise of it suited him, so these days he found it on grounds of his own choosing, on his own terms, and in his own kind of way.

Eventually the colonel went on: "Oh, I know that a part of it must have been the desire that anybody made like you would feel to become an independent operator. But wasn't there more too? A feeling that everything wasn't quite right at the top, somehow? Of wondering sometimes how some of the things you found yourself doing could serve the interests that it was all supposed to be for?"

"Mmm, kind of..." Fallon conceded guardedly. He glanced sideways with the mixture of uncertainty and reluctant admiration of one trying to divine a mind-reading trick. They walked on in silence for a few seconds while he thought about it. Then he gave a sudden nod. "Okay, you're so bloody close that I'll tell you," he said. "I've trained bodyguards for sultans in countries where women are owned like cattle and people can get their heads chopped off in public for breaking some medieval taboo. I've seen kids in Ireland whose dads starved themselves to death in prison because they believed they were right. I've seen too many good people wasted because somebody was more worried about what the public might think, or about looking good on TV.... Never mind wondering if it served the interests it was supposed to. There were times when I wondered if I was on the right side—or even if there was a right side at all. So sod all of it. I decided to be my own side."

They stopped as they reached a corner, and the colonel nodded in a way that said it was what he had been hoping to hear. "Part of my job once was to understand what made people like you tick. In some ways I got to know most of you better than you knew yourselves. I'm with a different organization now—a different *kind* of organization. It's international in scope, and probably more relevant to ensuring a decent future for all of us than anything you've ever been associated with." He paused for a moment, gauging Fallon's reaction. "I'll also add this.

What we stand for reflects all that you've shown to be important to you, only more so. And that, of course, is why the organization is interested, and why I was asked to approach you."

Fallon looked at Marlow suspiciously. "Did you put Perry onto me about this Zugendan business?"

"Yes, as a matter of fact. We knew that the Zugendans were looking for someone to organize a hit squad, and for various reasons it was important for us to stay close to the situation. That meant steering the job to someone that we knew, and you've been on the prospect list for some time now."

"So is Perry with this outfit too?" Fallon asked.

"No, he was just the messenger boy. He knows nothing about it."

"And how much more do I get to know?"

"No more for now. Everything in its time, when the time's right. You know the way these things work, Bernard."

Fallon stared past the colonel at the traffic on Gloucester Road. Why couldn't life ever be simple? Here he had been, ready to do the sensible thing for once and make a clean break from a job that had set all the warning bells going in his head. . . . And that was the moment that Marlow had to choose to reappear out of nowhere after years and plunge him right back into it. But at the same time, he was intrigued—as the colonel had known he would be, Fallon saw as he turned his gaze back and found the blue eyes twinkling at him intently. The colonel was playing it just right. He always had.

Fallon sighed. "I suppose there are times when life could do with a boost in the spiritual direction," he agreed resignedly.

"Does that mean you'll do it?"

"It means I won't make my mind up at least until after lunch. After that, well, you'll know the answer if I come out of Fortnum's with a stack of Dr. Livingstone shirts and a safari hat. You seem to have been keeping pretty good tabs on everything else I've been doing."

"Splendid." The colonel spotted an approaching taxi and raised his umbrella high to hail it. The taxi swerved in toward the curb. "Well, I have things to attend to. There's an industrial electronics exhibition on at Olympia this week. Meet me by the General Electric stand at ten-thirty tomorrow morning and let me know how things went."

"Electronics? I didn't know that was your line."

"There's somebody there that I need to talk to on another matter. Meanwhile, you'd better be getting on your way back to resurrect Boris." The colonel turned to look back as he was about to climb into the cab. "And do enjoy your lunch, Bernard."

Chapter Six

THE CALTHORPE ARMS WAS FILLED WITH A WEEK-day lunchtime crowd of noisy businesspeople when Fallon arrived, a little after 12:30. He ordered a pork pie and pickled onions with a cup of black coffee at the bar and, since the tables were all taken, carried his plate over to a stool by a shelf running along one wall. Across the corner was a mirror with a frosted design advertising Young's Ales, in which he could watch the door. He rarely touched alcohol during the day—and never when he had an appointment with the unknown. There was a door at the back of the bar, which upon checking in the course of a casual visit to the gents, he found led to a short corridor and side exit from the building.

He recognized her at once when she appeared twenty minutes later—it was indeed the woman he had glimpsed in the bar at Konstantiou's. She paused in the doorway to look back along the street as if wary of having been followed, and then came in and began threading her way through the crush, looking anxiously from side to side. She spotted him and changed direction to work her way over. Sure enough, he saw, she was five-foot-eight at least, her height accentuated by a slim build and long limbs, with high cheekbones and a narrow chin giving her face a heart-shaped outline. Her skin was smooth and closer to coffee-colored, with a flat lower face and clear, attractive features that derived as much from Arab as from Negro, Fallon guessed—the two races accounted for over eighty percent of the Zugendan population. She was wearing a dark green coat over a plain tan dress and carrying a brown purse with a shoulder strap.

"Mr. Fugleman. You get my message. I'm glad you are able to come." And yes, the curl at the edge of her pronunciation was distinctly French.

"I never could resist the mysterious," Fallon said.

"I was in the bar of Konstantiou's when you come in there, but I cannot talk to you then."

"Yes, I know."

Surprise flickered in her eyes for an instant, but she didn't delve further. Her face had something of a drawn look, and she hadn't smiled. Everything about her was tense. Fallon pulled out an empty stool and motioned with a hand. She sat down and hesitated. "It is not easy to know where one must begin."

"Well, you seem to know me. Who are you?"

"I am called Candy."

Fallon pursed his lips and nodded in an if-you-say-so kind of way. "A drink?" he suggested. "Maybe a bite of something to go with it?"

"Thank you." She looked at the empty cup and plate in front of him. "A coffee also . . . and a sandwich perhaps."

He got up to go to the bar. "Anything except ham?"

"It doesn't matter. . . . You are very perceptive, Mr. Fugleman."

"Part of the trade."

Fallon moved across the room and slipped into the space at the bar as a couple of men turned to leave. He ordered two more coffees and a round of chicken, and allowed his eye to wander casually around the place while he waited. There was no quick turning away of a head or averting of eyes—nobody who seemed to be showing an undue interest in them.

"What is 'the trade'?" Candy asked him when he came back with a tray and sat down.

Fallon passed her a plate and sipped from his cup without looking at her. "I've got a feeling you already know."

"You are a man who arranges for the hiring of professionals. . . ." Candy glanced about and lowered her voice instinctively. "Killers who work on contracts."

"That could describe any soldier."

"But it's what Ngoyba asks you to do?"

"Yes."

"And will you do it?"

Fallon leaned an elbow on the shelf and eyed her curiously. His first impression was of a realist who was under no illusions about how the world worked; and there was a hardness in her eye and the set of her face that said she'd had more than her share of knocks from it. Yet somehow he couldn't reconcile what he saw with his experiences of the dehumanized terrorist.

"Who are you, and why do you want to know?" he asked. She seemed at a loss to continue. To ease her predicament, he added, "I'm more in the business of preventing people from getting killed—people who don't deserve to be, anyhow."

It seemed to give her confidence the boost that it needed. "You have heard of the Zugendan Republican Front?" she asked.

"Yes . . . some."

"I belong to ZRF."

Which Julia had guessed already. But Fallon nodded reflectively as if the statement came as a revelation. "And is Ngoyba who he says he is?"

"I don't know what Ngoyba tells to you. He is deputy to a man called Embatto, who is in charge of state security."

"And what about Lichuru?" Fallon asked.

"Of him we are not certain. He is some kind of foreign adviser."

"To the president, Molokutu?"

Candy nodded as she bit off a corner of sandwich. "I see you know something about our country, Mr. Fugleman."

"I've got a reason to."

"And what do they tell you about us?"

Fallon shrugged and kept his voice neutral. "Only what you can read anywhere. You people don't have a very good press."

An intensity blazed in Candy's eyes suddenly, as if she had been waiting for this as a cue. Evidently there was a fiery side to her nature, which needed little to be touched off. "Those are all lies that the newspapers tell the world about us, *lies!* We do not indiscriminately murder our own people. It is Molokutu's government who terrorize. The ZRF is fighting for the people to be free from these parasites who use foreign money and guns to rob them. What good would we do for ourselves by making the people hate us and fear us?"

"The ZRF didn't plant the bomb that killed a lot of people in Jaquesville about two weeks ago, for instance?"

"No. That was a lie."

"Who did?"

Candy shook her head wearily. "To be certain is impossible. Some part of the government arranges it to put the blame on us."

"But wasn't the chief of police the target? Why would they bump off their own police chief?"

"Who knows what goes on . . . ? But it is not as they say. The people you hear about being cut to pieces in their homes, the crops that are burned . . ." Candy raised a hand to her brow and shook her head. "If you only understood more about the ZRF. If you knew its leader, Jovay Barindas, and what he teaches . . . then you would know why the ZRF could never do these things."

Fallon took his time draining the last from his cup, then sat staring at the wall. It wouldn't have been the first time that a ruling authority had beat terrorists at their own game by committing acts they could accuse the other side of and then use as a pretext for retaliatory measures. It fitted, too, with Julia's theory of somebody needing to justify to Molokutu the bringing in of outsiders to deal with the ZRF: it would strengthen the case for claiming that outside help was needed.

On the other hand, Candy's line could be simply an attempt to head him off. She didn't exactly come across as the epitome of ruthlessness, it was true, but then, in the real world they often didn't. Fallon could sense the fervor in her gaze as she watched him. She was no doubt sincere in what she said, and firm in her belief that the cause she had dedicated herself to was just. That was the problem. People never ever embarked willingly on actions that they perceived as wrong. Instead, they would find ways of convincing themselves that the direction their desires or their instincts compelled them in was right. The capacity of the human mind to see what it wanted to see was limitless. Every torturer and concentration-camp guard had an escape hatch for his conscience that enabled him to play with his grandchildren and sleep easily at night. And the true believers of the world would cling to what they were told, because they had to. . . .

"You are gone very quiet, Mr. Fugleman," Candy said.

Fallon pushed himself upright on the stool and braced

his hands on his thighs. Candy watched him with large, uncertain eyes. There was no way for him to decide whether she was genuine, or if the official line that he had heard the night before was correct, or if both sides were as bad as each other, which it had been his first inclination to suspect before Marlow entered the scene and complicated things.

But Candy didn't know about Marlow, and too ready a display of enthusiasm wouldn't have been appropriate to Fallon's role in the meantime. "Maybe you don't have to worry," he said. "I wasn't really sure I wanted to get involved, anyway."

"But you don't understand why I ask you here," Candy replied. "We *want* you to get involved." Fallon gave her a puzzled look. Her expression remained serious. "We make a counteroffer. Embatto wants to hire you against us, yes? Very well, we make the same offer—for you to help us against him. You work on the inside, for us. . . ." She exhaled sharply with the relief of having finally unloaded the burden she had come to deliver. "Voilà."

Fallon stared at the shelf in front of them. If Marlow had had any inkling that this was likely to happen, he had left no hint of what Fallon was supposed to do now. Presumably that was something that Fallon was supposed to work out for himself, which he would only be able to do when he'd found out a lot more than he knew at present. The place to do that would be in Zugenda, and the Zugendan authorities would get him there a lot faster and with far less difficulty than the ZRF could.

"We do find out things about this Mr. Fugleman that Embatto is so interested in," Candy said pointedly. "They say you work against the terrorists. Very well, that is what the Zugendan government are. Half of our children die before two years, while the gangsters who take their food live in palaces. Prisoners are shot in public as a warning to anyone who thinks of resisting them. A—"

"Yes, I've heard it all before," Fallon said. "And the usual poor sods get caught in the middle. It's a shame that it happens, but it's not the kind of thing that I or anybody else is likely to change anytime soon."

Candy's manner became openly sarcastic. "Or is it

that Embatto can pay better money? He should. He has more of it—stolen from our people."

"No, that isn't it."

"So you don't even want to hear our offer?"

Deciding it was time to relax the hard line a little, Fallon went through the motions of weighing up the situation at greater length than he needed to. "Do you plan on giving it to me here, right now?" he asked.

"Are you saying that you will listen?"

Fallon tossed out a hand carelessly. "Sure. What's the harm in listening?"

"But no, not here. Probably we say too much already. And it is not I who should explain."

"Who, then?"

"I am here in England with a colleague who is also with ZRF. We are staying at a—how do you say?—a safe house, of someone who is sympathetic to our cause. It is not far from here. There is where we must go."

"Right now?"

"Why not?" She stared at him questioningly with her clear, brown, unwavering eyes, not begging, but defiant and challenging. If it was a trap, he thought to himself, this would be the model setup. But it was the only way he was going to find out anything further. . . . And nobody had forced him into choosing this kind of bloody caper as a career.

He sighed and stood up. "Okay, Candy. Let's go."

They left the pub and took the back streets behind the Mount Pleasant sorting office, heading in the general direction of Pentonville Road along pavements still showing damp patches from the drizzle earlier. The sky was a typically British, sodden, sullen, featureless, battleship gray, without a patch of relief to hint that a sun existed. But the air seemed to revivify Candy's spirits, and her pace quickened as they walked.

"You know, you have to be really patriotic to want to come to this climate after Africa," Fallon said after they had gone two blocks.

Candy's features softened momentarily for the first time. "There is that too. You have been in Africa?"

"On occasions . . . in years gone by."

"With the military, yes?"

Fallon flashed her a look of mock suspicion. "Who's been putting out spies?"

"I can tell."

"Enough about me, then. So, what part of Zugenda do you come from?"

"What my background is need not concern us."

Fallon made a show of glancing nonchalantly up at the fronts of the buildings along the street. "Oh, how about somewhere in Kashinga province, up in the north, I'd say. How's that? Close enough?"

Candy stared at him. "How do you know this?" she stammered, visibly shaken.

Fallon shrugged. "Oh . . . I can tell."

They came to a main road. He took her elbow lightly to steer her across through the traffic. "So why do you need to stay in a safe house?" Fallon asked. "You're not illegal over here, are you?"

"No, but Zugendan security people, they are here. They watch for us everywhere. I take a big risk following them to Konstantiou's last night. But it is the only way I can find out where they meet you."

"Whose house is it?"

"All the time you keep fishing, Mr. Fugleman."

Fallon shrugged. "Well, you've got to try, haven't you?"

"Part of the trade, yes?"

"Right."

More side streets brought them to a row of three-story red-brick facades with ground-level doors set back behind iron railings. Candy went through one of the gates to a door with peeling blue paint that had a more tired look about it than most of the others. It wasn't locked. Fallon followed her into a passage with old wallpaper and a worn carpet on brown linoleum. The interior was divided into separate units. There were a couple of doors on the right-hand side, stairs on the left going up, and a narrower passageway between, leading to the rear section of the house. Underneath the stairway was a recess at the top of a lower flight of stairs continuing down to the basement. The place had an old, musty smell to it. It seemed a stale, preserved remnant of times now gone.

Candy stopped at the second of the doors opposite the stairs and produced a key from her purse. She opened the door, stepped inside, and held it open with her elbow for Fallon to go ahead of her. He noted the name "Dr. F. Velker" inscribed on a piece of card held in a metal frame on the door. As he moved into the doorway, his hand came up instinctively to finger the Browning Hi-Power automatic holstered in the armpit of his jacket. He had barely begun taking in the drably furnished, somewhat antiquated sitting room inside when everything happened at once.

Beyond an open door across the room was a black man with a gun aimed straight at him, and at the same instant as the sight registered, George's voice shouted, "*Watch yerself, Bern!*" from the direction of the front-door behind. Fallon knew he was too slow as he recoiled back from the doorway, but a shove delivered with the power of a swiping grizzly bear helped him on his way just as the sound of two shots cracked. He went into a roll on the passageway floor, aiming himself into the recess beneath the stairs, and came up on one knee with his gun drawn. The passage was suddenly filled with figures seemingly appearing from nowhere.

George, holding a drawn gun, was coming forward from the street door, which was now closed. The two Zugendan security men that Fallon had seen downstairs in Konstantiou's were there, both also with guns, one looking into the doorway that Fallon had been about to enter, the other covering from the bottom of the stairs. Seeing no immediate threat, Fallon straightened up cautiously and came forward from the recess. Candy was sprawled face-down inside the doorway, with Sullivan crouching over her on one knee. Her purse was on the floor by her head, its flap open and the strap still clutched in the fingers of her left hand. As Fallon watched, Sullivan removed an automatic pistol from her other hand and straightened up.

Now that his reflexes had let go, Fallon was able to appraise the situation. It couldn't have been George who pushed him out of the way—George had been too far back. From the force that Fallon had felt, it must have been Sullivan. And in any case George couldn't have seen the black with the gun, who had been on the far side of the doorway beyond this one. Therefore George's shouted warning must have been due to his misinterpreting the appearance of Sullivan and the others—fortunately George had been quick-thinking enough not to fire when he saw that Fallon wasn't endangered. Who, then, had fired the shots? They had sounded too close to have come from the inner room.

Frowning, Fallon moved past Sullivan, who was lifting Candy's limp form off the floor, and looked inside again. The black he had glimpsed was lying grotesquely on his back halfway across the far room, his upper face a mess and blood gushing from the back of his head onto the carpet. The Zugendan security man repocketing his gun told the rest of the story.

Fallon looked once more at the figure draped like a rag doll over Sullivan's arm. She was breathing, he could see now—so not shot, just knocked out. Fallon stooped and picked up her purse. A Zugendan passport started to slide out as he lifted it. He glanced at the passport instinctively as he pushed it back in and caught the name "Mosswano, Annette." One of the security men held out a hand, and Fallon handed the purse over.

And then another figure came around the corner from the stairway, slim, dapperly dressed in a tan suit and short raincoat, lighting a cheroot, and walked past where George was standing.

"Tut, tut, I'd have thought a man with your experience would choose his friends more carefully," Makon Ngoyba said. "How did they contact you?"

Fallon stared at him woodenly. "The girl was watching for me at Konstantiou's last night. She left a note. It looked like a chance to find out something about the opposition."

Ngoyba nodded and came forward to survey the inside of the room. He seemed satisfied. "Well, now you know the kind of people we're up against, Mr. Fugleman. Perhaps it's time that we resumed our negotiations?"

Chapter Seven

IT HAD TO BE ASSUMED THAT AFTER THE INCIDENT in Pentonville, the surveillance on Boris Fugleman would be intensified. Efforts to evade it would only have aroused suspicion. But Bernard Fallon, who lived in the next street and had nothing to do with him, could go about his normal business routinely and openly.

The next morning, as arranged, Fallon walked to the Olympia exhibition hall on Hammersmith Road and bought himself a ticket. He located the General Electric Company's stand from the program guide and made his way to it, and Marlow appeared at 10:30 precisely, ambling along the crowded central aisle between a polished welding robot and a revolving display of digital speed sensors and position encoders.

"Ah, Bernard, good morning..." The colonel's blue porcelain eyes read the expression on Fallon's face, and his affability evaporated. "What happened?"

"You got me into a fine ruckus. There were two people from the Front over here."

"Yes, I knew about them, as a matter of fact."

"Well, the girl—she called herself Candy—got nabbed by Zugendan security. And the fellow who was with her—"

"His name is Victor."

"*Was*. He's dead."

The colonel looked taken aback. Fallon could see at once that he hadn't known about it. "How?" Marlow asked, keeping his voice low.

"Would you believe that they tried to set me up, and Ngoyba and his cavalry showed up just at the right moment?"

"You'd better tell me about it."

They moved away from the central area along one of the crossways, where there were fewer people. As they walked, Fallon recounted the events of the previous day, pausing occasionally when others came within earshot, or while Marlow stopped to examine something that aroused his curiosity. He concluded just as they reached the outer wall, "Did you know about it—that the ZRF were going to pull a stunt like that?"

Marlow shook his head. "Most emphatically not. I know I got you into some dicey situations once or twice in the old days, Bernard, but something like this would have been over the line. I'm as surprised as you were."

Fallon nodded in a way that said he believed it. They stopped and turned to look back over the exhibition hall. "Okay, what's it all about?" he asked. "If I'm into it to the point where I've got bullets flying around my head already, then it's time I knew a bit more."

The colonel hesitated, then nodded toward a snack bar not far away from them, with a small crowd milling around the counter. "Could you use some coffee? Awful stuff, probably, but better than nothing."

They moved into the throng at the counter. Fallon bought two black coffees in Styrofoam cups, while beside him a tubby, pink-faced man in a wrinkled suit expounded enthusiastically to a companion on the virtues of event-driven real-time multitasking software. Fallon turned to hand one cup to the colonel, and they moved away toward a deserted area at the rear, by a freight-elevator door and some concrete stairs leading upward. The colonel sipped his drink and pulled a face. When he spoke, he seemed for a moment to have gone off on a suddenly different tack.

"Are you a history buff at all?" he asked.

Fallon shrugged. "I've heard bits and pieces: Guy Fawkes, Alfred and the cakes, 1066 and all that."

"You know, in many ways the world's taken some rather ugly turns since the end of the last century—which was just when a lot of people thought the future looked so bright. Two world wars; systematic brainwashing and propagandizing of whole populations accepted as normal; mass murder and mass terror as deliberate instruments of national policy, with victims numbered in millions . . ." He made a resigned gesture. "What went wrong, do you think? Just when we were on the verge of being able to feed everyone on the planet properly and achieve a decent standard of living everywhere, we seemed to throw it all away. Just when war was no longer necessary to compete for resources that had always been inadequate, we launched the most ferocious wars ever fought and created war-directed peacetime economies on a scale that was previously unimaginable."

Fallon shrugged. "What's new? You've seen the kinds of geniuses that end up in charge of everything. Now ask me again why I got out of it."

"I'll tell you what went wrong. Western culture had its share of faults, but on the credit side it had been groping its way toward an ideal that was probably unique in the history of human civilization: that of classical *individualism*—the notion that the individual's rights are sovereign, and the only legitimate function of the state is the purely passive one of protecting them."

Fallon tasted his own coffee cautiously, found it not too bad, and drank some more. He nodded. "Okay, if you say so."

The colonel went on: "By that principle, the state's power exists purely to restrain and deter those who would violate the rights of its citizens. It's not an instrument to be seized for imposing anyone's ideas of how everyone else ought to live." He made a throwing-away motion with one hand. "But instead of that, look what we've got. This century has seen assaults on personal freedom from every direction: dictators and their secret police terrorizing entire nations; fanatics and terrorists running amuck; people being robbed wholesale in the name of the people. A hundred years ago an Englishman could travel anywhere he wanted without passports or permission, take his money and spend it on anything he chose. If he behaved himself, he could live his whole life without seeing more of officialdom than the postman and the village bobby.

"What I'm saying is that probably the biggest unsolved problem at the root of it all is how to restrain government—any government—from abusing its monopoly on the legal use of force. That's a fearsome power to put in the hands of anybody, and despite all the noble intentions and solemn constitutions to try and contain it, it always goes out of control."

"Are you saying you know what the answer is?" Fallon asked, dubious that there was one.

"I'm not sure anyone could be certain of that, Bernard. But I think I know what it's not. . . . Because of that monopoly, brute force becomes the hallmark of governments, the only way they know how to think or operate. And when they turn it against what they perceive as a threat, it backfires on them. The democracies militarized to defend themselves against the socialist and fascist police states that were emerging in the first half of the century, and look how they ended up; there were our squalid little colonial wars; the French in Algeria and Indochina, then the Americans, later, when it became Vietnam. You felt the futility of it yourself. That was why you got out. You end up changing into what you set out to change. How many tyrants started out as revolutionaries against a tyranny? America went to war over a one-percent tax on tea and ended up with the IRS. Russia threw out an unpopular czar and got Stalin. Churchill ended up presiding over the creation of a welfare socialism that bankrupted the country. . . . Didn't Shakespeare say something about it being safer to be that which we destroy?"

"Did he? We didn't get much of that at the wrong end of Kensington."

The colonel smiled thinly and sipped from his cup. "*Macbeth*, I think." They began walking slowly along the side wall, toward the loading doors at the far end.

"So, tell me a better way," Fallon said.

The colonel raised his umbrella briefly to indicate the booths and crowded display stands lining the aisles of the exhibition hall. "Look at all those firms out there, all doing their best to earn a few quid and make a living. They *have* to do their best. Since they can't put a gun to anyone's head and force them to buy the product, they must compete to try and make what they're offering for your money a better deal than the other fellow's. Private enterprise. *Persuasion*, not coercion. Choice, not command of law. Capitalism is reviled for a lot of things, but what motivation for human behavior could be more honest and ethical than simply wanting to make a buck? You, the customer, accept the deal freely, and when you've paid the bill, your life is your own affair. Nobody cares what color you are, who you go to bed with, or what books you read, and you won't be tied to a stake and set on fire for saying the wrong prayers. When did a business corporation last flatten a city with bombs or conscript eighteen-year-olds to go and kill each other?"

"Some people would say they don't have to. They've got governments as agents to do it for them," Fallon commented.

"With some justification," the colonel agreed. "But why pick on them? State power has been used to push a lot of other interests too: flags, religions, political creeds, racial bigotries . . . any cause that could get its hands on it. Precisely *because* of their ability to coerce, governments end up so mortgaged to various interests who want to control them that they find it impossible to live by the principles which they were originally created to defend. We have no such power to sell, and therefore don't suffer from the consequences."

Fallon looked across sharply. So at last they were back to the subject of the mysterious organization that Marlow had alluded to the day before, which had been the point of Fallon's original question. They stopped at the end of one of the aisles and dropped their empty cups into a litter bin. Marlow clasped the handle of his umbrella with both hands and stared at it for a few seconds. Then he raised his head and looked out across the hall as he spoke.

"We're called Infinity Limited. There's a good reason, which I won't go into just now."

"I can't say I've heard of it."

"You wouldn't have. It's something that has grown in the course of several years now. Its aim is to combat violations of basic human rights and dignity, anywhere and in any form. It is international, and owes no allegiance to any state, political system, social or economic ideology, racial doctrine, religious persuasion, or any other form of dogma or creed. We adhere only to the principles of free individualism that I've already outlined."

Fallon's brow knitted into creases. "What are you saying this is?" he asked. "Some kind of *private* outfit that thinks it can take on international terrorism and dictators?"

"Among other things. Since we are not a blunt instrument licensed by any government to terrify guilty and innocent alike, we are obliged to use methods that are selective and precise. Not having any power to command, we operate purely as a free association of individuals, with no ties other than their own convictions. And that is the way we would wish things to remain."

Fallon watched a stand a short distance away from

them, where a mechanical arm guided by a TV camera was selecting metal parts from a heap piled haphazardly in a bin and inserting them into holes of the correct shape. At a console beyond, an attractive redhead in a crisp white blouse and black skirt was demonstrating something on a computer screen to a small audience of admirers.

"Well, that's nice," he said at last, turning back. "But what's the rest of the story? Nobody in the real world's going to put up the money you're talking about to make the world safe for some ideology these days. So who's paying, and what's in it for them?"

Marlow shrugged. "People who like to make money, of course." The question had evidently been expected.

"Ah, *now* it's starting to make sense," Fallon said. He stroked the side of his nose with a knuckle. "You know, you could have saved yourself a lot of breath by saying so in the first place."

Marlow nodded knowingly. "But that's not all there is to it. Yes, the bill's being footed by people who think that a world full of prosperous customers, instead of ruined farmers and starving refugees, would provide more opportunities to get rich in. That implies the *freedom* for anyone to make it—but with the way things have been going, there are too many incompetents queering the pitch, who only understand the language of tanks, the secret police, and the concentration camp.

"But economic freedom results in independence, which leads to all the other kinds of personal freedom too. And that's also reflected in the structure of Infinity Limited. We have scientists, artists, writers, thinkers: people committed to freedom of thought, freedom of expression, and the open exchange of ideas. And people like yourself, who got out of the system to do their own thing in their own way. You see, we all really stand for the same thing. But individualists, *because* of the very fact that they do value independence, have always suffered from dividedness, and the forces of regimentation and coercion have ruled . . . and look at the mess that's resulted. Well, that's what Infinity Limited has decided to try and do something about."

Fallon returned his hands to his raincoat pockets and looked away again for a while to think about it. "So who decides what the policy is?" he asked finally. "You're bound to get disagreements eventually. Someone has to give the orders. How do you end up any different from what you've been talking about?"

"For a start, nobody has the power to *order* anyone to do anything," the colonel replied. "If you accept a job that Infinity Limited wants done, it's because you think it needs doing, and it doesn't go against your own principles. There are no oaths of loyalty, and nobody tells you what your obligation or duty is."

"A hired hand in the special-skills department," Fallon commented.

"Which is what you're doing anyway," Marlow pointed out. "Only this way, you'd be pooling your talents with a lot of others who have the same fundamental goals, and thus helping to make all the effort that much more effective. That was what I meant yesterday when I asked you if you thought you were putting enough into life."

Fallon nodded that he accepted the point. "So, what's Infinity Limited's interest in Zugenda and the ZRF?" he asked, looking back at Marlow. There was something more than just curiosity in his expression.

The colonel frowned and took some time to consider his words. He seemed anxious for the first time. "About your story of what happened yesterday..." he said finally. "Tell me, how certain can you be that Candy and Victor set you up?"

"I didn't say they did," Fallon replied. "I asked you if you believed they did."

The colonel looked momentarily confused. "Why? Am I to take it that you don't?"

"No... I don't. And I don't think you do, either."

"So it sounds as if we *are* on the same side. I didn't want to bias you one way or the other when we talked yesterday. It seemed better to let you hear both sides first for yourself. We're with the ZRF. That's why I was getting worried about what you'd said."

"So, why the ZRF?" Fallon asked.

"Barindas represents a rather special case—unique, in fact. Practically alone among the new, postcolonial African leaders, he doesn't want power in order to impose his own version of nepotism, tribalism, a socialist utopia, or whatever. He just wants to establish a state that will protect its citizens' freedoms and leave them alone to evolve their own version of productive free enterprise."

"Is he a part of Infinity Limited, then?"

"We've been working with him for some time. His case is everything that a popular uprising to overthrow an oppressive regime should be. If we can help him throw out Molokutu, it could become a model to inspire the entire African continent. You've been there before, Bernard. You know the score. Think what a difference that could make to things."

Fallon turned to face Marlow fully as a number of things clicked into place. "It was you—your lot—who engineered the whole thing," he said, pointing a finger. "You found out that the Zugendan government wanted to put a hit team inside the ZRF. And you steered them to me, via Perry, so you could make the inside man that the government thought *it* had hired to penetrate the ZRF, in reality the ZRF's man working inside Zugendan security."

"Er... quite," the colonel agreed, forcing a genial smile.

Fallon gave a satisfied nod. Now they were getting down to the kind of specifics that he felt more at home with. "And what am I supposed to do when I get over there?" he asked. "Are we talking about turning their own plan around completely? They wanted to send a kill team in to decapitate the ZRF. We use it to take them out instead? Is that it?"

"If it proved feasible," the colonel said. "The initial goal was for you to assess the situation from the inside and see what kind of options exist." He pinched his mustache and frowned. "But from what you've said today, we seem to have a more pressing need. The ZRF must have been betrayed from the inside: Ngoyba knew who those two were, their safe house, and why they were here. Before anything else, we need to find out who the informant is. That will have to be the first job." The colonel glanced back at Fallon's face. "Er, I do take it that you're with us, then?"

Fallon nodded. "Oh, yes."

"Splendid!" Marlow brightened visibly. "You see, you do have noble principles deep down, Bernard. I knew you'd see things that way once you heard the rationale behind it all."

"No, it doesn't have anything to do with that. I'd already made my mind up yesterday."

Marlow looked surprised. "You mean when it happened, at Velker's place?"

"Yes. You see, it wasn't the ZRF who tried to set me up. It was Ngoyba." Fallon shook his head. "I don't like that—people taking me for some kind of a berk. I don't like that at all."

"How could you tell?"

"Well, here's my guess of what happened: Candy and Victor were here to make the ZRF's counteroffer. . . ."

"Yes."

"But Ngoyba's people were onto them. A few minutes before Candy and I got back to the house, somebody phoned and told Victor that Zugendan intelligence were on their way there to grab him. That was why he was holed up in the back room with a gun when we walked in. But because Candy was there he didn't shoot, and in that second of confusion they got him first. The whole idea was to make it look to *me* as if the ZRF had set me up to be taken out—in case I'd decided to accept Ngoyba's deal."

"That sounds feasible," the colonel agreed.

"That much was as they'd planned. But then they saw a chance to play for a bonus. Sullivan had KO'd Candy, and when George yelled from the door and I ducked under the stairs, one of them planted a gun in her hand and opened her purse to make it look as if she'd taken it out to back Victor up."

The colonel frowned. "But how can you know that? You said you were under the stairs."

"There was one small detail that they got wrong."

"What?"

Fallon took one hand out of his pocket and made an empty-handed gesture. "The card that she left with the hatcheck girl at Konstantiou's. The writing . . . And at the pub the next day, I saw it for myself."

The colonel's frown deepened. "What are you talking about?"

"She was left-handed," Fallon said. "They put the gun in the wrong hand."

Chapter Eight

FALLON MET NGOYBA ON A BENCH OUTSIDE THE monkey house in the Regents Park zoo a week later. In the course of several meetings during that time, he had indicated an acceptance of the official version of the affair in Pentonville—that it had been a ZRF trap—and agreed to go to Zugenda to hear the government's proposition.

"We have made arrangements for you to go via Copenhagen," Ngoyba informed him. "A contact at our Danish embassy there will furnish your cover-identity documents and entry visa. It would be better if there were nothing in the record to connect you with London."

Fallon nodded. Ngoyba had assured him that Candy's capture and the death of her colleague Victor meant that the ZRF back home would have no way of knowing what the outcome of events in London had been, or even if contact had been made with Fugleman at all. Since they could therefore have no way of knowing what Fugleman looked like, the original plan for him to penetrate the ZRF under some suitable guise could still go ahead.

Ngoyba was anxious to begin recruiting suitable specialists immediately, rather than wait until Fallon completed his reconnaissance in Zugenda. Then, if Fallon's assessment of the situation proved favorable, the team could be standing by and ready to move at once, without loss of momentum to the plan. Fallon had said he would leave that side of things in the hands of suitably qualified associates.

"About the hiring question," Ngoyba said. "Did you put out feelers on the circuit?"

"Someone called Stroller will be in touch in the next day or two," Fallon said.

"I assume he's reliable."

"Yes. I've known him for years."

"In view of the somewhat delicate nature of the operation, we would prefer that he didn't have overt contact with the embassy," Ngoyba said.

"Naturally," Fallon agreed. Since known acquaintances of Bernard Fallon couldn't be openly involved, anyway—the Zugendans were dealing with Boris Fugleman, and they would doubtless be keeping a watch on things—that suited him fine. He had decided to use somebody whose connection to Fallon could be easily dissolved after he initiated contact with the Zugendans.

Fallon had also insisted on having secure and private communications back to his contacts in London. In his profession, he had pointed out, his associates expected him to observe precautions. Although the Zugendans had hummed and hawed a little, they would have been surprised if he had done otherwise... and probably wouldn't have hired him.

"Our embassy will relay messages via the regular diplomatic link to Kinnube," Ngoyba said. "Your contact can use the telephone number that you already have.... Er, what would you like the embassy to do if anything urgent comes in from you? Is there a number I should give them?"

"My contact will call your people twice a day," Fallon said. Ngoyba nodded, having expected it. Worth a try, though.

Ngoyba went on to give details of the contact arrangements in Denmark. They left separately. Fallon departed for Copenhagen the next morning.

Years of a life spent in the open under hot sun had left Henri Monaux with tanned, leathery features and eyes that wrinkled into crow's-feet at the corners when he grinned, which was readily and often. He had bright, beady eyes, a full crop of black hair, graying somewhat prematurely for his years, and a short but ragged Gallic beard, also grizzling at the edges. Julia spotted his squat, solid frame easily as he came through the gate from Air France flight 27 at London's Heathrow Airport. He had seen her before she waved her hand and was already bobbing toward her through the choppy crosscurrents of arriving passengers and people meeting them. He threw one arm around her in a hug that left her breathless, pressed a wrapped bottle into her hands with the other, and kissed her heartily on the cheek.

"Ha-ha! You are looking as fine as ever, English madam from America. Here. That is for the two of us to get drunk with."

"Hello, Henri. You haven't changed." He was carrying a couple more pounds around the middle, she noticed, but it was hardly the thing to say.

"Today I got up early, ate breakfast out—croissant, eggs, some fruit, and a little wine—put on this suit fresh from the cleaner, and went to the airport in a white taxi," he informed her.

"How fascinating. But why are you telling me?"

Monaux grinned. "Because I know the way you are. Now I won't have to listen to you telling me and then have to rack my brains wondering how you knew."

"Oh, you spoil all my fun," Julia chided. They began walking back toward the terminal entrance.

"We're not taking the Underground today?" Monaux said, waving toward the escalator down to the Piccadilly Line.

"No, I brought the car. More privacy to talk."

"Already, you want to talk business? Don't you ever relax?"

"You're back in England now, Henri."

Formerly an NCO with the French GIGN counter-terrorist force, Monaux was another of the ex-military professionals that Fallon had met in his SAS days and stayed in touch with. He had been one of the team that had made headlines in Djibouti in 1976, when terrorists hijacked a bus carrying thirty French schoolchildren and threatened to slit their throats if political demands were not met. The GIGN snipers, all in radio contact with their commander, had waited ten hours for a moment to present itself when the five hijackers were centered in cross hairs at the same time before dropping them with simultaneous headshots. These days, he made a quasi-respectable living as a broker of hard-to-get armaments and related equipment, which meant that he usually had a good idea of what was going on in the private mercenary network.

They collected the silver-gray Mercedes from the multilevel parking area outside and took the exit tunnel from the airport. The lunaforming of the M4 was continuing, and after a mile or so they found themselves crawling in a tailback from a squeeze into single-lane traffic ahead.

"So what's this with Bernard that's so urgent suddenly?" Monaux asked, transformed now into a more serious version of himself. "He wants to put together a mercenary force?"

"Not quite. Just a small team. Strictly professionals."

"I'm surprised. I never thought of that as his line."

"It isn't. That's why we contacted you."

"Is he planning on expanding the business or something?"

"He has a special interest in this case. A rather personal one. Some people tried to kill him again."

"Oh . . ." Monaux nodded in a way that said everything now made sense.

"One does tend to take offense at things like that," Julia said.

"Anyone we know?" Monaux asked.

"Not very well. Bernard left for Africa yesterday on a fact-finding trip. It was part of the terms of a proposition he's been offered. He'll be given a fuller briefing over there. That's why he wants you to help take care of things at this end."

"Does that leave just the two of us?" Monaux leered playfully.

"George is in on it too."

"Aha! And how is the Yorkshire barbarian? He hasn't poisoned himself yet or drowned in his pints of dishwashing beer?"

"He's fine. I suppose we'll have the usual nonsense when you two get together again. This time I absolutely forbid any mention of black pudding."

Monaux pulled a face and got back to the subject. "Where in Africa are we talking about?"

"Zugenda."

"So . . . what's been happening there?"

Julia related the essence of the story while they were navigating the bottleneck, omitting references to Infinity Limited and other details that Monaux didn't need to know. For the time being, it was only necessary to ensure that anyone making surreptitious inquiries would be satisfied that he was raising an assassination team. There could be no leak of everything not being quite aboveboard if neither the members of the team nor their recruiter knew that part of it themselves. Monaux had been in the business long enough not to be offended when the time came to tell him more.

Julia concluded, "We'll know more when Bernard learns more himself. But basically he's looking for high-grade people who can be passed off as mercenary volunteers— in other words, probably with military backgrounds. In particular, he's interested in people who know how to get close to highly protected targets." Monaux nodded. "Also, he'll probably be needing a good radioman straightaway," Julia said.

"You mean, to send in now, without waiting for the others?"

"Yes."

"Is that how he's planning on keeping in touch?"

"No, he just thinks it would be wise in that kind of country. George thinks he might be able to get you someone—an old partner in crime of theirs."

The real reason was the existence of an informer somewhere in the ZRF camp. The first thing that Fallon wanted available was an independent communications capability of his own that he knew he could trust.

"So what's our channel to Bernard?" Monaux asked.

"Through the diplomatic link to the Zugendan embassy in London. He's worked out a procedure with them for using it as a drop."

Monaux nodded and fell silent for a while as he thought once more through all she had said. Then, changing the subject as if giving himself time to digest the information, he asked casually, "Was Bernard in Paris recently . . . a couple of weeks ago, maybe?"

A little too casually. Julia flashed him a suspicious glance as she drove. "Why?"

"Oh . . . just one or two things that I heard. Apparently there's a blood feud going on between the CCC and an Italian outfit that they teamed up with for a kidnapping that didn't come off—of the young daughter of a director of one of our electronics companies. I couldn't help but notice how some of the details sounded a lot like the way Bernard works sometimes—you know, making democracy safe for the world. . . . But it could be just a coincidence, I suppose." He looked at Julia and shrugged nonchalantly.

"Yes, I suppose it could. . . ." Julia dropped the pretense. "What's the score so far?"

"Two dead on each side, the last I heard," Monaux told her.

"How tragic."

"So it *was* him?"

"Of course it was."

Monaux pinched his nose. "But why did they use Bernard? It was a straightforward abduction case, wasn't it? Why couldn't our own people have handled it?"

"Apparently there are suspicions of a leak inside SDECE," Julia said. "So a phony official operation was set up as a decoy for his benefit while Bernard handled the real job secretly."

"Ah, now I see." Monaux nodded.

They drove in silence for a while. Monaux rested his arm along the window ledge and watched the outskirts of Brentford parading by in their regular, semidetached ranks. "You know," he said at last, "I've known Bernard for all these years now, and I still don't understand really what makes him do it." He shrugged in an unapologetic kind of way. "With me, I like the money and the life that it buys—and yes, it has its excitement too."

"You could say all those things about Bernard as well," Julia pointed out.

"Yes, I know. But with him there's something else too. Don't you think so?"

"Would you believe me if I said he's still an idealist?"

"Bernard? No. He's too much of a cynic, surely."

"That's what reality does to idealism. He used to think he was part of a battle to protect the Western world and its values. Today he still has the same values, but with more freedom to decide who represents them. Does that make sense?"

Monaux shook his head. "It makes life altogether too complicated. He should learn to be more like me, a . . ." He looked across the car perplexedly. "What's English for the opposite of cynic?"

Julia thought for a second. "I'd say an optimist."

Monaux looked surprised. "I thought that was the opposite of a pessimist."

Julia shook her head as she drove. "Oh, no. A cynic expects the worst, but he accepts that the best might happen. An optimist is the other way around. But they're both in touch with reality. The nice thing about being a cynic is that you're never unpleasantly surprised. Optimists are always being disappointed."

"Very well. So what's a pessimist?" Monaux asked.

"One who believes that only the worst can happen, so there's no point in trying. But it's unrealistic. The world isn't that bad."

"That's what Americans call the law of the Murphy, or something, yes? Everything always goes wrong."

"Yes. But it's also what sometimes causes things to go right. That's what makes pessimists unrealistic."

Monaux smiled uncertainly. "Now you're confusing me, Julia. Everything always going wrong sometimes makes things go right? How can that be?"

"Very simply. Being universal, Murphy's law sometimes works on itself, you see."

"Ahah! Now I see." Monaux nodded vigorously and smiled. "So the opposite of being a pessimist is...is what?"

"Seeing a world where everything can only go right, which is equally unreal."

"And what do you call him?"

"I suppose... Well, *you* should know, if anyone, Henri. A romantic."

Monaux laughed again and sat back to watch the road. "I should have known better by now than to start talking philosophy with you. Tell me, are you busy with another book these days?"

"But of course. It's about the victims of fraud and deception in urban development."

"Very good."

"Bernard likes it. He says the only problem is that with the way things are going, it's too historical."

"And is he still stealing your hard-earned fame and fortune?"

"Fortune, no. Fame, he's welcome to."

"It's a shame," Monaux grumbled. "You should assert yourself to the world. Come out of this shell that you hide yourself away in." He gestured expansively. "Be what you deserve. It's your right."

"Oh, come on, Henri, I prefer it this way. You know how I feel about all that vulgar nonsense."

Monaux shook his head. "You know, you're the wrong way 'round, you two. Bernard should be the American and you the Englishwoman. You would take well to it. That's why you came over here."

"It's possible."

"You don't think so?" Monaux said.

"I wonder if we ever really know why we do anything," Julia replied.

Chapter Nine

In Copenhagen, an official at the Zugendan embassy provided Fallon with a forged Danish passport in the name of Konrad Hannegen, along with papers and a visa identifying him as a zoologist authorized to enter Zugenda to carry out fieldwork. It was felt that such a cover would enable him to remain mobile openly once he was in Zugenda or to disappear for lengthy spells, as suited his convenience. Fallon spent a couple of days collecting an assortment of books, belongings, and other paraphernalia appropriate to the role and arranging with the embassy for a vehicle and suitable equipment at the other end. He then flew via Brussels to one of the Central African states bordering Zugenda to the south and spent another two days on the overland drive to the border.

The Zugendan border post was situated on the far side of a single-track steel bridge spanning a gorge of crumbly red rock, choked with thorny scrub. Driving a rented Land Rover painted safari style in zebra stripes and amply equipped with rations, field and bivouac gear, and supplies of water and gasoline in five-gallon cans, Fallon crossed from the customs hut where he had just completed exit formalities. He was wearing a short-sleeve khaki bush shirt, lightweight denims, and sunhat. The hills around the valley were sandy and dry, with jagged peaks of bare rock thrusting up beyond. Clumps of umbrella-shaped acacias, junipers, and stunted cedars crowded together in the depressions and faltered up the lower slopes, giving way to grass and scattered thornbushes higher up. The weather was sunny but cooling compared to what it had been, with a fussing wind marshaling the first scraps of cloud for the short rainy season, still several weeks away.

There was a barrier across the road, with a guard-

house and customs post on one side behind sandbagged
parapets. Across the way were a couple of other buildings
with vehicles parked haphazardly in front: a battered truck
roofed by a tarpaulin; a car, Fiat; another truck, painted
army olive; beside it a jeep mounting a .50-caliber machine gun. Barbed-wire fences extended to the edge of the
gorge on either side, blocking flank approaches from the
bridge. Beyond lay a charmless settlement of a score or so
tin-roofed dwellings harboring a visible population of scav-
enging dogs, goats, chickens, and half-naked children.
How anyone could scratch a living from the sunbaked,
stony dust in a place like this, Fallon couldn't imagine.

Three steel-helmeted Zugendans in khaki combat gear
appeared as Fallon stopped at the barrier. A corporal
wearing a sidearm came forward, hands on hips, his eyes
moving over Fallon and the vehicle in a cursory manner,
evidently not unduly surprised by the European's arrival.
The two others, both privates carrying carbines, stayed
back, eyeing him with greater suspicion.

"Good morning," Fallon said, peering through the
gold-rimmed spectacles he was wearing. "My name is
Konrad Hannegen. I was told that you should have heard
about me from Kinnube."

"You're the scientist?" the corporal said. His tone was
cool, but with a hint of curiosity—possibly at meeting a
"scientist" for the first time. "You're alone?"

"I hope to hire a guide when I get to Kinnube."

The corporal seemed less impressed than he had
hoped to be, and the initial flicker of interest died. He
indicated the customs post with a nod of his head. "We
have to see your papers."

Fallon produced a leather wallet and followed him
inside, while behind them the two privates began poking
about in the Land Rover.

The wall inside was graced with a large, framed
picture of President Molokutu wearing a military uniform,
with a brass caption plate shaped in the form of a scroll,
informing that he was the Father and Savior of the people.

"What does a scientist find to do here?" the corporal
asked, taking a stamp and carefully centering the imprint
in the square provided.

"I want to do a population census on a species of
antelope that lives in the highlands of the Glimayel region.

It's quite rare. Experts from several places around the world are concerned about it."

"Antelopes?" The corporal snorted. "You worry about animals? There are rebels who are killing people every day. Thousands starve. Why don't your experts care about them?"

"Your tribal squabbles are hardly our affair," Fallon replied, consciously provocative.

The corporal glared at him and thrust back a folded sheet of paper. "It's lucky for you that you have a personal letter from the minister. Your permit doesn't allow entry to the war zone, so stay away from it."

"I can assure you that I have no intention of doing otherwise."

One of the privates appeared in the doorway holding the .357 Magnum that had been concealed on the shelf below the Land Rover's dashboard. He said something to the corporal in a dialect that Fallon didn't understand. A glint came into the corporal's eyes for an instant, then dulled with disappointment when Fallon pointed to another slip of paper from the wallet. "It is authorized, can't you see? Look there."

"You come expecting trouble, eh?"

"Not at all. But I was advised to take precautions."

The corporal pushed the papers together and tossed them back, leaving it to Fallon to fold them and return them to the wallet. "I'd advise you to change your ways while you are in Zugenda. An attitude like yours can make trouble. I don't care about you, but we've got enough trouble already. Okay?"

"I'll bear it in mind." Fallon turned and held out a hand to the private. The colonel nodded curtly and muttered something. The private surrendered the Magnum. Fallon took it and went back outside.

Three other soldiers had joined the one by the Land Rover: two more privates and a captain in jungle camouflage and a maroon beret with a paratrooper's winged badge. The captain had narrow, overhung eyes, smooth features, and a thin mustache. When he saw Fallon emerge, he came around the Land Rover, moving with a jaunty swagger that was presumably part of the image. Fallon shot him an aloof look and climbed into the driver's seat without stopping. Undaunted, the captain lifted a foot onto the step of the Land Rover, at the same time resting his elbow on top of the frame holding the windshield. "Heading for Kinnube?" he asked.

"What if I am?" Fallon said. He stowed the revolver back in its niche, making a show of it as if daring the other to challenge him.

The captain followed it with his eyes but said nothing. "Just curious. That's my job. . . . What brings you to Zugenda?"

Fallon emitted an exaggerated sigh. "Please, do we have to? I've just been through all that." He nodded at the corporal, who had reappeared in the doorway. "Isn't that *his* job?"

"He's a scientist," the corporal supplied. "Come to count the antelopes."

"Not very friendly," the captain said, looking back at Fallon.

"If you must know, I don't like military matters, or the kind of people who get involved in them," Fallon said shortly.

The captain grinned, seeming to enjoy it all the more. He waved an arm loosely to indicate the jeep parked across the track, in which three more soldiers were now sitting. "We're just leaving in that direction. So I guess you've got yourself some company into town. What do we call you . . . 'Doc'? Any objections?"

"Do I have a choice?" Fallon asked resignedly.

"You should learn to get along with people better, Doc. Especially us. In this country it could be a lot safer."

"I thought that this isn't the war area."

The captain guffawed and said something to the two privates who were with him. They laughed hilariously. "You don't believe what them politicians say, do you? That stuff's for outside consumption. At least we'll get you as far as Kinnube alive."

"I'd have thought that with you I'd be worse off," Fallon retorted. "What reason would rebels have for interfering with me?"

The captain laughed again. "They don't need reasons for killing anyone. Where've you been, Doc? C'mon, I'll ride with you. It'll be a change to have someone to talk to." He let himself down into the passenger seat before Fallon could reply and held a brief shouted dialogue with the soldiers in the jeep across the road. The two privates who had come across with him ran back. One boarded the jeep as it lurched out onto the track; the other grabbed two rifles as they were held out and ran back to the Land Rover with them, handing one to the captain and climbing in behind Fallon with the other. "Follow them," the captain said, waving gradiosely like a wagontrain master.

It had to have been arranged, Fallon reflected as he pulled forward. For the patrol to have just happened to be there when he crossed over the border could hardly have been a coincidence. But sending an army escort specifically for a lone zoologist when there were no doubt more than enough pressing things to be attended to would have been too odd not to have provoked questions.

The corporal watched sourly from the customs-post door as the two vehicles receded bumpily in a cloud of dust. "Enjoy the company," he growled. He spat into the dust and went back inside, out of the sun.

From the border crossing, the road descended into less rugged terrain, though without undergoing any spectacular improvement in quality. The driver of the machine-gun-toting jeep in front swerved wildly around the potholes and boulders with the abandon of a kamikaze pilot bent on self-destruction, and at times it seemed to Fallon that no assembly of nuts and bolts could possibly hold itself together under the incessant wrenching and buffeting as he strove to keep up. But it seemed to be just part of a normal day's work to the black soldiers, and whenever the distance between the two vehicles began to lengthen, he was urged on by exuberant shouts of "Come on, we're losing them. Let's go! Let's go! *Allez vite!*" from the captain beside him, who by this time had introduced himself as "Raoul."

Although the upper slopes of the surrounding hills remained lifeless and arid, the landscape in general was greener than the images of parched dust bowls and dried-up water holes projected by the news media. But the potential of the land—in the region that they were passing through at least—was not being realized. In fact there were signs that it was reverting to wilderness. They passed whole areas where weeds and new growths of elephant grass were encroaching into abandoned crop fields. In other places they drove through the remains of deserted villages, houses burned and gardens overgrown, left to prowling packs of wild dogs. Raoul shrugged and explained that the people had been relocated. It was to prevent their being intimidated into providing food and respite for ZRF guerrillas.

"The Chinaman, Mao—he said they were like fish that swim in the sea of the people, right? Well, what you've got to do is drain the water away from the fish. Then you've got them stranded. That's what we're doing."

But farther on, they passed by well-tended cattle ranches where herds grazed behind high wire fences extending away into the distance, patrolled by armed guards. "Is this where the people are relocated to?" Fallon asked, feigning naïveté.

Raoul laughed. "You've got to be kidding, Doc. You need friends in the right places to get yourself one of these spreads. Or else be part of the family of someone in the government. This place here belongs to a brother of the minister of finance."

They came to a checkpoint with a makeshift barrier manned by more steel-helmeted soldiers, looking unkempt and slovenly. After a perfunctory exchange of words between Raoul and the officer in charge, the Land Rover passed through. Beyond was another village, but this time not deserted. It seemed to be undergoing a search, or maybe some kind of punitive action. A British-made Ferret scout car was parked in the center of the main street and, farther along at intervals, two Chinese three-ton military trucks and an armored personnel carrier. The villagers had been herded together at one end, under guard, some of the women wailing, others shouting angrily, terrified children clinging to their skirts. The men were segregated into a separate group. Fallon noticed several bloodstained shirts and bruised faces as the vehicle drove past. There were soldiers along the street, looking tough, festooned with grenades and pouches; others were inside the houses, some of which had had their doors broken down. Piles of personal belongings and furnishings lay where they had been thrown outside. One house farther back was in flames.

"The ZRF came one night and killed the headman and all his family right here in the square, in front of everybody," Raoul said, pointing. "Messy—I mean with knives and axes. So then everyone was scared and knew who was boss and did what they were told. Now they're getting it for helping the rebels."

"What are they supposed to do?" Fallon asked.

Raoul shook his head. "Why ask me? I don't know. Nothing needs to make sense anymore . . . if it ever did."

"What do you think?"

"I don't bother thinking. It doesn't get you anywhere. I just try to get the clean jobs and do what I'm told, okay?"

"What's the name of this place?"

"It's called Elinvoro. Why does it matter to you?"

"Just curious."

Raoul glanced across. "Don't look so uptight, Doc. It isn't your line of business. Things like this are necessary. You'd know, if you understood anything about it. You just keep to your own line, okay? Get yourself on upcountry and count the antelopes."

Beyond the village, the road widened and improved a little from the deep-rutted, rocky track that had brought them most of the way from the border. As the day wore on, Raoul became more expansive.

"You know what I'd really like to do if I had the chance, Doc? I'd open me a nightclub—in a big city somewhere, not some asshole place like Kinnube. You know, like you see in the movies. Walk around in a white tuxedo every night, lots o' chicks and booze. But you'll never do it up here, 'cause anyone who makes anything gets it taken away by the government, and that means you don't have no customers, anyhow. Reckon I'd have to go way down south, somewhere like that. Do they have good nightclubs in Denmark? Full of blond chicks?"

"I wouldn't know."

"Not your bag, huh? Nope, I guess not."

"What kind of things do go on in Kinnube?"

"Oh, you'll see when you get there. Where are you staying, at the Independence? That's where most foreigners go."

"Yes."

"You'll see it all there. We're a world sensation now, see. Everyone wants to come here with food trucks and get themselves on TV. But they're amateurs: pop singers, movie stars, rich people's kids who never knew food wasn't made in factories—famine groupies, driving around in cars from motor pools that the agencies provide, with radios and clipboards and getting to feel like they're important... except none of them don't know nothing. But I guess it makes 'em look good back home."

"You mean they don't have much effect?"

Raoul waved his free hand in the air. "Aw, everything's rotten. You need something, you go to the underground market. It's illegal, but everyone has to do it because there's no other way. If you want cooking oil, it's out. But if you pay two times, three times the official price that the government fixes, it appears. Most things you need, you don't find anywhere at any price. Everything has to have a signature, but you can never find the right guy. When you do, you pay. No one works. People take salaries from the government, but they only do work for themselves on their private lots."

"You work for them," Fallon pointed out.

"Sure," Raoul agreed unhesitatingly. "Because it's a regular way to eat. Hell of a lot safer than being at the other end of a gun, too."

Late in the afternoon they were nearing Kinnube when Fallon heard the whine of jets approaching low. Moments later a couple of single-engine fighters appeared above the trees, descending toward the west with their undercarriages already lowered. He identified them as Soviet MiG-19 types.

"Part of Molokutu's air force," Raoul said. "They're going into the air base at Mordun. That's a high-security area all around, Doc. You don't wanna go too near it." A mile or so farther on they passed a turnoff blocked by a barb-wired gate covered by machine guns and with two tanks placed some distance back, which underlined the point effectively.

After a few more miles, the road acquired a metaled surface. They arrived in Kinnube less than an hour later, by which time it was almost evening.

The capital was crowded and squalid, reflecting the effects of the bush war and the deteriorating economy. The houses on the outskirts had paint peeling from doors and timbers, with shutters hanging crazily and plaster flaking from cracked walls. While a few gardens continued bravely to maintain their shrubs and borders of yellow and red flowers, most were overgrown and littered with trash to become part of a scene where appearances had long ceased to matter. The shops that weren't boarded up or taken over by squatters were all but bare. On the corners groups of poorly dressed youths lounged, hands in pockets, bored, sullen, looking for trouble. There were posters on the walls extoling hard work, the virtues of sacrifice, and devotion to the party, along with the inevitable portraits of the Father and Savior.

They reached the city center. The taller office buildings and hotels that had once blossomed like desert flowers after a rainfall in the optimistic spurt of postcolonial growth that had come with the new era now wilted dejectedly above a shantytown of tin-and-packing-case huts that seethed with people of all ages like a collapsed nest of human termites. Fallon had seen it all many times before. As always, the sheer waste of human potential, especially the waste of young minds as starved of education as the tiny, brown potbellies were of sustenance, depressed him.

The jeep in front led them to the police station, where the people in the Copenhagen embassy had directed Fallon to report. Just before reaching it, they passed the Independence Hotel, just a short distance away on the other side of the street. One of its big advantages, Raoul said, was having a rear yard for parking that was guarded twenty-four hours. Under the prevailing conditions, leaving a generously equipped Land Rover on the street for a night wouldn't have been a good idea.

There were no problems at the police station, where a discreet word had been dropped from above of his impending arrival, and Fallon came back out after a few minutes, furnished with more of the stamps and permits to add to his collection, that officials in every socialist African country seemed to take such a delight in. He found Raoul's soldiers keeping back a curious crowd that had begun to collect around the Land Rover. There were the idlers who would congregate around a new attraction anywhere, the ubiquitous horde of children, beggars in various stages of living decay. Several girls with short, gaudy skirts and painted faces had come out of a bar next door, drawn by the promise of a potential customer with illicit foreign currency.

With an audience to perform before, and a roving-eyed interest in the girls, which he flaunted as part of the virility ritual symbolized by his military regalia, Raoul became more cavalier than ever, insisting on riding ostentatiously with his mysterious charge back along the street to the Independence and through to the fenced yard behind, where Fallon parked next to a newish-looking Toyota Land Cruiser. After making a ceremony of handing over the Land Rover and its occupant to the custody of the hotel guards that would have earned credit at Buckingham Palace, he left with a half-waved salute and a few parting words of advice to Fallon about keeping valuables out of sight and getting good references on anyone he intended hiring as a guide.

"Watch out for the ones who talk too much—the ones who tell you how good they are," he warned. "In this country if you really do a good job, others will speak for you."

A small gem of wisdom that a lot of the rest of the world could have benefited from, Fallon thought. He bowed his head stiffly and thanked Raoul for the company. Then, taking a large canvas carryall and a battered briefcase from the Land Rover, he turned and went into the hotel.

Chapter Ten

LIKE EVERYTHING ELSE IN KINNUBE, THE INDE-pendence Hotel had seen better days. It dated from many years back, having been renamed with the declaration of the Zugendan state and subjected to an overhasty attempt at modernization to celebrate the occasion. The lobby area needed redecorating and new carpeting, and some places where unfinished walls had been disguised by simply painting over the concrete were showing ominous cracks. But it was swept and clean and seemed to be doing as good a job as could be expected of presenting a brave face to the world in impossible circumstances. A coffee shop opened off from one side behind a cane screen. There was what looked like the entrance to a bar at the rear, with a group of African men in dark suits and women in bright, satiny dresses milling and chattering outside. A shoeshine "boy" dozed by his stand of bottles and brushes in one corner. A dusty shelf to one side of the desk displayed samples of basketry, earthenware, and crudely carved animal and human figures on offer at hopeful prices.

Fallon thumped the bell and waited. A sheet of pegboard to one side evidently functioned as the local trades directory and carried cards and scraps of paper advertising everything from taxi services and restaurants to "Engineers—We Fix Everything" in English, French, several variants of Arabic, and other scripts that Fallon didn't recognize. The windows and doors at the front, facing the street, were fitted on the outside with screens of thick steel mesh, he noticed—the kind used to protect against grenades. Peering over the top of the desk revealed a stout pick handle with leather wrist strap kept strategically close at hand. From the number of message slips in the pigeonholes at the back, he inferred that most of the current residents were out.

A short, balding, rotund man with a pockmarked face appeared; from his shiny black suit and the pens arrayed in his breast pocket, Fallon presumed him to be the manager. He bustled officiously with registration forms and bookings slips, making a show of checking Fallon's papers and the entry permits that had been endorsed at the police station.

"You are a zoologist?"

"That is what it says, so why ask?"

"What is your business in Zugenda?"

"Look, I only come to you for a room and a bed. The authorities who need to know why I am here are satisfied. What business is it of yours?"

"I have to know."

"Why?"

"It is our social responsibility to be aware of who our guests are. The police might come here asking."

"They already know. I've just told them."

"Sometimes the party needs to know."

"Then tell them to ask at the police station."

Not unexpectedly the room was Spartan, with a single bed covered by sheets and a plain blanket, chair, table, narrow built-in closet, and on the wall, incongruously, a framed print of *Monarch of the Glen*. But again it was reasonably clean, and it did have a private bathroom that included tub and shower, toilet, and washbasin all ingeniously formed from a single fiberglass molding—probably Japanese from the style and dimensions. The faucets disgorged a thickish red-brown liquid, which after some running lightened to speckly amber. Dubious as to whether it was likely to wash off any more than it would deposit, Fallon turned on the shower and experimented initially with just an arm; but the refreshing coolness soon overcame his reservations and he gratefully rinsed away the grime and dust of the day's drive. Then he put on some fresh clothes and went back downstairs to see what else the world had to offer.

The bar was beginning to fill for the evening when Fallon entered from the lobby. It seemed dim at first after the light outside, and was windowless but agreeably cooler. There was a central dance floor inside the door, at present taken up by tables where people were eating. The bar itself was to one side, with about half the stools occupied by an assortment of figures, including several of what looked like local whores starting out the evening. The decor was more congenial than his first impressions had prepared him for, the rest of the room being subdivided by screens of climbing plants and wicker into partitioned spaces crammed with a hodgepodge of furnishings, and a variety of rugs, bottles, baskets, leatherwork, and wood carvings adorning the walls. A Zugendan army officer was with a man in a civilian suit in one of the niches; three whites, also visitors from the look of their clothes, were talking loudly around a table in another, closer to the bar; there was a larger mixed group farther on. Fallon took one of the empty stools at the bar, ordered a schnapps, and removed his spectacles to polish the lenses with a handkerchief while he waited.

"Just get in?" A sallow youth with lank yellow hair, wearing jeans with a light jerkin, a gold Rolex visible below the sleeve, spoke across the corner of the bar. He was with a companion, lanky, vacant-eyed, listless looking, with an untidy beard.

"Yes," Fallon answered, making no attempt at being friendly.

"Where you from?"

"Denmark."

"I can exchange currency—English, French, American, you name it." His accent was from somewhere a lot farther south. "Getcha twelve Zugendan shillings to the dollar."

"I prefer to exchange it at the official rate, thank you."

The sallow youth sniggered. "Hear that, Stan? He wants to do it at the official rate."

"He's a sucker," Stan said.

"How about some stuff?" the sallow one said, looking back at Fallon. "Gota good connection. The real shit, man, know what I mean?"

"I don't use it."

"Need a girl? Coupla girls? Even getcha into Sadie's, and that's the best in town. Guaranteed clean."

"What's Sadie's?"

"That's the deluxe whorehouse around here. You have to be somebody to get in there."

"No."

The sallow youth seemed undeterred. "You have to

have connections to get along here. Stan and me, we got lots of friends—we got good connections all the way from here down to Jo'burg. Now that's *the* place. . . . You got problems, talk to me. We handle currency, dope, girls. Over here, money *talks.* You gotta have friends."

"You got any spare stuff tonight, Pete?" Stan asked.

"Not for you I don't. You've got too much in your head already."

Stan's voice became a whine. "Hell, Pete, I *need* some real bad. Ain't you got just one spare dime bag . . . ?"

Fallon's drink arrived. He picked it up and turned on the stool to face the other way. "Lousy uptight bastard," he heard Pete mutter behind him.

Farther along the bar, a knot of youngish-looking whites in khaki garb were talking earnestly about logistical coordination and contingency factors. "I *told* him!" one of them exclaimed in a carrying voice, spreading his hands in an exaggerated supplication. "I told him three weeks ago that it was crucial. But what can you do? The bloody man just grinned at me and said, 'Don't worry about it. We'll just ring up Sweden.'"

Fallon shifted his gaze to the nearby table where the three men were sitting. A walruslike man with rimless spectacles, wispy ginger hair, and an overgrown mustache was speaking. He had a European accent and put Fallon in mind of a Swiss cuckoo-clock maker. "Certainly, I agree, der overreaction was inexcusable."

"Overreaction? Shit, it was hysteria. What else is there to call it?" This was an American, broad but on the pudgy side, with a pinkish complexion.

The third man spoke, also American. He was well built, with clean-cut angular features, blue eyes, dark wavy hair, and wearing a lightweight tan suit with loosened necktie. His voice had a firm, self-confident ring, marking him the dominant one of the trio. "The thing should never have been turned into a PR spectacular in the first place. It was all politics." He scooped a handful of nuts into his mouth from a dish and munched them noisily. "You wanna know why they quit launching for two years after it blew up?"

"Okay, tell me. Why?"

"They had to. They never had any choice. They only had one shuttle."

"Vot you mean, vun shuttle?"

"That's crazy, Roy."

"No, really. See, that's how much the space program had gotten run-down. They were literally playing a shell game with the taxpayers. They had a few airframes, sure, but in terms of working, flyable guts, there was only ever one system. They switched it between different shells. Why else do you think it took ten thousand technicians three months to prepare for a launch? When they lost it, they *had* to shut down for two years while they built another. The rest was just baloney for the public."

"Where in hell d'you get this?"

"A guy I know, used to be in SAC."

"Why didn't it ever get out?"

"Come on, Gary, you've been around. You know how it is." There was a pause. "Say, here's a new face. Did you just arrive?"

Fallon turned his head. "Pardon? Oh . . . yes, today."

"No need to sit up there like a spare dong at a ball. C'mon and join the party. We're just shootin' the breeze."

Fallon appeared to consider the suggestion. "Very well. Why not?" He got up with his drink and went over. The cuckoo-clock maker moved around to make room.

The taller American went on while swigging from his glass of beer, without looking at Fallon directly. "Name's Leroy, here on assignment for *U.S. News and World*. This here's Gary. That's Dieter." Despite his invitation, Leroy's manner didn't strike Fallon as especially cordial. If anything, it was challenging and mildly provocative—the way of some people who like asserting themselves with strangers.

Fallon nodded his head a fraction. "Hannegen. Konrad Hannegen."

"Well, call me Roy, Konnie. That okay—Konnie?"

Fallon shrugged.

Gary, it turned out, was an agronomist from the U.S. Department of Agriculture, collecting soil samples and compiling a catalog of seed types. Dieter was another journalist, German, from a Hamburg-based current-affairs magazine.

"What kind of business brings you here?" Roy inquired, making it sound like the beginning of a cross-examination. One of the reasons Fallon had chosen the role of a prickly academic was that it gave him a means of distancing himself from anyone trying to get too close or inquisitive.

He replied, "Zoology. There are certain rare species of antelope in southwest Zugenda that I wish to study."

"Vere is it you are from?" Dieter asked, catching the slight accent that Fallon was affecting.

"Denmark originally. But I have lived mostly in England for many years now."

"Yes, I haff been there, of course. But I do not pretend to know it vell."

"How long are you here for?" Gary asked.

"In Kinnube a few days, maybe, until I find a reliable guide. Then up to the high country, around Glimayel."

Roy snorted derisively. "You won't find any of 'em reliable around here. Lock up everything you can't carry and don't turn your back. They all steal from everybody, then the army takes it from them, and the government takes it from the army. And don't believe anything any of 'em say. They're born liars, every one of 'em."

Gary nudged Fallon's arm. "Roy comes on a bit strong with newcomers." He winked and whispered, "It's not that bad really."

"Oh, really?" Roy countered. "Then what about what happened to Lizzie Boobs? That wasn't exactly being nice, small-town good neighbors. It doesn't happen in Ithaca, upstate where I come from."

"Who is Lizzie Boobs?" Fallon asked.

"Was," Roy said.

"Her name was Elizabeth Bouabbas," Gary said. "She was, what?" He looked at the other two. "Nigerian?"

"Ja, Nigerian," Dieter said.

"What does it matter?" Roy tossed in.

Gary went on: "Another reporter. She got herself into the Zugendan army as a nurse somehow, so she could get a firsthand line on the fighting up close to the rebels. But she got too close to them. She was found floating in the Tsholere River about a week ago."

"I see," Fallon said.

"The pieces of her that were left were found, anyhow," Roy told him, pulling a face. "That's the way these people are."

"It can happen viss any peoples, anywhere," Dieter

insisted. "Viss der Americans too. Do you vant me to give some examples?"

"She was right up at the front, miles from the hospital where she was supposed to be," Gary said. "I mean, I'm not condoning what happened, but she knew the score. She knew the way it is out there."

Outvoted, Roy dismissed the subject and raised an arm high, snapping his fingers at the bartender. "Hey, let's have some more over here, pronto, huh?" He looked back at Fallon. "I know one who's okay. A kid called Jonas—runs errands and stuff for me. He'll find you a reliable guide, if there is one."

"I'll bear it in mind," Fallon said.

The talk continued, with Roy setting the tone: the only part of Africa worth anything was the south, and the liberals were about to hand that over to communists, anyhow; tonight he was aiming at getting good and drunk, and why wasn't there any decent ass in this town? Gary played a loyal second and wondered how Pittsburgh had got on against Dallas yesterday. Dieter made intermittent attempts to talk about Denmark but kept getting eclipsed by Roy, which as far as Fallon was concerned was just as well.

Then a dust-caked figure wearing boots, baggy fatigue denims, and a sweat-sodden bush shirt came through the door from the lobby. He was a man in his early to midthirties, Fallon judged, white, with an unshaven but boyish face beneath the grime and a mop of sandy hair flopping over his forehead. On straps crossed about his body he was carrying a leather satchel on one side and a cluster of camera and accessory cases on the other. Although evidently from the same profession as Leroy and Dieter, he ignored them and went straight to the bar.

"The Boy Scouts have arrived, guys," Roy said in a loud voice. The newcomer took no notice and ordered a large beer. He spoke with a nasal twang, keeping his voice even and looking the other way, embarrassed, Fallon could see, but trying to avoid trouble. Roy persisted remorselessly. "Where's your monkey today?"

"Who is that man?" Fallon asked the others.

"You don't wanna know him, Konnie," Roy warned, abandoning his strident tone of a moment before. "Coon lover . . . thinks that we exploited them, and all that crap.

The truth is, if it wasn't for the White Man, they'd still be swinging in the trees. He's got a tame one that follows him around. Shit, he even says we're giving the rebs a raw deal." Roy gulped down more beer and shook his head.

Fallon watched as the man moved to an empty space at the far end of the room and sat down facing away from them. Then he turned his head questioningly toward Gary. "His name's Parnum," Gary supplied. "Australian free-lancer on a job for some news agency down there. He, ah, well, I guess you could say . . . pursues an independent investigative line."

"I think perhaps you are too harsh on him," Dieter said to Roy. "He makes too many excuses for them, maybe, *ja*. But in his eyes it is der objective reporting that he practices . . . being der professional. To der young idealist such as he is, these things are important."

"Professional!" Roy seethed darkly. "They're goddamn cold-blooded murderers. We all know that. How can anyone defend 'em, for chrissakes?" His voice had begun rising again, as if challenging anyone within earshot to disagree. "Hell, I mean, we all know what goes on."

"Easy, Roy," Gary muttered, putting a restraining hand on his arm.

"Roy has had a few this afternoon," Dieter said apologetically to Fallon. "But to be honest, Herr Parnum does get outspoken sometimes with der opinions that are not popular."

"Really?" Fallon said. He leaned back in his seat and sipped his drink while regarding the three of them. He hadn't come here to listen to accusations and justifications. He'd come here for information. And for the time being, he decided, he'd gleaned as much as he needed from this particular source.

"I think I've heard enough already," he said. Another advantage of peevishness was being able to terminate conversations like this abruptly when it suited him. He picked up his glass and rose. "Good evening, gentlemen. I thank you for your company." Then he walked to the partitioned space at the end of the room, where the solitary figure was sitting glass in hand, contemplating the wall. The youthful, dust-streaked face looked uncertainly up as Fallon's figure blocked the light.

"My name is Konrad Hannegen, just arrived today,"

Fallon said. He made a vague motion with his glass in the direction of an empty seat. "You're an Australian, I understand. Would you mind if I join you?"

The Australian's name was Roger Parnum. He had been commissioned to cover the Zugendan insurrection for Australian International News Services, of Sydney. As the German, Dieter, had said, his manner displayed much of the idealism of youth and the intensity that went with it. He was correspondingly forthright in declaring his position, and expounded his nonconformist views with a candor that was refreshing after the world that Fallon was more used to.

"I just think that the picture of the ZRF that the outside world gets is being distorted," he said. "Cheers, mate." He raised his glass and downed a third of his second beer, which Fallon had bought, and wiped his mouth with the back of his hand. "Mind you, I'm not saying they're angels. But who the hell is? Things have a habit of getting pretty brutal in the kind of conflict that this thing's turned into. But in this case, one side you never hear about, and the other gets blown out of all proportion. I'm just saying that given the realities of the situation, they're not the inhuman monsters that people are being made to think."

Fallon sipped another schnapps while he thought about it. "That could almost be taken as saying that the ZRF is being framed," he observed.

Parnum nodded candidly. "Mmm, yep, I guess you could say that, right enough. . . ."

"You don't seem to have any reservations about saying it."

"Why should I have? It's what I think."

"So, who is doing the framing, do you think? Have you any ideas about that?"

"If you knew the kind of harassment I get from Molokutu's babes in arms here, it might give you a clue."

"Are you saying the government is behind it?"

"Let's say I wouldn't find it the most surprising thing in the world."

Fallon waved a hand in the direction of the other group, who were still at the table at the far end, where two other men had joined them. "That, er . . . it isn't exactly the mainline version of the story that one hears," he commented.

Parnum snorted. "Oh, come on, sport, do me a favor."

"How do you mean?"

"What do they know about anything that's going on?"

Fallon shrugged. "They are professionals, too, in the same business, aren't they? Why should they all be out of step except you?"

Parnum leaned forward to the table and dropped his voice, at the same time motioning back over his shoulder with a jerk of his head. "Well, you can see for yourself the kind of cushy number they're on. . . . Nice break down in the sun, away from the high-blood-pressure-and-ulcers circuit, all expenses paid and overseas bonuses. This is where they do half their reporting from, the Independence bar. The other half is when a PR stooge hands out an official release at the press office three blocks from here. They're just conduits for the party line."

"But you can do better, eh?" Fallon made his tone and expression skeptical.

Parnum's answer was straight and unembellished. "I try to go where I think the facts are, sure."

"And where's that?"

Parnum's manner became evasive for the first time. "Oh, here and there. You know how it is."

"Do you talk directly to the ZRF?" Fallon asked. Parnum shrugged and drank some more of his beer. Fallon went on: "It mightn't be the way to make yourself exactly popular around here . . . not touting the party line."

"There is that side to it," Parnum agreed. "They'd like to see me on the next flight home."

"But aside from officialdom, do you find them easy enough to get along with?"

"Why shouldn't I? Sure, they're okay."

"You've got a helper, I'm told."

"Mamu? Yes, he's useful to have around. He's got notions about being a journalist himself one day."

"Leroy doesn't seem to share your sense of sociability."

Parnum shrugged. "Yes, well, you know the way the world is. I don't know where his kind of attitude comes from. We're not born with it. Kids don't have any of it."

Fallon sipped his drink and stared at the tabletop in silence for a while. At length he asked matter-of-factly,

"Did you ever know someone called Elizabeth Bouabbas . . . Nigerian?"

Parnum paused for an unnaturally long time before replying. "Where did you hear about her?" he said finally.

"Oh, the others mentioned her name briefly when I was back there."

"So you heard about what happened?"

Fallon shrugged. "I don't know. You tell me."

"What's she to you?"

"Nothing . . . I'm just curious."

Parnum took another long drink and looked at Fallon oddly. "You ask a lot of questions for a zoologist," he remarked.

Fallon was taking a liking to the young Australian. He had guts, anyway. Parnum's openness was more a declaration of principles and a gesture of defiance to the world to think anything it liked, Fallon was beginning to realize, than the naïveté that it could be mistaken for at first sight. He permitted the feisty Dane a faint smile. "I thought that a reporter would understand all about curiosity. After all, we're students of the same subject, aren't we? People are classified under zoology."

Parnum grinned knowingly into his glass behind his dusty mask in a way that said there was probably more to it than that, but wasn't about to make an issue out of it. He stretched a sun-browned arm along the seat next to him and lounged back. "I've never been to Denmark. Had some good times in Hamburg, though. I was there about three years ago, doing a series on the European defense industry. That was the place for some sheilas."

"They seem to be supporting quite a bit of a defense industry here," Fallon commented. "I saw some jets landing as I was on my way here, just a few miles east of Kinnube, it must have been." He rubbed his chin for a moment. "I don't know what types or anything. . . ."

"Probably MiG-19s from Mordun, the main air base. They're flattening every village in the war zone."

"There were some tanks too," Fallon remarked.

"The army has Soviet T-54s and T-62s. It's remained under Molokutu's direct control. But the Department of State Security also has its own, separate armed force. They have a couple of squadrons of armored cars in the city—mainly French Panhards that they got from Morocco somehow. Wheeled vehicles are usually better for urban situations and counterinsurgency work."

Fallon nodded. So Parnum did know his stuff. "You said in the city? You mean here, in Kinnube?"

"Yes. State-security headquarters is on the other side of the city center, along with their main barracks and depot. The whole thing forms a single complex. They probably wanted to keep a hefty presence on hand for riot control and that kind of stuff. SS mostly handles security inside the cities, but they do have a base a little way outside Kinnube, at a place called Djamvelling. They fly choppers from there too—also Russian. In fact they've got a few Russian technicians out there who look after the engines and electronics. You sometimes see one or two of them in here, but they don't come into town often."

Fallon was looking past Parnum at the far end of the room as he listened, and saw the manager that he had encountered at the desk come strutting in through the door, holding a sheet of paper. The manager looked around, saw them at the far end, and headed in their direction. Something in Fallon's expression must have showed, causing Parnum to turn his head. The manager drew up facing him, ignoring Fallon pointedly. "Mr. Parnum."

"Yes?"

The paper was brandished and pointed at. "There seems to be a mistake with the length of time you have indicated for your stay at the hotel. It says here that you will be departing on the fifth."

Parnum looked up and accepted it with a weary here-we-go-again sigh. "That's right. Or I might want to extend it a bit—if that's all right with you."

"But I'm afraid it isn't all right. Your reservation was only until tomorrow."

"Rubbish. It was confirmed to the fifth."

"Do you have a record of such confirmation?"

"You know bloody well I don't. It was what you told me over the phone."

"I think you must be mistaken. It was not I who took the booking."

"Bullshit."

"The room has been allocated to another party, who have written reservations. I must ask you to vacate by tomorrow, please."

"You and your other party can go to hell."

"I must insist."

Heads were turning across the room. Fallon looked toward the far end again and saw that two Zugendan policemen in khaki shirts and peaked caps were watching from outside the door. Now it was all starting to add up.

He focused back to the immediate vicinity and tapped the manager lightly on the arm. The manager turned, seeming to notice him for the first time, and regarded him disdainfully as if he had butted in on a private conversation. "Maybe I'd better check on my reservation too, if you've got problems," Fallon said. "I was thinking of extending it to the eighth."

"Please, I am already dealing with another situation."

"I just want to know if that would be okay?"

"Yes, that will be all right," the manager said curtly, and turned back toward Parnum. "If you persist in—"

"So I can have it till then?" Fallon interrupted.

"Sir, I have already told you that the room is available. Now if—"

"Well, I just changed my mind. So let him have it until the fifth."

"That would be impossible."

"Why?"

The manager spluttered something, balked, and looked toward the doorway in an appeal for help. Just then, another voice nearby said loudly, "Come on, Boy Scout. You heard the guy. He's just doing his job. Why do you have to give everybody a hard time?" Leroy had stopped on his way back to the other table from the men's room and was glowering at Parnum. Gary got up from the other table and came over to hover uncertainly in the background.

"Would you mind keeping your nose in your own goddamn business?" Parnum said to Leroy, his voice calm but sharp.

The drink had put the American in an ugly mood. He leaned forward and pushed his face close to Parnum's, breathing liquor fumes at him. "Just pack your bags and get out, then we'll all get along a lot better. And take a bath. You stink up the place."

Gary put a restraining hand on Roy's shoulder. "Come on, ease up. This is—"

Roy shook him away. "He should go and stay with his

friends. What's he doing living here and siding with them?"

The two policemen were inside the door now, looking alert and fingering the batons held in thongs at their belts. "There is no need," Fallon declared, jabbing hard at Roy's side with a finger. "We have already solved the problem."

Roy wheeled upon him. "Oh, yeah? And what's it to you? Are you another of 'em?" He pushed aggressively against Fallon's shoulder with a hand. "Well, maybe you'd better shove off too."

Gary tried to intervene again, but Fallon was already on his feet, shouting suddenly and slipping further into his mock accent. "Who you think you push like that?" He began jabbing Roy repeatedly with his finger again, in the chest, painfully, in a way calculated to make the American take a swing. "You keep your hands off me, you hear!"

"Quit poking me, you big shit!"

"You're drunk! Go away and mind your own business!"

"I said quit it!"

The exchange escalated in seconds. Fallon jabbed again, Roy smacked his hand away, and Fallon poked with the other instead. The punch came in a wide arc and Fallon rode it easily on a shoulder. The policemen were already running across the central open space, around the tables seating the diners. One of them stepped in between Roy and Fallon, deflecting the second swing as Roy aimed it. The other seized hold of Parnum's shirt and began hauling him roughly, although he was still sitting and had had nothing to do with the fracas. It was precisely the kind of situation that Fallon had hoped to create. He grabbed the policeman's arm and tore his grip away from Parnum. Fearing an attack, the policeman parried instinctively and struck out with his baton. Fallon ducked and hit him on the side of the chin, hard enough to jolt, but slower and less skillfully than he knew how. The other policeman was upon him in an instant. Fallon warded the first baton strike and took the next as a glancing blow on the face. The policeman that he had hit recovered his balance and closed from the other side, ready to even the score. But the fight seemed to evaporate out of Fallon suddenly, and he stood motionless, his arms raised protectively. For a moment longer the policeman stood in the now hushed bar, with a score of people looking on, his stick raised while prudence struggled against impulse. Then, tight-lipped, he produced a pair of handcuffs and clamped them savagely around Fallon's wrists. "You're under arrest," he growled.

A stab of pain lanced through Fallon's lower back as the other prodded him in the kidney area. "On your way."

"You too," the first said, nodding his head toward Parnum.

"He didn't have anything to d—" Fallon started to protest, but another prod sent him moving again.

Leroy's mocking tone followed them as they were hustled out into the lobby. "Well, what do you know? Maybe there's something to be said for this town after all. I guess they got their accommodation problem sorted out, huh? Have a good night, guys. Hey, I think there might be a few complaints about the room service by tomorrow morning. . . . Ha-ha-ha! Think that's good, Gary, huh?"

Chapter Eleven

THE CELL WAS ABOUT EIGHT FEET BY SIX, MOST OF which was taken up by a wooden cot with a straw-filled palliasse and single tattered blanket, both filthy and smelling of vomit. There was a sanitary bucket, unemptied, and a tin jug half-full of dirty water that looked to Fallon like an open invitation to a lexicon of tropical diseases. The evening was already growing cooler, and the thought of having to spend the night here was not appealing. He hoped there wouldn't be any snags with communications.

Less than an hour had passed, however, when he heard boots clumping along the corridor outside and stopping at the door, followed by keys clinking and rattling in the lock. The door was thrown open and a hefty black guard in blue shirt and navy cap motioned him outside with a curt jerk of his head. Two more guards were behind him, carrying riot batons. They took Fallon past a row of identical doors to the end of the corridor and up a steel staircase. The stairs led to a doorway opening through to another corridor, this time with a floor of linoleum tiles and a brown carpet along the middle, which seemed to be the connection from the cell block into an adjoining facility. Another short stairway and a more lavishly carpeted passage brought them to a door with a frosted glass panel. The leading guard tapped on the pane, a voice from inside called out something, and Fallon was ushered through.

The first person he saw was Sullivan, sitting to one side, close by the door as usual. Three other men, also black, two in civilian suits and one in military uniform, were waiting there too, sitting informally in chairs at the front of the room. There was a desk farther back, a side table with scattered papers, and several police training charts along with a map of Zugenda on the wall. One of the civilians greeted Fallon with an engaging smile of recognition. It was Makon Ngoyba, from the Department of State Security.

"You don't believe in wasting time, Mr. Fugleman," Ngoyba said after the guard had left and closed the door. "I know the plan was for you to get yourself arrested, but we assumed that you'd spend a day or two finding your way around first. I was just about to leave on a visit upcountry. It wouldn't have made a very favorable impression of Zugendan hospitality if you'd had to make a night of it."

Fallon shrugged and took an empty chair. "An opportunity presented itself. Taking initiatives is what I get paid for."

Ngoyba turned and gestured toward the two other men who were with him. "These are two of the people you'll be working with. Mr. Embatto heads the Department of State Security." Candy had mentioned Embatto when Fallon met her at the pub in London. Fallon had guessed he was the background figure behind Ngoyba. Ngoyba continued, "General Thombert, commander-in-chief of the army... Gentlemen, this is Mr. Fugleman from London, the man you've heard about."

They exchanged nods and some murmured words of greeting.

"I gather you've already met our zealous Australian," Ngoyba said, looking back at Fallon.

"Roger Parnum?"

"Yes—about the most inquisitive person around town that you could have picked. But he won't be in Zugenda for very much longer, so you don't have to worry too much. But watch him."

"So, what'll happen to him?" Fallon asked.

"Oh, nothing much. We know that he had nothing to do with starting the incident at the Independence. But we'll have to give him the minimum of a night to cool off. Anything less would look odd. He'll be out again in the morning. We'll have to keep you out of sight for a little longer, I'm afraid, for appearance' sake. But of course we'll find you somewhere more comfortable."

Embatto regarded Fallon coolly while he drew on a cigarette embellished with a personal gold monogram. He was a smallish man, with parchmentlike skin stretched across a bony face, giving it an appearance of a skull, the effect being augmented by thinning hair, a smooth high brow, hollow, high-boned cheeks, and a thin-lipped, humorless mouth. He was wearing a jacket of satiny material cut high-necked, Eastern style, and had tinted glasses that failed to conceal a disdainful remoteness.

"I regret the necessity of these somewhat melodramatic precautions," Embatto said. "But by now you will appreciate the nature of the opposition that we are confronting." He spoke with an exaggerated preciseness, punctuating his words with delicate gestures of fingers and wrist, as if inviting Fallon to share a private realm of exclusivity. "The ZRF have eyes and ears everywhere, some of them, I have no doubt, within our own organization, despite all our efforts."

"I've survived worse in my time," Fallon said.

This seemed to cue Embatto in a way that he had been hoping for. "And what kind of time would that be, Mr. Fugleman?" he asked. "What background are you from?"

Fallon had already given Ngoyba as much as was pertinent. He wasn't in a mood for a second employment interview and answered simply, "My experience is sufficient for your needs."

Embatto waved a hand. "Oh, I have no misgivings concerning your qualifications. I was referring more to your psychological disposition. We represent cultures that do not always see eye to eye on what they consider to be the desirable organization of the world and society. Our regime in Zugenda is committed to a path of people's socialism to set right the inequities and injustices perpetrated under the colonial era. The ZRF is being backed by outside interests in an attempt to reestablish the exploitive privileges which they have lost." He circled in the air with a finger and pointed it at Fallon. "Now, why should you, who are from the same side of the world that nurtures those interests, volunteer your services to us?"

Fallon replied evenly. "First, I didn't volunteer them. I was approached. And second, I don't support privilege. I'm all for equality, just like you. I don't discriminate between customers on the grounds of race, religion, color, or creed—which is the way I was told people should be. So we both believe in the same higher ideology, right?" It was the kind of answer they wanted to hear, and what

Fugleman's role required. His mouth turned upward at the corners for an instant, and he nodded. "I think we understand the same language."

The tinted glasses hid Embatto's reaction, but he seemed satisfied. He stubbed the butt of his cigarette in an ashtray while inhaling deeply. Then he looked across at General Thombert, nodded, and sat back in his chair, blowing out a stream of blue smoke.

Thombert was a big man with a heavy, unsmiling face, clipped mustache, and expressionless eyes that had been studying Fallon with the candor that comes from total detachment, neither liking nor disliking, accepting nor rejecting. Such terms were irrelevant to their relationship. Fallon was simply a given fact of reality, whom he could just as easily work with or have killed. His stare had the look of dirty-work specialists found in armies the world over.

He got up, moved over to the map of Zugenda pinned to the wall, and made a perfunctory sweep with his arm to take in the general topography: the mountainous region to the west, extending eastward into the lowlands in a ridge that almost bisected the country and defined the two provinces, Kashinga to the north and Sorindi to the south; the isolated plateau region of Glimayel, down near the southern edge of Sorindi, where the zoologist Konrad Hannegen was supposed to be heading; north from there the main river, the Tsholere, flowing eastward through Sorindi, with the capital city, Kinnube, straddling it at its confluence with a tributary.

"The war zone of active anti-ZRF operations is from here to here," Thombert began. He indicated a region outlined in red crayon, which covered the western highlands and most of the northern province, Kashinga. The dark, fathomless eyes met Fallon's dispassionately. "We're talking about an enemy that's vicious, ruthless, and fighting with his back to the wall, which means anything goes. The situation we've got is that ZRF mobility is confined primarily to this area. But if you're the expert on this kind of business that they say, you'll recognize this as ideal guerrilla country: rough mountain terrain, with poor communications and large, remote areas with plenty of cover to get lost in. The people have been intimidated into hiding the terrorists and feeding them, and there's a border to slip across into not unfriendly territory if things get too hot. They're slippery and elusive. They can pick their time and place to attack where we're thin; they vanish when we've got the odds; and they've got plenty of bases and hideouts to move between when we go after them."

What Thombert hadn't said, because no military commander would, was that he wasn't winning. In that kind of country, mounting conventional operations against determined, adequately organized resistance would have been ineffective with ten times the resources and manpower that a country the size of Zugenda could hope to muster. Fallon nodded but said nothing.

"A classical guerrilla operation," Embatto commented. "The two classical counters are intelligence and infiltration. And those are the weapons that we intend to use." He nodded at Thombert to continue.

Thombert turned to the map and indicated the Glimayel region again, forming the southwestern corner of Zugenda. Then he looked back at Fallon. "We had another reason for choosing the cover for you that we did. The Glimayel plateau is one of the most remote parts of the country, a mess of valleys and moonscape that you could lose an army in. It contains more than antelopes. That's where the ZRF's leaders are most of the time. They move between a network of hideouts and bases that they've got strung through that whole area. The regular forces that we send in there have never been able to get close to them. But a scientist, nonthreatening and working on his own, might."

Fallon nodded slowly, but at the same time with a distant frown beginning to form on his face.

"Konrad Hannegen doesn't need to have any connection with mercenary volunteers, or to know anything about recruiting them," Embatto said, watching him and anticipating the objection. "Your mission in the first instance will be to identify the targets and establish their normal locations, movement patterns, security arrangements, and to get yourself accepted in such a way as to be able to coordinate an operation from the inside, later."

"But that means being able to get close to the targets," Fallon pointed out. "This Hannegen line only gets me close to antelopes."

"Hannegen is also an academic," Embatto said. "Let us imagine him as freshly descended from his ivory tower, politically naive, and just stumbling upon reality for the first time in Zugenda. He is converted to the ZRF cause and sees his crusade as opening the eyes of the world—a not unlikely scenario. The ZRF are desperate for favorable publicity. With Hannegen's professional standing and the connections in Western circles that we can give him, he would have no difficulty in getting close to the right people. In all probability they would come readily to him."

Fallon rubbed his chin and stared at the map thoughtfully. The others watched him in silence. "Okay, so I'm down in Glimayel somewhere, the team have been brought together in England, and you're here in Kinnube. You're going to want to know what the practicability of the operation is. They're going to need to be briefed. How do we get everyone together?"

Thombert answered, still standing in front of the map. "When you've completed the reconnaissance phase of the mission, you tell the ZRF that you'll be back with others who can help promote their cause on the international scene, and you return to Kinnube. Once the plan is approved here and the final timetable agreed, you leave the country to brief the rest of your team on their parts . . . maybe back in England. Then you split up and go different ways that will bring you together again for the operation. Some of them would travel with you as the people you promised to bring back—they'd be the primary hit team, since you'd be able to get them to the targets. A backup group could come in individually across the border as volunteers."

"We could even fly some of them openly into Kinnube for you, posing as aid workers," Embatto chipped in. "They'd simply vanish into the bush."

Fallon smiled faintly at the audacity of it. It was feasible: foreigners came into the capital all the time; the ZRF would have no reason to suspect anything.

"And how do we get out afterward?" Fallon asked.

"Scatter and regroup for a helicopter pickup that night, with an alternate rendezvous for the following night in case of delays," Thombert answered.

Fallon nodded. There would be a lot of fine detail to

go into, naturally, but that covered things to his satisfaction essentially. "So, who are the targets?" he asked finally.

Thombert turned to the table and picked up a red-bound folder that had been lying there among some papers. "The operation to eliminate the ZRF leadership will be designated Trojan Horse," he said, handing the folder to Fallon. "A coordinated offensive by the security forces, designated Scabbard, will be launched to coincide with the amount of maximum disruption of the enemy, aimed at destroying them totally before they can recover. The specific objectives of Trojan Horse are profiled in there."

Fallon opened the folder and began leafing through the sheets of typewritten text and photographs inside. The first was of a gnarled, wizened face, with hair and beard both turning white. Without reading the caption, Fallon identified him as Jovay Barindas, whom Candy had mentioned, the founder and inspiration behind the ZRF movement, marked as the number-one target of the operation. Next was a face that Fallon also recognized, hard ebony, solid-jawed, and frowning: Haile Yolatta, the strong-arm man of the organization and chief of Barindas's military force. Listed after him was his deputy, Sam Letumbai, a younger man whose age was given as thirty-five. Next, a woman with long hair, youngish, maybe in her midtwenties, serious looking, who was new. The accompanying text gave her name as Marie Guridan and described her as running the ZRF's intelligence apparatus. Finally there was one white: a man with straight, fairish hair falling across his forehead in a studentlike mop, which with his heavy-rimmed spectacles added up to too young an image for the age implied by his features. The caption read "Dr. Felix Velker," which was the name that Fallon had seen on the door inside the house that Candy had taken him to. He looked up at Thombert questioningly.

"Yes, the English sympathizer," Thombert confirmed. "Eliminating him would cut off a lot of the ZRF's sources of external support."

"He's not in London?" Fallon queried.

"Actually he spends most of his time here in Zugenda," Embatto replied. "He uses his capacity as a doctor to set up various safe houses and meeting places for the ZRF. He can be elusive, but so far it has been more valuable to us to watch him than put him away."

Fallon ruffled back through the pages slowly. It seemed thorough. With an all-out military assault timed to coincide with the moment of maximum demoralization, the ZRF would very likely disintegrate irreparably. He looked up again and saw that Embatto was watching him keenly.

"Those are the ones we have never been able to pin down," Embatto said, gesturing toward the folder. "But they cast lines out in search of help, and that is how we will find them. For the line leads back to the fishermen. The problem with fishing for killer sharks is being sure of knowing which end is reeling the other in, wouldn't you agree, Mr. Fugleman?"

After the meeting, Fallon was taken to another room located upstairs in the same part of the building, as opposed to the cell block that he had come from. It had an iron-frame bed with sheets and blanket that were at least clean, and a washbasin with water that made a detectable effort to be warm. Shortly afterward, a warder brought him a palatable meal of lamb stew with sweet potatoes, and coffee. The door was left unlocked, making him no longer a prisoner and allowing access to a toilet along the passage outside. Unlocked doors, however, open both ways. Mindful of all the faceless people who might perceive interests of one sort or another to protect in this kind of situation, he improvised an intruder alarm from a tin tray wedged against the inside of the door, and tucked an empty bottle with the bottom broken off, found in a closet in the toilet, within easy reach beneath the edge of the mattress as a weapon before settling down.

He lay for a long time, staring into the darkness, evaluating the day's events for any emerging pattern. His strongest impression from the meeting that evening was one of thinly concealed animosity between Thombert and Embatto. By no stretch of the imagination could he see them as comradely brothers-in-arms marching to the same drum. Fallon had little doubt that the present unnatural marriage was purely one of convenience that both of them found expedient for the time being while they pursued different, and possibly conflicting, interests.

Although Thombert had done most of the presenting

of Trojan Horse, Embatto came across to Fallon as the more likely conceiver and principal architect behind the plan. If Julia's guess about the reasons for approaching Westerners was correct, then it would be Embatto who had put Molokutu up to the idea, and hence Embatto who was up to something that he wanted Moscow kept out of. In other words, he was playing a lone game of some kind against the other two. Interesting.

But the long drive from the border had been too exhausting for any further contemplation of such matters, and Fallon slipped away into a sound sleep. No untoward incident occurred in the night to disturb him.

Chapter Twelve

EMBATTO ARRIVED HALFWAY THROUGH THE FOL-
lowing morning, while Fallon was shaving after resting
late. He was wearing a pale blue suit of expensive cut that
made an incongruous contrast with the austerity of his
skull-like features as he stood in the doorway, surveying
the room through swirls of blue smoke from one of his
monogrammed cigarettes.

"I trust you are adequately rested, Mr. Fugleman,"
he said.

"I make it a rule to stick to cover at all times. The
name is Hannegen."

"As you wish. . . . I understand from our embassy in
London that Stroller has not contacted them yet."

"He will. He likes to work independently. They'll
hear from him when he's got something to report."

"I'm sure you are right."

Fallon rinsed the lather from his face and unscrewed
the handle of the vintage brass razor that he had been
given. "So, what's the plan in the meantime?" he asked,
picking up a towel and turning his head to glance over a
shoulder.

"Things are moving quickly. I have arranged a meeting with President Molokutu for you today. As soon as you
are ready, we will go to the presidential palace for lunch.
He wants to hear your views personally."

"Not to mention wanting to vet and approve the
goods himself, of course."

Embatto shrugged. "But naturally."

There was a short silence while Fallon dried the parts
of the razor and reassembled them. "Will we be seeing
General Thombert there too?" he asked, making his voice
casual.

"Not today. The general has been called away on urgent business upcountry."

Fallon nodded noncommittally as he slipped on his shirt and began buttoning it. The military, the state-security apparatus, and the presidency, all somehow involved in a tangle of conflicting and coinciding interests. But it was too early yet to try fitting them together. He picked up his jacket and indicated that he was ready. Embatto turned, and Fallon followed him into the passage to find Sullivan waiting there. "There were some personal effects that they took when I was booked in," Fallon said.

"They will be returned before you leave. We will be coming back here," Embatto told him. Fallon nodded. They began walking.

"How did your people in London find out that the ZRF were going to set me up?" Fallon asked.

"Oh, come now, Mr. Hannegen. I'm sure you have been a professional at this kind of thing for too long to expect us to reveal our sources without reason," Embatto replied evenly.

"I think it could be relevant to Trojan Horse."

"In what way?"

"Well, it could mean that you've got somebody inside the ZRF camp—somebody who's pretty close to the top." Embatto said nothing. Fallon went on, "Somebody like that could make it a lot easier for me to get close to the right people."

There was a brief silence, broken only by the sound of the footsteps echoing from the bare walls.

"Let me think about it," Embatto said finally.

They descended to the floor where the meeting had been held the evening before, and headed out of the offices and back through the connecting corridor to the jail block that Fallon had been brought to originally. But this time they followed a different route, toward the back of the facility and into what seemed to be a higher-security wing than the one containing drunks and petty offenders that Fallon had been taken to. It was gloomy and forbidding, with brown-painted doors and lower walls, the upper parts starkly gray. Fallon frowned and looked at Embatto in an unspoken question.

"Before we go to meet President Molokutu, there is

something else that I think you would be interested to see," Embatto said. He volunteered nothing further.

They came to a windowless room lit by naked light bulbs, where a number of uniformed guards were playing cards at a large, scratched wooden table in the center. At the far end was a desk with a typewriter, along with several filing cabinets and a tea urn. A man who had been standing near the desk came over to the door when they appeared. He was built on the smallish side, with skin a shade lighter than the average for Zugenda, and dressed in a white open-neck shirt with the cuffs turned back. Embatto introduced him as Mr. Tumratta. Fallon extended a hand perfunctorily.

"I don't shake hands with whites," Tumratta said. His breath had an odor of nicotine. Fallon withdrew the gesture and shrugged, at the same time mentally dubbing the new face "Ratfart." A couple of the guards looked over with disinterest and returned their attention to the game.

"Mr. Tumratta does have certain strong opinions," Embatto said. "But he is useful to us."

"Many have strong opinions," Ratfart said. He had a cunning, weasely look and a kind of permanent sneer that gave the impression of harboring an inner contempt for the rest of the world. His voice was high for a man's, almost shrill. "But what's rarer is the honesty of expressing them. Too many people are frightened of being known as they really are, which is why they can be intimidated. You don't frighten me, Mr. Fugleman, and you have yet to impress me. You see, already we know perfectly well how we stand, and all the pointless tedium of pretenses can be avoided."

"I'll try not to forget," Fallon said dryly, at the same time raising his eyebrows in Embatto's direction in a silent suggestion that they get this over, whatever it was.

"Come this way," Embatto said. Tumratta made a sign in the direction of the table and two of the guards rose to follow.

They continued to some railed steel stairs and ascended two flights to a concrete landing with several corridors leading off behind barred gates, and a half-height door opening into a small guardroom. Ratfart went ahead and said something through the door, and an armed guard in shirtsleeves emerged, jangling a ring of keys. He unlocked one of the gates, which rang hollowly as he swung it aside, and accompanied them through.

They walked almost to the far end, past heavy, solid-looking cell doors, each with just a small aperture covered by a sliding shutter, and halted outside one of them while the guard opened it. Embatto and Ratfart moved to the doorway. Fallon followed. A figure with dirty, matted hair was huddled in a corner on the bare floor inside, clutching a tattered blanket, its head bowed. Fallon didn't recognize her until one of the guards hauled her to her feet and held her as she sagged against the wall.

It was Candy.

But no longer the attractive, clear-skinned woman that he had met briefly in London. She looked frail and skinny now, but it wasn't just because of the soiled green shirt hanging from her shoulders and the thin, baggy, beltless pants that she had to hold up with one hand. It was the stoop of her shoulders and the shaking of her legs as she fought to stand. Her face was bruised and puffy, one side of her mouth split, and there were streaks of caked blood around her lips and chin. Fallon had seen the effects of electroshock interrogation before. The muscular convulsions that it induced made the victims bite their tongues.

"An obstinate one," Ratfart commented matter-of-factly. Fallon realized then that he was an interrogator. "We know she's part of a ZRF network here in the city, but we don't have her contact back to them . . . yet. We'll get it, though. It's early days still."

Embatto was watching Fallon's face intently. "She worked openly here, in Kinnube, as a medical technician," Embatto said. "It was her cover to steal drugs for the rebels. We want to know who her channel to them was."

Fallon stared at her. She was still looking at the floor with a numb expression and hadn't recognized him. "Why are you telling me this?" he asked.

Embatto shrugged but kept his eyes on Fallon. "I assumed you'd be interested in seeing what happens to someone who tried to kill you." But Fallon had the feeling there was more to it than that.

The words had caused Candy to focus on Fallon at last. Suddenly her eyes blazed with a spark of the fire he remembered, but it took her a moment to force words from her swollen mouth. "So you went with them," she hissed. "Bastard! I hope you burn. The others will find out who you are, and they'll find you. They'll—" One of the guards slapped her across the face and she fell back against the wall. But her hatred on seeing Fallon had given her a surge of strength. She tore the front of her shirt open to show her body, covered with welts and blemishes, and thrust one of her breasts out at him. The nipple had been bloodied by the electrode clamp, and the flesh was burned. "Those are the people you sell yourself to," she spat. "Do you want to see where they did the rest?"

Fallon looked at her expressionlessly for several seconds, then turned his head to Embatto. "I can tell you now who her contact is," he said shortly. "It's Roger Parnum. He's the ZRF's channel here."

"*Bastard!*" Candy screamed, hurling herself at him, her face contorted with fury. The two guards caught her, but she managed to slash Fallon's cheek with a nail and spat at him as they pushed her back into the cell.

"That's very interesting, Mr. Fugleman," Embatto said. "But how can you be sure?"

"That's part of my job too," Fallon said.

The others turned to go as the door slammed and the keys rattled. Fallon followed, raising a hand to wipe the glob of blood and saliva from his eye.

When the party was two levels back down the steel staircase, Tumratta and the guards left to return to the room they had come from. The others continued descending and emerged into an enclosed yard at the back of the prison, where a Mercedes limousine was waiting with two jeeps manned by soldiers. Fallon and Embatto got in the back of the Mercedes, which had rear windows of one-way glass. Sullivan climbed in alongside the driver, and the three vehicles moved off in convoy through a side gate. Outside the wall was a narrow street, and on the far side a rear section of a large building that faced onto one of the main thoroughfares a short distance along from the main entrance to the prison. As the car turned onto the broader street and passed the front of the large building, a sign by the wire-protected front doors proclaimed it to be the main offices and broadcasting studios of Zugendan National Radio.

Fallon had said what he had about Roger Parnum

compulsively, because he'd had to, to put a stop to what had been happening back inside the prison. It hadn't put Parnum in any greater danger than he was in already, for Embatto had already known. From Parnum's reaction in the bar, Fallon was fairly certain that he had not only known Elizabeth Bouabbas, but had worked with her actively to aid the ZRF—the role that Parnum had adopted would provide excellent cover for him as a communications channel back to them from Kinnube. And if Candy had also been working undercover in Kinnube, it made sense that Parnum would have acted as her contact too. Embatto possessed the same information, and Fallon had already assessed him as too shrewd not to have arrived at the same conclusion.

If confirmation were needed, Embatto hadn't questioned Fallon on his reasons; he had just accepted the statement. Therefore he had already known. He had known, but he hadn't told Tumratta.

"You are very silent, Mr. Hannegen," Embatto remarked as the limousine and its escorts proceeded out of the city.

"I suppose talking isn't really my strong point," Fallon replied.

"If a weakness, then perhaps one that many could profit from cultivating," Embatto said. He looked at Fallon curiously. "Who is Stroller? An old acquaintance of yours, of many years standing, I would imagine?"

Fallon tutted. "I'm sure you've been a professional at this kind of thing for too long to expect me to reveal my sources without reason."

"Touché." Embatto smiled and sank back into the upholstery.

Fallon turned his head away to stare out of the window, and silence fell again. The problem that he was frantically racking his brains over behind his outwardly calm facade was that from his reading of the situation, if he didn't come up with something drastic—and quickly—neither Parnum nor Candy had very much longer to live.

Chapter Thirteen

THE PRESIDENTIAL PALACE WAS SITUATED A SHORT distance to the west of Kinnube, on the northern bank of the Tsholere River. Formerly the regional gubernatorial mansion, it was a spacious affair consisting of an imposing central section with columned frontage flanked by two-story wings, lying among palm-fringed lawns and exotic shrubbery within a high wall patrolled by armed guards. There were two more gleaming Mercedes and a Cadillac parked in the forecourt. Inside was an entrance foyer complete with rattan chairs and tables set among potted rubber plants, with white-jacketed houseboys hovering in attendance and a male secretary perspiring in a three-piece suit behind a desk of Victorian immensity. The setting combined neoclassical pillars and plinths, Edwardian bookcases, a Queen Anne divan, and a gaudy baroque French cabinet: the hallmarks and trappings of empire collected indiscriminately and piled together—a strange sentiment to find echoed in the principal residence of an avowed Marxist state, Fallon thought. What struck him most was the complete absence of anything culturally African.

Molokutu received Fallon and Embatto alone in a private dining room at the rear, while Sullivan took up a position with the president's personal bodyguard in the corridor outside. Two more Zugendan security men sat at a sunshaded table beyond French windows opening out onto a terrace. Lunch was grapefruit and gingered melon, followed by spiced omelet and ham with fruit juices, toast, and coffee, served on bone chinaware from silver dishes.

The president was a heavily built man with coal-black skin, as dark as any that Fallon had seen. He had a wide brow left by thinning, receding hair, a fleshy neck and jowls, and large, thick-fingered hands that scooped the fork with careless, shovellike motions, picking food up from the plates and slapping it down again with casual disdain. His eyes were vigilant but remote, regarding Fallon as if from a distance, never letting down their guard. Fallon had the impression of innate shrewdness and cunning rather than intelligence—insensitivity wedded to strong self-preservation instincts. The kind of personality that makes effective dictators.

For the first half of the meal, Molokutu treated Fallon to a discourse on imperialism and the exploitation of Africa under the colonial system, the inherent superiority of the Marxist-socialist ethic, the nobility of the worker-peasant, and the West's obligation to atone for past injustices— which equated to pouring more cash into the state coffers of nations like Zugenda. It was all standard Moscow fare, delivered in a steady monotone and obviously recited so many times before that Fallon wondered if Molokutu was even conscious of the words.

Then the subject turned to the Zugendan situation and became more of a discussion with Embatto joining in. First came a repeat of the line that Fallon had heard first from Ngoyba in London and again the night before from Embatto: the government's policies were aimed at liberating the people from inequities and injustice; the ZRF, backed by external interests bent on regaining lost colonial privileges, were resorting to terrorism and all the other devices of unpopular minorities out to seize political control; Molokutu had decided to eliminate them finally, but to spare the people, this would be accomplished through a quick surgical strike in the way that Thombert had described, instead of by a long and bloody campaign of attrition along regular lines.

"Why come to us?" Fallon asked at this point. "Why not your own side—Russian *Raydoviki* or *Spetsnaz*? They've got people who could do this kind of job."

Molokutu snorted. "That's just what the ZRF want us to do. Then they could point to themselves as freedom fighters and get American weapons. We are not as blind as that." It was the answer that Fallon had been given before. However, the way that Molokutu glanced unconsciously at Embatto as he spoke and the faint nod of confirmation that Embatto returned told him that Embatto had fed the idea to him—which was in line with the way that Fallon had read things.

Then Molokutu played at being general for a while, rambling on about tactics and weapons and sprinkling the conversation with a lot of military parlance. He concluded, "Obviously the final details of where and when the hits are to be made, and how the operatives are to be extracted afterward, will depend mainly on what you find out in the reconnaissance stage. But how do you feel about the general plan so far?"

Fallon stared down at the table. Through the meal, he had been more preoccupied with finding a way to keep Parnum and Candy alive, and Molokutu's monologue had given him enough respite to form the glimmerings of an idea. And there would be no better place to plant the seed, he reflected, than here and now, while he had the president's ear.

"I'm not completely happy," Fallon said, looking up.

Molokutu and Embatto exchanged apprehensive glances. "What's the problem?" Molokutu asked.

"This idea of me going in as a born-again academic . . . It's too passive."

"How do you mean, passive?" Embatto queried.

"It relies on information finding its way back to the right people in the ZRF that I'm there, that I'm on their side, and that I can get them sympathetic publicity in the world outside. That could take a long time—and we've no guarantee that it'll happen at all." He gave them a few seconds to reflect on that. "Instead, word should be more actively steered in that direction. . . . The event needs to be *made* to happen."

There was a short silence. Molokutu nodded. "I hear what you're saying, but how would you achieve it?" he said.

"You really don't have any agents inside the ZRF?" Fallon asked.

"No," Embatto said. None that he was prepared to reveal at this stage, anyhow.

"A pity," Fallon said. "You see, ideally what I'd like is somebody in there who could make sure that the right people knew I was coming." He looked from one to the other, then shrugged, leaving the alternative to suggest itself in its own time.

Molokutu stared at his hands, then picked up his coffee cup and sipped distantly. Fallon could practically hear the gears clicking around in his head. . . . Slow, slow, slow, he thought to himself.

It was Embatto who finally voiced it. "Or if there were some way of feeding the information ahead that you were on your way to Glimayel and could be useful to the ZRF cause. Wouldn't that be practically the same?"

Fallon frowned and appeared to consider the suggestion. "Why? What did you have in mind?" he asked at last.

Embatto extended a hand in a palm-upward gesture. "The ZRF themselves have already provided us with somebody who would serve the purpose admirably." He turned his head toward Molokutu. "The Australian is apparently a conduit back to them, as we suspected."

"You mean Parnum?" Molokutu said. Fallon for his own part did a good job of staring in surprise as if wondering why he hadn't seen it before.

"He was the girl's channel back to the ZRF," Embatto said. "Instead of eliminating him, we can make use of him."

Molokutu's wide, black brow contorted into a frown while he chewed slowly and thought it over. "You mean we use his channel to prime them to receive Hannegen. How would we set up something like that?"

Embatto tossed up both hands. "We don't have to. In fact *we* don't have to do anything. Mr. Hannegen can do all that is necessary himself after they are both released. After all, they know each other already."

Molokutu turned his head toward Fallon. "What do you think, Mr. Hannegen?"

"It's a thought. . . ." Fallon set down his fork and wiped his mouth with a napkin. If they were prepared to use Parnum as a channel, at least it would give the Australian a temporary lease on life. "It doesn't feel a hundred percent yet, but we're thinking in the right direction," he pronounced.

That night, back in the room that he would be using until he could reasonably be allowed to be seen back on the streets, he pondered for a long time on the situation. Molokutu had agreed—grudgingly, and on condition that the account be settled in full later—not only to release Parnum, but to go a step further and have him deported from the country. That way, Fallon had argued, Parnum would be certain to recross the border into ZRF-held territory, and Hannegen would have his inside contact waiting for him when he, in his turn, showed up there.

Which left the problem of Candy. It was clear that what had to be staged somehow, if anything was to be done at all, was nothing short of a jail break. Fallon had pulled a few before, but this was going to be a tough one. The place she was being held in was a high-security facility, and even his one brief look at it had told Fallon that the job would be impossible without inside help. And Fallon's list of inside contacts so far consisted of just three names, all of them at first sight equally unpromising: Sullivan, Ratfart, and Embatto himself. Since Embatto held the authority, and Fallon couldn't picture either of the other two acting without his knowledge and say-so anyway, Embatto would have to be the one to work on.

That what he was contemplating was outrageous enough to have been dismissed out of hand by virtually the remainder of the human race didn't perturb him. Indeed, he had discovered that it was frequently the most outrageous approach to a problem—and therefore the last that anyone else was likely to have thought of or be looking for—that succeeded. He'd had a friend once, years ago, a life-insurance sales manager, who never tired of saying that "selling begins when the customer says no." Fallon had found it a valuable attitude to remember. In training in his military days, he had been taught repeatedly that "a belt buckle, a pen, a rolled-up newspaper—you're never unarmed. There's always a weapon." And with problems, especially the most seemingly intractable, there was always a way. It was just a question of finding the right angle.

As he lay, staring into the darkness, he asked himself what he was doing here, in a cell in an African jail, under a false identity, having agreed to work for both sides in a vicious war that wasn't his and wasn't a threat to him—and likely to be killed by either side if they became suspicious or sufficiently confused. It wasn't the first time that he'd found himself in this kind of bizarre situation or asking himself this kind of question. He had no interest in Zugendan politics, and despite Colonel Marlow's elegant discourse on the day after the shooting incident in London, he had little passion for the ideology of democratic institutions or theories of human rights. . . . His commitment had been made before then, anyway.

It hadn't been a result of any long-drawn-out process of weighing up one case against another. Fallon's more profound decisions—the ones that involved deep value judgments—rarely were. It had been an instantaneous reaction, like a switch clicking in his mind—at the time unconsciously, and not something he had become cognizant of until he came to sort out his feelings later—triggered by the sight of Candy lying on the floor, Ngoyba's security men with drawn guns, and Victor dead with his face shot away at Velker's house in London. Although Victor had been armed, it had been the image of defenseless victims crushed and degraded by organized, institutionalized violence—and beyond just them, not only the defenseless in Zugenda, but everywhere. That was what had got to him about them. Not their politics or their hopes for a just society.

There was another image that had once haunted him, years ago now, although he had long since overcome the trauma and could confront it with equanimity, if not comfort. When he was about twelve, growing up among the decaying Victorian terraced streets around the Portobello Road in the northern half of Kensington, he had witnessed a piece of brutality from the shadows in an alley behind a public house that had left a permanent mark on his developing mind. Three men had kicked and beaten another almost senseless, and then two of them held him pinned against a wall while the third slashed his face with an open razor. After they ran off, Fallon had emerged to stare in horror at the bloody figure left whimpering on the ground. But instead of fetching help, he had run home, terrified. That was something for which, even now, he had never forgiven himself.

Vowing never to be defenseless if he found himself in such a situation, he enrolled at a gym, took up boxing, studied weapons. Very likely it was that same deeply rooted fear of being a helpless victim that had led him first into the military and then to take on the toughest challenges that it had to offer. It was only when he finally earned the coveted pale-blue beret of the SAS that he had come to feel secure and at ease with himself again.

But he still had an aversion to cutthroat razors.

Chapter Fourteen

"IF I WERE THE ZRF, I'D BE SUSPICIOUS," FALLON said when Embatto appeared again the following morning. "Hannegen has got a story when he arrives, but so what? Stories are easy to invent. What credentials do I have to prove that I'm genuine? The story needs something to back it up."

"Such as what?" Embatto asked.

"Suppose you were to keep Parnum in custody longer after I get out. Then maybe I could kick up a lot of fuss publicly about getting him out. It might help create a stronger image of Hannegen in the ZRF's eyes. . . . You see, the ZRF don't have any positive proof of who I am."

There was a short silence. Then Embatto shook his head. "No, it wouldn't work. Parnum isn't even in on a petty charge. There would be no credibility in holding him. It would be too transparent."

Fallon pursed his lips, then nodded reluctantly. "True," he agreed.

"But I can see the kind of thing you mean," Embatto said.

Fallon moved to the sink to fill a glass with water and watched Embatto's face in the mirror. He took a swig and emitted a short, humorless laugh.

"What is it that you find so amusing, Mr. Hannegen?" Embatto inquired.

"We were too hasty."

"How do you mean?"

Fallon turned to face him. "Fugleman would have had the credentials. The ZRF approached *him* in the first place. Their agents got to him in London, but none of their people back here know it. We shouldn't have let him disappear from the scene like that. *He* could have convinced them in a way that Hannegen never would. . . . But why would they accept me as genuine now? They don't even know what Fugleman looks like." He gave an exasperated sigh, then seemed to dismiss the matter as a pointless exercise now. "Anyway, if I have to stay out of sight for a few more days yet, do you think you could find me something to read? How about as much background information on the ZRF as you're happy to share, for a start?"

Later that morning, after thinking alone in his office back at state-security headquarters for some time, Embatto called Molokutu's office and asked to see him urgently. An aide informed him that there was a meeting in progress with somebody from the World Bank. Embatto told the aide to inform Molokutu that he was on his way over and that he would wait until the president was free.

President Aloysius Molokutu stared across his desk in the upstairs study of the presidential palace. In the chairs facing him on the far side, Gaston Calombe, the Zugendan minister for the interior, and Colonel Esmil, from General Thombert's staff, listened with expressionless faces while between them the American from the World Bank, whose name was Irwin, continued his monologue. Irwin had a tendency to smile condescendingly while he spoke, which projected an air of knowing wisdom that was ill suited to his clean-cut, somewhat youthful appearance. It gave his words an evangelical thrust, and Molokutu didn't like being sermonized.

"It's a well-known fact that the sub-Saharan region has always been drought prone," Irwin told them. "And in the course of time the inhabitants evolved ways of dealing with it. The first way is to store surplus food from the good years to help tide over in the lean. The second is to sell surpluses for cash and use the cash to buy extra when you need to. And third, you transport it to where it's needed and exchange it for other commodities or labor—what's otherwise known as 'trade.' And in the past, those methods have proved themselves pretty effective."

He raised a finger and wagged it in the air. "But the policies that your government is implementing have virtually outlawed all of these measures on the grounds that they constitute 'hoarding,' or 'exploitation,' or are otherwise somehow against the public interest. Half of what does get grown rots because the labor to harvest it has been drafted, and the rest of the farmers are leaving the land because of the level that prices are being held down to." Irwin held up a palm. "Now, don't get me wrong, Mr. President. We do understand the importance of maintaining political viability in the cities. But before we could even consider any further credit, we'd have to have some reassurance that a policy shift in the direction we've indicated can be expected."

"We are on a war footing," Molokutu returned. "These measures are necessary to restrict the support that the rebels are able to extort from outlying areas. First we must win the war. Then we can talk policies. But if you deny us the means to preserve the state, what good will the policies be then? Our only alternative will be to turn further to the Soviets." He waved a hand above the desk. "There it is, frankly, but you force me to be blunt."

Irwin hesitated. "Let's not get too hasty about this. There must be some intermediate ground that we can explore."

Molokutu pondered for a few seconds. "Suppose I give you some tangible evidence that we are actively working on policy changes in the direction you'd like to see, to be implemented when the state of emergency is over," he offered. "Do you think that would help?"

"That's starting to sound more like the kind of thing we'd need. What did you have in mind?"

"You tell me. What would it take to convince them?"

"I think I already have. We're back to this." Irwin leaned forward and placed on the desk a folder bound in a buff cover, which had been resting on his knee. It was an analysis that he had produced earlier, containing statistics compiled by various agencies and experts, and a schedule of recommended action. "The first step should be for you to appoint a review committee to go through it. It would help a lot to see it being taken seriously, with a working brief based on the recommendations."

Molokutu considered the proposition. "I'll agree to that. What kind of reciprocation can we expect? I presume you're not asking us to demonstrate unilateral good faith?"

Irwin smiled apologetically and shook his head. "They'd have to see at least a preliminary report first. Then, possibly they might see their way clear to releasing a percentage of the package as an up-front deal."

Molokutu picked up the folder and handed it to Calombe without opening it. "Get a committee together to read this." He looked back at the visitor and pressed a button by the desk. "And now I'm afraid we have to terminate this. My head of state security has been waiting downstairs. These are difficult times."

Everyone stood up. "I'll put in a favorable interim report," Irwin said. "And in the meantime, I'll see if I can sound them out on a preliminary figure. But you understand I can't promise."

"That would be satisfactory," Molokutu said. An aide entered and hovered. Irwin shook hands all around and was escorted out.

Molokutu waited until the door had closed, then shrugged. "Well, it was worth a try. . . . There's only one way to keep the farmers where they belong," he told the other two. "Under the emergency powers I want a workforce quota assigned to every village in the affected areas. Any village that fails to muster its quota is to be burned and the inhabitants transferred to the communal camps. We'll get some decent work out of them that way, too."

"Do you want to approve a draft of the order?" Esmil asked.

"No, just do it and I'll sign it. You know the kind of thing well enough."

"What about this?" Calombe asked, raising the folder that he was holding.

Molokutu bunched his lips. "Well, you heard the deal. Get someone to read it. We always keep good faith, right? And it could be worth two million dollars."

Molokutu joined Embatto in a downstairs reception room five minutes later. He poured himself a Scotch from a decanter at a cabinet, added a splash of soda, and moved over to one of the room's high-backed leather armchairs. "You can tell they're not giving away their own money," he muttered, sitting down heavily. "They send boys to do men's jobs. . . ." He took a large gulp from the glass and looked up. "So what did you want to discuss?"

Embatto remained standing. "It's about Trojan Horse. I've been giving it some thought. I believe we can do better than simply using the Australian as a channel to feed the ZRF information about Hannegen." Molokutu looked interested. Embatto went on: "The cover as Hannegen doesn't carry enough credibility. He would be an unknown, and therefore not trusted."

"Maybe . . . But what can we do about it?"

"There is someone else whom they would accept completely—because they went to him in the first place, rather than the other way around."

"Who?"

"Boris Fugleman!"

Molokutu's brow knitted into a frown. "Fugleman? But he's out of the picture. As far as the ZRF are concerned, they never got to him in London. How can he reappear now?"

"None of them knows anything about what happened in London," Embatto reminded him. "All they know is that the two operatives that they sent there were lost."

"But how are we supposed to materialize Fugleman here?" Molokutu asked, still looking puzzled.

"We don't have to. He can materialize himself." Embatto licked his lips and gestured with a half-open hand. He was speaking more quickly than usual, obviously excited by his idea. "The plan as it stands is for him to approach Parnum in his role as Hannegen when he's released and get himself accepted as a ZRF sympathizer. But suppose, instead, that he reveals himself to be the Fugleman that the ZRF agents made their offer to! His story is that he's decided to accept it. There's nothing overt to connect Hannegen with us. It's simply Fugleman's cover for making contact with the ZRF again after his contacts in London disappeared."

Embatto paused and looked across. Molokutu stood up and paced slowly to the far end of the room, then turned, glass in hand. He was clearly intrigued. Embatto seemed to be containing something further, but he held back to await a response at this point.

"There's a problem with it," Molokutu pronounced finally. "They don't know what Fugleman looks like, but they do know that he talked to us. How are they to know that this Hannegen who appears isn't somebody working for us and claiming to be Fugleman? So why would they trust him any more than if he just says he's Hannegen?"

Embatto was nodding rapidly, having been waiting for that. "But there is one person they'll believe who can identify him positively: *the girl!*"

"The girl?" Molokutu looked nonplussed.

"Annette Mosswano. We fake a jail break and let them spring her! She and the Australian would both need to believe that it's genuine, but that shouldn't be too difficult to arrange."

"So now you're asking me to let *two* of them go?" Molokutu didn't look happy.

"What better way could there be for Fugleman to back up his story—and prove his ability? We've no further use for her. She was about to be liquidated anyway." Embatto shrugged. "So they get another of their operatives back as well as the Australian. It would be a small price to pay."

"But Fugleman went back with her to Velker's house," Molokutu objected. "Why should they believe that he'd want any part of an offer from the ZRF when the ZRF tried to kill him? They'd never buy it."

"She was knocked out cold," Embatto replied. "She doesn't know anything about what happened. All she remembers is vaguely that they walked into a trap that Ngoyba had set up. Fugleman's line is simply that he escaped. In fact, when you think about it, it actually makes his story stronger."

Molokutu contemplated his glass while he went over the whole thing again in his mind. He could see no further major problems. "Have you talked about it with Fugleman?" he asked finally.

"Not yet."

"I think it's better than playing the Hannegen thing through the way we'd originally planned. Okay, put it to Fugleman and let's get his reaction."

"I'll go and see him right away," Embatto said.

"I think it's brilliant," Fallon replied sincerely, back in his room at the Kinnube jail a little over an hour later. He nodded and looked suitably impressed. "Of course there'll be other details to work out. For instance, you couldn't hope to pull a break from a place like that without inside help. We'd have to come up with some sort of angle there."

Embatto waved a hand carelessly. "Oh... we can invent an accomplice that you managed to bribe while you were in here. After all, if your story is to be that you are really with the rebels, it would be the kind of thing that you might be expected to attempt."

"You mean, as if I were really double-crossing *you*," Fallon murmured in a faraway voice, as if still mentally feeling his way around it.

Embatto nodded rapidly and actually managed a thin smile. "It's an even more perfect way of implementing Trojan Horse."

"Very poetic. What made you think of it?"

"Who knows where these inspirations come from?"

"Well, let's start getting down to some details," Fallon suggested. "For a start I'll need a plan of the building, an indication of guard locations and when they're changed, and a large-scale map showing the immediate surroundings."

"I'll have Sullivan deliver them later today," Embatto promised.

Chapter Fifteen

WHEN FALLON ARRIVED BACK AT THE INDEPENDence Hotel, he discovered, not to his complete surprise, that he wasn't welcome, and his bags had been moved into a storage room by the lobby. "But I had a guarantee of a room before I left," he protested to the rotund, balding manager that he had crossed with before.

"I'm sorry, but we have no rooms for people who get in trouble with the police." The manager was on firm ground and evidently relishing the situation.

"That American attacked me. You were there yourself. You saw what happened."

"That is not for me to judge. All I know is that our other guests expect to be protected."

"But I have to organize a field trip into the bush. What am I supposed to do?"

"Try somewhere else. I have no rooms."

There was a tug on Fallon's sleeve. He turned to find a boy of about twelve or thirteen, who had been hanging around the lobby when Fallon arrived. The boy was wearing cutoff blue denim shorts with a torn red T-shirt and unmatched sneakers. "I know where there's rooms, sir," he said. "Lots o' rooms for sure. I'll take you there."

The manager smirked. Obviously there wasn't about to be any last-moment change of heart from that quarter. "Where?" Fallon asked.

"I carry your bag," the boy stipulated.

Fallon sighed and gave him half a Zugendan shilling.

"This way. Follow me. I take you to a better place 'n this."

They picked up the canvas carryall and briefcase that Fallon had brought into the hotel on his arrival and went out to the parking area at the rear. The guards that the hotel provided to keep a watch over the vehicles seemed to be effective, at least, and as far as Fallon could see, the Land Rover had not been touched. He stowed the bags, climbed in, and started the motor, while the boy hopped into the passenger seat. Fallon drove back up the alleyway beside the hotel building. "Straight on to end of street, then right," the boy instructed.

"What do we call you?" Fallon asked.

"Name's Jonas, sir. I take care of all the guests."

The American, Leroy, had mentioned Jonas as the hotel's self-appointed concierge and recommended him for finding Hannegan a reliable guide, Fallon remembered. "Do you happen to know the Australian who was staying at the Independence when I arrived there?" he asked.

"He's gone. They threw him out when he came back from the can, just like you."

"Do you know where he went?"

"Sure: the same place I'm taking you to now. I took him there too."

Well, that had been easy enough, Fallon thought to himself.

They crossed town to an area of sleazy bars and run-down houses, and pulled up outside a frontage of rickety clapboard with flaking paint. One side of the double front-door panes was covered over with plywood. The letters that were left on the signboard above read: TOB S HO EL. "It's called Tobins," Jonas supplied, following Fallon's gaze. They climbed out of the Land Rover. Jonas leaped nimbly ahead up the steps, opened one of the doors, and led the way in.

The proprietor was a burly, Uncle Remus–like character in green sweatshirt, tattered blue jeans, and sandals. "This is Xavier," Jonas said. "He take good care of you. He runs a number-one ten-star place." Then, to Xavier, "This is the scientist from the Independence. He doesn't like it there. Says he wants better place." Xavier grunted and gave Jonas another half shilling.

The entrance hall was dingy and dusty, with a table on one side evidently serving as a desk—there was a board fixed to the wall behind, with a line of hooks holding room keys. Xavier shuffled around to the far side and took down number three. "Terms is cash in full, in advance," he said.

Fallon muttered and produced his wallet. "What about my vehicle outside?" he asked.

"I know the man who runs the streets around here," Jonas said. "Nobody'll touch your stuff if he says so." He looked at Fallon pointedly.

"How much?" Fallon asked resignedly, reaching into his pocket again. But inwardly he had already decided that a pair of eyes and ears like Jonas's out on the streets would be a valuable asset to cultivate.

The room was tiny, with broken furniture and faucets that barely trickled. However, the air conditioner—surprisingly—worked. Fallon disconnected a wire inside it, then went back to the table in the hallway. After he had banged loudly several times, Xavier emerged from a room at the back.

"What de madder now? You wake up de dead, bangin' on de table like dat."

"The air conditioner is faulty. I want another room."

"Ain't nothin' wrong wit d'air conditioner. Ah checked it dis mornin'."

"Come and see for yourself."

"Then ah'll fix it."

"I'd still prefer another room."

"Can't have 'nother room."

"Why not?"

"Ain't got none, dat's why."

"Isn't that piece of paper an occupancy list? Look, half of them are empty. Why can't I have number eight, for instance?"

"Ain't no lights. 'Lectrician's gotta come fix de wirin'."

"What about nine, then?"

"Look, ah'll fix yoh air conditioner right now, okay? You gotta stay in t'ree."

Then a familiar voice came from the door at the rear of the entrance hall. "What-ho, sport." Fallon turned to find Roger Parnum grinning at him. "So they tossed you out on your neck too, eh? You got off light. I heard more than a few people say you'd be in for a few weeks at least. And believe me, in these parts that's not funny."

Fallon shrugged. "I told them it wouldn't look good to be arresting professors."

"Anyhow, come in and have a tot. You can say hello to Mamu too. It looks as if we're going to be all one family for a while, anyhow."

*   *   *

The room had a wobbly bed with one leg broken and propped up by a cinder block, a plastic-topped table and tubular steel chair, a chipped enamel washbasin that didn't work, and cockroaches. Fallon leaned against the wall at one end of the bed and raised the shot glass of Jameson Irish from the bottle that Parnum had produced. "Here's to my being free to walk the streets again."

Parnum, propped up at the head end, responded. "Cheers, mate." His eyes twinkled for a second. "You, ah, seem to have a way of getting into the thick of things that's surprising . . . for a professor, I mean."

"Just because one is an academic, it doesn't make him devoid of strong emotions or principles," Fallon said with appropriate Hannegenish stiffness. He sipped from his glass approvingly before Parnum could reply. "Very good. Your health."

"I prefer the Irish," Parnum said. "Smoother and less harsh. There's a lot of snobbery over Scotch, as with wines."

"Where did you get it?"

"Oh, there are still a few places around, you know. I've got a few friends left. It's amazing what you can find in the nooks and crannies around this town . . . as long as you've got the moola."

Mamu, the Sudanese whom Leroy had referred to as Parnum's tame monkey, nursed a small measure, generously topped with water, at the table, where Parnum's typewriter sat amid a pile of notebooks and heavily corrected manuscript sheets. Slimly built, with sensitive, sharply defined features but sunken eyes set beneath an older man's corrugated brow, he could have been anywhere from his midthirties to his fifties. He had previously been studying toward a doctorate in history at the Zugendan national university, but the university had been closed under Molokutu's regime as an alleged center for subversion. So Mamu had turned to journalism instead and attached himself to Parnum as a form of on-the-job training.

"It was Wylen who got Roger thrown out," Mamu said.

"Wylen?" Fallon queried. He did already know the name, from talking with Embatto, but there was no reason why Hannegen should have been told it.

"Leroy Wylen. The Yank with the big mouth, who got

us locked up," Parnum supplied. He clicked his tongue reprovingly. "And you weren't even properly introduced."

Mamu went on; "I heard it from the desk clerk. They didn't want the risk of Roger being around to say anything embarrassing while they're making the documentary."

"What documentary's this?" Fallon asked.

Parnum sighed. "Oh, they're getting a camera crew over to shoot for a TV production on the war. It's by invitation of the government, so it'll plug the usual line. Probably good for raising a few million back home too."

Mamu scowled angrily. "They make us an entertainment spectacular, in the same way that they treat an ecological problem . . . as if we were a helpless endangered species to be conserved by other people's efforts and donations. It never occurs to them that all we want is an end to the conditions that stop us taking care of ourselves."

"Don't look at Konrad," Parnum said. "He's only here to count antelopes, right?" He cocked an eye at Fallon and held it for a shade longer than would have been natural; then he added in a curiously provocative voice, "A strange kind of thing to be doing with a war going on, you'd think. But then Konrad, old mate, I'd say you make a pretty unusual zoologist all 'round."

Fallon returned his gaze evenly. "No more than you make a pretty unusual journalist . . . Or should I say, journalist, at least, with certain extracurricular interests?"

Parnum tried to conceal his sudden stiffening, but it showed. "What's that supposed to mean?" he asked shortly.

Fallon raised his hand and took a leisurely drink from his glass. Then, just when the tension seemed to have fallen a notch, he asked casually, "Did Annette use the name Candy when she operated with you here in Kinnube, or was it just for when she went to London?"

Parnum gulped at his own drink, far too hastily. In that same split second Fallon read from Mamu's face that he, too, knew what Fallon was talking about.

"I don't know about anything in London," Parnum answered. "And I've never heard of Candy."

"All right, maybe you don't," Fallon agreed. "But you do know Annette Mosswano. Embatto's people grabbed her in London three or four weeks ago. She was an agent for the ZRF, just like Elizabeth Bouabbas was. She worked here in Kinnube as a medical tech and procured drugs for the ZRF. But why am I telling you? You were her contact man back to them."

Parnum licked his lips dryly. "Look, I don't know what this is all about, but—"

"That's all right. There's no need for the act, Roger. Embatto already knows."

Behind his superficial nonchalance, Fallon was prepared for something sudden. Mamu fumbled inside his coat and Parnum was on his feet in the same instant, reaching for the jacket slung over the back of the chair. . . . But the gun had already materialized in Fallon's hand. Parnum stared at it grimly for a second, then drew back his arm. "Okay, I guess you've got us cold." He looked up at Fallon's face and shook his head distastefully. "I'd never have figured you for one. You seemed a pretty decent sort. Where are the rest of the jokers, out in the hall?"

Mamu, looking dazed, withdrew his hand from his coat, empty. "What gave us away?" he asked in a dull voice.

Fallon nodded at Parnum. "Your evasiveness when we talked in the Independence bar, for a start. The lone seeker-after-truth provided a good cover. It gave you a justification if your contact with the ZRF was uncovered. And you gave yourself away again a second ago by not reacting when I told you that Annette had been grabbed in London. In other words, you already knew about it. Right?"

Parnum nodded and licked his lips dryly. "So what's all this about Embatto knowing already?" he asked in a croaky voice.

"When we talked in the bar, you said they'd like to see you on the next flight home. You went where you weren't supposed to go and gave their government censor the finger. That breaks all the rules for an officially accredited journalist in a war situation and gave them every justification for throwing you out of the country. But they haven't. Why not? Because they'd rather keep you around until they can get rid of you permanently—perhaps on your next trip out into the bush alone, in the same way they did with Elizabeth Bouabbas."

Parnum frowned and hesitated as if unsure of having missed something. "You . . . don't exactly come across as telling us that we're blown," he said at last.

"I'd have thought that was obvious." Fallon looked down at the gun in his hand. "Oh, I just didn't want you two getting overexcited with those things you've got stashed away there." He slipped the gun back into his jacket and smiled apologetically.

"Mr. Hannegen, my nerves can do without things like this, thank you very much," Mamu said, closing his eyes.

Parnum reached for a cigarette from the pack standing by the Jameson bottle on the stand next to the bed. He lit one shakily, inhaled, then sat back down and took a nervous sip of whiskey. Mamu was watching Fallon with an intense but inscrutable expression.

"So how in hell's name do you come to know about Annette?" Parnum asked, pulling himself together again.

"I met her in London." Parnum's jaw fell open in surprise. Fallon waited for him to recover, then went on, "Do you know what she was doing there?"

"Not really . . . I just knew that she was going," Parnum replied. Fallon couldn't tell whether it was true, or if Parnum was simply keeping his guard up.

"Embatto's people tried to recruit a specialist called Fugleman to send a hit team in after ZRF's top echelon," Fallon said. "Candy was sent there with a man called Victor to try and call Fugleman off or else make him a counteroffer. As it turned out, Fugleman wasn't interested in either deal. But Zugendan security were onto it and decided not to take any chances. They killed Victor, grabbed Candy, and tried to eliminate Fugleman as well, but he got away. So now he's got a score to settle and wants to talk about the ZRF's offer . . . which means getting in touch with them again, somehow."

"How do you know all this?" Parnum asked him.

Fallon dropped the stiff intonation of Konrad Hannegen and reverted to his native London accent. "Because I'm Boris Fugleman. . . . Now can you see why I've come clean?"

Fallon took in the two incredulous stares and leaned forward to pour himself another shot of Jameson while they digested the revelation. Finally Parnum murmured in a still slightly dazed voice, "Well, it explains why you came across a bit bloody queer for a zoologist, anyhow."

"My pleasure, Mr. . . . Fugleman," Mamu said. "Or whoever you really are."

"It'll do for now," Fallon told him.

"I really am a reporter," Parnum said. "The rest came later, after I got to know the Zugendans."

"I guessed."

"Okay, so what are you telling us? You need to get across into ZRF country to make contact with Barindas's people and..." Parnum's voice trailed away as another thought occurred to him. He cocked his head to one side and looked at Fallon oddly. "Wait a minute. You said that you knew her in London as Candy?"

"Right."

"So how did you find out her real name?"

"And that she worked in Kinnube as a medical technician and procured drugs for the ZRF?" Mamu added, taking Parnum's point.

"I didn't until I came here," Fallon told them. "I found out quite a few things from a certain nameless source while I was in Kinnube jail. That's the big problem with regimes like Molokutu's. They breed enemies everywhere, even in the most unlikely places."

Parnum raised his eyebrows. "You don't waste much time, mate. I'll give you that."

"That's why such regimes are so paranoid," Mamu said.

Parnum stared distantly at Fallon for a moment, then snapped out of it abruptly and slapped a hand on his thigh in a businesslike fashion. "Right," he said. "So what next? Where do you want us to start?"

"I assume you've got some way of communicating back to the ZRF," Fallon said.

"Mmm...yes," Parnum admitted without volunteering any details.

"Well, the first thing I want you to do is tell them I'm on my way and that I want to talk."

"Okay."

"And another thing is to get you out of here before you end up feeding the fishes in the Tsholere River too," Fallon said. "You're living on borrowed time as it is." Parnum nodded tightly but said nothing. Fallon looked from him to Mamu and back again. "But there's one other thing to be done before that. You see, Candy was brought back here. She's in the special detention wing of Kinnube jail at this moment, and having a hard time. We're going to get her out."

There was a silence while the meaning sank in.
Finally Parnum shook his head as if to clear it. "But that's
a high-security facility," he protested. "You'll never get
anyone out of there."

"Not without inside help," Fallon agreed.

Parnum shrugged. "Well, we don't have anyone in
there. I can tell you that for—" His voice died and he
looked up. "Are you saying that this person you mentioned
is willing to help?"

"Exactly."

Parnum shifted on the bed and directed an uncomfortable look at Mamu. He obviously didn't like it.

Mamu was equally unenthusiastic. "Mr. Fugleman..."
He hesitated as if unsure of how to phrase something
delicate. "I'm not questioning your sentiments, and I'm
sure that you understand the realities here in Zugenda.
But the situation you have described is already perilous
enough without this... I mean, we are as distressed by
Annette's situation as you are. More so: we *knew* her.... But
such tragedies are daily fare in this country. She knew the
risks of the task she accepted."

"How can you be sure that this insider of yours is
reliable?" Parnum demanded. "You can't afford to trust
anyone you don't know here. It's the first thing you learn."

Fallon looked unsurprised. "But that's exactly my
point," he told them. They returned puzzled looks. "You
haven't had a chance to think it through yet, have you?" he
said. "As you so rightly say, *nobody* here can afford to trust
anyone. So why should *you* trust *me*? And more to the
point, why should Barindas and his people when I show
up there and tell them I'm Boris Fugleman?" He paused
and waited as a light of comprehension crept into Parnum's
eyes.

"Ah! Now I think I see...." Mamu breathed.

Fallon nodded. "It's not just out of the kindness of my
heart—although I agree it's a nice thought. But I *need* her
to back my story. And that's why I say we have to risk it
and hope for the best."

All that Parnum and Mamu knew, therefore, was the
"official" line that Fallon had agreed with Embatto. Hence
there was no risk of their disclosing anything more—for
example, if either or both of them should be unfortunate

enough to be captured in the attempt, which was something that Fallon had to allow for.

His other reason for telling the story "straight" was that he knew how people like Embatto worked. They trusted nobody and double-checked everything.

Since Jonas had taken Parnum to Tobins Hotel, it would have been a safe bet that Fallon would end up there in the same way. Unless he was very much mistaken, the business over the air conditioner indicated that Xavier had been told to put him in the room he had been given, and no other.

And that meant that his room and Parnum's room had in all probability been bugged.

Chapter Sixteen

IT WAS A MILD, SUNNY DAY OVER THE COTSWOLD hills near Gloucester, in the West Country of England. On a slope rising from rough, folded ground, a man and a boy sat concealed in a thicket of gorse bushes, watching three figures in the center of an open, grassy expanse below. A black shape was circling in the air about fifty feet above the figures, and the harsh note of a model airplane rasped up through the rural quiet.

"Are they the ones who smashed your plane up, Tommy?" the man asked. He was in his early forties, short and stocky, with sandy hair, a ruddy complexion, and was wearing a tweed jacket with a check shirt and knitted tie.

The boy was eleven, frail-bodied, with overgrown hair and a few freckles. "Yes. The biggest one in the middle was the worst. The mods that you showed me made it do all kinds of things that theirs couldn't, and they didn't like it."

The man pulled across the leather carrying case that he had brought with them on a shoulder strap and set it in front of Tommy. Tommy opened the flap and lid to reveal a panel of switches, control knobs, and dials. The man extended a telescopic antenna. "Right, let's see if you can remember the drill," the man said.

He watched as Tommy operated the controls, checked readings, and jotted figures on a pad. "Is that the full sweep?" Tommy asked.

"Right."

"I think I've got it centered on two-seventy-five."

"Lock it and wind up your power, then."

Down below them, the boy with the transmitter looked puzzled as he followed the course of the black racer. He peered down at his control box, jerked the joystick several times, and looked back up at the plane again.

"That's weird," he declared.

"What's up?" one of the others asked him.

"I didn't make it do that. Look, it's doing it again."

"What are you talking about?" the third demanded.

"This isn't working. Look."

"Give it to me."

Above them, the plane went into a steep climb, its motor straining to the point of a stall, and then rolled out into a power dive and regained speed rapidly.

"What are you doing, you silly sod? Pull out, you'll—"

"*I'm not doing anything!* It's doing it itself."

"Don't be stupid."

The plane pulled out at the last moment, climbed away again, and then turned and went into another dive, this time shallower, down to just above head height and coming straight at them.

"Stop it!"

"It won't—"

"*Oh Christ!*"

"*Whoooooah!*"

One of the boys turned and ran, terrified. Another ducked, while the biggest tumbled to the ground.

"Bloody good show, son," the man commented, jamming a pipe into his mouth and nodding approvingly.

"This is fun!" Tommy grinned.

No sooner had the trio below regrouped than the plane repeated the performance with an even lower swoop and scattered them again, causing all three to throw themselves down. One slid through a fresh cowpat, and another rolled into a clump of nettles. Bewildered, they picked themselves up to see the plane climb away once more, perform a victory roll, and disappear over a bluff on the far side of a hollow filled with briars.

Ten minutes later, the man and the boy were walking briskly down a path on the reverse side of the hill, the man carrying the case and the boy clutching his new trophy, when they saw a figure in blue jeans and a light windbreaker, sitting on a stone wall a short distance ahead, showing all the appearances of having been waiting for them. He had a pinkish face, fair, curly hair, and was grinning broadly. But the penny didn't finally drop until a familiar Yorkshire voice called out, "Aye, bloody good job too. Serve t'little boogers raht. Been learnin' some new tricks from that dad o' yours, 'ave yer, Tommy, lad? So 'allo again, Jimmy Reid. 'Ow yer been keepin'?"

"George, by God! Where on earth did you spring from?"

George got up from the wall and came forward to meet them. "Well, it so 'appens that I 'eard yer could use a few quid."

"Well, a little bit extra always comes in handy."

"Interested in a bit of business, maybe, are yer?"

"Oh . . . might be. You never know. What's come up, then?" They resumed walking on down the path.

"I've got a friend 'oo could use a bit of 'elp wi' summat."

"Oh, well, you know me, George; never could refuse a fellow soul in need. Good neighborship to all, that's what I say."

"Good. Let's stop off at t'poob when we get down to t'road. Tommy can 'ave a look at 'is new plane, an' I'll tell yer about it over a pint."

A Frenchman, an Algerian, and a Sardinian sat sipping Pernods at a sidewalk café on the south side of Rome. The first two were bronzed, well muscled, and alert; the other, lithely built and dusky skinned, with dark, droopy-lidded eyes and a heavy mustache.

Justin, a former officer with the French paras, was a picture of contented relaxation as he lounged back with an arm stretched across the back of an empty chair next to him and one foot crossed over the other knee, soaking up the sun and admiring the girls as they passed. The Sardinian, whose name was Emerel, remained tense, probing the surroundings with eyes that were never still.

"Relax," Justin told him. "You still see CIA and KGB everywhere. I told you, it isn't that kind of work. This is private enterprise we're talking now."

Emerel had a murky history of involvement with various political assassinations around the Mediterranean, including an assignment a few years back from Egyptian intelligence that had almost got Qaddafi. Strangely, it had been mainly the CIA's intervention that had saved Qaddafi. Emerel also knew from inside sources that whatever else their public posturings might suggest, the CIA and Qaddafi had cooperated in funding the FNLA Angolan independence movement against the Soviet-backed Cubans. Why, he didn't pretend to understand.

"I've seen too much of what goes on behind the scenes," Emerel said. "I take care of myself and trust nobody."

"This is a different league from the one you're used to," Benjedid, the Algerian, said. He was an ex-Legionnaire and an old acquaintance of Justin's. "These people are straight. I've had dealings with them before. I wouldn't have introduced you to Justin if I wasn't confident in them."

Emerel glanced at his watch. "Where is he, then? It's fifteen minutes after."

"He'll be here," Justin drawled. "He has a busy schedule."

"Did I ever tell you about—" Benjedid began, but stopped as Justin sat up suddenly, peering into the throng bustling along the sidewalk.

"Ah, I see him now," Justin said.

Emerel looked around as a squat, bearded figure in a light tan jacket and open-necked white shirt detached itself from the crowd and approached the table jauntily.

"Aha! My apologies for keeping you waiting," he greeted, and proceeded to pump the Sardinian's hand vigorously. "You must be Emerel."

"This is Henri," Justin said by way of introduction.

"I've heard good reports about you," Monaux said. He looked around as he pulled up a chair and sat down. "Well, looks as if it will be okay to talk here. We can get down to business right away. . . ."

Chapter Seventeen

MAMU WAS SCARED AS HE SAT IN THE FRONT passenger's seat of Parnum's mud-streaked Peugeot estate wagon. It was one of a number of vehicles parked on the street late in the evening by a row of demoralized-looking shops and offices and a bar, almost opposite the front entrance of the prison. He was scared because for the last three quarters of an hour he had been thinking of the things that happened to the unfortunates who ended up in such places, and that if anything went wrong with the operation tonight, he would probably become one of them.

Some years previously, when he had been a history undergraduate, he had met a man called Ehud, who had lived in Iraq as an undercover agent for Israeli intelligence. Ehud once told him the story of a woman in Baghdad who was visited one day by two security officials. "Go to the city mortuary," they told her, "and collect the body of your son." The son, a fourth-year medical student, had been arrested some ten months earlier as a dissident and taken to Abu Ghraib Khassa, the security wing of Baghdad prison. The news of his death was the first she had heard of him for six months.

The next morning she went to the prison, where over a hundred other people were also gathered to claim the bodies of relatives. She was shown into a room filled with mutilated corpses covered in blood. One had the marks of a hot domestic iron all over his chest and back; one's nose and ears had been cut off; another was without toes. Although Mamu had considered himself relatively hardened to the way of so much of the world, he had found himself disturbed for days after he listened to the story. Nobody, he told himself, should have to live with experiences like that Iraqi mother's.

There was the usual group lounging outside the bar, others squatting to roll dice on the sidewalk alongside, ones and twos walking on both sides of the street, a small knot gathered on the far corner, being eyed warily by the guards outside the prison gate. It had all the makings of a regular evening, nothing out of the ordinary to attract attention. Just the kind of evening the three of them had hoped for.

The Peugeot's horn was operated by a push switch at the base of the lighting control stem inside the steering column, which was normally held open by a spring. Fallon had loosened the rivet securing one end of the spring and wedged the mechanism in the "off" position with a straightened paper clip projecting out through a gap between two sections of the column molding. When the clip was removed, the spring would disengage and allow the switch to close.

Mamu checked the time on the dashboard clock and wiped the palms of his hands nervously on his thighs. Five minutes.

Kinnube's jail had been built on an urban site with limited space. It consisted of an irregular cluster of buildings with small, gloomy yards squeezed among them, and in several places the space between the perimeter wall and the main structure was quite narrow. One such place was to the side near the rear, where special-category prisoners were held in a tall, forbidding edifice of sheer brick walls and small barred windows. Mindful of the proximity of the streets and other buildings outside, the designers had decided to use height as an added measure of security, making it necessary for any would-be escaper or rescuer to penetrate several levels of formidable safeguards, no matter what direction they might try for getting in or out below. Nobody, however, had seriously considered the possibility of anyone's getting in from above. And as Fallon had observed when he drove out of the prison with Embatto to meet Molokutu, a rear projection of the Zugendan National Radio Building was situated across a side street outside the perimeter wall, immediately opposite the high-security wing.

Parnum crouched low behind the roof parapet, clutching the grapnel gun. Fallon was beside him, watching through

binoculars the two occupants of the guard tower at a
corner of the prison wall a short distance farther along the
street. He was wearing a dark, lightweight coverall with a
nylon rappel sling—a type of harness used by mountain-
eers for rapid descents—fastened over the top, and with
his hands and face blackened. They were both tense from
concentration and the effort of keeping their senses alert
for danger, and the conversation was sparse.

Parnum looked at his watch in the glow from a
penlight. "Almost time," he whispered.

"Right." Fallon lowered the binoculars and set them
down. "Let's go."

Parnum passed him the gun. It was short and stocky
like a grenade launcher, and fired a four-barbed aluminum
grapnel that opened in flight and trailed a lightweight
nylon line. The line was attached to a heavier-gauge rappel
rope lying coiled by Fallon's side. The spotlights on the
guard tower and the arc lamps projecting over the street
were directed downward at the wall, and had shades that
blocked the light in the upward direction. Thus, a line
stretched between the roofs of the Radio Building extension and the high-security wing of the jail, although passing within ten feet of the top of the wall, would be in
shadow.

On the far roof was a water tank and a steel access
door from below, set in a concrete fixture. The door was
normally bolted. Tonight, however, Embatto should have
arranged for it to be open.

In the street at the front of the prison, the group on
the far corner broke up and dispersed. Two policemen
came out of the coffee shop and stood talking on the
sidewalk. A hooker and her client emerged from the bar
and disappeared into the alley alongside. It was time.
Mamu drew a long, shaky breath, then reached across the
car and closed his fingers around the projecting end of the
paper clip. He felt his chest pounding uncontrollably. But
if he faltered now, he'd never muster the courage again.
He jerked the clip clear, and the sudden blare of the
Peugeot's horn shattered the silence of the street. The
dice players stood up from their game, and passersby
turned to stare. The policemen who had been standing

outside the coffee shop came running over. Mamu rolled the window down and looked out helplessly.

"What in hell d'you think you're doing, man?" one of the policemen yelled at him above the din.

"It's jammed. Can't you see it's jammed?"

"What did you do to it?"

"Nothing. A guy went into the alley that I wanted to talk to. I hit it to get his attention, and it stuck."

"Turn it off for fuck's sake."

"I can't. It won't turn off." Mamu hammered the end of the control repeatedly without effect.

"Gotta unhook the battery," the other policeman shouted, and moved around to the front.

"Open your hood," the other directed through the window.

Mamu threw up his hands. "How do I do that? I don't drive this car. Where is it?"

The policeman yanked open the door and stuck his head inside. "Don't you have any light in here?"

"How do I know? Where's the switch?"

"Shit, don't you know anything?"

"It just jammed. . . ."

The buildings along the side street and the prison wall across from them formed a sound guide that carried the noise. One of the guards in the tower came out to see what was happening, looked one way then the other, and went back inside. Through the glass wall of the guard post, Fallon could see the other lifting a telephone, probably to call the front gate.

He aimed high and fired, and the doubled length of line whipped out into the blackness above the lamps. The noise of the car horn echoing from the front street blanketed the report and also any metallic clink as the grapnel clattered over the far roof. He drew in the slack, felt the lines tauten as the hook found purchase, and tested it with a couple of hefty tugs. "It feels okay," he murmured to Parnum.

The line was doubled through a smooth link in the end of the grapnel, with one end attached to the rappel rope. While Parnum fed out the remainder, followed by the thicker rappel rope, Fallon hauled in the other end to draw the rappel rope out across the gap, through the link and back again, until the end returned to complete a doubled span with the stouter rope. While he was securing it, the sound of the horn ceased.

Parnum unfastened the thin line from the rope and handed it to Fallon, who tied it to the rappel sling that he was wearing. He then clipped the sling to the ropes with a couple of sliding snap links and was set to go. He checked his equipment inventory, which included a Browning automatic with silencer, two spare thirteen-round clips, knife, and hip flask, along with a second coverall rolled up around another rappel sling and an elastic belt. Satisfied, he peered over the parapet for a final look around.

"Good luck, sport," Parnum whispered, clapping his shoulder lightly.

Fallon straightened up cautiously, stepped over the parapet, and launched himself into thin air.

The rope dipped under his weight as he hauled himself away from the roof and out over the drop to the street far below. A car sped by beneath, stopped at the end by the front of the prison, and disappeared. Three men walked past in the shadows, talking loudly. Fallon hauled himself on along the ropes and after another minute or so was over the wall and as close as he would come to the guard tower. Although he was armed, he wouldn't have given much for his chances in an exchange with a trigger-happy guard from this position. For obvious reasons Embatto wouldn't have involved more than one or two people at the most, and even then, he and Molokutu were probably the only two who really knew what was going on.

But the guards stayed in their post and all remained quiet. Fallon moved on over the enclosed yard behind the wall, black and featureless in shadow. He was having to pull himself harder now as the ascent to the security-wing roof steepened, and to keep a constant grip to avoid slipping back. The night air was close and humid, and perspiration drenched him inside his clothing.

Finally he hauled himself over the parapet wall, unclipped his harness from the ropes, and tied off the end of the thin line that now ran back to Parnum, giving two tugs on it to signal that all was well. Then he crossed the roof and located the steel door. It was open.

The ladder beneath was in a small attic chamber, from

where a flight of wooden stairs led down to a room at the back of the landing at the top of steel stairs. They were the stairs that Fallon had climbed with Embatto, Tumratta, and the others on the morning after his first night's stay in the prison. Around the landing would be the barred gates giving access into the cell rows, and on the far side, the guardroom with the half-height door. According to the plan, the guard should have been drugged and unconscious.

Fallon eased open the door to the landing and peered through the crack. All was still. The half door into the guardroom was open, and from it a shaft of light angled down onto the concrete floor. A wider corridor, without a gate, entered the landing from the direction opposite. Fallon pulled the door open further, paused to listen, and emerged silently. He crossed the landing and moved stealthily along the wall toward the doorway until he could peer inside. His jaw tightened. The guard was unconscious, all right. Permanently so. He was lying beyond the desk inside the door, sprawled at the rear of the room in a pool of blood; he had been shot in the head and chest.

Expendable.

So, Embatto was making it look really good. And this way the "accomplice" could never talk.

Prominent above the desk was a round casing with a red alarm button. Fallon disconnected the wire from it and yanked out the cord of the desk telephone. There was a chart showing the layout of the building on the wall above the desk, but Fallon already knew the location and number of Candy's cell from the plans he had studied. He took the keys from the belt of the dead guard, then went back out and found the one that fitted the barred gate. It opened smoothly.

He moved into the passage of grim steel doors with tiny sliding shutters. As he passed one about halfway along, he heard a continuous, demented moaning on the other side. Farther on, a woman sobbing. Each door hiding its own story of tragedy, misery, and despair; a human being in the process of being slowly and deliberately destroyed; a life that someone had the power to erase. He wanted to open all the doors and let daylight in upon every one of the wretches behind them, to destroy this whole place and all the other places like it.

He came to the cell, stopped outside it, and inserted the

key. The lock turned. He pushed the door inward and paused in the doorway to readjust to the gloom farther back. Candy was huddled in a tatter of blanket against the far wall, hidden in his shadow. He moved out of the light. She pulled the blanket tightly around her and remained motionless, at the same time staring fearfully up at his silhouette. He took the flask from his belt and squatted down. Her eyes followed him dully, without care or comprehension. Her body reeked from lack of washing and untreated sores.

"Drink this," he whispered, putting the neck of the flask to her lips. She tasted the strong, sweet glucose preparation. Fallon held the flask while she drank more, supporting her head with his other hand. Her hair was sticky and dirty, with lumps that felt like clotted blood. "Don't ask questions. There isn't time. Just do as I say. Understand?"

She nodded weakly. Fallon wasn't even sure if she had recognized him yet. He let her drink for a while longer. A little strength seemed to return. She looked at him again in the light from the door, and he saw the confusion forming in her eyes. "*You?* Why—"

Fallon cut her off with a sign and unrolled the spare coveralls that he had brought. "Put these on." He straightened up and held out a hand, supporting her under an arm with the other. She tried to stand, but cried out with the sudden pain of trying to straighten her cramped and bruised limbs. Slowly but firmly Fallon urged her to her feet. He fastened the belt that had been inside the roll around the waist of her loose prison pants and helped her into the coveralls. Her body was shaking, and he could hear her catching her breath and wincing as she moved. Finally he buckled the second rappel sling over the top of her clothing.

The effort had got her circulation moving again. "What's happening?" she croaked hoarsely. "What does this mean?"

"It means we're taking you home."

"We? Who?"

"Later."

They emerged into the corridor, Fallon helping Candy with one arm and holding his pistol ready in the other hand. She moved slowly, and it took them a minute or more to reach the barred gate. Seeing it open and unattended, she looked at him questioningly; but Fallon, worried now about getting her up the ladder to the roof, merely shook his head curtly and steered her through.

Then, just as they reached the door on the far side of the landing, the sound of a door opening came from the wider corridor opposite the cell rows, and footsteps approached briskly. A guard came around the corner before Fallon could push Candy through the door and out of sight. Another man was with him, wearing civilian clothes. It was the weasel-faced interrogator, Tumratta—the one Fallon had dubbed "Ratfart."

The guard glimpsed them from the corner of his eye, and Fallon dropped him with two fast head shots while he was still turning; but even in that short instant, Ratfart ducked away and vanished into the guardroom before Fallon could shift his aim. Fallon crossed back over the landing after him, flattened himself against the wall beside the door, and looked into the room warily.

Ratfart had stopped just inside, momentarily paralyzed by the sight of the dead guard lying on the floor. Then he hurled himself toward the alarm button and stabbed at it frantically. Fallon stepped into the doorway and watched while Ratfart jabbed the button again and again without result. Then, realizing the futility, he turned fearfully. His expression took on an added dimension of bewilderment as he recognized Fallon's face. Fallon raised the pistol and aimed, feeling no more compunction than a pest exterminator.

But Candy appeared beside him before he could fire. "No," she hissed, taking the gun from his unresisting fingers. "He's mine."

Ratfart's eyes widened in disbelief and terror as he stared into the muzzle of the pistol and saw the same indifference on the two faces behind it as had innumerable victims as they watched the electrodes or the hot iron approaching. "No . . ." He shook his head wildly. "No, you can't do this! Not to me . . . Wait—"

Candy shot him three times low in the stomach and watched him writhe on the floor before finishing him off. The experience seemed to revivify her, and she managed the ladder without too much trouble.

When they were outside and back at the edge of the roof, Fallon clipped her sling to the ropes and attached the thin line that he had left tied. He signaled with a couple of tugs, and Parnum pulled her across from the other side. Fallon followed, hauling himself along and ready to help if she became stuck. Soon the two men were helping her over the parapet onto the other roof.

"Roger!" she exclaimed when she realized who it was. "How—"

Parnum held open a quilted jacket that he had waiting for her. "Here, get that gear off and into this. Don't try and talk now."

"Everything okay here?" Fallon asked, looking around as he unhitched his own equipment.

"Not a whisper," Parnum told him.

They collected their equipment silently, and Mamu picked them up in the Peugeot by a deserted lot a block away. It was only when they were safely on their way to the surgery that Dr. Velker had set up on the outskirts of the city that the tension eased and they became talkative again.

"So is this what you do for a living?" Parnum said. "Christ! And I thought it was me that needed his head examined."

"It has its moments," Fallon agreed.

"Well, it must pay a pretty fair whack, mate, that's all I can say. I should bloody well hope so too." Fallon didn't answer. He still hadn't agreed on anything with Marlow about that side of it. After a few seconds of silence Parnum said, "So, did it go off all right back there? Everything went as planned?"

Fallon nodded in a strange, grimly satisfied way in the shadows on the other side of the car. "Even better, Roger, me old cobber," he said. "Even better."

Chapter Eighteen

THEY CAME TO JACOB QUALEY'S HOUSE AN HOUR before dawn the next day. The first thing that Jacob knew was being torn from his sleep by the crash of the door being broken down as State Security Special Action troopers burst in and began kicking him to his feet from the floor, along with the four other men who had been sleeping on mattresses there—a cousin and three friends who had no work, nowhere else to go, and who had been sharing a meager communal pot.

He blinked in bewilderment, still half-awake. "What's the—"

"*Get up!*" the officer in charge barked. "All of you, over against that wall!"

"But what are we supposed—" A rifle barrel jabbed hard into his back silenced him.

"Face that wall. Put your hands high, against the wall."

There was a burst of firing. Jacob's cousin and one of the others fell against the wall and slid to the floor.

"The rest of you, turn around."

Three frightened men turned to face the soldiers and were mowed down. The officer's instructions had made it clear that not all were to be shot in the back.

A stifled whimper came from the next room. The soldiers looked inside and found two women cowering with several small children. They tossed two grenades in and closed the door. Before departing they left a grapnel gun, a couple of rappel slings, several coils of nylon line, a number of handguns, and some ammunition inside a closet.

By the time the city police arrived, the house was in flames and the Special Action squad had taken up covering positions around.

"It must have been them, all right," the SS officer told the police commissioner. "They started shooting as soon as we got here. Must have been jumpy."

"Is there anyone left alive in there?"

"It's hard to say. . . . They've been quiet for a while now. Maybe not."

"We'll wait five minutes, then move in and check it out."

"Whatever you say . . ." There was a dull thump and a *whoosh* as one end of the house flared up. "Hell, look at that. They musta had a bomb factory or something in there."

At the Independence Hotel, a busboy was clearing dishes from the tables on the dance floor, which was where lunch was also served. Apart from rumors of a break from the Kinnube jail that night, the morning had been quiet. In one of the booths, Leroy, Gary, and Dieter were sitting around a pot of coffee with a bearded, thirtyish American called Tom Hughes, one of the camera team shooting the documentary on the Zugendan war. The man standing and talking with them in a white shirt and dark pinstripe suit was from the Ministry of Information.

"I just stopped by to tell you that the stuff you left with us yesterday had been okayed by the censor. You'll be getting an official note later today."

"Glad to hear it," Leroy murmured over his cup. His tone conveyed that he had naturally assumed it would be.

"Were there any cuts?" Tom Hughes asked.

The official inclined his head and made a you-know-how-it-is gesture. "Some footage that was judged liable to misinterpretation by uninformed members of the general public was omitted from the final version."

"Oh," Hughes said, but he wasn't going to argue. Having to go along with this kind of shit was a pain, but if you didn't play ball, people complained somewhere, strings got pulled, and things happened. His predecessor had been shipped home on six hours notice. . . . And life could be comfortable out here.

Dieter motioned toward the coffeepot. "You vould care to join us for a cup, perhaps?"

The official shook his head. "I have other matters to attend to. I just stopped by on my way past to give you the word. Now I must dash. Good day, gentlemen." The others murmured responses, and the man from the ministry left.

Leroy stared after him with a misanthropic eye. "What in hell d'you want him sitting here for?" he asked Dieter.

The German shrugged. "Merely a courtesy."

"With them? It's wasted. A bimbo can dress up in suits and learn words out of a dictionary all he wants, but that doesn't stop him being a bimbo."

"Aw, ease up, Roy," Gary said.

Leroy poured himself more coffee. "Are we still on for cocktails with the general today?"

Gary nodded. "Not until the evening, though. There's some other people that he wants there too, but they'll be out of town until later. We said around six-thirty."

"That sounds okay. Then we'll still be in good time for the party at that other place?"

"Oh, sure." Gary looked across at Dieter. "Are you partying tonight?"

Dieter shook his head. "Really, I haff to write up my notes. Unt then, later, der interview I must do."

At that moment Jonas appeared in the doorway. He looked around, saw them, and hurried over.

"The yellow-haired Australian has been arrested again," he announced breathlessly. "They say it's to do with the jail break last night."

"When?" Leroy demanded.

"About an hour ago. The police picked him up at Tobins and took him to the station along the street from here. They were looking for the Dane too, but he's not around."

Leroy slipped Jonas a coin and looked across the table at the others as he downed the last of his coffee. "Hey, waddya know, guys? This could be interesting. What say we get on over there and see what gives?"

Inside the police station, Roger Parnum made an ineffective grab at the camera as the gum-chewing policeman in shirtsleeves pulled off the back and prised out one of the film spools. "Goddammit, you dumb bastard, that's exposed! You've ruined it. For Christ's sake watch that lens."

Another, in an unbuttoned tunic with sergeant's chevrons, slapped Parnum's hand aside. "You seem like you've forgotten you're under arrest, man. No, *you* watch it. You don't tell anyone what to do in here, got it?"

Parnum watched despairingly as another policeman tipped the contents of one of his accessory cases out onto the counter next to the pile of belongings that had been collected from his room. A half liter of Johnnie Walker, a container of talc, a bottle of after-shave, a calculator, an electric shaver, and a roll of U.S. currency bills had already been set aside as undeclared "contraband." The policeman picked up an audiocassette and began unraveling the tape curiously. Mamu looked on despondently from one side.

A door at the back of the room opened, and an officer with a mustache, big belly, and brow beaded with perspiration came through. He was wearing a disgruntled expression. "The word is that they've been cleared," he said gruffly. "Get 'em out of here."

The sergeant looked bemused. "You're kidding. Two guys of ours get shot. Now you're telling me we're supposed to let these creeps go?"

"I'm telling you those are the orders. How do I know what goes on? Seems like the SS got the ones who did it, up on the north side. There was a fight there early this morning." The officer threw down two passports and sets of stamped exit papers. "It says twenty-four hours as of now to get out of the country. If it was up to me, neither of you'd ever get out the door."

The sergeant looked balefully at Parnum. The Australian stared ahead impassively, inwardly almost ready to sob out loud with relief and wondering if this was more of Fugleman's doing. "Get all that shit cleared up," the sergeant growled, waving at the counter. Parnum and Mamu started bundling their clothes and other effects back into the bags. When Parnum reached for the leather cases containing his cameras, recorder, and other equipment, the officer stepped forward and held up a restraining arm. "That's confiscated material. It stays."

"It's worth thousands," Parnum protested. "You can't—"

"It was used for subversive activities. That's why you're being thrown out. Be thankful you're not going to a wall."

"But Christ—"

"On your way, before these guys run out of cool."

Parnum and Mamu collected their remaining things together and were jostled roughly out of the room. Outside, the inevitable crowd had gathered around Parnum's mud-spattered Peugeot, which was being watched by a number of police auxiliaries. Near the front were Leroy Wylen and a couple of his pals from the Independence. The sergeant shouted at everyone to move back, and the auxiliaries cleared a way through.

"What's going on?" Leroy demanded above the general level of chattering. He drew the sergeant aside and dropped his voice. "They're not letting those two go?"

"They've been cleared," the sergeant told him.

"But he's a goddamn reb for chrissakes! You've only got to read the crap he writes."

"There's an expulsion order for subversion." The sergeant shrugged. "I'd string 'em both up too. But I just have to do what I'm told."

Leroy came over to Parnum as he climbed into the driver's seat of the Peugeot. "How'd you swing that one? I hope it cost you an arm and a leg. Oh, I forgot, 'honest journalism' is supposed to be above bribery and that kind of stuff, isn't it."

"Hoping to see a firing squad, were you?" Parnum said while Mamu got in the other side.

Leroy leaned closer to the open window. "Don't tell me you weren't mixed up in that stunt last night."

"I guess you'll never know, will you?"

"Too bad they're kicking your asses out of here. Then you might have gotten a chance to find out how your friends really work."

"Oh, I know who *my* friends are, all right. Do you?"

Parnum started the engine and eased the car forward as the crowd parted to make way. His face remained expressionless, but beneath their wiry, sun-lightened brows, his eyes held a triumphant glint.

The report from the London embassy was that Fugleman's French associate was making satisfactory progress: he had done nothing to arouse suspicion, and the potential recruits that he had approached—as far as it was possible to verify—were legitimate. The tapes obtained from Tobins showed Fugleman to be adhering strictly to what had been agreed upon. From their chief's call to Embatto that afternoon, it seemed that the city police had drawn the desired conclusions.

"Wait for the final report from the police and then close the file on it," he told Ngoyba.

"What about the other suspects?" Ngoyba asked.

"Hold the ones that we wanted off the streets anyway. There's nothing to be gained from the rest."

"Does that mean we hold off from Velker's place?"

That was the last place that Embatto wanted raided just for the moment. "For the time being, yes," he said. "It's more use to us to leave it operating as normal."

"Rumors have got out already. What's the official line?"

"Straightforward: a terrorist group tried to break one of their operatives from jail; they had been penetrated by the security forces, were traced back to their hideout, where they attempted to resist arrest." Embatto shrugged and lit one of his cigarettes. "All of them were killed, and that's the end of the matter."

Chapter Nineteen

WITH HIS THICK, HORN-RIMMED SPECTACLES AND boyish mop of sandy hair, Dr. Felix Velker looked even younger and more studentlike in the flesh than in the picture Fallon had seen in General Thombert's file.

"I'm a doctor. I came out here originally to do doctor's work—my thesis was on tropical diseases. And as I got to know the ZRF better, I associated myself with their cause. It's the same cause of people anywhere who care about decency in the human race." His voice had a note of bitter resignation and futility.

Ironically, that was virtually the role that the Zugendans had conceived for Hannegen, Fallon thought as he steadied the head of the man stretched out on the couch and used tweezers and a cotton ball moistened with surgical spirit to swab blood away from the gash in his head while Velker stitched the flesh with a needle and forceps. The man had been beaten and robbed on the street in broad daylight that afternoon. Behind them, in the shadows beyond the desk lamp by which Velker was working, a girl dabbed water on the brow of a woman tossing deliriously in a fever. Around the room, other forms lay covered by scraps of blanket and linen on camp cots or makeshift mattresses on the floor. In a far corner, under another lamp, a youth was washing bandages in a sink next to a large pot of water heating over a kerosene burner.

Velker went on: "So I evolved into a political animal....I mean, you've got to try and do something, haven't you? To do something about putting the bigger problem right, that is. What's the point of setting a bone here and maybe saving a life there if crimes that maim and kill millions can be committed with impunity?"

"And Zugenda was a good place to start," Fallon said.

"Any of these socialist police states... How can ordinary people be expected to form any principle or ethic when the greatest violator of their freedom becomes the state itself? Anyway, I don't have much to offer as a military adviser, I'm afraid. So I devoted what effort I could to furthering their case in the international forum."

"How has the response been?" Fallon asked.

"Pretty miserable," Velker answered candidly. "You've seen the version that gets pumped into the world's head. I do what I can in London, but it's a bloody uphill battle. It's money that talks, as they say, and what do these people have?"

"Billions get poured into these countries," Fallon said. "What happens to it?"

"It just makes the problem worse. That's what all these do-good, bloody politicians don't understand—or don't care about, more likely, as long as it sounds good and polishes their image. All it does is subsidize dictators like Molokutu, who no longer need support from the people. The people don't matter anymore, and so they can starve."

"But it's all right for some," Fallon said.

Velker pulled the thread taut, raising a hummock of scalp, snipped the end off with scissors, and reached for a dressing. "Did you see the big ranches over to the east of Sorindi province on your way in?"

"On the way to Kinnube? Yes, I did."

"They belong to government officials and other favorites." Velker made a distasteful face. "They drive around in Mercedes-Benzes but still count their money the way their grandfathers did: in cattle. They don't sell them, or kill them to eat. The herds are there simply as displays of their owners' wealth."

"Thousand-acre bank accounts?"

"Exactly. And they pay experts to protect them. They put up fences, divert the water and block migration trails, and destroy anything inside that might carry disease or threaten the cattle. The people's lives are destroyed along with the animals, while a few enrich themselves with foreign money and foreign guns. . . . And this while they preach an ideology of equality!"

"How do they get away with it?"

"Through politics. Without the aid programs they couldn't survive. The people don't need them. They took care of themselves for ten thousand years—when they were left alone. It's the parasites who need the programs."

"And you think it would change if the ZRF did take over?"

"Oh, yes. Barindas means it. He'll deliver what he promises, if he ever gets the chance."

"That's what they all say. How can you be sure?"

"Still the professional cynic, eh. Mr. . . . What am I supposed to call you these days?"

"Let's stick with Hannegen."

"Very well. You see, Barindas doesn't have the kind of arrogance that makes some think they're fit to direct the lives of others. He isn't looking for the power to impose anything. But hearing these kinds of things from me isn't going to change anything. You have to get among them, get to know them. With luck you'll meet him yourself when you get down there." Velker smoothed the dressing over and straightened up. "There. This chap has been luckier than a lot that I've seen."

"It doesn't sound as if you'd give much credit to the atrocity stories that get told about them, then," Fallon commented.

"Largely fabricated, without a doubt . . . although, admittedly, you always get some ugly happenings in this kind of situation."

"Are you saying they never happened?" Fallon asked.

"I'm saying that the occurrences that have been getting all the publicity weren't the handiwork of the ZRF."

"Whose, then? Do you know?"

Velker dropped the instruments that he had been using into a tray. "Let's go into the back room and talk over a coffee," he suggested. He went over and rinsed his hands at the sink. "Can you manage on your own for a while, Arnold?" he asked the youth who was washing bandages.

"What if the gunshot case in the corner starts acting up again?"

"Give him another two mils if you have to . . . but that's all we can spare."

"Okay."

Velker moved to the girl tending the delirious woman while Fallon cleaned his hands. "Any change?"

"I think she's quieter now."

"Make sure that she keeps drinking water. Lots of water. She mustn't dehydrate."

"Yes, doctor."

Velker led the way through a door to a dingy back room that had an old kitchen dresser at one end, its shelves lined with bottles and jars. There was also a table and cabinet, both cluttered with boxes, medical books, and trays of instruments, a battered, leather-upholstered easy chair with its stuffing coming out, and a couple of wooden chairs. Fallon came in behind him and closed the door.

On the far side, away from the light, Candy, wrapped in a blanket and with the quilted jacket folded as a pillow, was asleep on a cot. Velker went over, checked her pulse at the temple, and then laid a hand on her forehead to feel the skin. "She seems stronger," he murmured. "Another good night's rest should help a lot." He adjusted the blanket, then moved over to a coffeepot simmering on a low cupboard in a corner and took down two chipped mugs hanging from nails in the wall.

He handed Fallon one of the mugs, then lowered himself into the easy chair, took a sip, and emitted a grateful sigh. Fallon moved a pack of field dressings from one of the wooden chairs and sat down. He tasted the coffee and nodded approvingly. "The real stuff. There are some perks in being a doctor around here, then?"

"Oh, God. Was that supposed to be a pun?" Velker asked tiredly.

"No, an accident. Sorry."

Velker snorted. "The dealer who got it for me is in jail. Have you heard about Molokutu's latest brilliant inspiration in progressive economics?"

"What's that?"

"He's discovered how to correct the deficiencies of capitalism by socialist decree; in other words, the optimum combination of private and state power. Quite simply, you set a quota for profits, just as you set a quota for anything else, and make it a punishable offense not to achieve them."

There was a pause. Fallon looked across at Candy. She seemed to be sleeping soundly. That was good. He was anxious for them to be on their way as soon as she was fit to move.

"We were talking about somebody framing the ZRF," he said, turning his head back again.

Velker nodded. "Yes . . . Well, I'll give you an example of what goes on. You must have passed through a place called Elinvoro on the way in."

"I did. The army was there, giving everyone a hard time. The story was that they'd been intimidated into helping the ZRF by having their head man and his family carved up."

Velker shook his head. "They weren't ZRF. They were from one of Embatto's Special Action detachments, disguised as rebels."

"How do you come to know?" Fallon asked.

"The ZRF captured one of them in an ambush on an SS patrol a week later, and a couple of the villagers recognized him. He'd taken a piece of shrapnel in the leg. I happened to be down that way and they got me to patch him up." Velker looked down at the mug in his hand for a moment and smiled humorlessly. "I gather that afterward he was, ah, induced to make an admission of the whole thing. . . . I did say that things always get ugly in this kind of wretched business. But the ZRF don't go in for indiscriminate terrorism."

"So the bomb at Jaquesville wasn't theirs, for instance?"

"Oh, you heard about that. The complicity isn't complete, of course—it never is. The local police chief—a man called Denyaka—had got a few whiffs of what was going on and couldn't condone it." Velker took a sip of coffee and shrugged. "So obviously someone decided to shut him up before he could blow the lid off."

"And found a way of hanging another one on the ZRF at the same time," Fallon completed.

Velker nodded. "Although I don't get the impression that it's had an exactly devastating impact outside. Such is the onward march of civilization that the world's getting inured these days to the idea of killing innocent people to get prime time on TV."

That had been pretty close to his own initial reaction too, Fallon reflected. "And then there was Elizabeth Bouabbas—I know she was part of the same cell here in Kinnube as you and Parnum and Candy."

"Yes . . . she was."

"I assume she got a bit too zealous."

An unnaturally long silence elapsed before Velker replied. Finally he said, "I think there might have been more to it than that. I think that possibly she was onto something."

"What kind of thing?" Fallon asked, shifting his weight forward on the chair and looking interested.

"I'm not sure—she worked mainly with Roger, you understand, and in this kind of business you stay out of affairs that don't concern you. But it had to do with certain kinds of weapons that Embatto's state-security people are supposed to have hidden in one of their bases somewhere."

"What kind of weapons? Do you have the types, designations?"

Velker shook his head. "I know nothing about such matters, I'm afraid. They're all hideous creations as far as I'm concerned. Apparently these aren't listed on the official inventory, for some reason."

Fallon thought for a few seconds. This sounded like something in Parnum's line, all right. But now that Parnum and Mamu had left, there would be no way of delving further until they met up again—if all went well—inside rebel-controlled territory. Then he remembered something that Parnum had mentioned when they first met in the bar at the Independence.

"Is this at the headquarters that state security have got here in Kinnube?" he asked. "Roger described it as a 'complex.'"

"That's the administrative offices, main barracks, transport depot, and an armory, which are all together in the city," Velker confirmed. "But I think the place that Elizabeth was interested in was Djamvelling. She took a lot of illicit pictures of the machines flying in and out."

"That's the place where they fly the helicopters from, isn't it?"

"Yes. It's about fifteen miles west from here: a state-security operations base for activities farther afield, outside the city—where the Special Action detachments are normally based. Nasty characters. They have their helicopters based there, used for counterinsurgency work out in the bush. Russian types . . . I can't tell you what kind."

"And that's all you know?"

Velker stared over the rim of his mug for a few seconds. "No, actually. Elizabeth had a box of notes and things . . . I mean aside from the usual journalistic stuff. She left it with me rather than Roger, because of the harassment he was constantly being subjected to."

"Have you still got it?" Fallon asked.

"Not here . . . But it's in a safe place. I take it you'd like to see it?"

"Yes. Very much."

The door opened suddenly and Arnold appeared. "Dr. Velker, I think we've got hemorrhaging out here."

"Excuse me." Velker got up, set the mug down by the chair, and hurried out.

Fallon sat thinking while he finished his own coffee. Then a stirring from the cot in the corner made him look across. Candy's eyes were open. Fallon rose and went over.

"Welcome back to the world. You're doing fine."

It took a few seconds for her eyes to focus. Then she murmured in a faltering voice, "It seems . . . I was wrong."

Fallon grinned faintly. "I'll get over it."

Candy's eyes moved to take in the room. "It's real, yes?"

"You'd better believe it."

"He's dead, isn't he? We killed him."

Fallon nodded. "He was just a sprat. Now we go for the big fish."

He ran a finger lightly along her brow. Her face softened into a contented expression, and she drifted back into sleep.

The next day Fallon walked across the city to state-security headquarters and took his time sauntering around the outside before going in, ostensibly to pick up signed permits for him to travel, as Konrad Hannegen, in the Glimayel region. The place was virtually a fortress, with wide streets on all sides denying cover to would-be attackers and affording open fields of fire for the defense, and sandbagged gun emplacements covering the main entrance and other gates. The five-story main building stood at the front, with reinforced lower walls and steel shutters on the ground-floor windows. The barracks, armored-car and truck depot, and other facilities of the state-security department's urban presence were enclosed in a walled compound behind. An outer wire fence ran along most of the perimeter, separated from the wall by a ten-foot gap, mined and filled with barbed-wire entanglements.

Once inside, he went through the formalities of filling in the forms for the permit to travel south, then produced a sealed envelope and handed it to the desk clerk to be passed to the official whose name was written on it. The clerk smirked knowingly and slipped it inside the file folder.

"It might take some time getting to him," the clerk said. "We are extremely busy." Fallon dug into his pocket again and added ten Zugendan shillings.

The envelope contained a long list of numbers. Later that evening the list was included as part of an outgoing message stream encrypted in a diplomatic code and radioed to the Zugendan embassy in London.

In London it was still late afternoon. Julia finished transcribing the list of numbers that a clerk at the Zugendan embassy had read out to her over the phone—she had called on the line officially assigned to "Smith, J.," who lived in Cornwall Place, so nothing amiss would come from its being traced. Even if the Zugendan diplomatic code was being read by somebody—as was quite likely—it was not an especially sophisticated one, and places like MI5 and GCHQ snooped into everybody's traffic as a matter of habit—the resulting plaintext would still be an encodement under a further system that Fallon used. Every number translated into a page, line, or word reference relating to one of the books that he had in his possession, which Julia had a copy of. The numbers would be indecipherable to anyone else who didn't know the title, making the arrangement effectively a one-time-pad system that couldn't be broken. Words not contained in the book, such as proper nouns, were spelled out from the initial letters of the words indicated.

When the list was complete, Julia hung up, unlocked the bottom drawer of her desk, and lifted out a biological text entitled *Taxonomie der Zentral- und Nord-Afrikanischen Säugetiere*. She drew over the list of numbers that she had recorded and began the decoding routine.

The message told her that, irrespective of the decoy operation that Monaux was unwittingly conducting to keep Zugendan intelligence occupied, Fallon thought he was going to need somebody who knew helicopters, especially Soviet ground-attack helicopters.

Julia checked some references in a catalog contained in the IBM PC, then removed several files from one of the cabinets by the far wall. After reading through them and verifying a few other details, she selected one, checked the time, then picked up the phone again and dialed a number in Tucson, Arizona, USA.

Chapter Twenty

THE FRONT ENTRANCE OF TOBINS HOTEL WAS locked and barred when Fallon returned, carrying a shoulder bag with several packages of additional supplies for the journey. Concealed inside one of the packages were the notes that Elizabeth Bouabbas had entrusted to Velker. A group of soldiers on the far side of the street looked on while he banged on the boarded-up window in the door and called irritably inside, but they didn't interfere. His Land Rover was still there and seemed to have been left alone. Jonas must have put in a good word for him to "the man" who ran the local streets. No doubt a bill would be forthcoming in due course for the service.

There was a shuffling inside and a jingling of keys. "Awright, awright. Ah's comin'. Ain't no need to bust it down." The door shook, rattled, and opened, and Xavier looked out, barefoot, wearing a pair of unfastened jeans and an undershirt. "What de hell kinda time d'yuh call dis, anyhow, wakin' up de whole street? Cust'mohs s'posed t'be back hours ago."

"What kind of hotel do you call this?" Fallon grumbled, stepping inside. "I pay for my room, and I come back to it when I choose."

"This a respec'ble place," Xavier said, closing the door and locking it again.

"It's a dump. Look at the floor. It hasn't been washed for weeks." He followed Xavier to the table that served as a desk, with a line of hooks on a board fixed to the wall behind holding the room keys. "Number three, please."

"Ain't no moh. Hadda move yuh."

"What do you mean?"

"Water pipe busted up over t'ree. All come through ceilin'. I moved yuh stuff into seven."

"Oh, very well. Which way's that?"

"I show yuh." Xavier produced a passkey from his pocket and led the way down a couple of steps into a dingy passage and on around a corner to the rear of the building. Following behind, Fallon reached surreptitiously inside his jacket as he walked. They stopped outside a door with "7" painted crudely on the outside. Xavier opened it and stood aside.

Without warning, Fallon dropped his bag and seized Xavier around the neck with one arm, at the same time drawing his gun with his other hand. He kicked the door open, and in the same movement shoved Xavier in front of him and charged through. One of the two men who had been waiting inside hurled himself back across the room from the end of the bed, where he had been sitting; the other remained calmly on the chair by the window. Without any pause or loss of momentum, Fallon veered sideways to get his back against the wall while he covered them, at the same time holding the vainly struggling and gasping Xavier in front of him as a shield. . . . And then his eyes widened in astonishment.

"Bloody 'ell. 'Ave yer been shiftin' a few tonight, Bern, or d'you always coom 'ome like that?" George asked, pocketing the automatic and straightening up from behind the washstand, where he had taken refuge.

Colonel Marlow was more approving. "I'm glad to see that you haven't lost any of your old touch." He was wearing olive fatigues and a dark parka. "Sorry about this rather unconventional way of appearing on the scene, but I know you appreciate the necessity of being a little discreet about these things at times. Er, don't you think you'd better let go of that poor chap before you choke him?"

Fallon complied unthinkingly. Xavier pulled himself away, massaging his bruised throat. "How'd yuh know they was in heah?" he muttered sourly.

Fallon answered mechanically, all the time staring at the two hallucinations as if half expecting them to dissolve away before his eyes. "The key wasn't on the hook. You used a passkey."

"Not the last word in luxury, I have to admit," the colonel said, sweeping an eye around the room but implying the hotel in general. "But it serves its purpose."

Fallon frowned at him in confusion for a moment, then turned his head to stare at Xavier. "Then you're—"

"Oh, yes, Xavier's one of Barindas's. I gather this is quite a town. Can't be sure of where anyone stands these days."

"Asshole done near broke muh neck," Xavier muttered, still peevish.

Fallon looked around. None of his things had been moved from the other room. Of course they had needed to switch. Number three was bugged. "You seem to have this habit of showing up at odd times," he said, allowing Konrad Hannegen to evaporate and reverting to his own self, regardless of Xavier's presence.

"Well, you have to agree that in the present circumstances it would hardly have been the kind of thing to publicize," Marlow replied amiably. "Oh, and incidentally, my congratulations on your initiative and ingenuity in getting the girl out. That wasn't something we'd expected. And I must say, I rather liked the way you took out Tumratta into the bargain. Nice touch . . . I trust she's recovering?"

"Yes. She's going to be okay."

"Splendid."

Inwardly, Fallon wondered who the source was that enabled the colonel to be so well informed on what had been happening.

Xavier shuffled back toward the door. "Well, if yous guys is done with tryin' to kill me, I'll get back to muh bed."

"Sorry about that, mate," Fallon tossed after him, and returned his automatic to its holster.

"Yes, please carry on," the colonel said. "Er, any chance of a pot of tea, is there?"

"Ah fix it." Xavier left. George moved over to the door as well to pick up the bag that Fallon had dropped outside in the corridor. He thumped Fallon lightly on the shoulder as he passed him. "Good to see yer again, Bern. Glad ye're all right. Been 'avin' fun, 'ave yer?"

"Lots. This place is as lively as Belfast. I'll tell you all about it soon enough."

Colonel Marlow raised his eyebrows at the remark, but he let it pass. He reached under his parka and produced a hip flask. "I do have a drop of something stronger while we're waiting. Anyone care for a noggin?"

"Yes. I need it." Fallon picked up a plastic beaker from the washstand and rinsed it. The colonel unscrewed the cap of the flask and used it to pour out a double measure of brandy, then poured another for himself. He raised the cap momentarily in an unvoiced toast and took a sip from it.

"Cheers," Fallon reciprocated. He savored the mellow, warming taste in his mouth for a few seconds, then passed the beaker to George and sat down on the end of the bed. "So, how did you two get in? Are you here legally, or what?"

The colonel shook his head. "The western border's like a sieve in places, especially with the ZRF to help you through. The Zugs try to stop the traffic, but it doesn't do them a lot of good."

Fallon nodded. Velker had described how in terms of ancient tribal loyalties, most of the guards on the other side had more in common with the Western rebels than with the ruling clique in their own capital. The borders had been drawn on nineteenth-century maps in London and Paris according to the political expediencies of the times, without regard for traditional ethnic groupings. General Thombert had accused the neighboring regime of harboring pro-ZRF sympathies, Fallon recalled, and given that as the reason for the relative ease with which they could melt away.

"Are you shacking up here?" he asked.

"No, but not too far away," the colonel replied. "Too much moving around wouldn't be wise, of course. All the same, it's surprising how much the people in this part of town manage to miss—even the ones that the authorities think they've got tamed as informers. Extraordinary, really." He set the flask down on the windowsill and leaned back in his chair, contemplating Fallon with a curious expression. Finally he said, "So now that you've had a chance to see the score here, what do you think?"

Fallon shrugged. "It's the old story. The ones with the power have got it because they wanted it enough to go to any lengths to get it—which is another way of saying they're the last ones who should have it. And it's the ones

who just want to mind their own business who end up paying and doing the dying."

"Care about things like that, do you?" the colonel asked, making an exaggerated show of nonchalance. Fallon didn't reply at once. After a few seconds the colonel prompted, "Enough to risk your neck breaking somebody out of a high-security jail and then setting up this whole con operation to help Barindas's revolution?"

"I suppose so. . . ."

"But why Barindas? It's not your war. Why get mixed up in it?"

"It pays."

"Oh, come on, Bernard. There's more too, isn't there?"

Fallon thought for a second, nodded, and took the beaker back from George. "What you said when we talked that day back in London, at Olympia. I think that what Barindas is doing is right. The world needs more of it. He isn't trying to use the ZRF to force anything on anybody."

"They've got more guns out there than the United States Marine Corps!" the colonel challenged. "God, there's enough stashed underneath this place to blow up Gibraltar. Don't you call that resorting to force?"

"No, that isn't what I meant." Fallon sought for words. "That isn't force that's being used to tread on anyone. It's to prevent people from being trodden on."

"Aha!" The colonel looked up. "In other words, resorting to force in order to defend one's freedom isn't the same as using force to attack somebody else's. There is a moral distinction that matters. Half the world's problems today are caused by people who shrink from making it."

"I don't know about that," Fallon said. "Philosophizing isn't my line."

"Ah, but it *is*, Bernard. It may not be something that you articulate to yourself consciously, but it's there. The whole pattern of your life-style over the last ten years affirms it."

"If you say so."

"It's right, what 'e says," George threw in.

"That's why Infinity Limited is interested in you," the colonel went on. "Because what you've been doing amounts to waging your own brand of war against the same things that we're against."

There was a thump on the door. George opened it

and Xavier shuffled in, carrying a pot and some mugs on a piece of board functioning as a tray. He set it down on the washstand, mumbled something once more about getting back to his bed, and left, closing the door.

George poured out the brew and spooned in sugar from a tin. "'Ere we are. It looks strong enough to dissolve the ruddy spoon, does this stuff. No wonder all these blokes around 'ere 'ave got frizzy 'air, if that's what they're drinkin'."

"Great." Fallon set down the plastic beaker and took one of the mugs.

George handed the other to Marlow and sat down at the opposite end of the bed from Fallon. Fallon settled back and looked at the colonel again. "Getting down to what's going on here, how much more can you tell us about the background?"

"Well, Julia is probably right. Something's going on that Moscow is being kept out of, and Embatto is behind it. Also, he's getting foreign support from somewhere."

"Is this where Lichuru fits in?" Fallon asked.

"We think so, but we don't know which direction it comes from. All we've got is that Lichuru deals with a person or organization of some kind that's referred to as 'Pyramid.'"

"Didn't yer say 'e was American or summat?" George asked, looking at Fallon.

"He could have been," Fallon confirmed.

"Which may or may not tell us something," the colonel said. "One of the reasons we're here is to see if we can make more sense out of it while you're off on your jaunt south."

There was a short silence while they tried the tea. "I've 'ad worse in some o' them Paki places in Bradford," George pronounced, giving them the connoisseur's opinion.

Then Fallon asked Marlow, "What do you know about the state-security base at Djamvelling?"

"State-security operational base. They also fly their support choppers from there: mainly Soviet types, Mi-4."

"Have you heard of any unusual weapons there— weapons being stored secretly?"

"No . . . no, I haven't." The colonel seemed very interested. "Why? What have you found out?"

"Did you know about Elizabeth Bouabbas?"

"Only what happened to her... Nasty business."

"You knew she was with the ZRF?"

"Yes. I did hear a whisper that she was onto something, but I never found out what it was."

Fallon rummaged inside the bag, which he had put down on the floor by the bed, and lifted out one of the packages that it contained. He opened the wrapping, removed the lid of a box inside, and took out the soup packets and a bag of pasta that were lying on top. Underneath was a wad of typed and handwritten sheets, some sketches and photographs, and photocopies of a number of other documents.

"This," Fallon said. He passed some of the papers across. "Stocks of M-47s and MGM-71 TOWs that she believed Embatto has hidden away somewhere."

"Hidden?"

"Yes. They're not listed on the official inventory that the accounting office sees, and they were never included in any procurement list approved by Molokutu."

Fallon waited while the colonel scanned the sheets. Both of the designations were American. The M-47, otherwise known as "Dragon," was a medium antitank missile used by infantry, capable of being carried and fired by one man. The MGM-71 Tube-launched, Optically tracked, Wire-guided variety was a more powerful version of the same thing.

The colonel looked up, and Fallon could see the question starting to form on his face.

"Right," Fallon said. "Those aren't the kind of things you need for counterguerrilla warfare. They're for use against armor. So why would Embatto want them? Barindas and the ZRF don't have any tanks."

Chapter Twenty-one

THE FOLLOWING MORNING, VELKER PRONOUNCED Candy fit to move. Less than an hour later the Danish zoologist, Konrad Hannegen, departed from Kinnube for the Glimayel plateau region, in accordance with his stated plan. Also as intended, he had found himself a guide: a tallish youth, attired in swirling folds of the traditional, nightgownlike djellaba, who had provoked sly smirks from the soldiers at more than a couple of the checkpoints they'd passed through on account of his boyish, almost effeminate features. The soldiers, however, had received word from above that the Dane would be passing through that way, and to give him an easy time. Apparently he had a friend in the government who was interested in his work. When he told the soldiers at one of the checkpoints what his work was, one of them had remarked sniggeringly to his companion that maybe the Dane liked good-looking antelopes too, as well as boys.

When they were well away from the populated area, they stopped to retrieve the two Kalashnikov AK47 assault rifles secured beneath the vehicle. The stay with Velker had improved Candy's condition considerably. Although she would be weak for some time yet, her eyes were brighter, and her voice had regained some of its former quality and firmness. Fallon had explained to her how the incident in London had been set up to appear as a ZRF trap, as well as his decision to go with Embatto's proposition in order to work for the ZRF on the inside, and how that had led to his being with Embatto and Tumratta at the prison. The realization that she had a genuine ally, along with the psychological feeling of being armed again and able to defend herself, did wonders for restoring her confidence and self-assurance.

"It feels good now we are out of the city," she said in

her French-accented way as Fallon drove. "All this wildness
out here reminds how the terrible things that are happening are for a moment only. They will pass." She gazed at
the slopes and folds of grassy hills, breaking up in places
into scars and buttresses of yellow rock higher up. The
Land Rover rounded a tight bend and scattered a troop of
baboons who bounded up onto a pile of boulders overlooking
the road, where they turned to chatter and screech their
indignation at the intrusion. A bench of black-and-white-
robed vultures on the branches of a nearby tree looked on,
indifferent and unmoving. A hawk circled lazily, riding an
invisible thermal fountain of air.

"Why do people need to fight and kill each other?"
she asked. "The world can give them everything they want.
But first they must work and build. Instead they destroy."

"Then they must want something else," Fallon said.

"What do they want?"

"Who knows? Maybe to make everyone else be like
them. Then, perhaps, they think they'd feel secure. That
seems to be most people's idea of how to improve the world."

"And you do not?"

"Want everyone to be like me?" Fallon shook his
head. "No, thanks. I can't think of anything that'd make
life more boring. Imagine it. What would be the point of
talking to anyone if you already know everything they
think? Everywhere you tried to go would be packed solid
with people who'd all had the same idea. No, I tell
everyone to go and enjoy the things that I don't like. That
way I can do what I want in peace."

"And what are the things that you like?"

Fallon lifted a hand from the wheel and waved it in a
throwing-away motion. "Oh . . . meeting mysterious wom-
en in pubs. Pulling off the odd jail break now and
again . . . The usual nine-to-five kind of thing."

"Now you are making the joke. What do you really do?"

"Fishing again, eh, Candy? Always fishing."

Farther on, the land grew more arid, the vegetation
sparser, the settlements that they passed through clinging
more precariously to existence. Attempts to plow at insanely
tilted angles high on the upper slopes testified of the
desperation with which the farmers sought to scratch
sustenance from the last of the exhausted soil. They passed

a group of men, women, children of various ages, sitting motionless outside a cluster of dilapidated shacks. Fallon could detect no flicker of reaction to the Land Rover, not hostility, resentment, curiosity, or even any interest. Their faces wore the blankness of total resignation.

"Why do they stay?" he asked Candy.

"Where is there to go?"

"Can't they do anything?"

"They starve, and they watch their children die. They sit in the dust and wait for a relief truck from Kinnube. Maybe one will come. Maybe not. They can change nothing." Candy went very quiet for a while. Then she resumed, as if resurfacing from a depth of thought that left her unaware of the minutes that had elapsed since she last spoke: "That's what the ZRF is for: the right of people to work for themselves—for their own good, without needing to have the permission or approval from anybody." She waved an arm vaguely. "This could be a garden. The knowledge is there to do it. All that's missing is the—how do you say, what it is that makes people work?"

"Motivation?"

"Exactly."

"Staying alive isn't a good enough motivator?"

"When everything that you produce over the minimum to stay alive is taken away? That is called slavery, whatever else you try to make it sound like. And yes, many people have died rather than submit to it."

They passed the refugees. Although this was not part of the official war zone where the most intensive fighting went on—that lay farther toward the north—for that same reason, it was the area that many of the refugees from both sides of the lines made their way to. Those from the rebel-held areas came to escape the bombs and rockets of the government forces, who commanded the greater firepower—the Ministry of Information presented it as demonstrating the spontaneous flight of the people from ZRF terrorism—and the "liberated" ones to flee the communal camps and evade conscription into the "peasants' militia," which was usually the condition for receiving rations.

Tens of thousands had made the trek southward to the Glimayel region, despite—or in many cases, maybe, because of—its inaccessibility, and heedless of warnings of the land's incapacity to feed them. The government did little to impede the migration, viewing the numbers as an added source of pressure to tax the guerrillas' resources. Not all who set out lasted the distance, and many of those who did arrived too exhausted by malnutrition and disease to last very much longer.

Although more were no doubt hidden among the tangled valleys and gorges along the route, keeping their indignity from the world while they died anonymously among strangers, the ones that Fallon saw were enough to crystallize all the faceless statistics into tangible reality—depending whose statistics one chose to believe; no two of the various UN agencies, volunteer groups, and national organizations involved in the macabre calculus had been able to come even close to each other in estimating the extent of what was happening.

The Land Rover passed them in bedraggled columns, trudging with oddments of belongings and their children through the dust by the side of the track; in a squalid camp of overcrowded tents and shanties administered by harassed relief workers; and huddling in derelict vehicles, lean-to shelters, and underneath awnings stretched between scrub and rocks. As always, it was the plight of the children that affected Fallon the most, with their prematurely aged and haggard faces, shriveled bodies, and spindly limbs—familiar enough sights by now, which the rest of the world was fed up with having to look at over dinner. Fallon had seen it before, real and close up—but just as a soldier with a job to do, minding his own business and not thinking too much about it then. He recognized the reddening of hair, paling of skin, and swelling of joints symptomatic of kwashiorkor, acute protein deficiency. There were the ravages of pellagra: anemia, lethargy, insanity, coma. . . . A world that imagined shortages to be inescapable impositions of nature was uncaringly squandering its most precious resource.

Candy seemed to read his thoughts. "There is the potential that could transform Africa," she said. "Every time an old man dies, a book is lost: This isn't just people being exterminated. It's a whole library burning."

Fallon nodded silently as he drove. For the first time, he thought, he was beginning to glimpse what Infinity Limited really meant.

*   *   *

In Kinnube, the room that Colonel Marlow and George were using as a hideout was upstairs in a dingy tenement a few streets away from Tobins. Its walls were cracked and grimy from cooking grease and the accumulated effects of years of countless, forgotten inhabitants; the window had been nailed shut when its disintegrating frame passed the point of being maintainable, and plaster flaked ominously from the ceiling laths. Its contents consisted of a creaky iron bed, the frame of another, supported on cinder blocks, a plastic-topped kitchen table, a wooden cupboard with one of its doors missing, and a couple of tattered wicker chairs. There was also a folding card table supporting a communications amplifier with ancillary electronics.

Colonel Marlow sat, wearing a telephone headset and tuning the system, while George watched from one of the chairs.

The system was laid out to confuse the authorities' constant efforts to track down the ZRF's radio facilities, using Soviet equipment brought in for the purpose. A wire from the rear of the unit went through a hole bored in the window frame and connected to an unused line in a telephone cable strung nearby. The line led to the actual transmitter, which was located in the attic of a building-materials storehouse several blocks away to give the people using it a reasonable chance of getting away if the signal was located. To further increase the odds, the installers had thoughtfully connected a number of dummy lines to the transmitter as well, leading away in different directions.

The transmitter was a low-power device whose primary transmission lobe extended toward the heights west of the city, where in more prosperous times the well-to-do had built their homes above the worst of the summer heat. There was also a sawmill there, with a motor-generator system to produce its own power, a little of which went to a microwave communications dish concealed in a water-tank tower nearby. The dish was aimed at a point in the sky where, eleven months previously, a European Space Agency Arianne launch vehicle had placed a Japanese scientific and communications satellite in geosynchronous orbit. The computer software used to control the satellite's communications processor had been written and tested personally by a Professor Aikatsu of Tokyo University, chairman of the committee responsible for the specifications given to the design team.

It just so happened that Professor Aikatsu also talked to his students frequently about individual freedoms, abuses of state power, the mass control of populations, and related issues.

"Hello, Simon. How are you receiving?" Marlow queried.

"Adequate," the voice in Marlow's headphones acknowledged. The channel that they were using switched frequency several hundred times a second according to a microchip-controlled algorithm synchronized at both ends.

"Good. Look, our man has dug up something that we need to follow up on," Marlow said. "It's to do with some weapons that found their way here in the course of the last three months. We need to discover the source."

"Fire away."

"I'm going to give you some serial numbers and batch references that relate to some unofficial shipments of M-47s and MGM-71 TOWs. They were apparently arranged by Lichuru via a contact in Greece. The only reference we have to the contact is 'Logger,' probably a middleman or dealer. What I'd very much like to know is where they came from. I think it could be Pyramid."

Marlow went on to read off the details. All he really knew about "Simon," despite meeting with him many times in an association that went back several years, was that he resided somewhere in the Tunbridge Wells area of Kent, to the southeast of London, and had financial connections in the City. Although Marlow had met other members of Infinity Limited when circumstances required it, Simon was his regular contact into the organization, connecting in turn to some general European level. Where the chain went beyond that, Marlow didn't know, nor where in the world the focal point of its activities lay—if, indeed, it was concentrated at any single location at all.

"I'll see what we can do," Simon promised when Marlow had finished. "How are things progressing there otherwise?"

"Not bad. Candy got a clean bill of health this morning."

"Good. Our friends were very impressed by the way your man handled it over there. He sounds like exactly the kind of material we need. So when will he and the girl be leaving?"

"They've already gone. I decided to get them on their way before anyone had a chance for second thoughts."

"Best. So, I'll see what I can find out for you on this other business. Anything else?"

"I think that's it for now, Simon."

"Good luck then. Give me a few days."

"Over for now, then. And out." Marlow shut down the system, took off the headset, and stared at the panel for a while longer. "Well, we'll have to wait and see if he comes up with anything," he murmured.

"Bern should be well on 'is way," George commented. "What's there for us to be gerrin on with while we're waitin'?"

Marlow looked down at the papers in front of him again and frowned. He now had a further snippet from a ZRF source apparently employed inside state-security headquarters in Kinnube. "It's beginning to look as if we were wrong about those weapons being at Djamvelling," he said. "They were flown to Djamvelling, all right, when they came into the country, but they're not there now. This suggests they were moved to Kinnube."

"SSHQ?"

"Yes."

"All right. We were wrong, then."

Marlow sat back and pushed the papers aside. "But Bouabbas was interested in *something* at Djamvelling. Look at all these photographs." He picked absently at a tooth with a thumbnail. "I wonder what the chances might be of getting somebody in to take a look around. . . . That would give us something to occupy ourselves with while we're waiting to hear from Bernard, wouldn't it."

"Yer mean inside that base at Djamvelling?"

"Yes. Perhaps you could look into possible ways of penetrating it—maybe talk to some of the ZRF about it."

George looked dubious and stroked his chin slowly. "I'll 'ave a think about it," he agreed.

Chapter Twenty-two

By NIGHTFALL FALLON AND CANDY HAD REACHED the southwestern plateau region. The military situation in the area was complex and fluid. By day, Zugendan patrols operated from fortified posts established at intervals along a single major road that followed a rift through the plateau to the border, while the night hours belonged exclusively to the rebels. In such circumstances, regardless of any word that Embatto might quietly have passed down about safe conduct for the Danish zoologist, for them to have gone driving around in search of the ZRF would have been inviting trouble. They had therefore arranged a rendezvous spot where the ZRF would come to them.

The Land Rover lay a short distance off the trail at a stony place that didn't show tracks, hidden from the surroundings in a hollow between boulders. It was after dark, so smoke wouldn't show, and Fallon had made a fire among the rocks, backed by a large boulder to reflect the heat toward the two sleeping bags unrolled over a ground blanket. Candy, mopping the last from a billycan of stew with a piece of bread, watched as he placed the pot of water on to heat and adjusted a couple of rocks forming an air tunnel in front.

"Usually you make it by digging out an opening in front to draw air in," he commented over his shoulder. "Under a bush, if it's daytime and there's smoke."

"Really?"

"It's called a Dakota hole." He sat back, next to where the two AK47s were propped close at hand.

"Where do you learn about things like that?"

Fallon grinned as he began smearing jam on biscuits. "You never stop fishing, do you, Candy?"

"Well, be careful you don't give anything away."

"Okay."

Candy took one of the biscuits and looked at him curiously for a few seconds while she bit into it. "All right, then, what are the things you think?" she asked at last. "What do you believe in? They say everyone has to have something."

"Oh . . . let's just say I'm pro-people."

"Then I try it another way. What are you against?"

Fallon jerked a thumb over his shoulder to indicate the general direction they had come. "What's happening to those people we saw today. What happened to you back in Kinnube. Anyone who has the power to make things like that happen."

"You mean governments?"

Fallon shrugged. "It doesn't matter. Governments, dictators, armies, religions . . . Anyone who's got that kind of power over other people's lives. People should be able to decide their own lives."

"You don't work for somebody's government?"

"I did once."

"In the military. You see, I could tell that first day. So you enjoy war?"

"I hate it. But sometimes what happens if you won't fight can be worse."

"Was it one of the proud British regiments with the big prestige that they tell us about, who will die before dishonor . . . or something like that?"

"Christ, no. We went off all that a long time ago. That's the French in you coming out again. I'd rather enjoy a bit of dishonor before death, any day." Fallon pushed a piece of branch farther into the fire with a foot. "How about you? Where are you from?"

"I thought you know that already. You tell me when we meet in London that I am from Kashinga province. How do you do it? Can you read a person, somehow, like a book?"

Fallon smiled to himself. "What part of Kashinga?"

"A village called Bakushal. It's not there anymore. They come one day and move everyone to one of the communal camps as part of the resettlement. They say it's to protect the people from the rebels, but what it really does is let them control the people more. Thousands have been moved into them. You don't get any choice."

She was getting more talkative, a good sign—the Candy that Fallon had met in London was coming back. "But you didn't go, eh?" he said.

"The huts are in tidy straight lines, like the way a bureaucrat thinks. They have wire around the outside, with guns ... they say, to keep the rebels out ..." Candy stared distantly into the flames. "No, I didn't go. That was when I moved to Jaquesville and join the Front. I had a sister there, Neraya. She and her daughter were killed by the bomb that exploded there."

"Oh ... I'm sorry."

"There was a baby also ... but he was dying already."

"The news said that the ZRF claimed responsibility for that," Fallon said. "But it wasn't them, was it? Most likely another undercover job by the Special Action groups. Denyaka was about to blow the gaff."

"You have been learning more about things here since the time we talk in London, Mr. Fugleman."

"Look, I know we weren't properly introduced, but try 'Boris.' That mister bit sounds so stuffy."

"Is Boris your real name?"

"No."

"Okay."

Fallon screwed the top back on the jam container and set it down. "So, what are you?" he asked, looking back up at Candy.

"How do you mean, what am I?"

"What do you believe in?"

Candy shrugged. "Nothing that I can tell you a name of. Anyway, they are unimportant—names. A name is just a name. There's nothing good or bad in it. Only things that people do can be good or bad."

"So what decides good or bad? I'm not much of a philosopher, you see."

"Oh, simple things ... There is no great philosophy. Villages that just come from people choosing to live together, that is good. Camps that they're forced to live in are bad." For a moment Candy seemed about to elaborate further, then she checked herself. "But why do I tell you these things? You already think the same way. Why else do you choose to work with the ZRF? Never mind who pays you, who are you really working for?"

"The innocent poor sods who always get caught in the

middle of this kind of mess," Fallon agreed, nodding. He stared into the fire, and after a few seconds went on in a faraway voice: "It's what happens to the kids that always gets to you. I remember a picture that I saw once in a book about the war. It was a photograph of a line of little Polish kids—not much bigger than toddlers, some of them. They were boarding a train to be sent to one of the Nazi extermination camps." He looked back at Candy. "It wasn't so much the thought of what was happening that was so sickening. Do you know what the worst part about it was?"

"What?"

"The innocent, trusting looks on their faces as they stood there clutching their toys and bundles, behind the woman warden who was directing them. How could any woman do a job like that?"

Candy looked at him in the firelight. For the first time she had the fleeting feeling of brushing close to the real person who existed somewhere inside the shield that necessity and habit had erected. "So once you thought you were helping to make a world that would be free from such things, yes?" she guessed.

He nodded. "Once. But sometimes it doesn't do to know too much about what goes on on your own side. Belgium and the Congo; the French in Algeria; all the dictatorships that the Americans prop up; the way Britain took sides in the Biafran war and lied about it. There was no easy black-and-white way to decide. Just closing your eyes and following orders wasn't the way. I'm not sure I know yet what the way is."

"You see. So you are the philosopher, more than you think," Candy told him.

"Am I?" Fallon sounded unconvinced.

"You know who will be the winning side, anyway."

"I do?"

"In time, yes. It is a strange thing, no? In the end, the oppressors are always buried by their intended victims."

Fallon looked at her, intrigued. "I bet you didn't make that up."

Candy smiled faintly and shook her head. "No, it was not me. It is one of the things that Barindas says . . . but he says it in better words."

"He's got quite a hold on you people, hasn't he?"

"Not what you would say, a hold. That is not his way.

He enlightens. He teaches us to think in ways that are strange for us . . . ways that are more European. But that is how we must learn to think if we are to grow and prosper in the world. We see him more as a teacher than a leader."

"He sounds quite a guy."

"Soon you will be meeting him now."

Fallon looked away and into the fire again. "I'm looking forward to it," he said distantly.

Fallon's first proposal was that he would stand watch all night. Candy insisted that she was feeling better and could do her share—after a full day of heavy driving, he needed rest as much as she did. Fallon relented and woke her at 2:00 A.M. after doing a four-hour stint. Minutes later, he rolled gratefully into his sleeping bag, stretched out his limbs and relaxed slowly with an ecstatic sigh, and almost at once dropped into bottomless, dreamless oblivion.

The boot thudding into his ribs knocked him rudely out of it.

He jerked upright, grabbing instinctively at where he had laid his weapon, but it was gone. An instant later he awakened fully to find himself staring into the wrong end of an automatic rifle.

There were seven of them that he could see in the glow from the embers: one holding the rifle on him, two others grappling with Candy, who was putting up a struggle, one poking through their kit, another looking on, and two more tossing things out of the Land Rover. The one standing over Fallon was grinning maliciously, his teeth glinting in the feeble light. He had a mass of hair tied down in a bandanna and a beard that jutted in two unruly tufts. Crossed over his chest were bandoliers of cartridges on top of a sleeveless combat vest. In addition, he was wearing torn pants and calf-length jump boots. The others looked just as unkempt, with an assortment of mixed clothing and weapons. The two at the Land Rover were laughing uproariously and throwing pieces of clothing from Fallon's bags in the air. The one looking on wore a forage cap and seemed to be the leader. Bush bandits, not guerrilla fighters, Fallon decided. They seemed to be on some kind of high.

"What's this we got here? Say, how about that?" One

of them turned and held a camera up in front of his face. "Take your picture, boss? Smile real pretty now, hee-hee."

"Don't bust it, asshole. That's worth money."

"Shit, just lookin'..."

The other tipped out the contents of a case of sample jars and slides for a field microscope and stirred them around with a foot to the accompaniment of tinkling glass. "What's all this fuckin' shit?"

The nearer one by the fire, wearing an unbuttoned officer's jacket with jeans and a beret, was giggling insanely to himself. He pushed aside items of rations and picked up the medical kit. "Gimme that," the leader in the forage cap snapped. He snatched the kit and began pulling out the vials of drugs and peering at them, discarding some and stuffing others in his pockets.

Meanwhile the other two had forced Candy back down on her sleeping bag, gasping and snarling as she fought to keep them off. One ripped open the front of her shirt, while the other pushed back her head. She bit savagely into his hand.

"Jesus!" He drew back his hand and slapped her back and forth across the face with it. "Bitch! See what she did."

The other pinned her arm with a knee and tore open the front of her pants. "Ha-ha! I guess you're just losin' your touch, Eko. Maybe she likes it rough. That right, bitch? Like it rough, do yuh, huh? That's just what you're gonna get."

"Back off. She's mine first." The leader unhitched his belt and moved over toward them. The two at the Land Rover had found a heavy crate bound in a tarpaulin and were lifting it down.

The one in the bandanna watched Fallon's eyes frantically estimating distances, and chuckled. "Get a good look, shithead. It'll be the last piece of ass you'll ever see. Then we'll have us some fun takin' care o' you." Inside the sleeping bag, Fallon had worked down the zip and was holding the flap closed with one hand.

"Turn her over," the leader ordered. The other two started wrestling Candy around onto her knees.

For that one brief moment, five of them were preoccupied all at the same time.... And then the one in the bandanna let his eyes stray for a moment to enjoy the spectacle.

Fallon fired the Magnum from the Land Rover's glove compartment straight up at him through the sleeping bag. The bullet entered beneath the bandit's chin and took a piece of the back of his head with it on the way out. The rest was the kind of fast, precision shooting that years of day-in, day-out practice in the SAS's "killing house" at Hereford had made reflexive.

A shot through the center of the startled face turning toward him dropped the bandit in the beret less than a second later, and another head shot dispatched the leader before the second body had hit the ground. But already, the pair by the Land Rover were grabbing for their weapons, while at the same time one of the two with Candy rolled away. Fallon fired after him, missed, and in the same movement hurled himself sideways, sleeping bag and all, into the shadows beyond a boulder. The other bandit who had been mauling Candy tried to pull her across in front of him as a shield, but she scooped the pot of hot water off the fire and flung it into his face. The bandit screamed and fell back, clutching at his eyes.

Four out of action, three to go, one apparently unarmed, Fallon checked mentally.

Wrong. Four to go. An eighth, who had been checking the gasoline cans on the far side of the Land Rover, appeared around the rear, and a burst of automatic fire tore into the shadows by the boulder at the spot where Fallon had vanished from sight. But Fallon was already ten feet from there, between another boulder and a thornbush.

But now he found that he couldn't move farther at all. The sleeping bag had clung around his waist as he rolled and somehow twisted underneath him, trapping his legs. Bullets were spattering off the rocks as the bandits sprayed the area randomly; he was unable to raise his body to free himself. Candy had followed his lead and vanished into the shadows away from the fire. Fallon caught a glimpse of the bandit who had rolled away from her, crawling to retrieve his weapon; but unable to move, Fallon couldn't risk giving away his position by trying a shot.

The firing became sporadic. Between the bursts, Fallon strained his ears to follow them as they spread out to cover his vicinity, but the continuing shrieks from the one that Candy had scalded masked their movements.

Four men with automatic weapons against one with a

handgun. Not good. In the darkness he worked the sleeping bag down from his waist and struggled to untangle it.

"See him yet?" the voice of one of them called out.

"He's in there someplace. Move around more . . . more this way."

"That you, Eko?"

"Yeah."

"Come on out, motherfucker. Don't think you're gonna get outta here."

"Where'd the bitch go?"

My fuckin' eyes! Christ, do somethin'!

"Mose, quit that goddamn noise, willya."

Apart from Mose, Fallon could make out three voices. Two were close together on the far side of the fire, and the last to appear was still near the tail of the Land Rover. It was the one he couldn't hear that Fallon worried about most.

Slowly, stealthily, he eased the sleeping bag down to his knees and at last pulled his feet clear. A couple of shots struck nearby and ricocheted off into the night. Then the bandit near the Land Rover called out again.

"Gimme cover. I'm gonna get in closer."

Fallon picked out the rock where the voice seemed to be coming from. He checked around himself for an escape route, then brought the pistol up and waited, holding it steady in a two-handed grip, trained on the spot where the bandit would break cover.

Mose moaned. Bullets slashed through the thornbush to one side of Fallon. Still, nothing moved.

"What are you waiting for?"

"Where's Chogu?"

"Still here."

Fallon waited.

Then something metallic clinked on a rock in between the two who were together.

"What the—"

The grenade exploded. At the same instant a flare blazed white, illuminating the Land Rover and the bandit beside it just as he emerged, and a sharp, almost continuous clattering echoed briefly from the darkness. The bandit was lifted off his feet and slammed back against the Land Rover before Fallon had registered the sound as the six-hundred-round-per-minute signature of an Uzi. Flash lamps came on in rapid succession to light the scene further. Figures moved forward among the rocks, and there were several more reports of single shots. A foot crunched in the dust close behind where Fallon was lying, and a voice said, "Sorry we're a bit late. Mr. Fugleman, I presume?"

Fallon stood up slowly. The man facing him looked to be every inch as rough and tough as the others, in bush shirt and beret, bristling with grenades and ammunition pouches, and holding a Sterling submachine gun casually in the crook of an arm. But the pants were intact, the shirt relatively clean, and suggestions of something out of the Hell's Angels or a Mad Max movie distinctly absent. *This*, he decided, was the ZRF.

"No," Fallon murmured. "On the contrary, I'd say you made it just in time."

"I don't think these are any big loss."

They moved forward to look at the aftermath. Mose was out of his misery, and the two hit by the grenade, if not finished immediately, had been now. The hail of bullets from the Uzi had stitched a line diagonally across the chest of the last and taken off an arm, along with most of the shoulder. Fallon was too familiar with the firepower of modern weaponry to be unduly surprised. He counted the bodies and cast a wary eye around as other shapes converged from among the rocks. "Be careful," he warned. "I think there's still one loose somewhere."

And then Candy stepped out of the shadows.

"No," she said, wiping clean the knife that she was holding. "There isn't."

Chapter Twenty-three

SADIE'S, SITUATED IN THE CENTER OF THE CAPITAL of one of the twentieth century's experiments in progressive, planned economies, was a monument to the most ancient form of free, private enterprise. The building was a large, rambling, four-story warren of rooms, nooks, passages, and stairs, which with its dingy lights, garish decor, and heavy and ornate furnishings preserved a vestige of the French influence in Zugenda's history. Since it figured prominently in the lesser-publicized side of the lives of many of the country's public figures, the establishment had not been especially afflicted by the general economic woes. For the same reason, it was one place where meticulous observations of comings and goings were not encouraged by the officials of any department of state, and where the likelihood of interference from without was negligible. All of this made it ideal for concealing faces that eyes elsewhere in the city might be watching for.

By nine o'clock in the morning, the last of the stopover customers had been sent on their way, the girls would be resting until afternoon, and the daily chore had begun of cleaning up the bottles, glasses, and other litter from the previous night's reveling, changing the linens, and checking the stocks of liquor, tobacco, hashish, and other stimulants for the evening ahead.

"Lila, could you come through to the office for a minute?" Dora called from the doorway of the private lounge that opened off the main downstairs salon. Dora was in her forties, full-bodied but still shapely, and with the poise and looks—even at that hour of the morning, and in a plain cotton dress with her hair up—which, together with a sharp head, had enabled her to work her way up from the ranks to management of the enterprise.

Lila, who was now off the regular working roster and

learning the business side, turned from a cabinet that she had been refilling. She was tall, long-haired and curvy, and wearing day clothes of blue jeans and a sleeveless orange top. She followed Dora along a passage and down a short flight of stairs to Dora's personal office, which Dora always kept locked. Dora opened the door with a key that she kept on a chain inside her dress, ushered Lila through, and closed the door behind them.

"I need you to run a message," she muttered, keeping her voice low. "One of the girls got it from the officer in state security who was here last night. They're going to take Velker in sometime later today. He has to get everyone out of there and lose himself right away."

"Oh, God, no."

"It sounds as if they've known about it for some time. . . . It had to happen, I guess."

"So what made them decide to move now?"

"Something to do with that jail bust."

Lila frowned. "Didn't they get the ones who did that?"

"Come on, that was a put-up. There's a lot more going on behind the smoke."

"I'll get going right away." Lila turned for the door.

Dora put a hand on her arm to restrain her for a moment longer. "Tell him to come here tonight, once he's sure he's clean of any tails. We can put him in the back rooms. It's probably the safest place in town to get lost in. He can worry about setting up in business again someplace after the heat blows over."

Lila nodded, left the room, and went out of the building through a side entrance. Dora came out into the passageway a couple of minutes later, locked the door of the office, and went back up the short staircase and through to the salon to see how the work was progressing.

Officially, Konrad Hannegen was supposed to have disappeared with his guide into the Glimayel highlands to count antelopes. Unofficially, Boris Fugleman was supposed to make contact with the ZRF rebels in order to convince them that he was really on their side, and to go through the motions of agreeing to help them get rid of Molokutu's regime. That this *was* in fact the case didn't alter the appearances that Fallon needed to keep up. There was no telling what eyes might be watching, and any account finding its way back to Embatto needed to confirm that the zoologist, Hannegen, had turned up in the area and expressed sympathy for the ZRF cause. Exactly what he thought he could do, or indeed that he was talking to the Front's leadership at all, didn't have to be public knowledge.

They started out at daybreak, following the aging, camouflage-painted Chevrolet pickup in which the rebels had come to collect them. It was evidently a seasoned campaign veteran, generously scarred and holed, with improvised armor fitted to the sides, a massive, welded roll bar, and chains instead of doors to permit fast egress under air attack. One of the rebels was detailed to ride with Fallon and Candy in the Land Rover as a lookout. As Fallon was by now coming to accept as normal, the driver of the truck in front forged ahead with suicidal abandon over rocks and potholes that any sane Western motorist would have considered obstacles to be negotiated with caution, if not insurmountable.

The squad sent to collect Fallon and Candy was led by Sam Letumbai—deputy to the ZRF's military chief, Haile Yolatta—whom Fallon recognized from the dossier he had seen in Kinnube. Fallon got to know more about him when they stopped by an almost-dried-up, pebbly watercourse for a midmorning brew—a custom that was apparently regarded with all due solemnity in this part of the world, presumably as a relic of the onetime British presence.

"This is a bit more than I'd expected," Fallon commented, accepting a mug of strong, sweet tea from the grinning, black-faced brigand, complete with Kalashnikov, who must have been all of twelve years old and was in command of the kerosene stove. "Having the second-in-command come out to fetch us in person. I thought you'd be busy."

Sam grunted. "Not if your deal is what the Australian says it is."

"Parnum? He must have made it back into the country a lot faster than I thought."

"Oh, he ain't showed up yet. He's on his way, though. We just got word ahead. Anyhow, goin' by what he said, it makes you kinda special. We just wanted to make sure you got all the way in one piece."

Sam had a lean, gnarled face with graying hair and eyebrows that gave his appearance an older touch than the early forties Fallon ascribed to him. He wore a military khaki shirt with a red neckerchief, and an Australian army slouch hat with the brim high on one side, adding to the dashing image that he seemed to like. But he carried it with the easygoing kind of confidence that distinguishes genuine competence from arrogance, which Fallon found reassuring. Fallon recognized the kind of personality that he had felt safest to have fighting next to him in years gone by. The others also responded naturally and spontaneously to the leadership quality that Sam's manner seemed to radiate, which manufactured its own authority out of respect, without need of heavyhandedness. If armies were democratic, all officers would have been from Sam Letumbai's mold. He was Fallon's kind of man.

"Where are we heading?" Fallon asked him.

"Place called Owanden—base that we use, up in the hills. That's unless we get word that it's changed to someplace else. Happens all the time."

"Will Barindas be there?"

"Sometime. He ain't right now. On his way, though. But he could take a day or two. Never can tell, the way things are."

There was a short silence.

"So, whereabouts are you from?" Fallon asked.

"Botswana, down the other end of Africa."

"Uh-huh. I know it."

Candy and Sam evidently knew each other. "He is a natural at everything," she said, sitting on a rock next to them in the shade of the truck.

Fallon sipped his tea. "How do you mean?"

"He grew up on a farm down there, and found he could do anything," Candy said. "Build houses, thatch roofs, fix motors, shoe horses, weld gates..."

"Just dabbling around," Sam threw in.

"You were good. What about all those stories you tell me? And it is true, *non*, that you spend two years at a mission school, just to learn how to read and write?"

"My pa yanked me outta there to herd goats."

"And that was when you ran away." Candy looked back at Fallon. "A contracteur who builds houses hired him and broke the South African law to train him in things that only whites are supposed to do down there. Can you imagine that—it's against the law to make a living?" She turned back toward Sam. "And then you got into trouble with the police and came north."

"And now generaling, eh?" Fallon said. "You seem to be picking that up pretty well too."

"Hell, all you need is a little bit o' sense."

"Sam can take a four-wheel drive apart and put it together again, but still he prefers the donkey's cart," Candy said.

Sam threw back his head and laughed. "When I get drunk," he explained, "I just fall in the back o' the cart and the donkey takes me home, don't matter where I am. Ain't no machine anyplace in the world you could name a price for that'd know how to do that."

Candy waved with an arm to indicate the area around them, Zugenda in general, the whole of Africa, her face more intense now. "But give them the education and the chance, what could all those people out there do? They are all people who understand this country. Africa can't afford to waste them."

It was Infinity Limited coming to the surface again, Fallon thought to himself as he listened.

Sam went on: "But instead, we get sent tech tourists." He pared off a piece of dried root that was good to chew. "There was this time when a bunch o' foreigners tried to get the people farther west to plant some kind of trees that won't grow there—too fancy, and they need lots o' water. In th' end, they went back to the good ol' acacias that was there when they started. See, them acacias can still make leaves even in the dry season, and there ain't nobody knows how. They got good-tastin' buds that th' animals like, so they get plenty good fertilizer all the time. Anyone from Cairo to Cape Town coulda told 'em that, but they never asked. Didn't need no tellin', see, 'cause they got *degrees*."

Sam spat a glob of juice into the dust and stood up. "Only problem is, them people who can't make a livin' 'cause there's too many people makin' laws, who don't know shit, tellin' 'em how—they got degrees too...'cept what matters with them is knowin' somethin' that's worth knowin', not talkin'." He ran a critical eye over his men, packing up, checking the truck, wiping weapons, and he shook his head. "That's why I reckon we'll win this war too. Them guys on th' other side, see, all they've got is tanks an' planes. Take them away, an' they don't know nuthin'. We got the people. An' when you've got one against the other, there ain't no doubt what's the way to bet. It might take a while, and it might cost you some, but I'll lay my money on people every time."

Back in Kinñube, Felix Velker was returning to his surgery, clutching a bag containing drugs and instruments. He had been to a farm outside the city to perform an amputation on a girl who had lost a hand in an accident at a ZRF bomb factory, steam-melting the explosive fillings out of unexploded government ordnance. As he emerged from the narrow alley that he normally used to cut across the adjacent block, four armed guerrillas stepped out of a doorway and blocked his path. They were all big men, obviously not sent to argue.

"SS are about to bust your place anytime," one of them said. "You have to come with us."

Velker blinked at them in confusion. "But I'll have to go back first. My supplies . . ."

"The place is being watched. You can't go back."

"I have patients there. I can't leave my patients."

Strong hands clamped around his upper arms from either side. "Sorry, Dr. Velker, but we've got our instructions. You're more valuable alive than as a martyr to medical ethics."

"But we can't just—"

"Back!" one of the others hissed, who had been watching along the street.

Velker was hustled back into the alley that he had just come out from just as the first truck filled with state-security troopers in combat gear rounded the corner and roared past in the direction of Velker's surgery. Two more followed. The boots clattering across pavement as the soldiers disembarked and the door being broken down were audible even at that distance. Moments later, the shooting began.

"Let's go," the guerrilla who had spoken first ordered curtly. They hurried away along the alley, keeping Velker, white-faced and tight-lipped, in the middle.

Chapter Twenty-four

IF THERE WAS ONE THING THAT GEORGE HAD learned to be wary of in the course of his dozen years with the British paras, it was the chinless-wonder breed of officers who got their men into sticky situations by playing hero games with two-way radios and sticking pins in maps they should never have been let within a hundred yards of. He'd seen them on tours in Northern Ireland: the day-trippers from desk jobs who wanted to go out with the patrols so that they could go back to England and tell everyone, "Oh yes, I've been to Crossmaglen." And one thing that he had come to value above all else was the officer who could be trusted, who trusted his men or got rid of the ones he couldn't, and who knew how to keep himself and everyone around him in one piece.

Although he had also learned from experience that the only true test was how a man measured up under fire, he had made up his mind that Colonel Marlow belonged squarely in the second category. Everything he'd seen had told him so; and in any case, Fallon's judgment was as good a testimonial as could be asked for as far as George was concerned. So he'd had no qualms about being left to work with Marlow after Fallon's departure.

"Looks ter me like there's some bloody 'orse around 'ere that's not too well," he muttered to himself, eyeing the water doubtfully as it trickled from the faucet on the standpipe outside the back of the tenement. He turned the faucet off, picked up the enameled jug, and went back inside. As he reached the bottom of the dingy staircase leading up to the room, a door at the bottom opened and the old woman who lived there started to come out. Seeing George, she backed in again apprehensively.

"Coom on, then, if yer coomin'," he said, standing back. But she peered at him fearfully through the gap for a moment or two and then closed the door. George continued up the stairs, shaking his head.

When he reentered the room, Marlow was still as George had left him, studying the sketches that George had obtained of the Djamvelling layout and defenses and jotting down notes. "It has to be something to do with the helicopters," he said without looking up as George closed the door. "They're the only thing unique there."

George inclined his head to indicate the general direction behind him. "We'll 'ave ter be movin' on. That old bird downstairs is about to shop us."

The colonel looked up. "I've been wondering about her myself. What makes you think so?"

"It's written all over 'er face."

"Okay, let's make it tonight. They've got another place lined up."

"It'd be a good idea anyway if y'ask me, after what 'appened at Velker's. They're tightenin' the screws oop now that Bern's gone." George put the jug down by the camping stove on a box in one corner and surveyed their stock of rations. "What were yer sayin' about choppers?"

"I'm pretty sure that's what Elizabeth Bouabbas was interested in at Djamvelling. From what I can make out, she was asking questions about equipment fitted to some of them."

George took out some crackers and butter and began opening a can of corned beef. "I 'ad a mate, once, in t' Greenjackets, who fell out of a chopper. It was when we were trainin' wit' Germans. The silly bugger coom down two 'undred feet right on top of an 'aystack an' walked away right as rain. Funny the luck o' some people, in't it? Especially a bloody fool like 'e were." George was happy to leave the theorizing to others. The sooner they had something real to shoot at, the better, as far as he was concerned.

Marlow thought to himself with a distant look, then looked back at George. "How much do you know about this helicopter chap, Czaryski, that Bernard is bringing over from the States?" he asked.

"'E's all right is Tam. Used ter be in Yank Special Forces, but ended oop in Afghanistan some'ow, teachin' t'lads there all about knockin' down them Russian jobs."

"Have you ever worked with him yourself?"

"Aye, once. It were summat that Bern got mixed oop with in Spain a few years back. One o' them deniable missions, with the USI. There was goin' ter be a train bombin', but it never 'appened."

Marlow's brow creased. "Wait a minute. I think I heard about that. Wasn't it when one of the extremist-right factions there planned to pin it on GRAPO, of the left?"

"Aye, that were it."

"So was it Bernard who booby-trapped the boat they used to move the stuff?"

"Aye."

"Then Czaryski must have been the stunt pilot who got him out. Is that what you're saying, George?"

"Aye."

Marlow knew that the Unidad Especial de Intervención counterterrorist unit of the Spanish Guarda Civil had been primarily responsible for foiling that attempt, but he had also heard unofficially that there had been a murkier side that the authorities were less forthcoming about. He felt a twinge of self-reproach. Evidently Fallon had not been quite the small-timer that Marlow had intimated during their first meeting in London.

"He sounds good. Very well, we'll give him a try," Marlow declared. "We'll make him one of the ones for Djamvelling—someone who knows what to look for. . . . Have we got anything back yet on ways of getting in?"

"Not yet. They're still scratchin' their 'eads."

Marlow got up, dissolved a couple of purification tablets in the water that George had brought in, and poured some of it into a billycan on the stove. "I gather that you and Bernard have been through some times together," he commented over his shoulder.

"We've 'ad a few laughs."

"The night that you and I arrived, when we were all together in Tobins, he mentioned Belfast."

"Right."

"You were there together?" George didn't reply at once, but carried on cutting the corned beef into strips, looking down 'as he worked. "Weren't you?" Marlow prompted.

"Well, 'e were SAS an' I was wit' paras," George

said at last. "But we were there at the same time, aye."

"When would that have been?"

"Oh . . . can't rightly say, it were that far back now. There were a couple of times."

"Let me see if I can guess: 1975, possibly?"

"That were one of 'em, aye." George avoided the colonel's eye and busied himself with wiping a pan.

"Early 1975? Second Battalion, was it?" Marlow didn't wait for a response this time. "Let me tell you a little story about something that happened to Bernard then—or rather I should say, to a friend of his. Bernard had been operating under cover as a magazine photographer, and he got to know a man called Tom Cullen very well—nice chap, absolutely straight. He ran an off-license and was also an active civil-rights campaigner. It was a sincere friendship. Bernard got to know the whole family well. Used to buy things for the kids."

"'E can be like that."

"But Cullen was arrested one night in a case of mistaken identity and hauled off to the grilling center at Palace barracks. No charge, but it was two months before he got out again. You know what an ugly business the whole thing is there. These things happen. . . . But anyhow, while he was inside, he went through some pretty ghastly treatment at the hands of a couple of the RUC Special Branch, and especially a pathological case by the name of Gorban—what's referred to as 'overzealousness' in the whitewashing reports. But in this case it went farther than usual and involved all the fingers of one of Cullen's hands being crushed in a door. Officially it was described as an accident. Cullen said it wasn't and went straight to the press. Then he received several warnings to drop the whole thing and keep his mouth shut, with threats to his family if he didn't. He didn't, and a couple of days later a car hit him and his wife, putting her in hospital for two months—quite deliberate, no question about it. It was a wonder both of them weren't killed." Marlow paused and sat down, holding an open can of instant coffee. "Shortly afterward, Gorban was found shot. The papers wrote it off as another IRA execution. Naturally so. What else would anyone think?"

"There was plenty o' that goin' on, right enough,"

George commented—but stonily, as if he didn't believe it himself.

Marlow looked across at him, watching his face intently. "But that's not quite all there was to it. You see, an army patrol heard the shots. And they almost caught whoever did it, but he got away over some rooftops. But he lost his gun in the process, and they found it. From the serial number, it was service issue." George's eyes failed to show any flicker of the surprise that would have been natural. Colonel Marlow went on: "And then, a strange thing happened. There was a mix-up somehow, and the evidence was lost. It vanished inexplicably in the course of being moved from Two Para HQ to the forensic lab. Nobody ever found it."

George scratched at an ear. "Aye, I do remember 'earin' summat about that."

The colonel finally forced a pained smile. "Come on, George, cut the bullshit. It was Bernard, right? And you lifted the gun. I knew he had an oppo in the paras that he worked with, but I never made it my business to probe deeper because I always respected my men's sources. But a few things you've said since I reappeared on the scene in London have added up. He was your mate, right? And he's seen to it that you've done all right since."

George bit his lip undecidedly. Clearly, he wanted to trust Marlow, but at the same time, all the instincts that he had built up over years rebelled against his saying anything.

Marlow went on: "If it helps, I'll mention another strange mix-up that happened too. You see, I knew who it was, because the serial number matched a list that passed across my desk. We were all a bit green once. I'm sure he wouldn't have used his own if it were today. But due to what must have been some clerical error somewhere, the weapon was confused with another one that had been lost in an unmarked car that came to grief in an across-the-border sortie. Extraordinary, really—I'd never have thought we could make mistakes like that." George turned his head sharply. The porcelain-blue eyes stared back at him with just a hint of a twinkle. "We all look after our own, eh, George?" the colonel said softly.

George emitted a heavy snort. "'E were a nasty piece o' work, that Gorban. I could tell yer a few more stories about 'im, an' all. It only took one like 'im to muck oop everythin' yer'd worked for in a year. 'E should never 'ave been put in a job like that in t' first place."

The colonel looked satisfied. "I just wanted to be sure that we all understand each other," he said. "Now, I don't think there will be any doubts. We're all in the same business now. . . . I rather suspect we have been, all along."

Chapter Twenty-five

OWANDEN LAY ON THE FLOOR OF A STEEP-SIDED rift below a line of ancient red cliffs, next to a string of mud-colored cataracts that sometimes flowed and sometimes didn't from a marshy, reed-choked lake that was sometimes there and sometimes wasn't. It was a typical, ramshackle collection of clay-brick dwellings roofed with thatch and tin, where people with their sheep, goats, chickens, a few cattle and small plots of maize and vegetables had wrested a living from the surroundings in a way that had probably remained changeless for generations.

But as Fallon followed the camouflage-painted Chevy down a deeply rutted road from a low pass toward the village, he saw ample evidence of the changes brought by the new presence of the guerrillas: several burned-out trucks and a Panhard armored car pushed off the road; camouflaged weapons pits and slit trenches overlooking the approaches and dotting the slopes above; a Soviet 73mm automatic antitank gun sandbagged beneath netting at the top of an incline from a sharp bend, where armored vehicles would be at their most vulnerable.

There was cratering at the outskirts of the village itself, and many of the houses were gutted or reduced to rubble. But the vehicles concealed beneath canopies stretched across alleyways and in huts with the front walls removed, along with the general activity around about, testified that the ZRF was far from being dislodged yet. However, as Fallon looked harder, he grew puzzled. The vehicles all seemed to be burned wrecks and chassis stripped of everything usable. Everyone he saw was armed, and in assorted mixtures of combat garb—there was no sign of any villagers.

Sam, who was riding in the Land Rover as a break from the jolting of the truck, explained, "This place been turnin' into what you might call a come-on. Kinda like a decoy for the gov'ment generals to stick pins in on their maps. Gives 'em somethin' to come fly over an' shoot up, an' sometimes send a raidin' column out to. Keeps 'em busy. 'Course, we make sure there's plenty o' stuff to shoot back. Give 'em a hard time. 'Cept for the guys in the dugouts, ain't no one livin' here anymore."

They followed the truck through a checkpoint with guards and stopped outside a large, partly demolished house near the center of the village, blast-proofed by earthen mounds and covered by a sandbagged machine gun beside the entrance. Fallon took it to be the local command post. Sam and one of his lieutenants went inside. The rest of the contingent in the truck climbed down and squatted down beside it on the shady side.

"You know this place?" Fallon asked Candy while they waited.

"I have been through it sometimes, yes."

Which meant there was another ZRF facility of some kind farther on, Fallon reflected. He didn't press the point. "So this was the kind of neighborhood you grew up in," he said, looking around and endeavoring to make light of it instead. "It's like the Western Front. No wonder you know about military things."

"We are at war. It is appropriate."

"Not what you'd call the most romantic spot in the world, though, is it?"

"Life does not permit the time, anyway."

"It's a lot different from what I remember. . . . Well, you've been there. You know what I mean."

"Cities are lonely places," Candy said.

"They can be, I suppose."

"Everybody must be alone sometimes. Here we can go behind our own fences. The city people have to make their fences inside their heads."

"How long were you in Kinnube . . . when you worked with Velker?" Fallon asked.

"Oh, it was not so long. Maybe two or three months." Candy went quiet for a while. "He takes too much risk. Security watch him, but he helps us and doesn't try to pretend. He should get out of Zugenda now. He has done enough."

"He's angry," Fallon said. "It's his way of defying them—the only way he can fight."

"It will kill him," Candy said matter-of-factly.

Sam Letumbai emerged from the command post again. He waved for his men to get back into the truck and came over to the Land Rover. "Okay, we're goin' on up to Tenyasha," he announced. "Barindas is on his way. Oughta be here tonight, or maybe sometime tomorrow—never can tell with these things."

"Sounds good," Fallon said.

"An 'nother piece o' news. Looks like that Australian fella and his pal made it all right too. Crossed over the border yesterday, and they're travelin' with Barindas." Sam looked at Fallon. "They got a friend o' yours with 'em that I was supposed to tell you about, name o' Reid. Came in from England."

"Not Jimmy Reid?"

"That's right."

"Bloody marvelous!"

Sam stepped back. "I'll be ridin' back in the truck for the rest o' the way. Just keep followin'."

"What's Tenyasha?" Fallon asked Candy as they pulled away.

"It's the name of the upper part of the valley," she told him. "In the dialect of this area that means 'Valley of Caves.' That's where we go now."

Above the lake and the marsh, the valley narrowed and the road degenerated to a dusty trail barely wide enough for the truck, threading its way among boulders and scratched across steep rockfalls. All the way, the valley walls rose in chaotic jumbles on both sides, with lower mounds flanking the floor. It had good defensive features, Fallon thought, ideal ambush country. A mile or two farther on, they came up behind two trucks laboring under loads of sacks and vegetables and had to follow them at a crawl until they reached a place wide enough for the trucks to pull over and let them by. And a couple of times they were forced to squeeze off to the side to pass other vehicles coming down in the other direction. "There is not much room to grow food at Tenyasha," Candy explained. "It has to be brought up from Owanden. Finding enough is always difficult."

After a few more miles they passed between two massive shoulders of rock, beyond which cliff walls rising and falling in a series of faces separated by gullies and scree slopes faced each other about a quarter mile apart. Shelves of fairly flat, scrubby ground extended outward a short distance from the base of the cliff line on either side, and then angled downward in steep, rocky slopes that met at a creekbed marking the bottom of the V-shaped gorge. A number of cave mouths, sheltered by overhangs, opened out onto the shelves on both sides, the largest being just past the rock shoulders. Farther up, the floor of the gorge rose, the shelves petered out, and the valley became narrower and shallower. In the lower part, in the vicinity of the caves, there were people about, and animals. Fallon realized that this was the ZRF's real operational base in the area—and almost certainly where the villagers from Owanden had moved to.

They were greeted by a squat, bull-necked man called Austin, whom Sam introduced as the local commander. He had a stubbly chin and a heavy growth of hair that stood out from his head like a fuzzy black halo, and was dressed in a U.S. Army olive shirt with camouflage pants. Austin led them into one of the caves, which seemed to function as a general barracks and mess area for the troops. There were cooking facilities near the front, and rows of palliasses and single- and two-tier cots receding toward the back, where the light from the mouth gave way to pools of dim yellow glow coming from electric bulbs strung below the roof. A side chamber near the front was separated by a canvas partition, behind which was what seemed to be the administrative area, with a couple of desks and a map table formed from boards supported between packing cases and oil drums. A screened-off space at the rear of this section contained several more bunks. Austin showed Fallon to one of them.

"You can stow your kit here," he said. "At least there's some privacy. It's where we put up visiting officers and guests. I think the Mr. Fugleman that I've been told about qualifies."

"It'll do just fine."

Austin indicated a partition at the back. "You can wash there if you need to clean up. Water's short, so go easy on it. There'll be food up front in about half an hour. We'll see you then."

The shower consisted of half an oil drum with holes pierced through the bottom, but no hotel-bathroom shower in Fallon's experience had ever been more refreshing. He changed into clean clothes, buckled on a pistol belt with the Magnum from the Land Rover, and made his way back toward the front of the cave to rejoin the others. Candy arrived a few minutes later, now wearing clean denim fatigues with a Colt sidearm and looking more the part of a guerrilla fighter.

Several people from the base joined the arrivals for the meal, which consisted of corn bread with a thick yam soup, a slice of melon, and hot tea—simple and frugal, but it worked wonders in washing away the aches and dryness of the journey. One of them was a German called Gustav Tannerling, who was apparently in charge of the ZRF's unlikely assortment of motor vehicles at Tenyasha and Owanden. He spoke flawless English and was tall, blond, and as true to the Nordic stereotype as any that Fallon had seen. He seemed to have led something of a checkered career, having gravitated to the ZRF after freebooting as a mercenary on various sides of a long list of Africa's postcolonial troubles.

"And what brings you here, Mr. Hannegen?" he asked across the board-and-box table inside the partitioned section of the cave. Fallon's revelation to Parnum—of his identity as Fugleman—was for the ears of Barindas and Barinda's closest aides only.

"Oh, much the same as yourself, I would imagine," Fallon replied.

"Come now, after all the special treatment?" Tannerling looked skeptical. "Sam Letumbai went out to collect you personally. You forget, I look after the transportation around here."

Fallon made a conciliatory gesture. Obviously he couldn't go around telling anyone who asked that he was really an undercover operator who had agreed to work for the ZRF inside Embatto's organization. He gave the "official" line that he had agreed upon with Parnum. "There's a plan to stiffen the ZRF war effort by bringing in a core of mercenary officers. I'm what I suppose you might call the advance guard, sent on a recce mission."

"You have a background in this kind of business?"

"Sufficient."

"Where will you be drawing your people from?"

"I have my contacts."

"I could probably make some recommendations from my own experience, if that would help."

"I think I can manage, thanks."

Tannerling seemed about to say something more, then changed his mind and smiled evenly. "I apologize if I seem inquisitive. Merely doing my job, you understand. It helps to have as much early warning as possible if transportation needs are likely to be affected."

"Of course."

Silence fell. Then Candy finished her drink and set the mug down. "Maybe I can show you around a little," she suggested to Fallon. "It seems we have some time free for now."

"Good idea," Fallon agreed.

"I'll catch you later, then," Tannerling said.

Candy and Fallon went back through the main part of the cave. "Are you sure it's safe, giving him a job like that?" Fallon asked after a silence as they walked.

"In this kind of war, one can never be sure of anything," Candy replied. "Tannerling knows his work. Barindas must take the chances. He is grateful for anyone he can get."

Fallon nodded, not overhappily, but he didn't pursue the matter further.

Outside, they followed a narrow, stony path along the shelf at the cliff base to the mouth of the next cave, which was slightly higher. Fallon noticed a line strung above the gorge and supported in a couple of places by poles, which looked as if it brought power from the other side. There were two large, round tanks on a ledge higher up on the nearer side, supported by wooden props.

"Where does the water come from," Fallon asked, indicating the tanks with a nod. "Not from that creek down there. It's almost dry."

"That has to be brought up in trucks, also," Candy said.

The next cave had two entrances that merged a short distance inside to form a single, vast cavern that was also devoted to living space. But whereas the first had looked reserved for fighting troops, the larger one was a seething mixture of men and women, young and old, and children of all sizes, scattered throughout a confusion of bedding, belongings, and makeshift furnishings and workbenches.

Virtually all of them seemed to be busy at something, cleaning and preparing food, laundering and mending, shoemaking, salvaging parts from mechanical and electrical assemblies, fixing tools.

"It's a big difference from those people we saw on the way here," Fallon commented. "They'd all given up and quit trying."

"That's the difference when people are allowed to work for themselves," Candy said simply.

They entered and followed along one side of the cavern to an area set aside as a school. A class of about thirty was attending a reading lesson. Fallon and Candy stopped to watch. Then two of the children, a boy and a girl of perhaps seven or eight, noticed Candy. Ignoring the protests of the teacher, they scampered across with delighted squeals of "Annette!" Candy picked them up in turn and hugged them.

"Have you come back to live here again?" the girl asked.

"No, I'm just visiting for a short while."

"Will you be teaching us while you're here?" the boy wanted to know.

"I try to find some time if I can."

"Where did you go?"

"Oh . . . a long way from here."

"Across the ocean?"

"Well, a little bit of ocean."

"Where did you go there for?"

"I tell you all about it later. But now, maybe, you should get back to your lesson."

Farther on, they encountered more faces that Candy knew, and some who stopped to exchange a few words. Fallon noticed a gradual change in her manner. The hardened ideologue that he had known since their meeting in London, embittered, perpetually tense and watchful, was giving way to a different personality. Secure once more among her own kind, she could let her defenses down to become her real self again. It was the first time since he'd met her that Fallon saw Candy really laugh.

Chapter Twenty-six

CRISTO ARYSKOLIS SENSED TROUBLE THE MOMENT he opened the door and saw the two men who came late in the evening to his apartment by the waterfront in Piraeus, the port of Athens. They were dressed soberly in dark suits and had that look of dispassionate purposefulness that goes with officialdom anywhere.

"You are the owner and captain of the motor vessel *Elaine*?" one of them inquired.

Cristo nodded. He had bought the boat only recently. His new business of ferrying tourists around southern Greece and among the Cyclades islands was already paying comfortably.

"Can we go inside, please? This concerns your professional dealings."

Momentarily confused, Cristo nodded again and stepped back into the hallway, failing to register that it was an odd hour for anyone to be calling on official matters. His wife looked out from the doorway of the lounge as the two men entered. From behind her came the sound of the western that the children were watching on TV. "It's to do with business," Cristo said to her. "We'll go into the back room." She smiled uncertainly, nodded at the two visitors, and withdrew.

Cristo closed the front door and led the men through to what doubled as a den and family room. There were a few shelves of books, a cupboard overflowing with toys, a table, and several chairs. "A little wine, perhaps?" he asked nervously, motioning toward the chairs.

"No, thank you." The one who had spoken at the door remained standing and moved to the window. It looked out over a section of the harbor, twinkling in the darkness with boats' lanterns and lights from the quay across the basin reflecting on the water. The other, who was carrying a light, underarm document case, sat down at the table and produced a notebook and some reference papers.

"A fine boat," the one by the window remarked. "It's a good season. Are you finding things profitable these days?"

"We . . . manage to get by," Cristo replied uneasily.

"Hmm, it's quite a step up for you, isn't it? I mean, a change in the right direction after that rust bucket that you were operating around the islands for years—and lucky not to have drowned in."

Cristo spread his hands and shrugged. "A man works hard, saves hard, stays honest. . . . God rewards him."

"Yes, and quite well too . . . Especially when you take into account that the credit papers were drawn up purely for you to claim deductions against and that the sale was in fact settled in cash under the table. I bet a lot of people don't know about that."

Cristo rubbed his shaggy mustache and shrugged again, this time without smiling.

"I wonder where the money came from to enable you to put down a wad like that. It couldn't have had anything to do with several particular loads that came in from Turkey over the last year or so, could it? Or the amount that you *really* chartered it out for to those Italians last summer? I bet a lot of people don't know about that, either. The taxation authorities here, for instance?"

Cristo felt his palms beginning to sweat. So that was it. Okay, he'd taken the gamble. . . . "I was going to come straight on it," he said pleadingly, looking to the one at the table and back again. "I just needed one year to put the business on its feet. That's all. I—"

"Well, we're not from the tax authorities, so you can save all that," the one by the window said.

"You're not?" Cristo said, surprised. Now he didn't know whether to feel relieved or more apprehensive still.

"But as you can see, we are people that they would dearly love to talk to." The ominous note in the visitor's voice was unmistakable.

Cristo's stomach knotted. "How much do you want?" he asked leadenly.

"Nothing. Just a little information."

Cristo licked his lips and nodded quickly. "If I can . . ."

"A little over two months ago, you landed a shipment

of thirty-two crates onto a beach in Libya. They were flown south to a helicopter pickup—"

Cristo swallowed visibly. "I don't know what happened to them. That was not my affair."

The man at the window moved back and leaned with his knuckles resting on the table. "No, you probably don't. But we're more interested in where they came from. Specifically, where were they delivered to you, and who commissioned you to do the job?"

Cristo shook his head. "I can't tell you those things."

The man standing tutted sadly and looked at his companion. "Such a shame. They'll seize the boat for sure, wouldn't you think?"

"Oh, at least. Maybe a stretch on top too. I hear they're clamping down everywhere."

"You must have picked them up somewhere," the first said, looking at Cristo again.

"Look, you don't understand," Cristo protested. "I didn't pick them up anywhere. I was told to meet another ship at a rendezvous ninety kilometers west of Crete. We transferred the cargo at sea."

"What was the ship's name?"

"It was all blacked out. I saw nothing."

"What kind of ship? Big ship, little ship? What kind of silhouette?"

"Freighter, ten thousand tons, maybe. Central superstructure, single stack."

"Who commissioned the job. Was it a company? Didn't you have a contact's name?"

"Nothing was written down. A man came to me one day at the docks, that's all. He called himself Milo and paid cash, half in advance. Then he came a couple of times again after that to make the final arrangements. They gave me the rest at the rendezvous. I never saw him again."

"What did he look like?" the one standing asked.

"Oh . . . normal, I'd say. He had a beret and a brown jacket. Fortyish, maybe forty-five."

"Was he black?"

"Black?" Cristo looked surprised. "No . . . just like you or me."

"How about a beard or a mustache?"

Cristo looked flummoxed. "I can't remember."

"Anything else notable that you can think of? Did he wear glasses, for instance?"

"No. At least, I don't think so."

The two visitors exchanged glances. "Not good," the one standing opined.

"He's holding something back?" the other agreed.

Cristo looked from one to the other, sweating visibly now. "I can't tell you any more! That's all I know." They looked at him with open disbelief. "Wait."

"Yes?" the one standing said.

"There was something else. Milo had a sort of a code word that he used for the job. I heard him use it when he was talking over the phone to somebody. He called it 'Flamenco.'"

The east side of Kinnube, north of the Tsholere River, was a run-down industrial quarter consisting largely of derelict warehouses and abandoned, overgrown sites littered with rusting sheds and machinery. A lot of squatters had established themselves there: vagrants, homeless families, refugees from the war zone, fugitives from the resettlement programs, living amidst a scattering of what personal effects remained to them and sometimes a few animals, picking a day-to-day living in one way or another from the options that the city had to offer.

On the bank of the river itself, backed by a decaying wooden wharf at which the hulks of a couple of barges were still tied, their decks long since rotted through and settled on the bottom, was a disused foundry building. When Molokutu's regime took over the country, it had been a going concern, if somewhat shaky; the flight of foreign capital under threat of confiscation had reduced it to its last legs and ten years of dictatorial power wielded by planners ignorant of even the rudiments of economics had done the rest.

By that strange process that operates in close-knit communities of telegraphing information without words needing to be spoken, it was understood that the foundry was not talked about and that people having no business there stayed away from it. Nobody heard the heavy crates being shifted when a truck unloaded behind its closed doors in the middle of the night, and nobody saw the armed, wary-eyed figures slipping in and out at all hours, sometimes alone, sometimes in small groups. A sack of flour or a carton of rations from government stocks would be brought out periodically and distributed. Nobody mentioned the ZRF.

In an upper room of the main building, Colonel Marlow, George, and an African called Crosby, who commanded the ZRF contingent occupying the foundry, were consulting over a map and some photographs and hand-drawn diagrams showing the state-security helicopter base at Djamvelling. With them was a deeply tanned, wiry man in his thirties, with alert blue eyes and shaggy hair that was normally sandy-colored, but which had been dyed dark. He was wearing a bush shirt with shorts, lightweight, rubber-soled suede boots, and a red bandanna.

Tam Czaryski had arrived the previous night after three days of being passed from one cell to another through the ZRF network, and his face and arms still showed traces of the dark brown pigment that had been applied to make him less conspicuous. He was originally from the Vietnam-era Special Forces, and since then, besides piloting helicopters, had developed a specialization in safe blowing, lock picking, bugging and tapping, alarm silencing, and other nefarious arts that could be marketed at a good price in certain select circles. He had last worked with Fallon and George on the job for the Spanish authorities that George had told Marlow about before they moved their location to the foundry.

"Razor-wire fences, clear-fire zone . . ." Tam shook his head and whistled. "Trip wire around the perimeter. That probably means mines."

"That's right," Crosby confirmed. He had a wild mane and beard coming together to surround his face, which with a flowing purple shirt, dark glasses, and ornate necklace made him look more like a renegade from Haight-Ashbury in the sixties than any popular notion of a guerrilla fighter. But he seemed competent. "There are electronic alarms and intruder detectors everywhere outside the clear zone too. We've lost a lot of people in probing raids on that place. And we've never even got close."

Tam tossed down the pencil he had been chewing on and looked at Marlow dubiously. "Tough," he pronounced. "There's no way anyone's gonna get in there without an army. And my impression from what you said is that anything like that would kinda defeat the object, anyhow."

"We just want ter know what they've got that they can put on them choppers o' theirs," George said. "We weren't really thinkin' about 'avin ter blow t'whole bloody place up. . . . Not just yet, anyroad."

The colonel nodded, unsurprised. "Exactly our conclusion, also. I was wondering, therefore, if something with a little more subterfuge might be more appropriate."

"How do you mean?" Tam asked.

The colonel gestured to indicate Tam's general appearance. "It's rather ironic. You've just washed off a lot of coloring that you needed to blend in. But for what I've got in mind, it's the very fact of being a Caucasian that would hide you."

Tam showed his empty palms. "I'm listening."

"By passing yourselves off as Russians. A number of Soviet technicians work at Djamvelling. I believe that many Africans have trouble telling the difference." The colonel looked at Crosby for confirmation.

"That's true in a lot of cases," Crosby said.

George, however, had caught the colonel's use of the plural and was looking suspicious. "'Ang on," he said. "Now just who are these 'selves' we're talkin' about all of a sudden? It sounds ter me as if we might be gerrin' a bit carried away with ourselves 'ere, does this."

"Oh, come on, George," the colonel said breezily. "You wouldn't send Tam into a place like that on his own without any backup, would you? I know you're strictly working with Bernard, but it's going to be a while yet before we see him again. And you and Tam have worked together before. Why not look on it as a little exercise to keep the cobwebs down while we're waiting for Bernard to get back, eh?" He looked from one to the other and took the two stony stares coming back at him as assent. "Jolly good. Well, the first thing, as I see it, is to find a way of luring some of them out for a few hours. . . ."

Chapter Twenty-seven

By the morning after Fallon's arrival at Tenyasha, the news was that Barindas and his party had been further delayed and were not now expected until sometime in the afternoon. Fallon spent the time letting Candy show him around more of the "Valley of Caves."

The hospital was overcrowded, with one surgeon, an Egyptian, and a pair of harassed-looking nurses, doing the best they could. There were plenty of volunteers to help as orderlies, but never enough qualified people. Drugs, anesthetics, everything was in short supply, if available at all, and adequate hygiene was impossible, as the heavy reek of infected flesh hanging over the place testified. Many of the patients were victims of antipersonnel mines, which more often than not necessitated a limb amputation, and there were some grotesque burn cases from napalm, the majority of whom, probably mercifully, couldn't be expected to survive. With insufficient fresh drinking water and rudimentary sanitation, dysentery was widespread and its sufferers were segregated into a separate chamber, where the stench was appalling and the effects of the disease covered the floor.

A few of the patients that Fallon stopped to talk to turned out to be defectors from the government forces. "The army's a shell," one of them told him, a former private who had lost a foot. "Morale's all shot to hell. They don't like what they're doing to the people, but who's gonna risk getting shot by making a thing out of it? If Barindas took over in the city and they thought he had a chance of staying put, they'd cave in. Half the guys would switch over."

Another—a rare prize to find—had been a junior officer with Embatto's state-security forces. His name was Patrice. Fallon and Candy found him propped on a straw mattress covered by a canvas sheet, with a traction sling supporting a shattered leg and hip. He was carving a wooden model of a tank for the children.

"It's state security that keeps the army in line," he said. "The army goes along with the hard line against the people because it'd rather be part of one side that's got the upper hand. It's a three-way balance, see. That way, none of them can get strong enough to try and take over—because it would pull the other two closer together against them. That's why Molokutu set it up that way."

"It sounds as if you're saying that if the ZRF didn't exist, Molokutu would have to create it," Fallon commented.

"Pretty much."

Fallon stared for a few seconds at the model that Patrice was whittling. It was an expert piece of work, and quite detailed. "You've done that kind of thing before," he remarked, motioning with a finger.

Patrice shrugged. "Just a pastime, I guess."

"You never worked at it professionally?"

"Nope. Never did."

"Ever think about it."

"Not really."

"Russian isn't it? T-54?"

"You know tanks. That was the kind I trained on."

Fallon looked puzzled. "I thought that the SS armored units don't have any tanks—just wheeled stuff."

"That's right. But we still got some tank training on the army's machines—about a week of it every couple of months."

"What for?"

Patrice shrugged. "Dunno . . . I guess somebody somewhere thought it would be a good idea to have some backup capability. They never told us what it was all about."

"What made you come over to the ZRF?"

"If you want the truth, I was pretty scared by the things I'd been told about what happened to guys they caught who didn't."

"Do you still think that now?"

Patrice grinned faintly and shook his head. "No. But I decided to stay on, anyhow."

Fallon was curious as to the kinds of weapons the ZRF had at Tenyasha. Candy told him that the armory was some distance farther up and on the far side of the gorge, away from the barracks area.

"Can we go there?" Fallon asked.

She seemed a bit hesitant. "Normally it is not a place that anyone just walks into. But since you are here to help, maybe GDF won't mind this time."

"Who?"

Candy explained that the armory was in the charge of a Chinaman called Sung Feng. He had come to Africa as part of the Chinese railroad-building aid program to Tanzania, grown disillusioned with the People's Revolution, defected, and stayed. How he came to be mixed up with the ZRF was anyone's guess.

"So why GDF?"

"That is what most people who have dealings with him here call him."

"Why?"

Candy smiled to herself in an odd kind of way. "You will see."

They crossed the gorge at the bottom of the valley by a wobbly plank bridge and ascended the opposite bank to a dusty track running along the base of the facing cliffs, just wide enough for vehicles. The first cave they passed was evidently used as a motor workshop—as they passed, Fallon could see a number of Land Rovers mounting various types of guns, and the carcass of a French Panhard. Candy confirmed that it was the transportation pool and repair shop that Gustav Tannerling managed. The electrical generating plant and radio facility were also there, in a separate section farther back at the rear.

The armory was a cave on its own about a quarter of a mile farther along, with two guards posted on the approach outside and a short distance below. Candy talked with them for a minute, then went inside with one of them to explain the situation to Sung Feng. While Fallon waited with the other, who didn't seem to speak any English, Gustav Tannerling appeared in the cave mouth and came down.

"Mr. Hannegen, good day. You are getting around and about, I see."

"I'll need to know what I have to work with. The sooner, the better."

Tannerling stood, hands on hips, surveying the valley generally.

"The degree of organization that they have achieved here is quite remarkable for blacks," he commented.

"Really?"

"But then, they were exceptionally fortunate. Austin spent several years in Europe as a student in his earlier years. As a race it's more in their nature to sit and wait for someone else to do something. That is why they have so many problems."

"And Austin has always got you around if he needs advice," Fallon said.

"Yes, of course. That helps also," Tannerling agreed, missing the sarcasm. He was being quite sincere. He went on: "I knew a man down in Zaire who was paid twenty dollars a page to translate American into English."

"How come?" Fallon asked.

"Military maintenance manuals. You see, the coloreds only do exactly what the instructions tell them. For example, if it says in the book 'remove carburetor'"—Tannerling made motions in the air of lifting a carburetor off its mounting—"'and replace.'" He reversed the motion. "They put it back again, ha-ha, and of course it still doesn't work. So what you have to do, you see, is learn to think the way they do. In the book, you change it to 'remove carburetor and *renew*'—then they'll go to the store and get another one." He waved a hand to and fro in front of his face. "But to try and get them to think for themselves is quite impossible."

Candy reappeared, accompanied by a smallish, jerky-limbed Oriental with a bony, hollowed face and a sharp chin sporting a wisp of a beard. He was wearing a U.S. Army baseball-style hat and khaki jodhpurs, together with a suspicious scowl, as he came stomping out to accost what he evidently regarded as an intruder to his domain.

"Huh? What vis? Who vis new ferra you bling heah?" he said to Candy. "You know vis prace high-seculity prace, my goddamn fuckin' lesponibility." From the way he seemed to be ignoring Tannerling, Fallon sensed that the atmosphere between the two of them was not of the best.

"He comes here to see Barindas in person," Candy replied. "I assume it will be okay. Sam Letumbai came himself to bring us here yesterday."

"Hum, ho, is so, eh? You send messengah boy next time, get okay flom Feng."

"Yes, Feng. I am sorry. I will remember."

"Hum." The Chinaman peered at Fallon. "Okay, so you wanna see good stuff, brow Morokutu sowdiers all up sky, huh? You come forrow me." Feng turned and led them inside.

There were piles of rifles and automatic weapons of all kinds and calibers: Russian Kalashnikovs, lots of Israeli Uzis, standard NATO-issue Belgian FNs, British stens and Sterlings, American M1 and M2 carbines. Feng's collection of rarer specimens included some Remington-870 shotguns—an old acquaintance of Fallon's from his SAS days—a few Mauser Model-66 bolt-action sniper's rifles, favored for a long time by the French GIGN, and a crate of Czech Skorpion submachine guns. There were M16A1 Armalites, M79 grenade launchers, Very flare pistols, and more single- and double-barrel shotguns. Arrayed in another section of racks and boxes was a similarly diverse selection of pistols, ranging from Walther PPKs and PPs, to Webley navy revolvers of World War I vintage.

Fallon picked up one of the FNs and tested the mechanism, checking for dirt in the barrel and carbon specks on the gas regulator. It was clean, oiled, and the parts slid smoothly.

"Hah, so you fink you know sump'n about goddamn gun?" Feng said in a challenging voice. "You fink you good plofessionaw sowdiah, eh? You see prenty gun befoh? You show."

"Oh, a couple here and there," Fallon replied. Holding Feng's eye so as not to be able to see the weapon, he stripped down an AK47 by touch in a matter of seconds and then reassembled it. The glint in Sung Feng's eye changed, and he bowed his head a fraction in a gesture of deference.

"A show of manners wouldn't be out of place," Tannerling said haughtily. "Mr. Hannegen is here expressly at Barindas's personal invitation."

"Who ask you, stuck-up klaut plick? Go back your own side and kick brack ass. No ass gettin' kicked alound heah."

"He is good with explosives," Candy whispered

in Fallon's ear. He noticed that she had to bite her lip.

Fallon turned away and smiled to himself. It seemed that the super race had an equally dim view of Asiatics as of blacks, but with Feng it didn't cut any ice. He ran an eye over the heavier stuff by the far wall: Russian and European 7.62mm machine guns, 50mm cannon, section and medium support mortars, Soviet Sagger and RPG7 infantry-launched antitank and antiaircraft missiles.

Explosives were kept in a separate cave, under guard, several hundred yards away at the remotest end of the base. Apart from stocks of various ammunition types for the main weapons used by the ZRF, they included hoards of several kinds of antitank mines, with several cases of the plastic-cased Torpex type, immune to conventional metal detectors. For sabotage and demolition work there were boxes of haystack- and beehive-shaped charges, together with reels of Cordtex detonating cord, delayed-action detonators, time pencils, D10 cable and exploder generators, Russian MUV igniters, camouflet sets, for booby-trapping roads, and stacks of slabbed C4 plastic explosive and TNT in thousand-gram blocks and smaller primer blocks. Fallon surveyed the scene, prodded and poked here and there, and nodded in a satisfied way.

Feng proudly showed him an itemized inventory list, with all additions and withdrawals dated and signed. "Aw done plopah, plofessionaw," he announced. "No see any sroppy man'gement heah."

There were grenades: fragmentation, smoke, and CS gas varieties, and several patterns of antipersonnel devices and mines, including claymores. But the types stored in an area by one of the walls were strangely unfamiliar. Fallon peered at them more closely, then picked one of them up. It was made from what looked like a sawed-off Russian 125mm artillery shell. He looked up at Feng curiously.

"Ah só, vely good." Feng showed two rows of discolored castellations that had once been teeth. "We not one of your fird-rate op'lation. Morokutu sowdiers send us prenty good stuff flee. Dumb to ret go lustin' away in glound, so we fix. We fix pletty goddamn fuckin' good, eh?"

"Much ammunition that the army fires doesn't explode," Candy explained. "GDF has a recovery workshop.

His people open up the duds and melt out the TNT to make their own things."

"Not the sort of thing to mention on your life-insurance application," Fallon commented.

"Criminally reckless," Tannerling opined.

"Huh? Watchoo know 'bout exprosive? You stay wiv oily geahboxes. Find prenty mo' climinaws in gleat Hitlah faddahland."

"Perhaps it's time we moved on," Tannerling suggested, ignoring the barb. "Have you seen the motor workshop yet?"

"We passed it on the way up," Fallon answered.

"Allow me to show you more of what we have inside."

"I'd be interested."

There was just the one workshop up at Tenyasha, Tannerling explained as they walked back down the track. Most of the vehicles that the ZRF had in the area were kept dispersed around Owanden, which made sense in view of the impossible traffic situation that would have resulted from overuse of the track up to the gorge.

They arrived at the cave that Fallon and Candy had passed by earlier and went in. The space inside was larger than the glimpse from outside had suggested, and contained, in addition to the vehicles that they had seen earlier, several Russian trucks abandoned by the Zugendans and rebuilt, and a Swiss Mowag, minus its turret. Tannerling also showed them the motor-generator system located behind the workshop, in a partitioned area that also contained switch gear and an electrical store. The radio facility was in a separately partitioned room behind the generating installation, with a lead up to an external antenna on the clifftop. Besides using radio for their own communications, the ZRF found an invaluable source of intelligence in the interception of official Zugendan government and military traffic.

On the way back through the workshop, the group passed a youth of about sixteen, clad in shorts and a grease-stained T-shirt, who was doing something to the engine of one of the Land Rovers. They watched him working deftly and surely, and such was his concentration that he didn't notice them for some time. When he looked up suddenly and saw Candy, he tossed down the wrench he had been using and came over, as if to give her a hug;

then, mindful of the state of his hands, he drew back to rest content with a broad smile.

"Annette! I thought you were still overseas someplace."

"I only got back recently. You're looking well, Imo. How is your father?"

"He's up north somewhere. Last I heard, he was okay."

"This is Mr. Hannegen. He's here to help us."

"Hi."

"Hi, Imo."

Tannerling had been poking around critically in the Land Rover, as if looking for something to fault. Finding nothing, he grunted, muttered a few words about keeping tools together, and went over to a bench where another African was filing a part from a dismantled transmission.

Imo was Candy's nephew, the son of the sister that she had told Fallon about, who had been killed by the bomb at Jaquesville. Imo had already been active with the ZRF at the time. Having no further reason to stay, his father, Jomar, had left town after the tragedy and was now with one of the fighting units in the war zone.

Imo was all swagger and cockiness, but with the ready good humor that came from ebullient self-esteem rather than any inner insecurity. Fallon took to him immediately. He could see, too, why a consistently good performance from somebody like Imo would only irk Tannerling all the more.

Fallon inclined his head in the direction of the Land Rover. "Where'd you learn that?"

"Oh, I was figuring to be a mech at one time, back when it was still worth it," Imo told him. He turned back to resume what he had been doing.

"Is that your Land Rover that showed up yesterday, the one with the fancy stripes?" he asked, glancing up at Fallon.

"Yes, that's right."

"You didn't get that anywhere near here."

"I rented it—from across the border."

Imo nodded while he carried on working. "Uh-huh. So is that what you went out of the country for, Annette, to bring him back? Did you two travel back together?"

"Not exactly," Candy said.

Imo sighed and shook his head. "I guess some people just have it lucky. I'm stuck here, working my ass off, getting covered in grease all day, and having to put up with the kraut. You get to see exciting foreign places. Don't seem right to me. What do I have to do to get myself a bit of fun like that too?"

Fallon and Candy's eyes met briefly. "Oh, I wouldn't lose too much sleep worrying over it if I were you, Imo," Candy said. "It isn't all quite the kind of fun that you imagine."

Chapter Twenty-eight

BARINDAS AND HIS MODEST ESCORT OF GUARDS and lieutenants arrived in the middle of the afternoon in an aging Renault and a Nissan eight-seat minibus. With him was Marie Guridan, the woman that Thombert had described as running the ZRF's intelligence activities and whose face Fallon recognized from the photograph that he had studied. Roger Parnum, Mamu, and Jimmy Reid with several cases of equipment were also with the party, as Fallon had been led to expect. But Haile Yolatta, the ZRF's military boss, was on operations somewhere in the war zone.

Barindas had indicated that he would attend to business first and appear for the crowds later, so no advance warning was spread of his coming. The arrivals made their way through into a group of walled-off chambers above a rockfall at the rear of the cave that the ZRF troops and officers were billeted in, which was where Barindas's quarters were located when he was at Tenyasha. It was a restricted-access part of the cave, with a single approach up from the main floor, which was always guarded; a small rear entrance, also guarded, opened high up in a side rift off the main gorge. There, Barindas, Marie Guridan, and Parnum joined Fallon, Candy, and Sam Letumbai over a meal. Austin had gone down to attend to business in Owanden, and Jimmy Reid was resting after his journey.

Barindas had a slim, fragile build that was deceptive in view of his energy, and wore loose, flowing clothes of the local pattern, and a small tarboosh. Because of a pigment deficiency in his eyes, he also wore sunglasses most of the time. His gnarled face, with its shock of white hair and white beard, retained a relaxed, untroubled look despite the rigors of the journey, which had been at a forced pace over hard terrain. Fallon's first impressions were in keeping with the general image that he had built already: of a man who was first an idealist, governed by principles that were inviolate, and who was therefore never swayed from his chosen course by the kind of pragmatic considerations responsible for the fickleness that characterized much of contemporary politics.

At the same time Fallon could see how perilous such a disposition could be in the present circumstances if it were allowed to become the sole determinant of policy. As he listened to Barindas's visions of how, one day, the whole of Africa might not only feed itself but become an industrial superpower, he could understand the charisma that the leader exerted on the people; but it was also clear how essential was the balancing role played by Haile Yolatta. With their complementary appeals, the two of them together would make a formidable combination.

Parnum had already satisfied Barindas and his colleagues that they were talking to the Fugleman whom they had sent their agents to London to contact. Candy and Fallon related the happenings there and subsequently in Kinnube, and Parnum joined in to describe the jail break. Barindas listened intently, expressing disgust and sympathy at what had befallen Candy. Fallon went on to summarize his conversation with Velker and the mystery concerning Embatto's secret stock of antitank weapons, since Parnum already knew something of the story. Barindas revealed that Velker's surgery had been raided and the doctor had gone to ground. Since nobody mentioned Infinity Limited, Fallon omitted any reference to Colonel Marlow and George. That was something he could go into later, he decided—probably something to be restricted to Barindas himself and Marie Guridan.

That brought them to the first major issue to be addressed, which until it was resolved would make all further plans worse than useless: the spy in the ZRF camp.

"What happened in London seems conclusive," Barindas agreed heavily. Parnum had already outlined the story to him, but Fallon got the impression that despite the evidence, Barindas had been hanging on to a hope for some other explanation.

"Ngoyba knew that your people were there and why they were there, and he set them up," Fallon said, nodding. "You can't even think about making a serious move against the regime with the situation as it is."

"Someone with access to top-level information . . . or someone that information passes through," Marie Guridan said in an obvious allusion to communications.

She was an intense, passionate woman, leaner than in the picture that Fallon had seen in Thombert's dossier, and with her hair cut short now. Her large, round spectacles seemed to magnify her statements, which she uttered in a crisp, clear way that declared her position unambiguously and brooked no compromises. She had a youthful face and wore khaki shorts revealing long, smooth legs and enhancing the student image that had already formed in Fallon's mind. Very intellectual, he didn't doubt, and probably a hard worker. The classical, dedicated revolutionary. But he couldn't help wondering if her experience could match the position she held.

Letumbai made a resigned gesture with one hand. "There's people in a lotta places who that could cover. This isn't the only base we've got. We move around all the time."

"What about the really sensitive stuff?" Fallon asked, looking at Barindas. "Do you have your own comms man who travels with you?"

"His name's Hardy," Barindas said. "He was hand-picked for the job. I'd vouch for him personally." He looked around. "If you can't trust your own communications person, all's lost anyway."

"I'd like to talk to him, anyhow," Fallon said.

"Of course."

"That's why I brought Jimmy Reid over," Fallon explained. "This spy almost certainly uses radio to report back, whether his official job is to do with communications or not. Some of the gear that Jimmy's brought with him is to scan for illicit transmissions going out in frequency bands that you don't normally use."

"Okay . . ." Letumbai said. He sounded a shade dubious, but at the same time willing to hear Fallon out.

Fallon half turned on his seat and waved an arm to indicate generally the part of the cave that they were in. "My suggestion is that we set him up in here without making it public knowledge. He could run an antenna lead up to the crags at the top of this cliff. Nobody goes up there. I had a look around this morning."

"But we don't even know if this spy's at Tenyasha," Letumbai said. "That was my point."

"I know, but it's just to let Jimmy familiarize this guy Hardy of yours with the equipment and give him some practice with it." Fallon looked back at Barindas. "The equipment isn't that bulky. It can stay with you when you leave. Then Hardy can take over the job, so you'll be able to check out each place you go. It'll take time, I know, but we have to start somewhere."

"Well, we certainly can't make any progress until this is cleared up," Barindas said.

"True," Parnum agreed.

Fallon was watching Candy's eyes and reading the thoughts behind them as she sat tight-lipped, saying nothing. What had happened to Victor in London, and to her afterward, had been caused by somebody's treachery. Fallon had already been present on occasions when she had killed two men. He didn't need two guesses as to what her verdict would be if and when the informer was exposed.

The next matter they turned to was the ZRF's counteroffer that Candy had put to Fallon in London, and which Fallon had told Parnum and Mamu, before their departure from Kinnube, he had accepted; in short, what Fallon's mission for the ZRF was supposed to be.

Candy, of course, knew by now that Embatto believed Fallon to be working for him. And Barindas and Marie Guridan almost certainly knew it too, because Colonel Marlow knew, and Infinity Limited was in touch with Barindas; also, because their counteroffer had been for Fallon to work within Embatto's organization for the ZRF, and Fallon could hardly have accepted without first being installed with Embatto himself.

As far as Parnum was concerned, however, Fugleman had simply entered Zugenda as Konrad Hannegen in order to renew his contact with the ZRF after his channel to them in London was lost. Fallon hadn't revealed any more to him and Mamu than that, primarily because in this kind of situation, the less a person knew, the less they could be induced or forced to disclose.

Fallon related the Zugendans' plan as it had been presented to him by Embatto and Thombert. "Zugendan intelligence in London will certainly have been trying to find out everything they can about the recruiting operation that my people are running from there. And it's possible that they may have tracked down some of the contacts. If so, it's okay because they're legitimate. The operation there is a decoy act to satisfy Embatto's people while I'm getting established on the inside in Kinnube."

Parnum was looking perplexedly from one face to another as he listened, but he refrained from interrupting at that point.

Fallon was about to continue when he caught a motion from Barindas to attract his attention. "Now, Molokutu and his confederates believe that the object of that exercise is to dispose of us and others," Barindas said, indicating himself, Guridan, and Sam Letumbai, and at the same time grimacing to show what he thought of the idea.

"That's about the shape of it," Fallon said, nodding.

"On the basis of what you have just told us, I would like to suggest that possibly we can make better use of these people than merely using them as decoys. You said that when your reconnaissance here is done, you are to return to Kinnube to report. Also, Embatto has proposed bringing one contingent of these assassins into the country via Kinnube." Barindas turned his head and gestured to the company in general. "Very well. Why not allow him to go ahead and do so? In fact, Mr. Fugleman might be able to prevail upon him to enlarge that part of the operation such that a considerable number of the team arrive by that particular route. Thus, Mr. Fugleman and they might find themselves all in the capital, and therefore in close proximity to some of the most unpleasant among our adversaries, all at the same time. The situation would appear to offer certain opportunities. I, er, trust you take my point."

Fallon stared at Barindas with a mixture of new respect and surprise. He was beginning to see a deeper side of the wily old African. An idealist, yes, but not the kind of hopeless romantic that Fallon knew from previous experience he could spend half his time saving from harebrained notions, and all too often lost his patience with. He had come to terms with the real world and wasn't trying to create perfection. A step in the right direction would be accomplishment enough for one lifetime.

A faint smile softened the corners of Fallon's mouth.

The audacity of Barindas's suggestion was the kind of thing that appealed to him. He swallowed the last of a can of British army compo-rations treacle pudding and wiped his mouth with a knuckle. "I'll give it some thought," he promised.

"I find it a distasteful way of approaching one's goals," Barindas confessed. "But in this case I'm forced to agree with Haile's view that we are merely playing by the rules as our enemy has written them."

By this time Parnum could contain himself no longer. "Look, I don't know if I'm being a bit slow, but let's see if I've got this straight," he said, and leveled a finger at Fallon. "You came a bit less than completely clean with Mamu and me when we were in Kinnube, is that what I'm hearing?"

Fallon nodded, not really apologetically. "You know how it has to be sometimes, Roger."

"Embatto knows you're really Fugleman?"

"Yes."

"And he thinks you're really working for him, but pretending to be agreeing to work for us, pretending to work for him. . . . Right?"

Fallon's brow creased as he went through the convolutions. "I'm not sure. I think so," he said.

Parnum raised a hand to his brow as if unsure of it himself either. "But . . . wait a minute. What would *he* believe we believed? That is, what would you tell Embatto that you'd given us as his reason for bringing these people into the country."

"I'd tell him that I'd told you they were really on your side and were coming here to take him out," Fallon replied.

Parnum's bemusement only increased. He started to speak, thought it through again, and frowned hesitantly. "But . . . that's exactly what you *are* telling us."

"Yes," Fallon agreed cheerfully.

Barindas looked at Parnum sympathetically. "I know," he said. "I've been round the same loop myself. I wouldn't recommend even attempting to unravel it. It merely wears out one's mind. All it boils down to in the end is, do you trust Mr. Fugleman, or do you not?"

Fallon picked up his mug and downed a long draft of coffee, wondering whether to go the whole hog at this point and tell them who the inside accomplice in pulling off the jail break had really been. No, he decided finally, it would be stretching credulity too far. If the complexities were such that they were forced to take him on trust as things were, revealing that would add nothing to the solidity of his credentials. He had concocted the whole business simply to save Candy's and Parnum's necks, and that had been accomplished. It didn't affect the general plan from here on.

There were some things, Fallon told himself, that it just wasn't worth getting into and having to explain.

Chapter Twenty-nine

FORT GEORGE G. MEADE, HEADQUARTERS OF the U.S. National Security Agency, stands on a thousand-acre site halfway between Washington, D.C., and Baltimore. It consists of a tan, nine-story headquarters building towering between the jutting arms of the original green-stone-and-glass, A-shaped operations building, and almost twenty other anonymous buildings. A double set of ten-foot-high Cyclone fences topped by barbed wire, with an electrified fence running between, encloses the complex, and armed guards with attack-trained dogs patrol the perimeter. The roofs of the buildings are cluttered with satellite communications gear, long-wire antennas, log-period antennas, parabolic microwave dishes, and two enormous radomes, one pockmarked like an enormous golf ball, the other smooth like a Ping-Pong ball. There is a permanent population of around 3,500, which increases fifteenfold with the daily flood of commuters.

"C Corridor," the main thoroughfare of this establishment that might properly be called a city, since its full-time residents exceed in number those of 130 other cities and towns in the state of Maryland, stretches the length of three football fields and includes a bank, credit union, travel agency, drug and cosmetics store, library, ticket service booth, shoe repair shop, dry cleaners, and a barber shop. The complex also has its own bus service, medical facilities, police and fire departments, a college, a TV station, a post office, and a power station. In cavernous, city-block-size expanses below the headquarters-operations building there exists what is probably the greatest concentration of computing power that the world has ever known. Whereas most government departments and large corporations measure the space taken up by their computer operations in square feet or even thousands of square feet,

NSA measures its in acres. The CRAY-1 supercomputer constituting NSA's "Loadstone" facility is capable of executing two hundred million calculations in a second, or of transferring between its processing circuits and memory the equivalent of 2,500 three-hundred-page books.

Although it has the highest budget and the greatest number of employees of any of the institutions that make up the U.S. intelligence community, NSA remains the most secret of America's secret agencies. Its business is code making and code breaking: scouring the stratospheric realms of higher mathematics and statistical theory for secrets that would make their own encryption technology the securest in the world; and wresting out the information buried in the communications of others: Soviets, Warsaw Pact, Third World, friend, foe, and neutral alike—in short, the ultramodern realization of one of the primary tasks that governments have set themselves since time immemorial, of uncovering what others don't want them, or anyone else, to know.

A stupendous flow of data feeds this self-contained information-processing industry. It comes from listening posts and interception points all over the world; in spy ships at sea, planes in the skies above, and from satellites hanging silently in space beyond; from monitoring stations in Japan, Germany, Turkey, and the Arctic, eavesdropping on telemetry signals from the Soviet test-firing ranges; from a receiver in the back of a van in Berlin picking up diplomatic exchanges; from the mammoth Wullenweber antenna sprawled across the Scottish highlands like a twentieth-century electronic Stonehenge, with its four concentric rings of antenna masts, the outermost with a diameter of a thousand feet.

NSA also has listening posts near all four of the main satellite ground stations carrying international and commercial communications in and out of the United States— in West Virginia, Washington, Maine, and California—and at the microwave links that terminate submarine cables connections. The chatter of Soviet transport pilots, a home communiqué from the Kuwaiti ambassador to Algeria, a Chinese importer telephoning an order to a supplier in Malaysia—whatever the net snares is funneled through the agency's own supersecret communications network to a synchronous satellite position 22,300 miles above the equator, and beamed down at a pair of giant dishes hidden in the woods behind Fort Meade to become fodder for the computerized army of analysts, linguists, mathematicians, and code breakers.

The largest single entity within the sprawling organization is the Office of Signals Intelligence Operations, which comes under the control of the deputy director for operations. Its brief encompasses the entire spectrum of electronic eavesdropping from intercept to final cryptanalysis, and covers every level of secrecy from high-level, computer-encoded military and diplomatic systems to low-level radio telephone.

One of the most important of the supporting groups within "DDO," as this operation is known, is designated PO5. This is the agency's consumer staff liaison—NSA's point of contact with the various other agencies in the intelligence community. From this office the collected intercepts and decryptions that constitute the product that the whole awesome industry is set up to mass-produce are distributed to the end users.

Into this point, also, are delivered the "watch lists" of key words, names, subjects, or phrases, that the end users can flag to be plucked from the data streams by the batteries of tireless and ever-vigilant computers. The material filtered through the watch-list sieves can comprise not only the latest intercepts coming in from the worldwide catch, but also anything from the thousands of miles of taped records accumulated in NSA's voluminous archives.

A couple of days after the two strangers came to visit Cristo Aryskolis in Athens, a high-priority watch-list request came into PO5 from one of the smallest of NSA's clients: the Intelligence and Research Bureau of the Department of State. The request had originated from a Nathan B. Durnside, one of the assistant secretaries.

Durnside had for a long time been concerned about some of the U.S. policies toward the popular revolutions against established orders and other shifts of power taking place in developing parts of the world. In particular, the repeated insistence on trying to prop up unpopular and repressive regimes whose days were clearly numbered had not only alienated whole nations that had once looked upon the United States as the model for all revolutions, but had also left an uncomfortable number of its own citizens openly cynical of their government's motives and unconvinced of the sincerity of its claims to being upholders of the principles that the country had been founded on.

None of which was to say that he would have favored dragging the country into war over it.

Durnside believed that the primary function of a duly limited government was to protect the rights of its citizens. While intervention in the defense of others outside that society might be considered morally praiseworthy, it was not an *obligation*, however just their cause—and not least because going to war was more likely to entail the surrender of more freedoms than it was ever likely to gain.

But helping and supporting other peoples in their own fights against tyranny was another matter. Such external subversion—provided that it avoided outright falsification and renounced terrorism as a means—was ethically defensible and as American as the Fourth of July, since the colonists of 1776 would almost certainly have been defeated but for the money, supplies, and arms furnished to the rebels by France and Spain. In this light, one of the major weaknesses in the way the West had handled the postwar international situation seemed to be its failure—either through indecision or muddleheadedness over the principles that were supposed to guide policy—to proclaim and pursue such expedients openly and unashamedly. If governments were not prepared to show such an initiative, Durnside had agreed with certain acquaintances who had made themselves known in the course of the previous year or so, then perhaps there was room for others to try.

Durnside's request to NSA called for any references to a particular word, occurring during the previous six months within a context of ships and shipping, freight transportation, or weapons and munitions, or possibly mentioned in connection with Libya, Crete, Greece, the eastern Mediterranean, Zugenda, or to the words "Aryskolis," "Piraeus," "Embatto," "Lichuru," *Elaine,* or "Pyramid."

The word that the request specified was "Flamenco."

Chapter Thirty

THE MORNING AFTER THE ARRIVAL OF BARINDAS and his party at Tenyasha, Fallon found Jimmy Reid getting organized as agreed. His equipment had been brought in before dawn from the Nissan minibus, and he was setting up a receiver and scanning unit on a trestle table in a partitioned room in one of the rear chambers above the rockfall.

"Rested up, then, mate?" Fallon asked, pulling up a chair roughly nailed together from packing-case braces and sitting down on it reversed, with his elbows resting on the back.

"The man is reborn," Reid said. He put down the screwdriver that he had been using and turned to face Fallon more fully. "It's been a while. What have you been up to that you dare admit to?"

"Oh, this and that . . . So obviously George found you okay."

"No, he found me rather broke, actually."

"I heard things were a bit tough."

"George hasn't changed much."

"Does he ever?"

Reid took out a pipe and began searching his pockets for his tobacco knife. "So . . . what got you mixed up in this little lot?"

"Oh, it's a long story, Jimmy. It all started in a pub in Pentonville."

"Paying the rent, and all that?"

"Can't grumble. Well, you can if you like, but nobody wants to know, do they? So what was it with yourself? Didn't the business work out in the end?"

Reid pulled a face. "Not too well. It seemed fine for a while, but the costs and the taxes took a chunk. Then there were all kinds of new regulations coming out all the time that only the big boys could afford to comply with. That's what it was all about too, if you ask me. Keep the little chap in his place, same as always."

"That's too bad. But there should be a good wad from this caper if it comes off. Might even set you up for another crack."

"Oh, I don't feel so bad about it, Bern. At least I had a go. How many can say that? Once you've come to terms with it, it's not such a bad way to be: a contented failure. Leave all the ulcers and the heart attacks for the others, that's what I say. It's not worth it. At least I get to see the kids grow up."

Fallon grinned. "That's the way.... How are they doing?"

"Joanie's off to university this year. Going to be an architect, she says."

"We could do with some common sense in that line. What about Tommy?"

"Oh, him! Bright as ever. He's going to be an electronics buff too, by the looks of things. I tried to talk him out of it, but they don't listen, do they? Anyhow, what's the score?"

Fallon went on to sum up the part of the meeting the previous day that concerned Reid. Just as he was finishing there was a rap on the door. "Yes?" Fallon called out, rising.

"It's Sam. I've got Hardy with me."

Fallon unlocked the door and opened it. Sam Letumbai came in, preceded by a lithe, wiry African of about twenty-five. He was the color of ebony and seemed to Fallon to radiate a quality of primitive, unspoiled splendor that even the olive shirt and blue jeans that he was wearing failed to mask. Here, Fallon thought, was the noble, aboriginal African if ever he had seen one, a living tribute to an age of savage magnificence that had yielded man as its crowning triumph, and which now would exist no more.

But it turned out that he spoke with a Liverpool accent and his parents were Jamaican. His full name was Hardy Coal, which he assured Fallon was genuine—Reid of course knew him already from their journey to Tenyasha together with Barindas's party.

Sam had already explained the situation. When Fallon

had locked the door again, Hardy produced a folder filled with papers, and a wire-bound notebook. "Here're the schedules of bands that the military and SS forces use for their field traffic, and also the regular ZRF frequencies," he said, showing a sheet to Reid. "And this is what we've got on their call signs and formats, protocols, and code-word usage patterns."

"Good," Reid said.

"Got all you need?" Fallon asked.

"It'll give us a start, anyhow." Reid shuffled through the papers, gave a satisfied nod, and picked up the screwdriver that he had been working with. "Right," he said to Hardy. "Give me a hand to finish getting that power unit hooked up at the back. Then we can try some fishing."

Later, leaving Reid and Hardy busy at work, Fallon stopped by the school and found Candy coaching a class of eight-to-ten-year-olds to reproduce a somewhat disharmonic rendering of "Frère Jacques." Fallon delighted them by supplementing the lesson with a couple of cockney pub songs, which he left her the task of polishing up as best she could. He then walked farther up the valley to watch a mixed squad of guerrillas practicing with rifles and demolition charges.

Early afternoon found him sitting among some rocks by the plank bridge crossing the trickle that was left at the bottom of the gorge, alone apart from a couple of indifferent goats and some noisy chickens, stirring the gravel with a stick and going over everything once more in his mind to see how much closer the pieces were to fitting together.

At the center was Molokutu, installed as a client of the Soviets ten years ago, but now openly courting the West for all the dollars he could get. That added up to unreliability both ways, and therefore an unsatisfactory state of affairs from either side's point of view. But he was solidly entrenched, nevertheless, because of the three-way balance of the potential destabilizing forces around him: the army, the state-security organization, and the ZRF. The Soviet system achieved stability in the same way, through the self-regulating triad of the party, the army, and the KGB.

Now, what would be the effects of the various moves

afoot that were threatening to disrupt the balance? Fallon asked himself.

First, Embatto stages a systematic campaign to exaggerate the ZRF terrorist menace and convinces Molokutu and Thombert of the need for decisive action. As part of that action, he comes up with the novel proposal of sending in a specialist hit team to take out the ZRF leadership. But not specialists who would have links back to Moscow—he recruits them covertly in the West. At the same time, Embatto is secretly building up a sophisticated antitank capability within his own state-security forces. The ZRF have no tanks. Only the army does.

Fallon pushed together a pile of sand with the tip of the stick, nodded to himself, and knocked it down again.

So, if he moved with speed and surprise, Embatto would be in a position to paralyze both of the other two forces of the triangle: the army by eliminating its superior armor with his secret hoard of weapons and by persuading Thombert to send half of it away from the capital on a "coordinated offensive" at the crucial moment; and the ZRF by eliminating its leadership just when the confusion elsewhere would present the rebels with their greatest opportunity.

That was it. The clearest answer that seemed consistent with all the facts was that Embatto was planning to get rid of Molokutu—and no doubt Thombert as well, since his existence afterward would constitute a permanent threat—and take over the country himself.

Some questions still remained, of course. First, Lichuru and whoever was backing Embatto. There was still no pointer to who or what "Pyramid" was. Fallon's inclination was to dismiss the Soviets as candidates. For one thing, they would have resorted to far more straightforward and less subtle means than what was going on if their object was simply to replace one puppet who wasn't performing satisfactorily with another; and for another, Embatto wouldn't have had any reason to complicate things by going elsewhere for the hit team. But it had to be somebody substantial, nevertheless, because Embatto seemed sure of his ground. It was all very well for him to come to the West to avoid alerting Moscow to what was about to happen with one of their clients; but did he not worry that they might try and do something about it afterward? If so, he showed no signs of it, which suggested that he had good insurance of some kind. . . . But for now, Fallon could only leave it to the colonel and Infinity Limited to follow up on that side of things.

Second, even with the army scattered and its strength in Kinnube neutralized, Molokutu would still command a formidable capability in the form of the air force based at Mordun. It was inconceivable that Embatto wouldn't have taken that factor into account too, and included a means of dealing with it. . . . And suddenly the attack helicopters at Djamvelling took on a new significance. If this was the kind of thing that Elizabeth Bouabbas had been getting too close to, Fallon reflected, it went a long way toward explaining why she had ended up the way she had.

He nodded to himself and jabbed the point of the stick decisively into the dust. "That's it," he murmured aloud to himself. "It all fits. The only big question it doesn't answer is: *when?*"

The sound of someone approaching interrupted his thoughts. He looked up and saw Marie Guridan coming down the bank toward him. She had been conferring with Barindas and Letumbai and their staff all morning. "So this is where you're hiding," she called ahead. Fallon continued watching her curiously as she picked her way over the rocks.

"Thinking," Fallon told her. "One of the most valuable things you can enjoy in this world we've created with mass communications, information, and entertainment is being without any of them: peace, quiet, and solitude. And guess what? It doesn't even need batteries."

"What have you been thinking about?"

"Oh . . . this and that. What brings you down here?"

"I was going across for something I left in the minibus when we came in. . . . It was an excuse to take a break, anyhow." Guridan sat down on a boulder. "I've just heard about your contribution to the advancement of transcultural art."

Fallon blinked. "I'm glad. What are you talking about?"

"The songs that you taught to the children this morning."

"Oh, right . . . They'll probably be astounding tourists with them for years."

"What's the Bull and Bush?"

"An old pub by Hampstead Heath, in London. That's

where young people used to go to screw. A lot of cockneys were made on Hampstead Heath."

"And they sing songs about it?"

"Why not? It's one of the happiest and healthiest pastimes we've discovered yet: a good thing to sing about. I've had to listen to songs about things that were a lot worse."

Fallon started to wonder if he was getting a glimpse of another side of the intense woman who ran the ZRF's intelligence operation. But then her face became serious again, and she asked, "How are things going with the radio?"

"Hardy and Jimmy Reid are looking into it. I left them talking about header blocks and megahertz."

Guridan crossed her arms and gripped her shoulders, as if she were feeling cold. "You know, with the number of people that pass through here, we hardly expected Tenyasha to remain a secret forever. We've been fairly sure for a long time that Embatto has agents operating here ... but the kind of treachery that we are uncovering now is another matter. How anyone could betray us to a man like that is inconceivable to me."

"Why do you say Embatto, particularly?" Fallon asked curiously.

Guridan looked momentarily taken aback. "Oh, different things ... We plant information and watch to see where it surfaces. ... And then there's the fact that the government forces have never pushed farther than Owanden in their sweeps. It suggests that they've been trying to conceal how much they know, perhaps to avoid compromising their sources until it suits them to reveal otherwise."

"Such as by a surprise attack on this place one day," Fallon said, nodding.

"Quite."

"A lot of the world believes a lot of nasty things about the ZRF," Fallon reminded her.

"Yes, manufactured things that are picked up by the global media. But for anyone who is from here, it's different. They know what really happens." She stood up, maybe to release the exasperation now visibly building up inside her. The old intensity was back again, Fallon saw. She turned away and raised her hands appealingly. "But no, it's only the ordinary people outside who are misled.

This is the part of it all that mystifies me the most. We all know what Molokutu stands for, and yet it's the *West* that keeps him in power. His regime is destroying this country, and the people who matter in the Western governments *must* know it, never mind what their newspapers tell everyone else. Yet it seems deliberate. The conditions that are attached to the loans make any real economic or political progress here impossible. You're creating a tyranny that's propped up by welfare. Is that what the taxpayers in America want, who are being made to foot the bill?"

Fallon gave her a long, appraising look. Finally he said, "What I was thinking about when you arrived was, who's up to what in Kinnube, and what's going on behind it all? And what I reckon is this: Embatto's about to stage a coup to get rid of Molokutu and take over. That's why he set this whole thing up."

Guridan turned back sharply to face where he was sitting. "What did you say?" The question was mechanical. For a moment she just stared at him. Her face was set in an expression that showed shock and astonishment, yet at the same time was clearly not disbelieving. Fallon didn't quite know what to make of it.

"Embatto's setting up a takeover," he repeated. "Before he can do it, he has to take care of the ZRF and he has to take care of the army. That's what all this is about." He went on to describe his line of reasoning, recapping on the evidence and showing how it all fitted together.

Guridan listened with few interruptions, all the time regarding him unwaveringly through the large, round spectacles that magnified her eyes. "I can't fault it," she whispered, nodding slowly and distantly as she went over it again in her mind. "And it's consistent with all of our other information."

Fallon threw the stick aside, stood up, and stretched. He stared at the dry, crumbling rock buttresses and cliffs on either side of the gorge, and the frown on his face deepened. "So who is Pyramid? If it's not the Soviets, the most likely other place is somewhere in the West. But from what you've just said, Western money is also bankrolling Molokutu and keeping his regime in power—whatever his politics are supposed to be. Why should the West at the same time be both supporting somebody and backing a plan to get rid of him?"

And why Embatto? Fallon asked himself. He had seen enough already to have no doubts that a regime under Embatto would, if anything, be even worse in suppressing just about every freedom that the West was supposed to stand for. If the West were in any way sincere about its preachings, he told himself, surely the ZRF should qualify in every way as the *ideal* force to support as a replacement for Molokutu. But instead of supporting the ZRF, all the Western influence that Fallon was aware of seemed directed at misleading world opinion and secretly backing a man who intended to have its leaders assassinated.

So here were a few more pieces of the puzzle, and whichever way he tried twisting them and turning them, he was unable to bring them together in any way that made sense.

Chapter Thirty-one

IT WAS CROSBY WHO EVENTUALLY CAME UP WITH A way of getting some of the Russian technicians away from Djamvelling to supply George and Tam with a pretext for getting in. A couple of technicians usually went out to supervise the recovery operation if a helicopter crashed—especially if the machine was not badly damaged. The next question, therefore, was how to arrange a not-too-serious accident within a reasonable distance of the city. Tam proposed an answer to this one, based on a trick that he'd learned the hard way from the Viet Cong. Further discussion of the plan established that they would need a couple of uniforms as worn by Soviet technicians, likewise a couple of ID cards, and a vehicle of the type used by the Zugendan military, with correct markings, insignia, and registration plate number, which would pass before eyes that would have no reason to be suspicious.

The vehicle involved the most work but presented the least difficulty, since the Zugendans used various versions of the Soviet BRDM armored staff car with assorted modifications, and the ZRF had a few rebuilt models hidden away around Kinnube. A thorough paint job after a day of surreptitious observation and photography by two of Crosby's men hidden in a culvert at the last bend in the road on the approach to Djamvelling took care of that need. The surveillance also revealed that Russians passing through the gate tended to be haughty in their attitude toward the African sentries and were usually waved through with only a cursory check, often without the vehicle even coming to a complete halt.

A number of individuals in Kinnube who had been into the base for one reason or another—to collect trash, deliver supplies, perform repair or construction work—were traced and questioned. From their combined recollections Crosby was able to draw a fairly detailed plan of the layout. While this was going on, a batch of laundry went missing at the Mordun air base, which just happened to contain several Soviet fatigue uniforms; it just so happened that a lot of native help worked at Mordun, in the kitchens and for other domestic chores.

The IDs were copied by a forger in Kinnube from an original carried by a Russian technician who had been unfortunate enough to have been riding in a Zugendan army truck that hit a mine just over a month previously, all of the occupants of which had been killed in the ambush.

The morning after all the preparations were complete, an army unit mounting a routine sweep against the rebels in a forested valley about thirty miles to the south ran into unusually heavy opposition. Instead of melting away after a token exchange as was their usual practice, however, the ZRF apparently elected to make a stand and shoot it out, and from the amount of noise and commotion, they seemed to have concentrated a considerable force. Very soon, the army commander decided that he needed reinforcements. . . . But he also noted that the rebels had positioned themselves poorly, with a narrow, tree-filled pass as their only avenue of escape if the fight turned against them. But visible among the trees were several clearings large enough for helicopter drops. The commander radioed for support and specified the coordinates of the LZs.

A flight of six machines duly appeared. But the down draft from the first to descend set off a pressure-sensitive mine in the *top* of one of the trees by the clearing, destroying its rotor. The crash was from a low height and the damage modest. The ZRF force must have been smaller than had been supposed, for by the time the army ground troops arrived on the scene, they had indeed melted away. The soldiers secured the area accordingly, and shortly afterward a recovery vehicle departed from Djamvelling with an escort of several vehicles that included two BRDMs. A ZRF observer in the culvert by the roadside noted the registration and sent it via field telephone to a burned-out farm a few miles away that had been turned into a temporary paint shop. Shortly afterward, a BRDM with similar markings and the same registration number, and carrying a black driver and escort in state-security uniforms and two Caucasians dressed as Soviet technicians, came back around the bend and approached the gate.

The crew of the Russian 12.7mm heavy-machine-gun covering the roadway from a sandbagged emplacement opposite the guard post watched with bored indifference as Homassu, the ZRF driver, slowed the vehicle to a crawl. A corporal stepped forward and raised an arm.

"Troost us to pick a day when they're bein' bloody careful," George muttered, loosening the automatic at his belt.

"Just take it easy," Tam breathed in the seat next to him. Seymour, the bespectacled escort riding alongside Homassu, gripped the Zugendan-issue assault rifle propped by his knee nervously.

But then they saw that the guard corporal had held them back to let a despatch rider on a motorcycle through from the other direction. When the gateway was clear again, he waved them forward. "What's up?" he inquired in the local dialect, peering in through one of the two hatches at the front as the BRDM drew alongside the guard post.

"They had to come back for something else that they need," Homassu said. "I don't know... some kind of tool set." The corporal cast a cursory eye over George and Tam, who ignored him, and then stepped back with a lazy wave of his arm. "We'll be coming back out pretty soon," Homassu said as he eased forward.

"Uh-huh."

And so, a whole night of intense work with mapping pens and carefully blended inks by the forger in Kinnube had been for nothing.

Past the gate, the main barracks buildings and administration offices were set around a parade square to the right, with canteen, storehouses, armory, and a transportation depot clustered behind. Most of the activity visible was in this direction: a squad in shorts doing physical drill on the square; an instructor demonstrating the use of mine detectors to another group on one side; and drums being unloaded from a truck. Homassu steered the other way, toward the two large, olive-painted sheds that served as maintenance hangars for the helicopters, and the dispersal banked with earthen mounds for protection against ZRF mortar and rocket attacks.

With luck, Homassu and Seymour would be able to talk them through any encounters with Africans. The trouble would begin if they were accosted by Russians. However, the number of technicians at Djamvelling was not large—the helicopter aircrew were all African—and of those who were on duty that morning, hopefully most had been called out to deal with the wreck. In short, the chances seemed at least even.

The majority of the machines at Djamvelling were the Mi-4 "Hound" type, a basic twelve-seat military helicopter used by the Soviets since the 1950's in transport, ground-attack, and antisubmarine roles and supplied to clients the world over. The ones that they drove past had rear clam-shell doors for admitting small vehicles or artillery pieces, and were fitted with ventral gondolas housing 7.62mm machine guns and rocket-firing pods on external pylons. "Pretty standard stuff," Tam commented to George as they rounded the first hangar to be out of sight from the main part of the base. "Nobody's gonna make a big deal about covering any of this up."

On a pad away from the hangar were two of the smaller Mi-1 type helicopters, probably used for observation and training. In front of the hangar was an open concrete apron on which the machines that had returned from the aborted airdrop to the south had just landed. Soldiers in combat gear were stringing out in a loose gaggle heading back toward the barracks section of the base, while the pilot of one machine, in helmet and flying coveralls, was talking to a couple of mechanics and pointing at something in the engine compartment. And that wasn't so bad—with people around, the arrivals in the BRDM felt less likelihood of attracting unwanted attention. There was no sign of any Russians.

The doors along the front of the nearer hangar were open; the one beyond was closed. Homassu drove along the front of the first, where they could see two machines inside, one with its rotor and engine removed, a miscellany of parts and assemblies along the back, and some benches to one side where several mechanics in coveralls were working. They pulled up at the far end. Tam climbed out on one side and stood looking casually around, George

lifted out a large leather carrying bag containing assorted
tools and gadgets, while Seymour got out at the front.
Looking purposeful and confident as if he were in command of the place, George walked with Seymour into the
hangar and began poking around the helicopter that was
partly stripped down. Tam sauntered over to one of the
combat machines that had just landed and spent a few
minutes looking over it before coming in to join them.
Homassu had remained in the BRDM.

"Interesting," Tam said in a low voice. "And there's
the same thing on this one." He nodded toward the
machine that George was looking at.

"What's that?" George asked him.

Tam pointed at the brackets and fittings beneath the
nose and on either side of the fuselage, next to the
external pylons. "See those mountings here, and those
connection points? The armament that they've got fitted at
the moment doesn't use them. It means that it's rigged for
fast changeover to a different weapons system."

"Can yer tell what kind?"

"Something a bit heftier than what they've got now."
Tam squatted down to pull the plastic cover from an
electrical outlet in the fuselage, and examined the pin
configuration. His eyebrows lifted. "More interesting still.
This is U.S. pattern, not Russian."

"Bloody 'ell."

Tam straightened up, leaned inside the helicopter
door, and lifted a floor plate to trace the connecting cable
on the inside. "Gimme a medium screwdriver," he muttered
back over his shoulder. George found one in the case and
passed it to him. Tam began taking off the cover of the
terminal box. Seymour moved around to the other side to
make it less of a gathering.

"This is for priming something that's a lot more
sophisticated than the Fourth of July rockets they've got in
the racks outside," Tam said. He stepped back and slipped
the screwdriver into a pocket. "It's for handling smart
hardware."

Just then, one of the mechanics came across from the
workbenches at the far end and said something to them.
Although the words were unintelligible, the tone didn't
sound challenging. Seymour came back around and replied. The mechanic talked to him briefly. Seymour came

over to Tam and George. "He's apologizing for the delay on something. A part broke and is having to be remade. It will be ready tomorrow."

Tam hesitated to say anything. They were within earshot of the mechanic, and even if he didn't speak English well, he would surely be able to distinguish it from Russian. But George instructed in a firm, no-nonsense tone. "Aye, well tell t'booger it 'ad better be, else we'll 'ave 'is guts for bloody garters an' string 'im off top o' t'flagpole out there by 'is knackers."

Seymour translated as best he could, and the mechanic, evidently satisfied, nodded quickly and hurried away.

They moved to the rear of the hangar and had a look over the items at the back, which included the dismantled block of one of the Shvetsou radial engines, another engine assembled in a wheeled cradle, assorted rotor and gearbox mechanisms, and a dismounted gondola housing dual automatic cannons, but they didn't tell Tam anything new. There was an electrical store and workshop adjoining, but a superficial inspection from the doorway revealed only regular radio and navigation equipment.

They drifted toward a small door in a rear corner, on the side flanking the adjacent hangar. Crosby's map showed an area outside at the rear where scrap was brought to await collection. "What I really need to see is some ordnance," Tam said. "I wanna know what that fancy gear back there's for. But I don't see any."

"Maybe they keep it in with the rest o' the regular explosives," George said.

"That has to be the humps," Tam said. He meant the concrete bunkers, dug partway into the ground and topped by mounds of sand, that were sited on the far side of the base, away from the buildings and the helicopters, inside wire-fence enclosures with guards at the gates. He shook his head. "But if they've been making their own modifications, they wouldn't fetch something from that distance every time they needed to check something out. There's gotta be some test samples around here someplace."

Outside at the back of the hangars was a yard with racks holding stocks of metal rods, tubes, and I-sections, alloy sheeting, and other materials, and farther back an untidy jumble of twisted metal and junk machinery. While

Tam ran a cursory eye over the collection, obviously not expecting to find anything earth-shattering, George moved on to the rear of the other hangar, which also had a small door similar to the one they had come out of. The only difference was that this one was bolted and secured.

"What d'yer make o' this, then?" George inquired. Tam came over and looked. Their eyes met in an unspoken agreement.

"Well, we didn't come here to look at the sculptures," Tam said. Seymour looked around nervously but said nothing as George hoisted the leather carrying bag from his shoulder and Tam began examining the locks.

The door was steel-plated, with two hefty deadbolt locks set one above the other. There was no obvious alarm wiring, but then they wouldn't have expected the connections to any contact strips to be obvious. They didn't have time for niceties; the only other option was brute force and to hell with it. George produced a battery-powered drill and bored straight into each of the cylinders in turn with a half-inch, carbide-tipped bit. Tam extracted the tumbler pins from the wreckage with a pick, but the door still didn't give. Leaning with full strength on a two-foot crowbar, George forced the edge of the door far enough from the frame for Tam to locate the two bolts still holding it on the inside. The choices were either a lot of laborious working through the crack with a hacksaw or a swift but noisy attack with a wafer-thin, diamond-edged grinding disk.

There was what sounded like a compressor running somewhere inside, which would go a long way to masking the sound. "Fook it," George declared. "Use the wheel and let's gerron with it." The disk shrieked intermittently, and in less than twenty seconds the door swung open.

Tam led, George followed, carrying the bag, and Seymour closed the door and brought up the rear with the rifle. A passage led between storerooms and a machinery compartment from which the noise was coming. The passage opened into another running crossways, with doors opening into several workshops. Just after Tam had passed one of them, a hefty figure in a boiler suit appeared in the doorway behind. His eyes had barely begun to widen when George's fist cracked into his jaw. He buckled without a sound. George caught him and steered him back into the doorway and down to the floor as he fell. He closed the door and straightened up with an apologetic shrug. "Weren't really the time fer 'avin 'a chat, were it?" Tam turned away and resumed in the direction he had been leading.

At the end of the passage he stopped and raised a warning hand, then inched forward cautiously. George moved up behind him. Seymour hung a few paces back, covering.

Just ahead, the passageway opened out into the main-floor area of the hangar. A pickup-size flatbed truck was parked nearest them, and beyond it, standing in the center, was another Mi-4 helicopter. But instead of being armed with just the machine guns and simple rocket pods of the machines they had seen outside, it had four pods on an extended system of inboard and outboard pylons, each with four launch tubes, and beneath the nose a chin housing with its covers removed to show a rotary-barrel, Gatling-gun-like cannon mounted to fire forward. Scattered around it were some pieces of test equipment, a portable bench with tools and a vise, and a rack holding several projectiles, each five feet or more long. Another of the missiles was partly dismantled on the bench. Tam took in the sight and whistled quietly.

"Bingo?" George asked behind him.

"That's it," Tam whispered, gesturing with a hand. "Those are laser-designated ATMs. It carries sixteen of 'em. That cannon fires thirty-millimeter rounds. Armor Piercing Incendiary with a depleted uranium core—two thousand a minute. It can penetrate any kind of armor. That whole machine's a flying tank killer."

"What about 'im at back?" George muttered, nudging.

Only then did Tam realize that he'd allowed himself to become so mesmerized by the sight that he'd failed to notice the African mechanic at a bench by the rear wall, who had turned and was staring at them uncertainly. It would look too suspicious if they ducked back into the passageway now. The only chance was to brazen it through, Tam decided. "I'm going for a closer look," he hissed, and strode out across the floor with all the haughtiness he could muster. He reached the helicopter, stood looking at it for a few seconds, his hands clasped behind his back, and then stooped forward to make a show of examining the cannon.

And then an unmistakably American voice barked, "What's this goddamn Russian doing in here?" A stockily built, craggy-faced man in shirtsleeves stepped into sight from a recessed area behind some electronics cabinets and advanced threateningly. An African in a stained white work coat was behind him. Tam faltered and looked automatically toward where the other two were following; but George had magically disappeared, and there was only Seymour, looking confused where he had come to a halt halfway across the floor from the end of the passageway.

"Who in hell a—" The American's voice cut off in midword as George, who had ducked around the far side of the flatbed truck, stepped out behind him and felled him with an edge-handed blow to the base of the skull. For a split second Tam just stared.

"Coom on, then. Shit's 'it t'bloody fan. Let's get our arses out of 'ere!"

The African in the white coat had produced a pistol and aimed it at Tam, but he ducked away as Seymour brought the rifle up, and both missed in their haste as they fired. The African dived back behind the cabinets, but the mechanic who had been at the bench by the far wall was already making a bolt for a side door. Tam broke out of his stupor and ran toward a small foot door set into the main hangar door. Seymour wavered between following after Tam and shooting the mechanic, then tried to do both at once, missing again and slipping on an oily patch of floor instead as a consequence. Tam reached the small door. It opened. George, racing behind, scooped Seymour off the floor, and a bullet pinged off the door frame as they followed Tam through.

Homassu had seen Tam come out the front of the adjacent hangar and was already backing the BRDM across. "We're blown!" Tam yelled as the three of them piled in. "Gotta make the gate before the alarm gets there. Don't go crazy, though."

They drove back the way they had come past the other hangar, but as they rounded the end it was clear that they were already too late. On the far side of the base they could see uniformed figures running out of the guardroom and taking up defensive positions, while in the background others were closing the gate. Seconds later an alarm siren began wailing and the figures on the parade square scattered toward the periphery. Homassu crashed the BRDM to a halt. In the back, George and Tam had grabbed rifles. Armed figures were spreading out from several points to secure the perimeter. Others were advancing toward the helicopter area. Homassu backed up, turned, and drove around the hangar again onto the apron, where a dozen or so figures had now appeared. Tam fired a burst from the BRDM's rear side hatch and they ran back inside.

"What do I do?" Homassu shouted desperately over his shoulder.

They looked around frantically. Right in front of them were the machines that had recently returned, fueled up and with motors already warm. "What about one o' them?" George bellowed, grabbing Tam's shoulder and pointing. "We'll 'ave ter go oop. It's the only bloody way we've got."

"Do it," Tam yelled. Homassu drove to the machine farthest from the hangars and pulled up alongside. They all scrambled out. As Tam leaped up into the pilot's seat of the Hound and Homassu threw himself in on the other side, a knot of soldiers appeared from behind the far hangar and opened a ragged fire. George and Seymour dropped to a kneeling position and returned it, and the soldiers retired to cover. Farther back, an armored car was being brought up.

Then the engine of the helicopter spluttered, coughed, then roared into life. "Okay!" Tam's voice yelled through the din. "We're on our way."

George and Seymour piled in through the waist door as the machine lifted off. Tam skimmed the ground to keep the other machines in the line of fire for as long as possible, then made a wide turn out across the field and behind the earth banks of the dispersal area. Then the boundary fence was rushing at them, falling below the windshield only when they pulled up at the last moment. There was the cleared zone outside the perimeter, then bush and trees streaking by a matter of feet below, an open stretch of rocky grassland, and finally a sense of space around them at last as Tam followed the line of a creekbed between deepening walls, and the floor dropped away beneath.

"Bloody 'ell," George breathed, propping the assault rifle between his knees and wiping his brow with a handkerchief. "They never tell yer about this part of it, do they, them travel agents?"

"I trust that your curiosity is adequately satisfied, Mr. Czaryski," Seymour said shakily.

"It'll do for now, anyway," Tam replied.

They zigzagged for a while to confuse any reports that the security forces might put together of the direction they were taking, and then worked their way north a little over twenty miles to a village called Lommerzo that Homassu had lived in until a couple of years before. After circling the area for a while to check for any military presence, they landed in a disused quarry. Homassu immediately went off to raise help. The main worry of the others while they waited, after landing a state-security helicopter in Zugendan and Russian uniforms, was of being ambushed by a local chapter of the ZRF. Nothing disturbed the peace until Homassu returned with a score of villagers, however, and by nightfall the four of them had been fed, provided with a change of clothes, and the machine hidden away under camouflage in a steep-sided gorge choked with scrub and thorn trees a short distance from the quarry.

Back at the foundry, Crosby was given a message shortly before midnight and announced to an anxious Colonel Marlow that all four were safe and on their way back to Kinnube.

The four arrived at the foundry in the early hours of the morning. Crosby listened to their story and at once was for getting out. "State security have just had one of their bases busted into and a chopper stolen!" he expostulated. "They're going to be tearing this whole city apart. We have to get everyone out now."

Colonel Marlow, however, wasn't so sure. "That was a secret facility," he pointed out. "*Unofficially* secret: in other words, kept from Molokutu, like the ATMs they've got at SSHQ. Sφ what's Embatto going to do? He can't go charging around making a big fuss about it, can he? It would give away whatever his game is. He'll obviously be doing his damnedest to find out what he can, but when you think about it, he can't actually *do* very much. I think we can afford to sit tight."

Tam and George concurred. Crosby remained uncomfortable, but in the end he agreed to go along with it.

Later that day, Lichuru sent a coded message to Pyramid summarizing the incident. If reports from the Soviet technicians at Djamvelling of something secret going on there had aroused the curiosity of somebody in Moscow, then the intruders at Djamvelling might genuinely have been Russians, he suggested. But the greater fear that he expressed was that they might have been sent by the Iranians. If that were the case, the whole of the forthcoming operation might be compromised. He also advised that he would like to come to New York in person sometime in the near future to discuss the possible implications and to formulate alternate strategies for dealing with them.

Chapter Thirty-two

To support his "official" reason for being there, Fallon spent some time circulating around Tenyasha ostensibly to check on equipment, ammunition stocks, manpower reserves, training methods, and other matters that would be of interest to somebody intending to introduce a cadre of mercenary officers. Two days after Reid began introducing Hardy Coal to the scanning equipment that he had brought, Fallon arrived halfway through the morning at the armory. He told Sung Feng that one of the problems he saw was an insufficiency of heavier equipment for the kind of offensive that he had in mind. They especially needed longer-range infantry missiles to counter what Molokutu was able to buy from outside.

"You goddamn fuckin' light theah!" Feng agreed heartily. "Need maw big stuff. Awmah-piahcin' missaw, take out Morokutu tank. Need moh aiah-glound missaw, bling down lots MiG bombah. *Poom! Bam!* Prenty good kick ass then, you see!"

On his return to the lower part of the gorge, Fallon was intercepted by a boy who had been sent out to find him. Barindas wanted Fallon to come at once to his quarters in the upper chambers at the rear of the rockfall. Fallon arrived there fifteen minutes later to find Barindas waiting with Marie Guridan, Sam Letumbai, and Jimmy Reid. Reid pushed across a sheet of paper on which were scrawled some notes, a few figures, and a time of day.

Fallon looked over it quickly, and then his eyes widened as he realized what it meant. He looked up at Reid, who was watching him. "You've got him," Fallon breathed. "Christ, that was quick. I thought it would take a lot longer than this."

"Well, we must have hit lucky for once," Reid said. "It went out this morning: a ten-minute transmission in coded Morse. I can't give you the plaintext, although it seems to be based on a fairly basic cipher—not enough material."

"I don't suppose there's any way of telling where it came from?" Fallon said.

Reid shook his head. "I don't have the gear here to do a direction fix. From the signal strength it can't be very far away... but I suppose we'd have guessed that much, anyway."

Sam Letumbai waited for a few seconds, then shrugged. "Look, I don't know if maybe I'm missing something, but one possibility seems obvious to me. When we talked about what went wrong in London, we said that one place the leak could have come from was somebody who handles our communications, right? Well, the guy who does that here is the kraut, Tannerling."

There was a silence. Fallon got the feeling that Sam wasn't the only one that the thought had occurred to. It had crossed Fallon's mind even before Reid had finished speaking.

"There's nothing from this to prove that it came from across the way," Reid pointed out cautiously.

Sam waved a hand in a way that said yes, but why waste time on trivia? "Hell, it was in Morse. The guy's a pro."

Barindas looked at Fallon. "He does ask a lot of questions," Fallon said. "And for another thing, he doesn't fit. He doesn't have any ideological stake in this war, and I doubt if you're paying him the kind of money it'd take to make him work for blacks. That could mean he's here for a different reason."

"How do you mean, make him work for blacks?" Barindas asked. "He can be arrogant at times, I agree, but no more so than many others I've known who share his presumptions."

"I'm white," Fallon replied. "You haven't heard the way he talks when there aren't any blacks around."

"This still adds up to no more than unsubstantiated suspicions," Barindas insisted.

"But we're in a war situation," Sam said. "Sometimes waitin' until you're sure of everythin' is the way to guarantee you'll be too late. It's people's lives we're talkin' 'bout. What about Victor and Annette?"

But Barindas wasn't prepared to yield ground. "Yes,

lives—and principles," he returned, his voice taking on a sharper note. "We are talking about condemning a man. If we are contemplating the killing of innocent people merely as a precaution, then our methods are no different from Molokutu's and we might as well forget the revolution right now. What can we show in the way of *proof*?"

"Hell, I didn't say anythin' about killin' anyone. All we need to do—"

"It's all right, there's a chance I might be able to get you some proof," Jimmy Reid said, intervening before an argument developed. He indicated some papers lying in front of him. "Hardy's given me some intercepts of other illegal stuff that he's picked up in the past. As I said a minute ago, they use a pretty basic cipher. Now, if this German fellow is our man, we could probably identify the pattern of suitably structured information contained in an outgoing transmission . . . for example, something that included lists of numbers, especially with plenty of recurring digits."

"You mean we could plant something on him and then watch for the pattern?" Fallon said.

"Yes, exactly. But since I don't have any DF gear to pinpoint the source, all I'll be able to give you is a list of the signals that go out, and the times. But if there was some way of checking his movements so that we could correlate the times when he's alone in the radio room . . . See my point?"

Everyone looked at Barindas. He nodded, indicating that that would be good enough. "So I take it you would prepare some suitable material for him?" he checked, looking at Reid.

"Yes. I could start on it right away."

Barindas looked at Fallon. "Then, since you have been making yourself visible already as an intended procurer of mercenaries, perhaps we could use that as a means of conveying it."

"You'd like me to do the planting," Fallon said.

"Precisely."

Fallon pursed his lips for a moment. It seemed straightforward enough. "Sure," he agreed. "Let's see if we can get something by this afternoon." He leaned back and rubbed his chin as a further thought came to him. "In fact,

I might be able to take care of the other part that you mentioned too, Jimmy."

It was early evening when Fallon strolled into the motor shop, where Tannerling was busy in the partitioned section at the rear that he used as an office.

"You seem to have been very busy, by all accounts," Tannerling commented. "I hear that our fighting force is to acquire a new look."

"Well, that's what they pay me for," Fallon answered.

"What kind of new look do you have in mind? Will there be any radical restructuring of the units?"

"Because of the support situation, a drawn-out conventional campaign isn't the way," Fallon replied.

"I quite agree."

"I see something more along the lines of independently operating, fast-moving groups, highly trained for stealth and hard hitting."

"How large would they need to be, do you think?"

"I haven't really decided yet. I'd need to talk with Yolatta first, as soon as I get a chance."

"Who would train them?" Tannerling shook his head. "I can assure you that these people don't have the knowledge and capability."

"But the kind of people that I can bring in do," Fallon replied.

"What kind of people are they?"

"Oh, the usual kind that you'd expect, ex-professionals: the Legion, SAS, Special Forces and Rangers, some techs. . . . Probably a lot like yourself."

"Primarily European, I presume?"

"Mainly. . . Or American."

"Well, thank God for that."

Fallon looked at the German obliquely for a few seconds. "You don't exactly have the highest opinion of them, do you?"

"Is it surprising? I mean, you only have to look at the record. Before decolonialization this country was ordered and reasonably prosperous, and things were improving. But now look at the mess they've made of everything since. They think that all there is to being civilized is being driven around in limousines and wearing tunics with brass buttons on. All that independence has achieved is to give mediocre, little men a power over others that is utterly beyond their competence or intelligence, the ultimate expression of which is reversion to the kind of barbarism that we're seeing now."

"Why, ah ... Out of curiosity, what are you doing here?" Fallon asked.

Tannerling shrugged lightly. "Much the same as you, I'd suspect. It avoids the more normal kind of soul-destroying rut. And it pays. But getting back to the subject, how will transportation needs be affected?"

"It'll become even more important for the kind of fast movement that I'm proposing," Fallon said. "One thought is to set up a network of caches of fuel and spares at strategic points. I've got a list here of the map references that seem suitable, and the minimum that I think ought to be held at each. Could I leave it with you for an opinion?"

"Certainly."

"The other thing I've been looking at is the deployment of ZRF units in the field. I think they're spread out too far from the capital to give the urban population the sense of constant ZRF presence that we need, so I've drawn up some suggested changes. I'd appreciate your thoughts on how it would affect transport and logistics support before we involved Yolatta in it. Could I stop by with that tomorrow?"

"By all means ..."

The farthest outposts of the base were a half mile away in the upper gorge. Beyond, the floor became a steeply rising series of ledges and scree mounds, and the walls petered out into jumbles of crags and fissures. The guerrillas trained there in the daytime, but apart from when they staged a nighttime exercise, nobody went up there after dark.

Evading the sentry positions, which he had noted and memorized, Fallon moved silently and invisibly through the rocks and across the slopes a short distance above the center of the gorge. Even if Tannerling were to act without delay that night, he would still need time in privacy to encode the information that Fallon had supplied, before it could be sent. Fallon estimated that it would be at least midnight before the risk of missing anything became appreciable.

There was no moon, but the skies were clear and the starlight sufficient to give him bearings. Keeping to the deeper shadows and the folds of dead ground, he followed the directions that Candy had given him and worked his way higher up and around to the side of a cluster of large boulders heaped together in a neck of the gorge between broken walls of rock. Nothing had been visible from below, and it was only when he had reached a position slightly beyond the neck that he came in sight of a subdued red glow. He changed direction to come down from behind it. As he drew closer the sound of rock music became audible, turned low but carrying in the still night air. Fallon grinned to himself in the darkness and shook his head. Apparently the compulsion of youth to return a derisive finger at authority in any form imposed by the world of adulthood was universal. And when the gesture took the form of flouting the stern discipline of a guerrilla base, the appeal and the lacing of danger were all the more irresistible.

A low fire, built behind the boulders and out of sight from the base, turned out to be the source of the glow. The music was coming from a portable radio-cassette player. There were maybe a dozen or two of them that Fallon could see as he moved closer, teenagers of around Imo's years, perhaps on average slightly older. A few were dancing, but most were just standing or swaying to the music. Some kind of brew was being passed out in cans scooped from a large earthenware bowl near the fire. Their weapons were stacked within easy reach against the rocks on the far side.

Imo was to one side of the group with another youth and two girls, as self-assured as ever and doing most of the talking. They were so engrossed that Fallon was able to come almost right up to them through the shadows without their noticing.

"Pretty lousy lookouts you've got," he murmured from a few feet behind Imo. "I could have been Aloysius Molokutu himself."

Imo spun around in alarm, and one of the girls gasped. "Hell, we're busted," the other youth groaned.

Then Imo saw who it was. "No, I don't think so," he told the others. "This guy's okay."

"How'd you find us up here?" Imo asked, looking uneasy.

"Well, you don't exactly have to be a bush tracker."

"Are you on your own?"

"Of course."

Some of the others had noticed Fallon and were watching curiously, but they hung back from approaching any nearer. Then the one who was dispensing the brew from the bowl called over, "Could your friend use a jar, Imo?" Imo looked at Fallon uncertainly. An apprehensive hush descended all around.

"Any Watney's bitter?" Fallon asked.

"Fresh out of it," Imo replied.

"All right, then. I'll take whatever's going."

Imo grinned. "Yeah, another one over here," he called back. "Make sure it's the best."

"Yessuh! Comin' right up." The atmosphere relaxed, and the talk picked up again.

A girl brought a ration can across, half-full of a dark liquid that smelled slightly of aniseed. It was sharp and sweet with something of a dry undertaste, not unpleasant.

"So, what gives?" Imo asked.

"I need a favor."

Imo shrugged. "Any friend of Annette..."

"Can we talk?"

"Sure."

"Excuse us," Fallon said to the others. He put an arm lightly across Imo's shoulder and steered him a short distance away from the fireglow. Just then, a couple emerged from the shadows in front of them, holding hands. The girl was about to say something, then saw Fallon, clapped a hand to her mouth to stifle a gasp, and hurried past, giggling. The youth who had been with her turned and disappeared hastily.

Imo gave a sheepish shrug. "That's our lookout," he said in a resigned voice.

Fallon looked back at him. "Can you find some guys who are reliable and know how to keep their mouths shut?" he asked, speaking in a low voice.

"I reckon that'd be no problem."

"There's somebody that I want watched," Fallon went on. "But it would have to be low-key, without him suspecting anything. Could you handle that?"

"Is this legitimate?" Imo asked guardedly.

"It's for Barindas personally."

"That's good enough for me."

"Okay, it's Tannerling."

"Can I ask why?"

"Sure, but I won't tell you."

"Okay, I get it."

"Obviously I'd like you to handle it because you work close to him. Now, until further notice, I want a record of where he is and where he goes, okay? The exact times are important. Don't leave anything lying around that gets written down. Pass the findings back to Annette twice a day. If you need to contact me, do it through her. I don't want us to be seen talking together. That's why I came here. Is that okay?"

"When do you want this to start?"

"Right away."

Imo nodded. Fallon waited as he went back to his companions and led several of them aside. "The party's over," Fallon heard him murmur. "We need some help, right away."

Chapter Thirty-three

IN AUGUST 1956, THE WEST VIRGINIA STATE LEG-
islature enacted into law the Radio Astronomy Zoning Act
to provide a National Radio Quiet Zone as a sanctuary
from the electromagnetic interference normally encountered
in the proximity of urban areas as one of the consequences
of modern living. There are no high-powered radio or TV
stations in the zone, and airliners are routed around it,
eliminating the intrusions of their radars. For the electronic eavesdroppers of the NSA who were instrumental in
pushing the idea—along with others from the Naval Security Group and the Naval Research Laboratory—the static-
free site promised to be ideal for a project par excellence
that had been stirring the imaginations of theoreticians for
years: a gigantic radio ear, sensitive enough to pick up
Soviet radio and radar signals by detecting their reflections
off the surface of the moon. A go-ahead and initial funding
were awarded in 1959 by a Congress still smarting from
the Russian space "first" of Sputnik I, and work commenced in the remote Allegheny Hollow of Sugar Grove
(population forty-two) on what was to have been the
largest movable structure ever built: a 36,000-ton steel
dish, sixty stories tall and six hundred feet in diameter.

The scheme was eventually scrapped after running
into mammoth cost overruns and other problems, but the
intelligence community's interest in the site remained.
Twenty years later, by one of those curious coincidences
that never fail to arouse proverbial grins among the cynical, three other large microwave dishes, belonging to the
Communications Satellite Corporation, came to be located
at Etam, less than sixty miles from Sugar Grove. Through
the installation at Etam pass more than half of the commercial international communications entering and leaving
the United States, consisting of hundreds of thousands of

telephone calls, telegrams, and telex messages daily, pouring to and from 135 countries around the globe.

The first item that the NSA supplied in response to Durnside's request from the State Department was from an intercept logged three months previously, originally encrypted in a diplomatic code used by the Iranians, which the computers at Fort Meade had cracked apart and spat out in pieces a long time ago. From the source and destination codes, which had been identified from analysis of other traffic, the message was stated as being from the Iranian chargé d'affaires in Washington to a department of the Foreign Ministry in Tehran. In part, it read:

> AS FAR AS CAN ASCERTAIN, EXACT DATE OF FLA-MENCO NOT YET FIXED. MINARET HAS CONFIRMED TO BEACHBALL THAT A TRANSSHIPMENT OF WEAPONS CAN BE MADE IN EAST MEDITERRANEAN VIA SOMEONE RE-FERRED TO AS LOGGER. DISAGREE PLAN TO APPROACH HERON DIRECT. ALL RIGHT FOR YOU, YOUR ASS NOT ON LINE HERE. SUSPECT HERON'S MOTIVES. WILL CHECK FURTHER AND ADVISE.

Through further inquiries with the source, Durnside learned that the references to "Heron" meant nothing to anyone, but the name had been flagged for cross-checking. "Minaret," however, was a code name that had appeared in Iranian communications before and was thought to be somebody in or connected with the Zugendan government. One of the names on the list that had been tenta-tively assigned to it was none other than that of Robert Lichuru. And "Beachball" was known from other intelli-gence sources to mean the Welman-Forbes & Knaurrserchen group of trading banks, centered in New York and Zurich.

The details that Durnside passed back to Infinity Limited were the beginnings of a trail that began with a number of methodical people collecting and collating the kinds of information available to anyone in the New York Public Library from such sources as *Standard & Poor's Register of Corporations, Directors, and Executives*; Dun & Bradstreet's directory of businesses; *Nelson's Directory of Wall Street*; *The Wall Street Journal Index*; *Funk & Scott's Index* of industries and company activities, and the public information rooms of the SEC. Following this, several New York brokerage houses received calls from individuals seeking to make appointments with analysts specializing in certain aspects of commodity trading and investment banking. The findings uncovered pieces of an Iranian connection to WF&K that extended back over a number of years, which some people appeared to have been going to considerable pains to conceal. From there, the lines of inquiry began branching overseas.

Besides possessing an extensive information system of its own, Infinity Limited had fingers that found their way into intelligence services not only in the West, but also the Third World, and in several instances, even the Eastern Bloc. Operating in an atmosphere that was largely free from the internal and interagency rivalries that bedeviled the organizations of every nation, it was often able to assemble a more complete account of all the linkages and ramifications surrounding a given subject than could be gleaned from any of the partial pictures possessed by any one of them.

This ability had got Infinity Limited into the business of "information trading," as certain professionals in the trade, who knew nothing of the organization's background and didn't especially want to know, became aware that there were people around who had access to information in some extraordinary places. And they didn't threaten; they didn't blackmail; and they didn't want money. Merely in return for a little cooperation—which usually meant no more than supplying a few snippets that they were curious about for their own reasons—they would frequently help a baffled analyst or a harassed case officer break an impasse far more quickly than doggedly going it alone or sticking to the rules would have done.

The man who had always called himself simply "Ignazio" arrived punctually at 11:00 A.M. at the fourth-floor suite of Maximilian Hesse, commercial security specialists, in a recently completed office building not far from Milan's Central Station and the Pirelli Building. Hesse received him personally and ushered him through to the plush inner office with its expansive mahogany desk that combined a side extension for a computer terminal, contemporarily designed decor, and styled metallic lighting. They sat down in comfortably enveloping recliners finished in brown suede, by a backlit alcove housing several futuristic sculptures. Max proffered a cigar box. Ignazio accepted.

"Something to drink?" Max suggested.

Ignazio shook his head. "Maybe a coffee, black, one sugar."

Max leaned across to one side and used an intercom to transmit the order out, adding a Campari for himself. "Now?" he invited, sitting back in the chair and interlacing his fingers. "Don't tell me you've managed to come up with something already?"

In reply, Ignazio drew an envelope from the inside of his pocket and passed it across. "The address is in there, and also details of where the documents are hidden. The place belongs to an old girlfriend of his who surfaced again about six months ago. She's got a new name and hairdo, but that's all there too."

Max opened the envelope and took out the two sheets of paper from inside. A smile spread slowly over his face as he read. Ignazio watched in silence. "The legal owner will be very grateful," Max said. "And I am, also . . . and impressed." His eyes flickered at Ignazio with unabashed curiosity for a second or two. "Where did you get this?"

"Oh, it came out of a computer in Marseilles. Let's just say that the police in a number of cities have had their own reasons for keeping track of the girlfriend."

Max's smile broadened. He inclined his head in a mildly deferential gesture in a concession to leave things at that. "And there's no fee?"

"Just a favor, as I said."

"One day, I want to know who you're with," Max said. "I want to know who works in such an unusual way as this."

"One day, perhaps you will."

Max set the papers aside, leaned back, crossing one leg over the other, and steepled his fingers in front of his face. "Obviously, a contact like you can be an invaluable asset to someone such as myself. Tell me, can these people of yours acquire all kinds of information?"

"What we can acquire and what we might be willing to divulge are two different things."

"What kinds of thing wouldn't you be willing to deal in? Give me an example," Max invited.

"Oh . . . terrorism, for instance," Ignazio replied. "That's something we wouldn't give any aid to. Either the outlaw variety, or when it happens to constitute the government."

Max spread his hands. "But there you have put your finger on the problem yourself. One man's terrorist, another man's freedom fighter. Who decides?"

"We do," Ignazio replied simply, refusing to grant that there was anything to debate. "There are principles that distinguish between the two, which are very simple and very basic. Half of today's problems result from failure to apply them by people who should know better."

Max studied the other in silence, his smile giving way to a curious, more serious expression. Somewhere, he felt the stirring of fragments of thoughts he had once pondered and scraps of things read long ago, buried long since beneath the daily deluge of making a living. It was interesting. Maybe he would try to get to know more about this strange person when there was time. But for now, the deluge of making a living had to take precedence once again. He had an appointment for lunch and some calls to make beforehand.

He showed his palms. "What can I do for you?"

Ignazio sat forward in the chair and rested his elbows on his knees. "I'm interested in what you might be able to tell me about certain things that took place some time ago, now—about twelve years, to be exact."

Max raised his eyebrows in surprise. "Yes?"

"Before you set up your own company, you were vice-president responsible for security at Welman-Forbes and Knaurrserchen's European headquarters at Zurich, isn't that right?"

"Yes . . ."

"A series of meetings took place in Switzerland with some executives from the American side of the organization."

Max shrugged. "That's nothing unusual. Like most international outfits, they've got people from both sides going backward and forward all the time."

"Yes, but it also happens that certain individuals connected with the then-current regime in Iran were also in Zurich at the same time. We're trying to establish whether that was just a coincidence, which we very much doubt, or if there was some covert contact. If so, which of the names from the American end were involved, and if possible, what the common interest was."

Max looked uncomfortable. "Now we're getting into an area of serious professional confidences."

"I understand that."

"I don't know what the information might be used for."

"I hoped I'd given you some indication of where our values lie."

"What makes you think I might even have such information?"

"If special covert arrangements had to be made, you would have been responsible for making them."

Max drew a deep breath, then exhaled it sharply. "I don't know. . . ." He picked up the envelope and the two sheets of paper from the side table and held them out. "Maybe I should let you keep this until I have thought it over."

Ignazio waved a hand. "Keep it. Whether you decide to read it or not can be between yourself and your conscience. For my part, I don't think that the right to justice of the person who owns the documents should be conditional upon an affair that is between you and me."

Max smiled again, this time ruefully. "You don't seem to have many scruples when it comes to exerting moral pressure," he observed.

"None at all," Ignazio agreed readily.

They met again a day later and lunched together near the cathedral. "Yes, there were covert meetings that involved some Americans—not all of whom were from WF and K—and the Iranians," Max said. "But would you believe me if I tell you that I wasn't informed who the Americans were? I just made the arrangements. I dealt with one man only on that business. His name was Theobald Sorgen. He was from Zurich."

"He retired nine years ago," Ignazio supplied. "And he died of a heart attack eighteen months ago."

"You see. You know as much as I do already."

"Not quite," Ignazio said. "There were a number of references in classified communications and records to 'PGMs.' Can you tell me anything about them?"

Max sat back and chewed distantly. "Yes, that's right," he said at last. "They brought in an expert from Germany.

I can't bring his name to mind right at this moment, but I'm sure I could find it for you. Would that help?"

"I think it might help a lot," Ignazio said.

Max chewed another mouthful of pasta and refilled his wineglass from the carafe. "What are PGMs?" he asked.

"A rather strange line of diversification for a banking group to get into," Ignazio replied. "It's a more widely used term nowadays, but I suppose a few people on the inside could have been using it as far back as twelve years ago. Have you heard of the new, 'smart' missiles that can recognize a tank from several miles away and lock themselves onto it? It stands for Precision-Guided Munitions."

Chapter Thirty-four

"THERE'S NO QUESTION ABOUT IT?" BARINDAS ASKED. "You're sure, both of you?"

Fallon and Reid exchanged brief looks that left no doubt. "It all fits," Reid answered. "The pattern correlations, the confirmations that he was in the radio room alone both times. As far as I can see, it's an open and closed case."

There was a short silence. "So, what are we going to do about it?" Barindas asked.

"Why is there a question?" Candy spat. "Shoot him. And that's better than he deserves." She had brought the latest details from Imo.

"I'll go with that," Sam Letumbai said. "Hell, he got Annette grabbed, Victor killed, and who knows how much else. . . ."

Marie Guridan chewed on her lip and looked inquiringly at Barindas, like a gladiator waiting for a thumbs-up or -down from the emperor.

"I understand your sentiments," Barindas agreed. "And while I can't pretend to any disposition to tender mercies either, I do find myself asking if it would be the best way of serving our interests." He looked quickly from one to another. "If we eliminate one agent, they'll eventually install another that we'll have to go through the process of finding all over again. Perhaps we could use him to our advantage instead, by feeding him information of our own choosing—perhaps to assist Mr. Fugleman in his mission."

Fallon, who had been sitting silent and thoughtful throughout the exchange, looked up. "I'd like to try going a bit further than just using him," he said. "That's a bit too passive. We could do a lot better."

"How?" Barindas asked.

"By being able to *control* him, instead." Barindas looked interested. Fallon explained, "I'm wondering if we could get ourselves a controlled information channel, all the way back to whoever Tannerling reports to in Zugendan intelligence—who I think might be Embatto himself. Let me think about it for a little while."

The African girl stood back nervously, holding the hand drill. Gustav Tannerling wrinkled his nose and peered at the mounting frame of the alternator in the Renault that Barindas had arrived in. "What are these holes doing here?" he demanded. "You're supposed to be fitting a clamp. It doesn't need holes."

"Imo say that's the best way to fix it. He tol' me. He say them clamps never work how they s'posed to. Always come loose, then the cable pulls out there." She pointed. "He say the best way is make holes an' use bolts."

"Imo?" Tannerling's color darkened, and his voice rose to a shout that caused the others working in the shop to look around. "*Imo* does *not* give the orders in this place. Is that clear? *I* decide how things are done here, and nobody else. How many times do I have to tell you people something before it sinks in? Well, don't stand there. Take that imbecilic expression off your face, go and get another clamp, and fit it the way *I* showed you."

"Yessuh." Looking terrified, the girl hurried away.

"And when Imo gets back, tell him I want a word with him," Tannerling threw after her, scowling. His voice rose again. "*Did you hear me?*"

"Yessuh."

Tannerling moved around to the rear of the Renault to check a replacement suspension unit that had been fitted. As he straightened up and looked out across the shop, one of the other girls who worked under Imo's direction looked away quickly and returned her attention to the bracket she had been fitting to a tailboard mounting. Tannerling frowned to himself. For the last day or two he had been experiencing the uncomfortable feeling of being watched. He walked away to the makeshift desk to update a couple of parts lists. Outside, dusk turned into dark with tropical rapidity. Some workers left. Others arrived to begin the evening shift.

After a quarter of an hour or so had passed, he looked

out around the shop again. Everyone was busy. He glanced at his watch, then moved between the benches and partly dismantled vehicles to the rear, and past the generating installation and electrical stores toward the radio room. The only approach was along a short corridor, which meant that with the door of the radio room open, a person inside could see anyone coming. Tannerling had laid it out that way purposely. On the far side of the shop, the girl who was fixing the tailboard mounting paused to check a dimension on the sketch that she was working from. She also noted the time on the slip of paper folded inside.

Tannerling sat down at the bench in front of the transmitter cabinet, aging Racal RA17 HF receiver, and ancillary equipment. He put on the headphones and laid out the standard schedule of frequencies that he used to test the circuits. But after glancing one last time along the approach corridor, he took from the pocket of his bush shirt a sheet of already encrypted five-digit number groups and smoothed them out in front of him. Then he removed one of the crystals controlling the preset transmitter frequencies and replaced it with another tuned to operate in a band well separated from the ones used by the ZRF. He activated the channel and reached for the Morse signaling key.

Reading off the numbers and tapping them out had long ago become reflex. He was beginning to see now why Embatto had attached so much importance to Skater—which was Zugendan state security's internal code for Fugleman. The intelligence people in Kinnube had probably known more about Skater's background even before he arrived than Tannerling had been able to furnish since, and possibly they had been aware of the plan for bringing in a cadre of mercenary officers too. But the details that Skater had been working out with Barindas and his lieutenants were all obviously new and should prove invaluable. It had been an astute move on Embatto's part to realize that someone in Skater's position would naturally gravitate to and confide in a fellow white man for a second opinion. That much alone should be worth a hefty bonus.

Feeling satisfied with his work of the past few days, Tannerling finished sending his report and completed the transmission with a validation code known only to himself and Embatto, which confirmed the message to be genuine and not sent under duress. He received the correct acknowledgment in response and signed off.

It was only when Tannerling had switched off the equipment and removed the headphones that a narrow door at the rear of the room, which gave access to an enclosure containing emergency batteries and a charging unit, opened quietly. There was another way into the battery compartment, where cables ran in from the outside—a bit of a squeeze, but out of sight from the workshop. Tannerling was still looking away in the direction of the corridor and didn't notice. Then Fallon emerged fully and closed the door behind him with his heel. Tannerling whirled around at the sound and found himself staring into the muzzle of a Magnum.

"*Eine Kleine Nachtmusik?*" Fallon inquired lightly, eyeing the radio and the phones. Tannerling's hand moved instinctively toward the coded sheet on the bench. Fallon shook his head and moved the fingers of his empty hand in a beckoning gesture. "Slowly," he cautioned. Tannerling tensed for a moment, assessing the odds, then handed the sheet over. Fallon pocketed it and waved his free hand in an upward motion. Tannerling raised his hands hesitantly. Fallon relieved him of the Colt pistol that he was carrying, then checked quickly for other weapons, keeping his eyes on the German all the time and his own gun well back. "Now the crystal." Tannerling removed it from the set and handed it over. Finally, Fallon eased himself down onto a steel tool locker, one foot on the floor and the hand holding the Magnum resting comfortably on his other knee. "Okay," he said. "Let's talk."

Still visibly shaken, Tannerling lowered his hands. "Can I smoke?"

"Burst into flames if you like."

Tannerling took a pack of cigarettes from his other breast pocket, put one in his mouth, and lit it with a match.

"I take it that our mutual friend Julius is now a happily reassured man," Fallon said. "Good. I don't like not being trusted. It isn't a nice feeling."

Tannerling drew in deeply, held the smoke for a few seconds to absorb the effect of the nicotine, and then exhaled long and slowly. The charge seemed to help him pull himself together. "It appears I must congratulate you, Mr. Fugleman," he conceded grudgingly.

"Ta very much."

"What gave me away?"

Fallon shrugged. There was no reason to reveal everything. "I had to assume he had someone on the inside here. I couldn't afford to carry on making plans with Barindas without taking some precautions to check it out."

"So... why me?"

"You ask too many questions, Gustav. And you don't fit. What are you doing here? A pro mercenary from way back? You don't have any stake in the ZRF cause. So you must be in it for the money, which says it has to be the Zug government. Barindas doesn't have the kind of bankroll that would persuade you to work for blacks. On top of that, you overplayed the part. The mean bastard isn't the real you. He wouldn't have let GDF get away with it like that the other day. You come close, though, mind you."

"How could you be so specific about who?" Tannerling gestured in the direction of the radio.

"That you're with Embatto?"

"Yes."

"He's the only one with good information on what's going on here. Thombert might be nominally in charge of the military details, but Julius gave him the plan."

Tannerling frowned. "Plan? I don't know what plan you mean."

Perhaps not, Fallon thought. "Don't worry about it," he said.

"And who are you with?"

"If it mattered, would you expect me to tell you?"

"I suppose not." Tannerling drew on his cigarette again, still evidently nervous, and considered his options. There wasn't much to consider. "And so, what happens now?" he asked finally.

Fallon uncrossed his legs and settled himself more comfortably on the tool locker. "Did you ever hear of the Double Cross system that the British ran against your lot in the war?" he asked. "They picked up just about every one of your blokes as soon as they landed and turned well over half of them. That was one of the main sources of the disinformation that was fed back about D-Day."

"Well, what of it?"

"The choice they offered was, either work for us or we'll shoot you." Fallon shrugged in a way that said the rest should be obvious. "That's the choice I'm offering you." He said it in a nonchalant tone which conveyed that the outcome was of no particular concern to him.

Tannerling drew quickly on his cigarette again and stared hard at the gun in Fallon's hand. It seemed that he was already considering the proposition seriously.

"Or I could let Sam Letumbai's mob handle it in whatever way they saw fit," Fallon said, to help him along. "Some of them would just love to be let loose on you. There's a lady here right now that would happily slit your throat—and I can't blame her. Then there's Victor, who went to London and never came back."

"I don't know what you're talking about."

Fallon looked at him skeptically for a second or two, then shrugged. "No, possibly you don't. That's something we can talk about later. But what it means in the meantime is that you're on pretty creaky ice, my old china."

There was a short silence.

"If I agree, what would be your insurance?" Tannerling asked. In other words, why should Fallon have any trust in such an arrangement? It was an important thing for Tannerling to know. His neck depended on his credentials now.

Fallon replied, "Well, for one thing, your continuing good health is more important to you than a paycheck—and you know as well as I do that we're not just talking about right now, but longer-term too. If you agreed to a deal and then screwed us on it, they'd find you. And I'd imagine some of them could be very ungentlemanly, given a good reason." Tannerling didn't doubt it. Fallon made a brief gesture with his empty hand. "But why risk it? You don't care which side comes out on top at the end of all this."

"Why should you?" Tannerling asked.

"Maybe I don't," Fallon said. "Perhaps I just work for people who can write bigger checks than Julius." Tannerling raised his eyebrows. Fallon gave him an unsavory look. "Forget it. Nobody's going to be talking about any bonuses. Be grateful if you come out of it with your skin."

Tannerling thought over it again and nodded. "Very well. I accept. What do you want me to do?"

"Nothing for now, except give me all you've got of what you've been sending to Embatto. And obviously, everything that you send back from now on will come from me."

Fallon watched the German in silence, giving him time to assess the implications and waiting to see what he would do next. Tannerling just drew deeply on his cigarette again, held it for a few seconds, and then exhaled with a shakiness that was audible.

What he didn't do was say anything to establish whether Fallon was really working for the ZRF, or if he was enacting a charade to let Tannerling know that he had been blown, while at the same time preserving his own cover. And that told Fallon that Tannerling had not been a party to what Embatto thought was his secret—that Fallon was really working for him.

Which was how Fallon had hoped things would be. It meant that Tannerling was genuinely insecure. And that was Fallon's real insurance.

Chapter Thirty-five

WITH THE LEAK TO EMBATTO NOW PLUGGED—IN fact, controlled, which had greater possibilities—plans for the future could proceed. A council of war was held the next morning in Barindas's quarters above the rockfall to review the situation and decide the next move.

The first item on the agenda was the need for security precautions to be kept up, which everyone recognized—there could be no guarantee that Tannerling had been Embatto's only source. Scanning the radio spectrum was something of a hit-and-miss business that could by no means be guaranteed to catch everything—the net they were casting was of a coarse mesh that much might slip through. And in any case, as thousands of years of effective operation of the world's second oldest profession amply testified, there were many other ways of communicating information from place to place apart from by radio. The whole of the Glimayel region was swarming with refugees and displaced people, every one of them equipped with eyes and ears, and it was inconceivable that the authorities wouldn't have found ways of exploiting the obvious opportunities.

That was why Fallon had avoided confronting Tannerling openly. It also meant that restrictions upon the German's freedom of movement would have to be kept to a minimum, and even that much couldn't be made public knowledge.

"Obviously we can't put guards on him," Fallon told the meeting. "Just detail a couple of people to watch him from a distance. I wouldn't go any further than that."

"Any changes of the regular pattern could alert state security's signals operators," Jimmy Reid said. "Routine transmissions still need to go out at his scheduled times. And he has to send it himself—a good Morse man can recognize an individual signature."

"Good point," Fallon said. "We'll need to keep up a supply of material for him. Send it indirectly to Tannerling via Imo. We don't want to risk anything being seen passed too obviously. Jimmy and Hardy can handle any genuinely sensitive ZRF material using the facility they've got next door." Sam Letumbai, who was recording the proceedings on a pad, made a few notes.

Barindas had been listening for the most part and not contributing much to this part of the discussion, which concerned details that he was happy to leave to his lieutenants. When a silence descended, signaling that these ends had been tied up, he sat forward and placed his hands on the trestle-supported board that served as the conference table.

"Very well, so we have the German tamed and in our pocket. Now let's look more to the future and talk about how we are to exploit the situation. We now know that Embatto's real reason for persuading Molokutu and Thombert on the necessity of an all-out effort against ZRF terrorism was to draw the army's attention away from Kinnube and at the same time use Mr. Fugleman's people to neutralize us while he makes his bid to take over." He clasped his hands together and looked around invitingly. "The question is, how are our own plans affected in the light of this new knowledge?"

After a few seconds Sam Letumbai said, "Well, the way we've got it set right now is that when Boris goes back to the city to check in, he makes a case for bringin' over the hit team early, while he's still there—at least, the part of it that's comin' in through Kinnube. That way we'll have a bunch of them together there at the same time, and instead of waiting for anything more to happen, they can take out—"

Barindas pulled a face. "You know I detest these euphemisms, Sam. If we're talking about killing people, please let's be frank and say so."

Letumbai nodded. "They get rid o' him and as many else that's part of it as they can manage. So the coup never happens." He shrugged. "What's wrong with leaving it as it is?"

"Maybe we will," Barindas replied. "But I think this is a time to reappraise our options, nevertheless."

"You'd still be left with the war to win," Fallon mused, nodding.

Marie Guridan glanced quickly around the circle of faces, her eyes large and intense in her round spectacles. After the lull had persisted for a few seconds, she said, "I think we can do a lot better than that." The others looked at her. "What Sam has described amounts to turning the first part of Embatto's plan around on him—which was our thought from the beginning. But what we've learned more recently presents new opportunities. If we seize them boldly enough, I think we might have a chance here to wrap up the whole campaign."

Intrigued looks greeted her words. Barindas nodded at her to continue. She went on, speaking quickly and earnestly now: "Why stop halfway? Why not turn *all* of Embatto's plan back on him? If half the army will be remote from Kinnube and out of his way, it'll be remote from Kinnube for *us,* too. In other words, maybe the chance is there for us to create exactly the same chance for *ourselves* as Embatto thinks he's creating for himself."

Barindas began to smile faintly as he saw what she was getting at. "Go on," he said.

Guridan nodded. "When Thombert moves his force *out*—away from Kinnube for his offensive—we move *in* . . . not only our fighting units, but also us, the ZRF leaders." She gestured toward Barindas, Sam, and herself. "Bring in Haile from the war zone. We let Embatto go ahead and take on Molokutu's tanks, and we wait while SS and the army destroy each other in the city. With luck, Embatto might even get rid of Molokutu for us. Then, when the moment's right, we come out into the open in full force." She looked around quickly again. "We take the Radio Building and go public, as many key points as we can. It's as good a chance as we're ever going to get. We can't take another year of this attrition."

There was an exchange of questioning glances and raised eyebrows, punctuated by a few murmurs. Generally the reactions seemed positive. "What do you think, Mr. Fugleman?" Barindas inquired.

Fallon thought through the salient features again and nodded. "It's got possibilities. I get the impression that army morale is pretty low right now. Once things started swinging our way, we could see a lot of defections."

"That'd sure help," Sam agreed.

Then Fallon sat back, stroking his chin, and seemed

less sure. Barindas raised his chin in an unvoiced question. "A lot of it depends on Thombert sending enough of the army far enough away not to be able to intervene," Fallon said. "But exactly what does a 'coordinated offensive' mean? You see, he might interpret it as just stepping up activity everywhere, without any large-scale troop movements away from Kinnube at all. With the ZRF scattered the way it is, and its leaders never in the same place for more than a few days, the target is too diverse."

There was a silence, finally broken by Sam Letumbai muttering, "That's true."

"I don't see much we can do about it," Guridan said.

Fallon thought for a moment longer. "Maybe there is. . . . Use Tannerling, now that we've got him on a leash. A deception operation. We make them believe that the ZRF is disengaging from the war zone and regrouping here, in the Glimayel region . . . perhaps setting up a more permanent HQ in Tenyasha." Fallon gestured to take in Barindas and Sam as well, and his posture changed as he warmed to the idea. "In fact we could even make your arrival here the first phase of it. Something like that would give Thombert a tempting enough target to draw a large force. And it would also give a reason for the action in the war zone to slacken off when the fighting units move into the city. So we'd have an automatic cover for the real operation."

"How many men are we talkin' 'bout movin' into Kinnube, an' how we gonna get 'em there?" Sam Letumbai asked, frowning. "An' what would be their targets?"

"We'll work those things out with Haile," Guridan answered. "For now I'm just concerned with the overall idea. How do we all feel about it?"

Barindas was staring distantly at the far wall of the cave. "Yes, it sounds feasible to me," he pronounced. "And it does have a certain appeal of justice about it. Very well, let's begin looking into it in detail right away. And we need to involve Haile as soon as possible. Sam, will you locate him and take care of that side of it?" He looked at Fallon, who had sat back abruptly and was scratching the back of his head in a mystified fashion. "You seem unsure of something, Mr. Fugleman."

"I'm not sure what part my people are supposed to play now," Fallon said. "By the time Embatto makes his move, they'll have dispersed into the bush and I'll be out

of the country. So we can't be in Kinnube to take care of
the top management."

The others seemed to have missed the implication
also. "Hmm, true," Barindas declared. "But I think you've
done enough for us already. Let you and they carry on
exactly as you have just described. It would continue the
decoy operation admirably. We will take care of what's left
of the opposition. It is our war, after all."

Possibly in honor of Barindas's presence, somebody
had produced a case of American Michelob beer. Fallon
secured himself a six-pack along with some cheese, butter-
substitute spread, crackers, and a can of pilchards, and by
late night had retired to his bunk in the screened section
behind the officers' area to relax. Marie Guridan appeared
in the doorway to find him propped on his cot, contented-
ly munching between mouthfuls of beer and browsing
through a book. He set it aside when he saw her, sat up,
and swung his legs aside to make room.

"Hi." She pushed aside the mosquito netting hanging
across the doorway, came in, and sat down on the other
end of the cot.

"Have a beer and a bite. Let's make it a party," Fallon
said. He passed her one of the cans and a mug from a shelf
fixed to the partition. She half-filled it with beer and
picked up the book he had put down.

"Biology? I didn't think this was like you. You don't
have to be this particular, you know. Maybe you're starting
to take Mr. Hannegen too seriously."

"Oh, that's just me. Always curious." Fallon raised the
can he was holding and drank. "It brings home how much
there is to life that you never even get a chance to know
about. When I remember all the things I was going to do
one day, years ago now, and never got around to. Why
does time seem to go faster as you get older?"

"They say time goes faster when you're enjoying
yourself too," Guridan pointed out. "So maybe that's
telling us something."

"Maybe . . . So how's it all going?"

"They're still talking about target priorities to go for in
the city. Mordun might present a problem. But this is
where we really need Haile. Barindas wants Sam to go and
meet him in the war zone to update him on what's

been happening. We need to get Haile out—either here or to Kinnube, depending on what the time scale is."

"We don't know that yet," Fallon said. "It's to be agreed when I report back to Embatto in Kinnube."

"Anyway, that's what they'll want to talk about tomorrow. I stopped by to tell you."

"Thanks. I'll give it some more thought."

She hesitated for a moment, looking at him uncertainly. "There was something else too."

The suddenly confidential note in her voice caused Fallon to raise an eyebrow as he looked at her over the top of the can and chewed a mouthful of pilchard. "What?"

"Have you noticed anything odd about Candy in the last day or two?"

Fallon's brow knitted into a frown. "Odd? How do you mean?"

"I'm not sure. She seems withdrawn, somehow."

"I can't say I've really noticed."

Guridan bit her lip. "I think it might have something to do with Tannerling. She didn't take at all well to the thought of him still walking around free like that."

Fallon shrugged. "Well, she has got a pretty good reason to feel less than what you might call charitable in Gustav's direction, let's face it."

"You . . . think she'll be all right?"

"Oh, she's a good soldier. She might not like it, but she'll live with it. You worry too much."

Guridan smiled sheepishly. "Perhaps you're right. This kind of work makes people see ghosts everywhere. . . . I was just concerned."

"That's okay. I only wish that more people were, more often," Fallon said.

Chapter Thirty-six

"THIS HEAT TAKES SOME GETTING USED TO AFTER England, I don't mind telling you," Jimmy Reid said. "Phew! It's like walking around wrapped in a wet blanket."

"We're near the rainy part of the year," Fallon told him. "It gets a bit close."

"What we call rain, anyhow," Sam Letumbai said from where he was standing on one side, looking at a large-scale map of Zugenda pinned to the wall. "Do people there really get tired o' havin' rain for weeks at a time?"

"It's all right for the likes of George," Reid grumbled. "I suppose he's tucked away in a pub back there somewhere." He leaned back in his chair and gazed at the wall wistfully. "God, what wouldn't I give for a pint of bitter right now!"

Fallon hadn't said anything about George's being in Zugenda. For now, Reid didn't need to know. They were sitting in front of the equipment that Reid and Hardy Coal had set up in the new radio room. He gestured at the columns of numbers on the sheet of paper that Reid had in front of him. "What have we got? Anything new?"

"Nothing that'll change your way of life."

There was the usual background of signals traffic between the base and various units out in the field, groups training or out on maneuvers, and calls up and down the valley to Owanden. But these took place in well-defined frequency bands. It was anything irregular—outside the standard channels, and therefore, presumably, having something to hide—that Reid was more interested in. But he hadn't learned a lot.

"I say we shouldn't wait for you to go back to Kinnube before we start moving the troops in," Sam said. "Closer it gets to the time, the more Embatto's gonna be tightenin' things up there. The time to move in is now, before the door starts closin', not after."

"Do you want to move Barindas and the others there now too?" Reid asked him.

"Why not? Now he's been seen at Tenyasha, it kinda backs up the story that this is where the HQ's gonna be. The longer Embatto's people carry on thinkin' he's here, the less they're gonna be lookin' in other places. So the better the chances we'd have of movin' him there."

"Makes sense," Fallon agreed. He got up and moved a few paces away from the equipment at which Reid was sitting. "But that's not what's bothering me." He stared at a calendar illustrated by scenic views of England, pinned to the pressed-chip message board next to the map. The calendar was six years out of date, but Reid liked the pictures. They had been going over the plan from the day before, now that they'd each had time to think things over. It still didn't feel quite right, somehow. Fallon was trying to put his finger on why.

"What we need to do is mount some kind of misinformation operation," he told them, turning. "Now that we've got a high-level controlled source, we need to discredit all the rest. Then we can feed Embatto anything we want to."

"You mean about makin' him think that we're movin' our HQ operation here?" Sam said.

"Right."

"What kind o' misinformation d'you mean?"

"I'm not sure."

Over at the equipment table, Reid produced his pipe, clenched it between his teeth, and then went into the inevitable routine of patting the pockets of his bush shirt to locate his tobacco knife. "Suppose we were to put out a false story that the HQ will be somewhere else . . . ?" he said at last. His voice trailed away for a moment while he explored that line; then he nodded to himself. "But at the same time, we make sure that enough other information also finds its way back for Zug intelligence to deduce that it's really going to be Tenyasha—which is what Tannerling is already telling them. So they'd interpret the other version as an attempt by us to mislead them, which any other sources they might have operating here were taken in by. . . ."

Fallon was already nodding. "But not brother Gustav. So *his* credibility is established. They buy the Tenyasha story, and that keeps them busy while we're installing Barindas and his merry men in Kinnube. . . . Yes, I like it, Jimmy. That's exactly the kind of thing I think it needs." He turned to look at Sam. "What do you think?"

"You don't think it might be complicatin' things too much?"

"No. I think it's what the plan needs."

"So, what's this other information that's s'posed to find its way back to make 'em figure out that the other story's wrong?"

"I don't know yet," Fallon replied. "I mean, Christ, we've only just thought of it."

"Let me think it over for a while too, then," Sam said.

Fallon moved closer to the map and studied it, then raised an arm in a sweeping motion. "Okay, then, Sam. But what we need while you're thinking is another place that an HQ could believably be set up at, somewhere preferably on the other side of the war zone. That would make it look as if we'd picked it deliberately to draw attention as far away from Tenyasha as possible. Any ideas?"

Sam turned back to the map and looked at it for a while. Then he raised a hand and with a fingertip traced a circle around a small area of the northwest, dark with closely spaced and richly convoluted contour lines. "My suggestion'd be somewhere like that," he replied. "It's called Boake Rift—an out-of-the-way part of Kashinga province, up here to the north. Rough, dry country. Mountains. Lots o' places where somebody might try hidin' a base in."

Fallon leaned forward to peer at the region that Sam had indicated. "Yes, it looks rugged enough, all right. And another thing I like about it is—" He broke off and looked around as he caught a glimpse of a figure passing by on the far side of the netting across the door. "There's Barindas. Let's see what he thinks about it before we go any further." He crossed the room quickly and drew the net aside to poke his head out. "Jovay, have you got a minute? We've been talking about something that—"

But the figure that had turned and was looking back

at him in surprise was not Barindas, but Mamu. "Yes?" he said.

Fallon, however, didn't answer, but was looking at him strangely.

"Did you want something, Mr. Fugleman?" Mamu asked.

"I could have sworn...Come here for a second," Fallon said.

Mamu retraced his steps and stopped in the doorway, looking puzzled. Fallon stood in front of him, stretching his hands out and measuring the width of Mamu's shoulders as if sizing him up for a suit, and then stepped back a pace and looked him up and down from head to foot and back again.

"Please, what is going on?" Mamu demanded.

"It's amazing," Fallon said.

"What's so amazin' 'bout Mamu?" Sam asked.

Fallon looked back over his shoulder. "I think we might be able to keep everyone thinking that the ZRF leaders are holed up in Tenyasha for a lot longer than you hoped, Sam," he said. He turned back to Mamu, who was looking at them bemusedly. "Mamu, we're going to make you a star," he said. "Come in, sit down, grab yourself a beer, and let's talk."

Chapter Thirty-seven

IN THE CITY OF MUNICH IN SOUTHERN GERMANY, Dr. Hans Möller stopped dead on the path halfway across the lawns in front of the university's geology-department building, and stared openmouthed. His small stature, bald dome, and wide eyes, rounded by the effect of his rimless spectacles, together with the tweed jacket and check shirt, made him almost a caricature of a scientist.

"Missiles? But I am a petrologist. I specialize in the study of minerals and metal-bearing ores. What makes you imagine that I would know anything about missiles?"

The man called Ignazio, who had arrived from Milan that morning, replied, "Your name was given to me as an expert who was involved in some confidential dealings that involved certain American-European financial interests."

Möller shrugged. "Yes, I divide my time between teaching here at the university and acting as a private consultant to industry, particularly in the mining field— although I haven't done much of the latter for some time now, since I am involved in a considerable amount of private research and writing these days. What of it?"

"According to my information, you have also been consulted for expert advice concerning PGMs."

"Platinum Group Metals, yes . . . But you still haven't told me what this has to do with missiles. Are you sure there isn't some kind of mistake?"

Ignazio stood holding his briefcase, and stared hard.

So simple an error, so simply put right. Yet neither he, nor any of those that he had spoken to, nor presumably anyone beyond them, had thought twice about it. He sighed and turned away. They resumed walking. Möller gave him a puzzled look. "Forget about missiles," Ignazio said heavily. "Yes, there was a mistake. You don't have to worry about it. But tell me about the Platinum Group Metals instead. I'm still interested."

"Platinum, of course, is rarer than gold and more useful commercially," Möller replied. "The rest of the group comprises palladium, rhodium, iridium, osmium, and ruthenium, so called because they usually occur together. Their main uses are as catalysts, for example automobile converters, oil refining, and chemical processing. Also, electronic switching equipment and components."

"Are they all valuable?"

"Yes, because of their extreme scarcity."

"Where do you find them?"

"The world's production is practically concentrated in two countries: the USSR and South Africa. That makes the West's position rather precarious in the eyes of some authorities in the field. An alternative to redress the situation would be ocean extraction, for example, for which the technology is being developed . . . but we're talking long-term now."

Ignazio's pace slowed as the implication registered. "Or mightn't another solution be to develop a new source?" he asked.

"Yes, if you could locate some worthwhile deposits."

"If you did, would it be a valuable asset to whoever controlled them?"

"Oh, extremely so—politically as well as in pure commercial terms."

Ignazio stopped again and looked at Möller directly. "The situation that interests me concerns some meetings that took place in Switzerland about twelve years ago. They involved people from both the European and American sides of the WF and K banking group, and some Iranians. They also included yourself." He paused for a second, and then added as a pure guess, "Among the things discussed were certain areas of what is today the republic of Zugenda."

Möller's manner at once became wary. "Who told you this?"

"It was put together from a number of sources."

Möller gave a humorless snort. "If they're also the sources that told you it had something to do with missiles, I'd have my doubts about them if I were you."

"Very well, then, you tell me the story."

"I haven't said that I know anything about it."

Ignazio could see no choice but to try the direct approach. "You've read the papers, seen the news. You know the kind of things that are going on there today," he said. "A lot of misery, a lot of suffering, a lot of dying. I'm with an organization that's trying to do something about it."

"Well, there are enough volunteer groups advertising for funds. Send your money to them."

"That isn't the way to help, as I think you know. After all, you've seen the place yourself, haven't you?"

"That was twelve years ago. All I—" Möller stopped, realizing how he had been trapped.

Ignazio pressed his advantage. "You were there to carry out a survey—for the people I just mentioned, right?"

"I'm beginning to find this offensive. Kindly leave me alone."

"Oh, let's not be too hasty," Ignazio urged. They resumed walking once again. He went on: "The problem is political at its roots. To be any good at all, the solution has to be a political one. Therefore we need to know the background from which the present tragedy developed. It's twelve years ago, now. Whatever the survey was for, the result hasn't materialized. What does it matter to you today? Just a dead and forgotten report somewhere, paid for and filed away. I am concerned with people whose lives are things of the present. All I'm asking for is some information. It can't possibly make any difference to you now. But the outcome could make a lot of difference to them."

They ascended the broad steps outside the geology building and passed through the main doors into a large foyer area that included a collection of rocks and ores in glass display cases. Möller stopped with his hands braced on a brass guardrail, staring at an exhibit of malachites, cheyssilites, and agates. "That was a private assignment," he said finally. "I was generously paid to keep the results confidential. And that much is more than I should be telling you."

The survey must have turned up something, Ignazio told himself, otherwise there would have been nothing to be confidential about. "A new find, that would surely have been of considerable interest to your colleagues as well as to the scientific world in general," he said. "And you weren't allowed to publish a paper on it? Didn't that strike you as odd?"

"I've already told you, I had accepted a generous retainer." Möller showed his teeth briefly. "I presume that interests such as those we are talking about have their motives. Anyway, I didn't make it my business to question them then, and I have no desire to do so now."

"So the findings were not insignificant," Ignazio pressed.

Möller looked at him balefully for a second. "Fabulous," he murmured. "Somebody will end up dominating the whole north-central region of Africa from there one day. They're just biding their time. *That* is what's at the back of your political situation, Mr. . . . Ignazio." Möller turned away abruptly, as if regretting having spoken. But Ignazio moved around and addressed him from the other side.

"Do you still have a copy of the report?"

"No. There were only four, I handed them all over, and I had to sign a confirmation that there were no others. And if there were another, I wouldn't let you see it. We're dealing with people who can be rough." He began walking quickly toward the door leading through to the main corridor on the far side of the foyer. Ignazio caught up with him a few seconds later.

"What makes you say that?"

"It doesn't matter."

"It might to me."

"That is your own affair. I've already said as much as I'm prepared to. And now, good day."

Ignazio caught the door into the corridor to prevent Möller from passing through. "Just one more question, then."

Möller sighed. "What?"

"Which executives from WF and K were involved? How many of their names can you tell me?"

"None. I met only two of them personally, and one of them is now dead. They were introduced to me by first names only, which I have no doubt were fictitious. And even if I did know the name of the other, I wouldn't tell you. I don't like being pestered like this, Mr. Ignazio, and I don't like you. I'm not sure that you are getting the message."

"Could you identify him from a photograph, perhaps? I happen to have some with me."

"No. Go to hell." Möller began walking again. So did Ignazio.

"Very well, forget that we said anything about WK and K, or anything that took place twelve years ago. I could have told you that I am from a law firm and that we are simply trying to trace a man that we believe worked for one of your client companies because he has been left some money. Would you please oblige by looking at some pictures and seeing if you recognize any of them?"

"Don't be absurd. I know you're nothing of the kind."

Ignazio caught Möller's sleeve and checked him again. His tone lost its flippancy suddenly and became very serious. "Before you go marching away like that, I advise you to reconsider your position," he said in a low voice. "It would not look good for you if the chief executive of Welman-Forbes and Knaurrserchen in New York were to receive a personal letter asking for more details concerning some interesting information that had been blabbed by a certain doctor of petrology in Munich, now, would it? Especially since, as you intimated, they can react somewhat unpleasantly if the situation demands. . . ." Möller hesitated and blanched visibly. Ignazio went on, speaking in a low, urgent whisper, "All I want is an identification, if you can. Whatever happens after that, I promise you that your name won't come into it. It's no more than a policeman might ask, who is trying to find one of your former students. What have you got to lose?"

Möller bunched his mouth. His face took on a purple hue and seemed to swell. For a few moments he struggled to keep his indignation under control, and then nodded. "Let's go up to my office," he said tightly.

Chapter Thirty-eight

IT WAS LATE EVENING IN THE VALLEY OF TENYASHA. In the glow of the setting sun reflecting red off the dry rocks of the gorge, the familiar slim, white-bearded figure with dark glasses and white hair showing beneath his red cap strode along the track crossing the slope below the main general-quarters cave. He was accompanied by Austin, Roger Parnum, and a few aides. Some of the people working or resting around the cave entrance stopped what they were doing and looked up to watch their leader pass. When some children ran down toward the track to see him more closely, he stopped walking and looked at them. His party stopped with him, some of them exchanging uneasy glances. The children came to a confused halt and stood, awed. The two women who had come down after the children slowed their pace and hesitated. When they saw that he was smiling, they moved to come nearer, but Austin and a couple of the men with him stepped forward to keep them at a distance. The leader, however, motioned for them to stand back.

"It's all right," he said in a voice that carried. "They offer their lives. The least we owe them in return is a little courtesy. If we must be afraid in the heart of our own camp, all is lost anyway."

The women came closer with the children. Seeing this, more adults from above came down, and soon a small cluster had formed around the group, waving and calling out affirmations of loyalty and support. Some shook his hand and exchanged ZRF slogans.

"What do we want for Zugenda?" he asked them.

"Freedom to think! Freedom to speak! Freedom to work!"

"What are we fighting for?"

"The freedom to be people!"

He held a hand high, giving them the thumbs-up sign that had become another of Barindas's personal symbols, and went on his way, followed by a forest of extended thumbs and an outbreak of cheering, joined in by others watching from higher up.

As the party walked away, Austin turned his head and gave the leader a strange look that was a mixture of admiration and relief. Parnum leaned closer and murmured, "Not bad, mate, not bad."

"How long did he say this would go on?" was the quavering reply.

"If we can't hack it, this is the time to find out, not later," the Australian said.

"*We?* I fear I must educate you to some of the minor realities of this situation."

"It'll work out okay. You worry too much."

In the chambers above the rockfall, Barindas, in a loose-sleeved smock and sandals, cradled a mug of strong, black coffee and watched as Fallon turned from the map and schedule of places, dates, and times pinned to a wall board. Jimmy Reid was with them, also Sam Letumbai, Marie Guridan, and a few of Barindas's lieutenants.

It was not an unusual practice to allow an unmasked hostile agent to continue operating without interference, but making sure that he had access only to controlled information. It saved the trouble of having to track down an unknown replacement if the first were apprehended, and it provided a convenient way of misleading the other side. "But it means that the agent has to believe that the information he's passing back is genuine," Fallon said. "We need one who's been fully turned: willing to send information that he knows is false. And now, we've got one."

"And you are confident that he will cooperate?" Barindas checked.

"Yes. He doesn't have any ideological stake in the outcome of all this. Anyone could be watching him. His only concern is to keep his skin in one piece."

Barindas got up from where he had been sitting, stretched his arms to relieve them of cramp, and moved over to a crate by one wall, where a pot of tea was standing. "Complications, always complications." He sighed, pouring himself a measure into a ceramic mug. "You know, it's a funny thing," he said over his shoulder to the company in general. "The beginning and the end of life are such simple, straightforward affairs. It's the part in between that involves all the complications. Why can't people live as simply as they come and go?"

Fallon grinned and stood up to get a cup for himself and one for Reid. "I'm not so sure about that. It's always amazed me how complicated some people can make the beginning part too."

A buzzer sounded by the table at which Sam was sprawled. He touched a button to activate an intercom. "Yep?"

"Barindas and the others are back." It was the guard from the post at the end of the approach passageway. The rule was that nobody was admitted without permission from inside.

"I wonder how it went," Guridan said. Barindas waited. Fallon stared expectantly toward the door as the sounds of footsteps and voices approached.

Parnum entered, followed by Austin. Both were smiling broadly. Behind them were more of Barindas's staff, and among them, Mamu. . . . But he didn't look like Mamu. His hair was bleached white, he had acquired a short beard, also white, and he was wearing dark glasses with the kind of clothes typically worn by Barindas, all the way to the round red cap on his head. He seemed to be exhausted, but doing his best to keep up a brave face about it.

"Ah, a bravura performance, I presume," Fallon said, reading their expressions.

"It went off a beaut!" Parnum exclaimed. He turned to Mamu. "You see, I told you you were a natural."

"A real professional," Austin declared.

"I remember reading somewhere that some professionals never get over their stage fright," Mamu said. He accepted some tea proffered by one of the aides and sat down gratefully. His hand shook as he raised the mug to his lips, and he had to steady his grip with the other.

Barindas smiled and looked relieved. "It looks as if I may have a rival," he remarked. "I shall have to be careful."

Sam glanced at his watch. "That's great. But let's not forget the rest of it." He looked at Guridan and indicated the piece of paper containing the material to go out via Tannerling. "That needs to be on its way to Imo. You'd better get movin'." She nodded and reached for a lockable document holder on a shelf.

Fallon looked at Parnum as the Australian sat down and emitted a sigh of relief. "It went okay, eh?"

"Oscar performance, mate. An Oscar performance. Maybe Mamu isn't cut out to be a journalist after all."

"On the contrary, the life has never appealed more to me than right at this moment," Mamu said.

A strong corroboration of Tannerling's story would be if Barindas and his staff were seen to remain there, and were reported as doing so by any other sources that Embatto might have. And for as long as the Zugendan authorities could be kept believing that Barindas was still there, they would have little inducement to look for him elsewhere—such as within the capital itself. The morning's experiment with Mamu seemed to indicate that the deception could be kept up convincingly for some time after Barindas left.

Marie Guridan closed the document holder and stopped by Fallon on her way toward the door. "Is Candy okay?" she inquired in a low voice. "I haven't seen her for a while."

"Sure, she's okay. I think she said something about going up to GDF's and looking over some of his toys."

"Oh, an' see if Imo's done with the Renault while you're at it?" Sam called across to Guridan. "He was s'posed to be puttin' in a new generator."

She nodded and moved toward the door.

"I've got things to do too," Austin said, joining her, and they left together.

Barindas came back to the table and sat down, stirring his mug of tea. Fallon came over to hand Reid his, but remained standing with his back propped against the wall. There had been enough talk about plans and details. He was curious about the bigger picture that Barindas saw beyond all the immediate concerns. "What do you plan on doing at the end of it all, Jovay?" he asked. "Suppose the ZRF do make it and you get rid of Molokutu. Then what? What do you see for Zugenda after that?"

"Oh . . . not just for Zugenda," Barindas said. "Eventually I see a whole new future for all of Africa."

"Okay, for the whole of Africa then?"

Barindas stared at the mug in his hands as if pondering how to begin. At length he said, "I don't understand why what is happening is happening. . . . You have seen how the people are dying. Yet the silos in Kansas hold enough surplus grain to pave Zugenda from one end to the other. And the farmers there fight for higher subsidies to compensate them for not growing more. The even worse part is that Africa could grow enough, easily, to feed two or three times its population. Over half of the world's metals come from Africa. Can you imagine the supercontinent that we have the potential to become? But all that comes to us from outside is ever-more-destructive armaments and the politics of strife."

"So what would you like to bring in?"

"Obviously, the means of progress."

"You mean capital, industry?" Reid said. "Western know-how, that kind of thing?"

Barindas waved a hand back and forth rapidly. "No! Those are results, not causes. Hanging a few trappings of advancement onto a backward culture won't help it to grow, any more than dressing a pigmy in giant's clothes. What I would like to see is something more fundamental: a spirit, an attitude. The quality of mind that produced your Renaissance and enabled Europe to lift *itself* from barbarism. Infuse that into Africa, and we will evolve an advanced industrial culture in our own way, stamped with our own uniqueness and to our own style. The details of how you happened to do it aren't important." Barindas sighed and waved a hand again, but despondently this time.

"Instead, we got Marx: 'To each according to his needs. From each according to his ability.' So if I think that I 'need' what you have, then you have the obligation to give it to me, and I have the right to take it. That is the creed of the mugger and the thief. We indoctrinate a generation with that kind of teaching and wonder why they grow up believing they have a right to expect the state to steal for them. Is it any wonder that we end up with what we see?

"Yet what puzzles me the most is that enough people who matter *know* what is happening, and they know the reasons why. When colonialism was ending, we sent our young people to the West to learn of the methods that had made it rich. But instead of being taught how to create wealth, they were fobbed off with doctrines of redistributing it. What use is that to countries that don't possess any worthwhile wealth to redistribute? Yet it's an effective way of preventing the Third World from turning into a serious competitor, is it not?"

Barindas looked up. "But what of yourself, Mr. Fugleman? You must admit to being the kind of unique individual who prompts people to be curious. Tell me, what kind of belief system do you subscribe to? I can't accept that a man of your dedication could be without a guiding ideology of some kind."

Fallon pulled a face and drank a long draft from his mug.

"What's your ism, in other words?" Reid prompted.

Fallon shrugged. "It's not isms that are good or bad. Cruelty, hate, envy, greed, power lust . . . Things like that are bad, however they're disguised or excused. Capitalists see the same evils in communism as communists see in capitalism; every religious fanatic sees heretics in all the rest. But it's the wine that's good or bad, not the labels on bottles it comes in."

"Then there's your ism," Barindas declared. "You're a classical liberal."

Fallon raised his eyebrows. "I am?"

"You're certainly no socialist."

"He's a ruddy cockney, that's what he is," Reid declared.

"Not really. Just an ordinary London lad."

"Ah yes, and that reminds me, what is this word 'china' that you call people sometimes?" Barindas asked. "I've been meaning to ask you. Mr. Reid told me it has something to do with Londoners' slang. Is that correct?"

"Kind of. . . It rhymes: china plate—mate: pal. See?" Fallon pointed to the sun helmet that he had hung on a peg by the door. "Or I might ask how you like me titfer over there."

"Titfer?"

"Tit for tat—hat. See, it rhymes."

"So is that why you call Tannerling a berk?" Sam asked. "Where in hell did that come from?"

"That's less polite," Fallon said. "Berkeley Hunt—cunt."

"Shoulda guessed."

"Now I see." Barindas looked even more bemused.

The buzzer sounded again. "Yep?" Sam acknowledged, flipping the intercom switch.

"Austin and Marie Guridan," the guard's voice announced.

"Okay."

Austin appeared in the doorway before anyone had a chance to say anything further. The expression on his face was grim. Guridan, tight-lipped, was right behind him. Imo was there too, breathless and flustered, looking as if he had run all the way from the other side of the gorge. "Tannerling! He's been shot. . . . I think he's dead," he blurted out between gasps.

The body was still as it had fallen, slumped across the RA17 receiver, its hand still clamped in a death grip on the Morse key. He had been shot twice in the head. Blood from the wound covered the papers on the work surface and was congealing in a pool on the floor. The bullets had entered from behind and to the right, which meant that they had almost certainly been fired from the door of the battery compartment that Fallon himself had hidden in. The document holder that Guridan had left with earlier was under Tannerling's elbow.

The two Africans who had been detailed to watch him stood nervously just inside the door from the short passage leading out to the workshop area. "We were down in the shop, talking to Imo," one of them said defensively. "Our orders were to stay out of sight and make it look natural."

"Who found him?" Fallon asked.

"I did," Imo answered from the doorway.

Fallon pointed at the document holder. "How did he get that? I thought you were supposed to give it to him?"

Imo nodded. "I already had, down in the shop. He brought it up here on his own. Then I came up after him a few minutes later to get the keys for the Renault—he had them in his pocket. And that's how I found him."

"So Marie had already left."

"She was talking to me on her way back," Austin said. "Imo ran into both of us when he went across to find someone."

Sam Letumbai ducked back into the room from the

battery compartment. "Yep, I reckon that's where it came from, all right," he said. "Ain't no sign of any gun, though."

"Whoever it was must have got out through the shaft that carries the antenna leads outside," Austin said. "He could have climbed down from the ledge that the generator cables run out along."

Fallon stared hard at the corpse slumped grotesquely in the chair, remembering the other things he'd heard and searching frantically for any way to avoid the conclusion that was already shouting in his mind, but which his mind didn't want to face. But it was Marie Guridan who voiced it.

"Unless it was a 'she,'" she said woodenly. Sam frowned and shook his head, not following. Guridan looked at Imo. "Have you seen Annette at all this evening?" she asked. She looked around the circle of faces. "Has anyone?"

They exchanged questioning, apprehensive looks.
Nobody had.

Chapter Thirty-nine

CANDY REAPPEARED A LITTLE OVER AN HOUR AFter the body was discovered. When questioned, Sung Feng confirmed that she had come to the armory earlier in the evening to examine several weapons that she was interested in. However, she had taken a couple of rifles to the range higher up the gorge in order to test the night sights that they were fitted with, and there was nothing to fix her exact whereabouts at the time Tannerling was killed.

She denied that she had done the shooting, but made no pretense of any regret that it had happened—even if the plan to establish him as a controlled source was dashed as a consequence. Some believed her; others didn't; most were unsure. For his part, after listening to the questions and answers, Fallon tended to stick with his initial impression that she wouldn't have let personal feelings override operational needs. Somehow the method of the killing didn't fit with the defiant directness that was part of Candy's makeup. If she had wanted to do it, he couldn't help feeling, she would have done it openly, face-to-face, the way she had killed Ratfart, not in the back, from hiding; and if challenged afterward, she would have admitted it and told them to go ahead and do whatever they wanted to.

And she wasn't the only one for whom he could see motive. There were others around who could be expected to have the kinds of grudges and resentments that resulted in killing somewhere or other every day of the week: the Africans that he had bullied and insulted; even Imo wasn't beyond suspicion; and who could hope to guess what might go on at the bottom of a mind as unfathomable as Sung Feng's?

The remainder of the evening served only to demonstrate the futility of further argument and speculation, and when all there was to be said had been said, it was clear that they were not about to get any closer to establishing the truth. A story was prepared for general dissemination the next day, stating that Tannerling had been uncovered as a government agent and shot while attempting to escape. At least that version would be unlikely to arouse undue suspicions if it found its way back to Embatto.

Concerning more immediate matters, the purpose of the deception operation surrounding Tenyasha had been twofold: first, to establish Tannerling's credibility, which meant discrediting any other sources that Embatto might have operating; and second, to divert the attention of Zugendan intelligence while Barindas and his staff were secretly being installed in Kinnube.

Although the first of these objectives was now frustrated, the second could still be pursued as planned. As Fallon and Reid had proposed, a rumor had been put out that a consolidated ZRF headquarters was being established north of the war zone in the valley known as Boake Rift, while Tannerling had transmitted several messages stating that the real location was to be Tenyasha. The plan had been to then discredit the rumor by planting other information that would reveal the Boake Rift story as hoax, and Tannerling's continued presence was in no way essential to its accomplishment.

The decision reached the next morning was to carry on as planned without delay or diversion, which meant getting Sam Letumbai away on his mission to meet with Yolatta as quickly as possible and not allowing the Tannerling affair to interfere with it. Accordingly, Sam left with a small party of guerrillas shortly after noon in the same Chevy pickup that he had used to collect Fallon. With him he took a pouch of the kind carried by ZRF couriers, which would be left on a dead body at the scene of one of the clashes with government forces in such a way that it would be sure to be found. One of the documents contained in the pouch was purportedly a personal letter from Barindas to Yolatta, referring among other things to large-scale troop movements southward and giving code words relating to secret plans for consolidating the ZRF headquarters at Tenyasha. There were also references to a cover operation being carried out at Boake Rift.

The second part of Letumbai's mission would be to collect and brief a detachment of ZRF who would drive north to Boake Rift itself, where they would go through the motions of making preparations to receive a large-scale move there. Space would be cleared for stores, accommodations made ready, and communications facilities set up.

But Zugendan air reconnaissance would detect cracks in the facade: slips apparently caused by an inexpert and too hasty attempt at deception. A flaw in the camouflage here would reveal the weapon concealed beneath to be a wooden imitation; a sloppy piece of carpentry there would betray a storehouse as an empty shell; the vehicles driving around and around to make the place look more inhabited and active than it was would be a little too obvious. The monitoring activities of Zugendan signals intelligence would also support the same story: ZRF radio traffic from Boake Rift would remain at a mediocre level, confirming that nothing of much importance was happening there, but transmissions from the vicinity of Tenyasha and Owanden would show a significant increase during the coming week.

Any unknown sources operating in Tenyasha would continue to report an operation involving a place far to the north. Only the version that Tannerling had sent would be corroborated by Embatto's intelligence staff—from the captured documents, from their photo reconnaissance, and from their signals intelligence.

The situation as far as Candy was concerned presented something of a problem. On the one hand, it seemed impermissible for somebody who was a primary murder suspect in many eyes, and who was unable to furnish a satisfactory alibi, to continue walking about freely and normally. If nothing else, the need for the ZRF leadership to be seen to exercise its authority seemed to demand an active response of some kind. On the other, the lack of conclusive evidence precluded anything drastic. So in the end she was confined to quarters in the restricted chambers above the rockfall until Barindas decided how the situation would be resolved. Fallon stopped by there early in the evening on the day of Sam Letumbai's departure. It was the first opportunity he'd had to talk to her alone.

"Do you think I did it?" she asked him. She was sitting stretched out on the steel cot, her back propped against the partition wall and her arms folded loosely on her chest. Her manner was more a challenge than a plea. If anything, she seemed angered that her dedication to discipline should have been questioned at all.

Fallon answered from where he was leaning against the cave wall on the opposite side of the narrow cubicle. "Oh, I don't doubt that you would, if the circumstances were different, but I don't think you did. The way it was done wouldn't be your style. And you wouldn't have let the cause lose a useful asset like that, just to even a score."

"You think maybe somebody does this on purpose to make it look like me?"

"You mean were you framed?" Fallon bunched his mouth and shook his head. "I don't see any reason to suppose so. You just picked the wrong time to go shooting."

"So why don't Barindas and the others believe this?"

"They don't know what to believe. But you were named, and they can't be seen not doing anything. And even if they did think it was you, they could hardly go making a big spectacle about it. The official story is that he was caught as an SS spy. So how could they explain getting upset with you over bumping him off? My guess is that they'll just give it a few days to blow over and quietly get back to business as usual."

Candy nodded, evidently prepared to accept it at that. "I'm still glad that somebody did it, whoever it was," she couldn't resist adding.

Fallon snorted and grinned briefly. "I figured that much already."

She unfolded her arms and stared for a moment at her legs stretched out in front of her on the cot. "So what is your timetable now?" she asked finally, looking up.

"A few more days to get things finalized here, and then back to Kinnube to report to Embatto," he replied. "Go through the motions of working out the plan for the hit team, and then Konrad Hannegen's work is done. Leave the country as planned, and keep up appearances by showing up back here later. By then, your people should all be in Kinnube and ready to go. Embatto will make his move when he gets a message from me saying that Trojan Horse is accomplished. . . . And that's when the fun should start."

"It will be different with you gone," she said. "And after so soon."

"Oh, it won't be for long if my guess is anything to go by."

Candy leaned her head back against the wall and looked at him pointedly for a few seconds. "I want to go with you when you leave," she said. "To Kinnube."

Fallon stared at her as if she had taken leave of her senses. "Back there? But look at all the bloody trouble we've just been through to get you here!"

"I know, but I have to."

"Why, for Christ's sake?"

"There are things there that must be finished. . . . And you drive out of there with the boy who is the guide, yes? Many people see it. The boy will need to be there too, when you go back."

Fallon shook his head. "The boy took off. It happens all the time. That's not a good enough reason."

"We will need a new safe house in Kinnube for Barindas and Yolatta. Dr. Velker is the one who can arrange it, but someone must talk to him about what has been agreed here. I know him and his contacts. It is best that it should be me who goes there."

"I know him too. The Kinnube network can arrange it without you." He shook his head. "For you it would be insane. You know what would happen if Embatto's lovelies got their hands on you again."

"I am not so sure. I think that if I go there with you, then they leave me alone even if they do recognize me. If Embatto believes you are with him, it blows your cover if he does anything else, no?"

"There's still no reason for you to go."

Candy sighed and closed her eyes for a moment. Fallon sensed the pretexts falling away and waited for the real reason to reveal itself. "Look," she said. "For years, all my life has been working for ZRF. Now, if everything works out in the way we all hope, everything that it has all been for will be decided in Kinnube. That is what I have fought for, and that is where I have to be when it happens. You understand that, yes? Because I know you are the same kind of person."

Fallon drew a long breath, hesitated for a second, then nodded in a way that said he understood. His voice lost the slightly impatient note that it had been assuming. "Yes, I know how you feel. But a lot of other people have been fighting for the same thing too, and they can't all be there. . . . And don't underestimate what might happen at this place. You could find all the action you need right here, and more. We've made it their prime target. If Thombert's armor gets through from Owanden, they're going to need every fighter here that they can get. So if you really want to do something for a lot of the people that this is all supposed to be about, this might turn out to be just as important a place to do it in as Kinnube."

Candy eyed him reluctantly. "You're sure it's not because you think I might have killed Tannerling?"

"Of course that's not it, and you know it."

She sighed again, resigned this time. That there would be no unbecoming show of pique at the decision, Fallon already knew. She had stated her case, and would accept the verdict, even if less than enthusiastically. And that strengthened his feeling that she would have accepted the verdict on Tannerling in the same spirit too.

As Fallon had predicted, the Tannerling affair faded into the background amidst the hectic planning and discussion in the days that followed. Word came in from the field that Letumbai and Yolatta had rendezvoused as planned, and the restrictions on Candy's movements were quietly eased. Not entirely satisfied with allowing things to rest at that, Marie Guridan pursued a low-key line of questioning and investigating around the base, but it led nowhere. Privately, Fallon consigned the whole matter to a long line of life's unsolved mysteries.

Fallon had now been at Tenyasha for almost a month, and he began preparing material to present when he got back to Kinnube on the feasibility of Trojan Horse. He would have to return as Hannegen, since that was how he had left. The most likely development then, he guessed, would be for Embatto to clamp him under arrest following reports of his open sympathizing with the rebels while he was in the Glimayel, ostensibly to satisfy the ZRF's expectations, but in reality to keep Fallon safely out of circulation and cut off from any opportunity of mischief while he remained in the country. Embatto's intention after that would probably be to have Hannegen officially deported as the fastest means of getting him on his way to meet up with the team and brief them. Embatto would later expect Fallon to recross the border into rebel territory with some of his associates while others appeared via other routes—and for the benefit of the various sources reporting to Zugendan intelligence, they would. But nothing in the elaborate assassination plan that Fallon would propose would really matter, since events would be following a different course.

There still remained the need for Fallon to have some way of coordinating with Barindas and Yolatta after he met with Embatto and Thombert. He would head for Tobins Hotel again, he decided, and if it turned out that he was still at large when Yolatta and Barindas reached the safe house that Velker had moved to, Fallon would be contacted accordingly. In the more likely event of his being detained, however, he would request use of the Zugendan diplomatic link to London to give his associates advance notice of the arrangements and to fix his return date. Thus, he would be able to convey the essentials via Julia, the colonel, and the ZRF network in the city.

The only question left outstanding, then, was how to get Barindas himself to Kinnube. He constituted an irreplaceable piece of merchandise, and the idea of sending him toward the city with a truckload of armed desperadoes readily identifiable as guerrillas was simply too risky. There had to be a better way.

"Why not come with me?" Fallon suggested at a meeting a week after the Tannerling shooting, when the issue came up.

Barindas blinked in surprise. "I'm not sure that I understand you, Mr. Fugleman."

"I'll be leaving for Kinnube in a couple of days time. And since Julius has been considerate enough to make sure I get safe conduct, it would be a shame not to take advantage of the fact, wouldn't it?"

Barindas turned his head in the direction of the others who were present, as if waiting for them to tell him why the suggestion was preposterous. But none of them could.

And so, two days later, Fallon, once more at the wheel of Konrad Hannegen's Land Rover but alone this time, followed a different truck full of ZRF guerrillas down the track toward Owanden to begin his journey back. For the benefit of the valley's inhabitants—and especially for any interested eyes that might be watching among them for reasons other than loyalty and enthusiasm—Mamu, already an adept at impersonating Barindas, put in an appearance to see them off.

He collected the real Barindas the following day, at a rendezvous where he had been brought by a small escort of trusted aides. Barindas was dressed nondescriptly, his beard shorn and the white of his hair grayed, and would ride with Fallon as simply an old man that he had taken up with on the way. He seemed to like the role. It made him feel closer to the people, he said.

Chapter Forty

"CALLING WEST PALM BEACH CONTROL, THIS IS Piper Aerostar N313BA. Am fifteen miles north at seven thousand feet, for landing. Come in, please."

"Roger, Aerostar 3BA. We have radar contact. Squawk at one-three-zero-zero and enter right downwind for runway three-three. You have traffic at three o'clock at three thousand feet. Call on final."

"3BA, Roger."

Eugene Wollack eased the plane into a shallow descent as the downtown cluster and the sprawling built-up strip along the oceanfront approached and passed by below on his right. Sunlight glinted from the glass cliffs of the hotel towers, and the white sands stood out like fresh snow against the azure sea. South of the city, he banked into a lazy starboard turn. The ocean slid off to the left, and a green carpet patterned with lakes stretching inland across southern Florida moved into view ahead. The airfield crept in from the side and centered itself, with the city now forming the skyline in the distance behind.

"Hello, Tower. Aerostar 3BA downwind."

"Roger, 3BA. Clear to land. Make a left turn after landing and use runway two-one to taxi back to ramp. Contact ground control on one twenty-two point seven."

"3BA."

The background scene flattened and receded with the changing perspective, giving way to a busy highway flanked by hotels and malls, then rooftops scattered amidst well-tended gardens as the plane straightened into its final descent. The runway flattened itself into an onrushing, elongated trapezium, expanding to engulf the nose, and then the wheels bumped down tidily astride the centerline. Wollack whooped jubilantly and sang aloud to himself as he taxied off the main runway and followed the perimeter track to the parking area.

The heat felt like an oven door being opened when he stepped down onto the tarmac. "Oh man," he muttered approvingly, "New York could sure use some of this."

He heaved three bags down from the rear baggage compartment and secured the aircraft to the anchor rings set in the ground. The station wagon from the reception building drew up just as he was finishing, and a heavily built Cuban in white shirtsleeves climbed out. "Mr. Wollack, good to see you back. It's been a while now."

"Hi, Manny. Yep, too long. How've you been doing?"

"Pretty good." The Cuban opened the rear door and lifted in the bags. "Just these?"

"Just the three. Has a car arrived for me?"

"It's here. A Porsche, that okay?"

"Sounds just fine," Wollack said. They walked around to the front of the wagon and got in.

"What is it this time?" the Cuban asked as they pulled away. He grinned knowingly. "Business, pleasure, or maybe a little bit of both?"

Wollack leaned back in the passenger seat, savoring the sunshine and warm, lazy air and the sight of cypresses and palm trees. "Work? Hell, screw work, Manny. This is strictly pleasure." He threw his head back and laughed. "Lots of pleasure."

Twenty minutes later, Wollack drew up beneath the canopied entrance outside the Hyatt front lobby. A bellhop carried the bags and led the way through to reception while a hotel valet parked the car. A pretty redhead with a trace of freckles smiled at Wollack from one of the positions at the check-in counter. "Can I help you, sir?"

He glanced at her name tag. "Hi, Barbara, honey. Name's Wollack. Call me Gene. Reservation for a week, right?"

"One moment."

He eyed her approvingly while she tapped at computer keys and studied mysterious oracles on a screen. After a few seconds he looked away and surveyed the lobby area, his jaw chomping on a piece of gum while his fingers drummed a restless tattoo on the countertop.

"Suite with a Jacuzzi. Seven nights, departing on the

eleventh, is it?" She had a trace of an accent that he couldn't quite place.

"There should be a bar too. Stocked."

"Er. . . right. That's taken care of. Would you fill this out, please?"

Wollack entered the information required on the registration card and passed it back.

"Thanks. . . Oh, and I need your phone number."

"What for?"

"It's our normal procedure. If you leave something behind, or if anyone needs to get in touch after you leave."

He scribbled a number in the box. "Do I get yours too?"

"Sorry. I'm not on the bill."

"Hey, come on. We could fix that. When's your night off, eh? Ever try a martini in a Jacuzzi?"

"Eighteen-twenty-five," she said to the bellhop who was hovering. And watch out for this one, she said to herself inwardly as she handed Wollack his key with a reproachful smile, at the same time mentally tagging him an asshole.

The suite faced out to sea and had a lounge and a bedroom with a king-size bed as well as the bathroom with the Jacuzzi. After dismissing the bellhop with a generous tip and unpacking, Wollack mixed himself a drink and took it through into the bathroom. He took a long shower while the tub was filling, and afterward stretched out to relax with his drink while the warm, pulsating water washed away the cramps of the flight. Then he used the phone by the tub to call a local number.

"Hello?" a female voice answered.

"Hey, baby! Guess who?"

"Gene, you made it!"

"Flew in about an hour ago. Boy, do I wish you were where I am right now."

"Where are you right now?"

"In a Jacuzzi with a drink—on my own."

"Say, that's too bad. We'll have to do something about that."

"I'll say we better had. So, are you still okay for later?"

"Well, sure. You gonna pick me up here?"

"Wanna bring a friend? Let's make it a real party. What do you say?"

"I see, feeling kinky, eh?"

"What else? Anyhow, it's a nice suite with a real big bed. It'd be a shame to waste it on two."

"Do I get a little extra consideration if I come up with someone?"

"Hey, come on, let's not get sordid. You know me. I'll take care of you."

"I'll see what I can do. Make it about seven for dinner. How's that?"

"You're wonderful. Seven it is."

"Talk to you later... Oh, tall, short, dark, fair, black, brown, or what?"

"Surprise me."

He hung up, tossed back the last of his drink with a self-congratulatory flourish, then got out of the tub and hummed exuberantly while he toweled himself dry. Then, slipping on a bathrobe, he picked up his glass and went back into the lounge for a refill... and stopped dead in his tracks.

The man sitting in the armchair by the door leading out to the veranda nodded approvingly over the glass that he had been cradling. "Not a bad voice. Good Scotch too. Sounds like quite a party you're throwing."

He was late-fiftyish, stockily built with broad shoulders under the pale green, slightly crumpled suit that he was wearing, even in the Florida heat, with an ample spread of midriff straining against the belt. He had a fleshily rugged face with hard, alert eyes, a squashed ear, and saggy jowls. He looked pugilistic. The hands holding the glass were meaty and huge like jointed pepperoni, the kind that could pulp apples.

"Who the fuck are you?" Wollack demanded, at the same time feeling less certain of himself than he tried to sound. The first word to flash through his mind was "mob"; he wondered fleetingly if a forgotten gambling debt had just caught up with him from somewhere.

"Oh, you can call me Al. It's not my name, but it'll do for now."

"How'd you get in?"

"Not down any chimney." The voice was like gravel being poured into a bucket.

Still struggling to reengage his mental gears, Wollack marched stiffly across to the bureau by the wall and picked up the phone. "Then I'm sure you won't be very surprised if I call hotel security."

Al shrugged but made no move to stop him. "Then you'll never know what the deal was, will you?" Wollack hesitated and looked back at him. Al took his time and sipped from his glass. "And that could be kind of a shame for somebody in your situation, who could use a break, maybe. . . . Private planes, fancy cars from Europe, swinging broads, a little coke—all very nice. But it's all on borrowed money these days, isn't it, Eugene? How much longer can you keep it up? Starting to sweat a little at night yet?"

Wollack withdrew his hand slowly from the button pad as he listened, then turned to face the stranger fully. "Who—" he began, but Al cut him off, still speaking in the same gruff, matter-of-fact baritone.

"Twelve years ago you were Welman-Forbes and K's five-star wonder boy. VP and executive member of the board at thirty-two, all set to fly high. Well, you still fly, I guess, and you still get high, but not in the kinda way that Pa thought too much of. Musta been quite a blow to find out he'd disinherited you when he died. And now the other sharks have cut you out, eh? But you still can't kick the life-style."

"Where are you from, the goddamn CIA or something? If it's any business of yours, I've resigned temporarily, following a policy disagreement. In other words I'm taking a long vacation. Is that okay with you?"

"Bullshit. For three years? Let's get real. There's still blood all over your back. They threw you off the ship, and you can't keep treading water much longer."

Wollack replaced the phone on its hook. "What do you want?" he asked guardedly.

Al waved a hand in the direction of the bar. "Have another. You look nervous." Wollack walked over to the side of the room and shoveled ice into his glass. When he poured from one of the bottles, his hand shook noticeably as the shock started to wear off. Behind him, Al lit a cigarette and replied, "You were involved in some meetings that took place in Switzerland twelve years ago. Secret meetings. They included people from a consortium of other outfits who were in it along with the bank. A guy called Theo Sorgen was there, but he took a coronary over a year ago."

Wollack had stiffened visibly. "What if I was?" he asked uncomfortably over his shoulder.

"What can you tell me about them?"

"Why should I tell you anything?"

"All right, I'll tell you some more. There were some Iranians involved too. It was to do with metal deposits in a certain part of Africa—Zugenda, if you want to be exact about it. There was an expert who was commissioned to do a report on it."

"Did he tell you all this?"

"No. We don't know who he was."

"Who's 'we'?"

"You don't wanna know."

Wollack moved away from the bar and sat down on the couch facing the room from the far side of the window. "What do you want to know?"

"Who the rest of the people were. Also, a photocopy of the report, if you can get one. We know that four copies were delivered."

Wollack gulped quickly from his glass and thought about it. "What do I get out of this?"

"Revenge is sweet. Why protect a bunch like that? You can torpedo their ship."

"That's nice, but I don't run on torpedo fuel."

"Ten grand for the names. Another ten if you can get the report."

Wollack pursed his lips dubiously. "That doesn't exactly pay off a lot of mortgage."

"And we're not exactly a welfare agency for playboys who are running on empty. Hell, it's a donation. You're not exactly in a position to be turning down any offers right now."

"The report might be a problem. I don't have the same access these days . . . but I know people."

"That's your problem. We pay on delivery."

Wollack drew a long breath. "Twenty each."

Al shook his head. "For a few lousy names it's a steal already. There could be more later if we end up doing business." He reached into the jacket of his suit and produced a thick white envelope which he held up enticingly between finger and thumb. "You could go ahead and give me the names right now."

Wollack stared at the envelope hungrily and bit his lip. But already at the back of his mind he was thinking that he could do better than twenty thousand from this situation. "Do I get to think it over?" he asked.

Al put the envelope back in his pocket and took out a small notepad. He wrote on the top sheet, tore it out, and handed it over. "Leave a message on that number for Al to call the Hyatt. Tomorrow evening at the latest. I'll be around until then."

He got up, tossed a spare room key down onto the table by where Wollack was sitting, and walked unhurriedly to the door. "Have fun with the broads. But you're wasting your time with Barbara downstairs. She's Irish, very Catholic, her husband's a trucker, and they've got five kids. Just thought you'd like to know."

"Er. . . thanks," Wollack stammered.

"You don't have to," Al said, turning to close the door. "Just protecting our assets. You were in banking. You understand."

Wollack sat staring at his drink and thinking furiously for twenty minutes after Al had left. Then he got up, called the hotel travel information desk, and checked the times of flights to New York that evening. He booked a provisional reservation and then called a Manhattan number. A male secretary answered. The voice that Wollack was put through to reacted disdainfully to his name.

"Don't give me that crap," Wollack said impatiently after they had talked for a few minutes. "Don't you see what this means? They're onto you, you turkeys. They know you're trying to screw them out of the operation in Africa. If—"

"Please," the voice interrupted, "this is a public line. Try to be more circumspect."

"Then we need to sit down and talk, because this time *I'm* the one who's got the lead, and *I'll* tell you what the terms are. Okay?"

There was a pause. Finally the voice said tightly, "What are you proposing?"

"I'm arriving in La Guardia at eight-fifty-five, Eastern

flight twenty-eight from Miami. Have somebody meet me. We can talk tonight."

"I'm sorry, but it may not prove possible to locate the others at such short notice. Might I suggest—"

"Then make it possible. Look, I have to get back to the contact by tomorrow night. I'm not asking any favors. It's your asses on the line, so you'd better have somebody there."

When he had finished the call, he repacked his smallest bag with an overnight kit and change of clothes, and on his way out left a message with the desk that he would be staying with friends away from the hotel until late the next day, which he figured would explain his absence to Al's satisfaction if Al should try to get in touch for any reason. As an afterthought he gave the clerk ten dollars to call a local number and cancel the night's arrangements for him, explaining that he'd had to leave town on a business emergency. Then he drove back to the West Palm Beach airport and took off in the Aerostar for the seventy-mile flight south to Miami.

A limousine was waiting for Wollack at La Guardia. It took him to a staid but expensively furnished town house on the Upper East Side, where three men were waiting in an oak-paneled drawing room with high bookshelves, faded paintings in heavy, ornate frames, and wingback chairs upholstered in maroon leather.

"The deal is this," Wollack told them when they had been through the preliminaries. "They've caught a sniff of what's going on, and you can't afford to jeopardize the operation at this stage. You can deal them back in, head them off, or try to stall, but whatever you decide, you have to deal through them."

"What kind of guarantee do we have that you won't screw us the same way as you're screwing them?" one asked.

Wollack spread his hand appealingly. "I'm here, aren't I? I could have blown all of you out of the water. There's my proof of good faith."

"And what's the rest of the deal?" another queried.

"Full reinstatement with back pay, and my original cut in the operation—in other words, nothing more than if we'd have stayed on the rails together in the first place.

That's what I call real generous. Let bygones be bygones, eh? Considering what you stand to lose if the rest of it goes sour, you're not going to do any better than that."

The talk went on late into the night. It was agreed that Wollack would return to Florida the next day to meet again with Al. His line would be that he was willing to cooperate, but it would take time for him to work out a way of getting his hands on the report. In the meantime he would supply Al with some names, and the consortium would take it from there. By the time it was discovered that the names had no connection with the consortium, Al would no longer be a problem and Wollack would be far away.

It was almost 1:00 A.M. when Wollack checked into the New York Hilton. Farther uptown and to the east, meanwhile, the discussion continued.

"Irresponsible, unreliable, and dangerous," the oldest of the three pronounced. The other two concurred. One of them called a number in Fort Lauderdale, in southeast Florida, a few miles north of Miami.

"Do you know what goddamn time it is?" a sleepy voice answered irritably.

"I'm sorry, but this is urgent. We have a job for you, which must be completed before early afternoon tomorrow. . . ."

Wollack left to catch a return flight from JFK midway through the next morning. While he was eating his lunch thirty thousand feet above the ocean east of Norfolk, Virginia, a man in white mechanic's coveralls drove a pickup truck into the parking area for private aircraft at Miami airport and placed a package in the space behind the rearmost seats in a Piper Aerostar that had been left there the previous evening.

Wollack's trace disappeared suddenly from the radar screens when he was halfway back from Miami to West Palm Beach. The crew of an air search plane that was sent out spotted a patch of floating debris, and a Coast Guard boat recovered fragments that identified the aircraft type. Damage was consistent with a midair explosion. The body was found washed up on a beach fifty miles farther north almost a week later.

Chapter Forty-one

GENERAL NAGUIB THOMBERT TURNED FROM the large picture window looking out from Molokutu's study in the presidential palace, and stood with his hands clasped loosely behind his back, regarding the company with fishlike, dispassionate eyes. "We've begun mobilizing for Scabbard, but do we move north or south?" he asked. The eyes shifted to single out Embatto, who was sitting with Ngoyba in chairs pushed back from Molokutu's desk. The only other person present was General Waroon, chief of the air force. "Reports from three sources say that the ZRF are concentrating at Boake Rift. But you're still standing by the one from Drummer, who said it's Tenyasha. And now Drummer's dead. What makes you so sure he was right and the others aren't? I need to know for sure. We can't risk sending half the army to the wrong place."

"Yes, but remember that those same three sources also confirm Drummer's original observation that Barindas and Guridan are still at Tenyasha," Embatto said.

Molokutu gestured at the papers lying on his desk, which had been recovered from the ZRF courier's pouch. "There's the letter to Yolatta right here. Barindas says it's Tenyasha. Who should know better than him?"

Thombert's gaze flickered down at the desk suspiciously. "I always have doubts about documents from dead enemy bodies. They're too easily planted."

Waroon indicated the aerial reconnaissance photographs also on Molokutu's desk, which he had shown and interpreted earlier. "The activity at Boake Rift is being faked. The guns in those pits are crude mock-ups. There's nothing under that camouflage netting. It certainly suggests that the activity there is an elaborate deception."

"Which the other sources fell for, but Drummer didn't,"

Molokutu concluded. "Barindas's people found out, and so they got rid of him. It all hangs together."

Thombert sighed heavily, turned to gaze out of the window for a few seconds, and then turned to face the room once more. "I'm not satisfied that rebels would be that devious," he declared. "It's my responsibility to have the army in the right place when we go with Trojan Horse. I want to put a team down on the ground at Boake Rift to check it out from close up. We could have the answers by tomorrow night."

Molokutu looked around and saw that there were no objections. "Okay," he agreed. "It won't do any harm to be double sure."

"I have a further suggestion," Embatto said to Thombert. "We have a prisoner who was caught near Kinnube yesterday with a schedule of ZRF supply requests in his possession. The figures suggest that considerable activity is anticipated around Tenyasha, and comparatively little up at Boake Rift, which would appear to endorse our contention. However, we could turn him over to you. Let's see what your interrogators make of it."

Thombert looked inquiringly at Molokutu. The president nodded. "Do it. They might get something," he directed.

A reconnaissance unit consisting of six Zugendan army commandos landed from a helicopter that night, twenty miles from Boake Rift. An overnight march brought them to a line of crumbling cliffs and shattered rocks looking down into the valley where the new ZRF headquarters was supposedly being relocated. On reaching the valley, they split into two three-man squads, one of which crept down to reconnoiter from closer range, while the other remained positioned on a ledge higher up behind them on the cliffs as a covering party.

From various vantage points, the reconnoitering party observed that the antiaircraft guns and missile launchers inexpertly concealed in weapons pits on the higher slopes around the valley were mock-ups fabricated from pieces of wood and metal piping; that the tents and sleeping quarters housed under the camouflage nets were, for the most part, hospitals for the wounded, or simply empty; that the trails crisscrossing the area had been made mainly for show, since there was no guerrilla force worth talking about in the area; and that the groups of figures that aerial photographs had revealed marching and drilling with weapons were older men and women, convalescents, and other noncombatants.

And ZRF eyes had followed them all the way.

Behind some rocks near the crest line of the cliffs, Jomar Mosswano lay prone, cradling the stock of the Armalite against his shoulders. Another ZRF guerrilla, a deceptively frail-looking veteran called Suzi, crouched on one side of him, sighting through a gap between the rocks, while on the other, the section leader, whose name was Dominic, watched a point down in the valley through binoculars, waiting for a signal. It had taken them two hours to work their way up above the Zugendan commandos' covering squad. Two other guerrilla parties should also be in position by now, one on either flank. A warm breeze was coming up from the sunbaked rock below, carrying the distant sound of hammering from somewhere in the valley.

Suzi eased herself over onto her side to relieve cramping muscles in one of her legs. "What are we waiting for?" she muttered impatiently. "They're sitting ducks down there."

"Maybe the others aren't covered tight enough yet," Jomar said, meaning the commando squad lower down the valley side.

"That shouldn't have taken half the time it took us to get up here."

"It would be more difficult with this group higher up able to watch everything," Jomar pointed out.

"What are we holding for?" Suzi asked, raising her head to address Dominic.

"Orders," Dominic said, not very enlighteningly, without taking his eyes from the binoculars.

"It's the only action we're likely to see up here," Suzi complained. "Everything's supposed to have moved to Tenyasha. I heard that Barindas is there now."

"I have a son at Tenyasha," Jomar murmured distantly. "Sixteen, a fine son too. Imo, his name is. He's a mechanic. . . . There were more of us, once."

"Too much talking," Dominic told them. They fell quiet. In the niche below them, the three commandos moved intermittently, making observations, using their radio. They had picked their spot well: hidden from below, and with a covered escape route along a gully. As Jomar stared down at them, he searched within himself for feelings of remorse or regret over what was about to happen. He could find none.

Suddenly Dominic stiffened. Suzi rolled back over to aim again and looked at him expectantly. Jomar's finger curled around the trigger.

"Okay," Dominic breathed. "We take out one and two. Fire wide on three."

Suzi looked across incredulously. *"What?* We're gonna let one of 'em get away? I don't—"

"Just do as I say!" Dominic snapped.

Jomar and Suzi aimed, waiting. Dominic reached for his own FN as backup.

"Fire."

The Armalite juddered solidly against Jomar's shoulder, and over the sights he saw the target that had been designated "one" pitch forward and lie still. For his wife, Neraya, he told himself grimly. Beside him, Suzi got off two rounds, then her weapon jammed. *"Shit, no!"* she screamed. Jomar shifted aim to number two, who was turning to look back, and squeezed the trigger again. The figure convulsed and crumpled. For Miralee, and the baby. . .

The third soldier was already on his feet and leaping for the cover of the gully, but Jomar fastened onto him before he had made it to the first rock.

"Wide," Dominic's voice commanded.

Jomar bit his lip, aimed a few feet higher, and peppered the area with a scattered burst. The sound of more firing came from somewhere farther along the crest line, but again, too far away to be effective. The third commando was under cover and worming his way back toward a stretch of dead ground behind a crag. But the guerrillas didn't close in, and he got away.

The other group of three, farther below, hearing the firing above them and losing radio contact with the covering group, terminated the mission. Since they hadn't come under fire themselves, they assumed that they hadn't been spotted. Two of them, however, were picked up off by snipers in the process of extricating themselves from the valley. The third made it to the rendezvous with the pickup helicopter, where he also met up with the survivor from the covering group. The two of them returned safely to base to deliver their report.

Kembo had never known that a human being could endure so much pain. If he had known, he might not have volunteered to let himself be arrested carrying the papers. Every one of the bruises from his lacerated shins to his swollen mouth and eyes was its own source of dull, throbbing agony. Every inflamed cut and welt burned like a raw wound being seared in a flame. His muscles no longer responded when he tried to move.

First, they had stripped him of his clothes in a bare, concrete room, then beaten him with fists and truncheons and kicked him with their boots—three or four of them at a time, taking turns. They had tied him to a board and tilted him facedown into a bath filled with stinking sewage water and vomit, forcing his head under until he lost consciousness. Then they would revive him and repeat it, over and over. . . . They had whipped him with electrical cord—metal-filled plastic that cut into the flesh and tore. When they threw him back into the cell to recover, he forced memories into his mind of his sons, stood against a wall and machine-gunned with fifty others from the village, and told himself again that he was doing it to avenge them, and the thousands like them. He had been able to do little enough for them in the past. Maybe this made up for it.

The blow exploded against the side of his head, shooting pain through him like a long nail being driven into his ear. A hand grabbed his hair and yanked his head back so that he was staring straight into the light. He could feel blood trickling over his broken teeth. The shape of one of the interrogators loomed closer, indistinct and featureless in silhouette.

"You're lying. Why don't you tell us the truth when you can see that we know you are lying? Barindas is not moving to Boake Rift, is he? We already know that. Where is he really being moved to?"

Through the haze that filled his head, Kembo could make out the interrogator's fist rising to strike again. Behind him, the other was swishing the electrical cord against his palm. This must be enough, Kembo thought to himself. Surely they would believe that they had broken him now. He had been told when he volunteered that it would be vital that they believe. He had seen the ZRF units out in the bush opening their hidden caches of weapons and preparing to move upon Kinnube. The day was very close now. Barindas would be depending on the army's having been lured away. It was important that the interrogators believe. . . .

It took all Kembo's effort to muster a breath through his cracked lips. The interrogator held back.

"No more," Kembo gasped. He swallowed and tried to speak, but his mouth could form no sound.

"Well?" the voice barked.

"The . . . the things being done at Boake Rift are fake."

"Yes?"

"To deceive . . ."

"And where is the real headquarters being transferred to?"

"To . . ."

"Come on, tell us. Where?"

"To Tenyasha . . . The caves at Tenyasha."

"You see, you could have saved yourself a lot of pain. And isn't it true that Barindas, Letumbai, Yolatta, and the other leaders have already moved there?"

"I don't know. I was only involved in the things at Boake Rift."

A report was delivered to General Thombert at army headquarters within the hour. "Order mobilization for plan Hopscotch," he instructed his adjutant. Which meant the first phase of Scabbard—the offensive to coincide with Trojan Horse—with Tenyasha designated as the target.

Chapter Forty-two

THE LAND ROVER BUCKED AND SLITHERED ITS way down a trail of loose rocks and potholes hidden by red dust, which Fallon's map insisted was a road. He drove in silence, preoccupied with negotiating the bends and obstacles, while Barindas sat wedged in the passenger seat beside him, one hand clutching an AK47. But at least they were past the shanty camps and the refugees. Although Barindas had seen too much in the course of the war to be shocked, the sights had left him moody and dejected.

At the bottom of the slope the rocks gave way to smaller, more firmly packed stones, making the going smoother and enabling them to talk again. This was the first real opportunity that Fallon had had to talk to Barindas alone.

"How long have you been mixed up with Colonel Marlow?" he shouted across, above the engine and the pounding of the wheels on the dust.

"And Infinity Limited, you mean?"

"So you know all about them too?"

"I'm not so sure about 'all' . . . but sufficient, presumably, anyway. It has been for a number of years now. Zugenda tried to establish a democratic system when it became independent. The first prime minister was a socialist called Chrensy."

"Yes, I've heard of him."

"As a reaction to colonialism, the tide of popular feeling across most of Africa then was to the left. I founded an opposition party that felt a more liberal policy, one that would take advantage of the productivity of free enterprise, would serve the nation's real needs better. We needed investment and results, not slogans. But Molokutu took over before the next elections, and Chrensy was murdered. Zugenda became a single-party state with all opposition suppressed. We were driven out into the bush and became a guerrilla army. We would probably have just faded away if it were not for the equipment and funding that Infinity Limited provided in later years. I still don't know who was behind most of it."

"What brought Molokutu in?"

"Force and terror. It certainly wasn't anything to do with popularity. He armed and equipped one of the mountain tribes who have always been hostile to the plainspeople of Sorindi. The speed and violence of the coup left no time for anyone to organize effective resistance. We were paralyzed."

"Weren't the Soviets behind it?" Fallon asked.

"That's the story that the world accepts today, and the Soviets are quite happy to improve their standing in Third World revolutionary circles by accepting the credit. And they have exploited Molokutu's posturing by supplying equipment and sending some technicians here. But really, that all came later."

"You don't think it was them, then?"

"I'm not sure. If they were involved, they weren't alone. I can say that much. There were also some Western connections that have remained obscure."

Fallon's brow creased as he tried to follow. "But why would anyone in the West want to install a Marxist?"

Barindas smiled humorlessly as he stared ahead through the windshield. "I can see that you are still not completely wise to some of the ways of the world, Mr. Fugleman," he said. "I invite you to consider for a moment how the game works. You see, he doesn't have to really *be* a Marxist. He only has to say he is. Now he can steal anything you like for you, because the world will expect him to confiscate and nationalize everything in sight as a matter of policy. And that way you can get away with it because the world has been conditioned not to challenge the morality of anything that's claimed to be done in the name of the people."

Fallon took his eyes off the road for a second and stared across.

Barindas shrugged and tossed up a hand as if it should have been self-explanatory. "The whole socialist ideology is tailor-made for theft on a cosmic scale. Look what Lenin was able to grab with it: all of the property, industry, and agriculture of a sixth of the earth's surface, along with its entire population. And people still flock to it in millions because they believe that the loot will be shared out. You don't imagine that a force with that kind of power and potential would be left to genuine reformers and honest idealists, do you?"

Fallon was about to reply, when the rumble of a series of muffled reports came from somewhere ahead. The broken terrain both blocked and amplified sounds, making it difficult to judge how far away they were. They carried more the duller thud of incoming shells bursting than the sharper crack of gunfire. The explosions had been sounding intermittently for the last hour or more. He slowed to a halt and listened, his eyes searching the skyline and his face set in a frown as he sought to decode the sounds.

"What do you think it is?" Barindas asked.

"I'm not sure."

Several minutes previously, he had caught the flash of sunlight reflecting off of something shiny higher up on the line of crags they were approaching—a glass of some kind, maybe, an eyepiece of a pair of sand goggles, or possibly the polished metallic part of a weapon. He hadn't said anything, but he was certain that they were being observed. But there was only one way to get where they were going. He let up the clutch and eased the vehicle into motion again.

Barindas continued: "That's the universal tragedy. Systems of thought that have the power to move the masses precisely because they do inspire visions of how things could be better invariably become targets for unscrupulous elements that seek only to command and control the people. So it was with the early Christian church, or the French Revolution, or China's revolution. Where I see the hope for Infinity Limited is that it doesn't seek to improve the world by changing human nature—you won't change human nature. It accepts people as they are, with all their faults and vices, and builds from there. Its premises are founded in reality."

"You mean by not being pacifist?" Fallon said. "People will resort to force when they think they're right."

"Of course they will. Who would willingly submit to the force of somebody whom they believe to be wrong? The reason why communities within a nation manage to function with a reasonable degree of harmony is because instead of trying to settle their differences themselves, they agree to abide by the arbitration of the state, which can back its decision with a force that's greater than any of them. In other words, you arm the law, not the litigants. And as well as anything tends to in this world we're stuck with, it works.

"But when it comes to disputes between nations, they all try to enforce what they perceive as just, which means being the judge not only of their own rights but everyone else's too, and hence claiming the rights which they deny others. The result is what it can only be: impasse and war. What's needed is something that stands above the litigants in the same kind of way that law stands above individuals. I think that Infinity Limited could be the beginnings of it."

"And possessing the kind of force you're talking about?" Fallon sounded dubious.

"I'm not convinced that brute strength is the way to do it these days. Most modern weaponry is impotent, anyway—neutralized by the other side's. If what you want to do is—"

Barindas stopped speaking as the Land Rover came out of a bend at the foot of a steep rock bluff, and they saw armed figures in the roadway ahead and to the sides. There were vehicles parked behind, along both verges and some pulled off the road, and more activity on the slopes above, where weapons positions were visible. There were jerry cans and ammunition boxes scattered around, opened rations cartons, signs that the unit had been here for some time.

As the Land Rover approached, a bearded soldier wearing a black beret waved them down.

"They look like ZRF," Barindas muttered. "Should I reveal who I am, do you think?"

Fallon shook his head. "Not unless you have to."

The Land Rover drew to a halt. The soldier in the beret moved around, while others covered from a few yards back.

"Who are you two? What's your business here?"

Fallon replied stiffly, "My name is Konrad Hannegen. I am a naturalist. This is my guide."

"Where you comin' from?"

"My work involves certain researches in the Glimayel

region. Now that is completed, and I am returning to Kinnube. I have a guarantee of safe conduct from the authorities."

The soldier sneered. "That won't do you much good from shootin' distance. There's an army column about five miles farther on this way. The road up ahead's under shell fire."

"Are they coming this way?"

"I ain't too sure. Guess that's what we're tryin' to figure out. You'd better pull off the road over there."

"What for? I have just told you we are going to Kinnube."

"Maybe you don't hear too well. I just told you that the road's under fire from here on. You ain't goin' nowhere for a while."

Another group materialized from the slopes above, led by an officer wearing a tank commander's smock. He repeated the same questions; Fallon gave the same answers. While this was going on, some of the other soldiers moved around to peer curiously at the equipment inside the Land Rover. One of them fingered a spare pair of boots of Fallon's covetously. Another was looking inside a canvas sack.

It was the kind of situation where any sign of submissiveness would have been the only encouragement needed. Fallon was about to make some protest when Barindas snapped suddenly from beside him, "What kind of liberation of the people do you represent? Do you call yourselves soldiers, or are you common thieves?" They looked at him, startled. The officer's face hardened, and for a moment Fallon thought there would be a confrontation. Then Barindas said, "When I was a young man, we knew such a thing as honor. Is this the way that Jovay Barindas tells you to treat travelers?"

The officer glared at him for a moment longer, then nodded curtly and motioned the troopers back. "The old man is correct. We are not bandits." He looked at Fallon and waved toward the spot that the soldier in the beret had indicated. "Still, you'll have to stay here for now. Pull off over there."

Fallon complied. The ZRF unit was evidently preparing a defensive position and it was obvious that they couldn't permit him and Barindas to proceed on their way having seen as much as they had.

The officer and two of the troopers conducted them to a spot out of sight from the road, where a camouflage net stretched across a depression between several large boulders formed a shaded refuge that seemed to function as field kitchen, dressing station, and command post for whatever was going on in the vicinity—although most of the equipment seemed packed, strapped, and ready for an instant decampment.

They were offered the inevitable mug of tea, and now that protocol had been established, Fallon donated the spare cases of rations and medical kit that would no longer be needed. At this, the officer's manner became more affable, and tea was supplemented to become a meal. He introduced himself as Olemo. "Do you know, I saw Barindas once, about six months ago," he informed Barindas as they settled down. "You remind me of him."

"Yes . . . so I've often been told," Barindas replied dryly.

"Where do you come from?" the officer asked Fallon.

"From Denmark."

"Is that anywhere near Russia?"

"Not really."

"We had many Russians here several years ago—after Molokutu took over. They were behind the whole thing. But the people weren't keen on them much. The Westerners we'd had before were more popular: French, English, and especially Americans. We loved the Americans."

"Why was that?" Fallon asked.

"Russian families don't hire anyone. Americans have a cook, a nanny, a night watchman, a driver . . . maybe ten helpers. And each one of them could have ten people dependent on him. So every American fed a hundred Zugendans."

"They still try to," another guerrilla said, overhearing. He was propped against a pack at the rear of the hollow, nursing an arm in a bloodstained sling.

"Yes, but these days it goes to Molokutu instead. They probably paid for that piece of steel that you've got inside you."

They waited beneath the netting for another two hours. There was no further shelling. Messengers appeared and went, the radio came to life intermittently, and muttered conferences were held at the far end of the redoubt. And then a Zugendan army spotter plane came over and spent some time circling the area. Fearing an air attack, Olemo decided to abandon the plan for an ambush and disperse his force. "We'll be leaving here shortly, so you'll be able to carry on," he told Fallon and Barindas. "If you're asked, you say nothing about us."

Fallon looked from side to side with a puzzled expression. "About who? I haven't seen anybody."

"You've got the idea. Normally I'd tell you to watch out for bandits, but all the activity has probably caused them to make themselves scarce too. So with luck, you should have a safe run through to Kinnube."

Fifteen minutes later, Fallon and Barindas set off in the Land Rover once more. They met the advance guard of the army column a few miles farther on. The Zugendans detained them while they checked with Kinnube by radio, but as soon as they reported the name of Hannegen and received a response, their manner improved considerably. Nobody asked any questions about the old guide who was traveling with the Dane, and they continued on their way in the company of some trucks and an escort that were returning for supplies.

The column that they had run into seemed to be a spearhead to secure the route for a larger forcer, for several miles farther on they passed a column of tanks and trucks packed with troops moving the other way. And in the bases and depots that they passed as they got nearer to Kinnube, they saw lines of tanks, trucks, and guns being assembled in evident readiness to move out. The preparations for General Thombert's "Scabbard" offensive were apparently already under way. And the main thrust of it seemed to be southwest, into the Glimayel region.

Chapter Forty-three

FALLON AND BARINDAS ARRIVED ON THE OUT-
skirts of the city late in the afternoon. State-security forces
were in greater evidence on the approaches than had been
the case when Fallon left, presumably taking over from
some of the army units being moved farther afield. It
meant that Embatto's timetable was advancing.

It had seemed only prudent to assume that the progress of the Land Rover would be followed and reported.
Arrangements for spiriting Barindas away before they entered
the city proper—to a safe house that Velker had prepared
but not disclosed—had therefore been made by radio with
the ZRF Kinnube network before Fallon and Barindas left
Tenyasha. In the outskirts of the city, they entered a narrow,
crowded street where an exchange mart was being held,
with stalls lining one side and traders displaying wares on
makeshift tables and blankets spread out on the ground.
For some reason, the throng of people seemed to thicken
itself around the Land Rover, reducing its progress to a slow
crawl amid a mass of jabbering, gesticulating people,
waving trinkets and oddments of clothing, and begging for
alms. When the vehicle finally extricated itself at the far
end, its passenger had disappeared. Fallon drove on alone
into the center of Kinnube.

As he waited in line at the last checkpoint before
entering the central district, he recognized the figure with
the thin mustache, wearing a captain's insignia with camouflage smock and paratrooper's badge on a maroon beret,
standing watching from next to the barrier. The captain
spotted him and sauntered over.

"Well, if it isn't Doc, the animal man. I heard about
the trouble you got y'self into." Raoul shook his head and
clicked his tongue. "Shouldn't have gotten mixed up in

that kinda stuff, Doc. Shoulda stuck to counting the antelopes."

"The man attacked me," Fallon retorted with Konrad Hannegen testiness. "What was I supposed to do? Those two buffoons of yours only made things worse. I thought they were supposed to protect innocent people."

Raoul guffawed. "How long you been here now, Doc? Come on, gimme a break."

Fallon waved to indicate the activity ahead. "What's going on? I passed lots of tanks on my way to the city. There are troops everywhere."

"Oh, I dunno. There's supposed to have been more trouble with the rebs. I know for sure there's been a lotta people arrested." Fallon wondered if that meant that maybe Molokutu was catching whiffs of something in the wind.

Raoul pivoted to survey the street routinely. "So how'd it go out in the hills? Got back okay, huh? Do you know you're crazy? There's an old saying out here that the gods keep a special eye out to take care of crazy people."

Fallon paused before answering, as if weighing up whether to speak what was on his mind. Finally he said, a trifle gruffly, "There is much suffering among your people. Many go hungry. The children . . . An outsider has to see it to realize how bad it is there."

"Uh-huh." Raoul nodded. "Seeing the real world at last, eh? Gonna write some scientific paper about it now, tell all the other smart people how somebody oughta do somethin'?"

"But it's your own government. . . . The ZRF don't bomb crops."

"I only know what they tell me, Doc."

"Why do their dirty work? Why do you take orders from them?"

Raoul shifted his eyes evasively and lowered his voice. "Hey, you know better'n to say things like that. You might have been in the police station that time, but you haven't seen what goes on. You've gotta know how to survive in a place like this. What you do is keep with the side that's got the guns, see. You don't stick your neck out, and you don't ask questions. That's the way I play it. That's the way to stay alive and make sure you'll still be around after it's all changed."

"Ah, so it will change, then?"

"It's got to," Raoul muttered. "This kind of shit can't go on forever. Everyone knows it."

This was the kind of indicator of mood that Fallon had been fishing for. "How many others feel that way?" he asked.

Raoul shuffled uncomfortably. "Look, no more questions. I shouldn't be talking like this."

But Fallon persisted. "Suppose Barindas took over tomorrow, here in the city. How many of you would be with him?"

"Why should you care?"

"I told you before, I'm a scientist. Scientists are curious about everything."

"You got no business asking stuff like that."

"What about your nightclub—the pretty girls and the booze, the white tuxedo?"

Raoul grinned briefly. "You've got some memory, I'll give you that."

"Will you ever see it with things the way they are?"

"No way." Raoul leaned closer. "This system will never let you have what you want. To them, you're just a tool to be used to get *them* what *they* want." He gestured vaguely at the other soldiers behind him. "They've all got their own nightclub inside their head somewhere: a farm, a nice house with kids, open a restaurant, own themselves a truck, whatever." He nodded. "Okay, if you want to know what I think, if they felt it was for keeps and they weren't going to lose their necks a day later, they'd go with it. Does that satisfy your curiosity? And now, just forget that I said it, 'cause I didn't say nothin', okay?" He turned and waved to the soldiers at the checkpoint to let Fallon through. "Now beat it, Doc, before I forget that you're not such a bad kinda crazy guy."

It was reassuring to hear, even though there was no way to be certain that what Raoul had said characterized the mood of the army as a whole, or even that Raoul himself had meant it. As Sam Letumbai had told Barindas, to wait until they had *all* the facts would guarantee being too late.

Since he had expected that Embatto would want to deprive him of any opportunity of further contact with the ZRF, he was mildly surprised not to be arrested and whisked away immediately on entering the city. But he arrived back at Tobins without incident, and Xavier showed him to the same room—keeping himself well back, Fallon noted with amusement, when he opened the door.

Fallon's next aim, if he remained at large long enough, was to meet Yolatta to coordinate final plans when Yolatta materialized in Kinnube, which, according to the tentative timetable that had been worked out when Letumbai left Tenyasha, ought to be at any time now. But he didn't doubt that the place was under surveillance, as he himself would be wherever he went. But that had been anticipated. To preserve the secret of Yolatta's whereabouts, Fallon had been told that the procedure for establishing contact would be communicated to him after he arrived. It was Xavier who gave him the details.

The shadows were lengthening as evening approached in the valley leading up toward Tenyasha. At one place, the track came out of a defile and entered a stretch that was overlooked by broken slopes on one side, flanked on the other by a rocky depression with a floor of short elephant grass and sandy gullies, and commanded from ahead by a high crag. As an ambush site for motorized columns, it was a natural.

Austin watched from one side of the track as Sung Feng finished boring a six-foot-deep, one-and-a-half-inch-diameter hole in the center and extracted the bit of the camouflet set. Next, Feng inserted a small primer charge and detonated it electrically, creating a cavity at the bottom of the entry hole without disturbing the road surface. He then showed Candy, who was assisting him, how to feed the prepared pieces of plastic explosive down through the hollow camouflet tube, and stood back to let her continue the process until the cavity was filled. Finally, he withdrew the tube, lowered a compact detonator onto the charge, and filled the hole with displaced earth to act both as tamping and camouflage. The result was virtually invisible, even from a few feet.

"You got that okay?" Austin said to Candy. "You can carry on tomorrow morning and do the rest the same way?"

"It will be fine," she said.

"Okay, let's get the rest of this stuff tidied up for

tonight," Austin said to the helpers who were doing the lifting and carrying.

Feng looked on as they sorted out reels, packs, and boxes, and began loading them into the truck parked just off the track. "Pletty good stuff when vis go up," he told them. "Charge make twenny-feet-acloss goddamn fuckin' clater. Evelythin' totarry obritelated. You see."

Austin nodded and turned, hands on hips, to survey the other squad working down in the depression to one side, where they were setting up a nightmare composition of trip-wire grenades, antipersonnel mines, fragmentation bombs, and booby traps that would be lethal for anything that tried to move. Feng's reasoning was that when the mines went off, blocking both ends of the column, the soldiers in the personnel carriers would disembark and deploy. While they were doing so, ZRF machine guns would open up from high on the broken slopes to the right . . . but seemingly sited too far back to be effective. The soldiers would therefore seek cover on the far side, among the gullies and rocks in the depression—and run straight into the mine field. That would be the signal for the mortars, preregistered on the killing zone and the stretch where the vehicles would be immobilized, to open up from the reverse side of the crag.

When they arrived back at the caves an hour later, by which time dusk had fallen, Marie Guridan informed them that the code word had been received from Kinnube that Barindas had arrived there safely and made his rendezvous with Velker.

The ZRF were unusually active across the whole area to the west of Kinnube that night, as they had been for several nights in a row now. Military posts were hit with rocket and mortar attacks; columns camped for the night were harassed by infiltrators and sniper fire; army patrols sent out to lie in wait along nocturnal ZRF supply routes found themselves walking into ambushes themselves instead. The pattern was such as to keep the government forces busy up and down the major highways and around the bases and strong points along them. Meanwhile on the lesser-used tracks and paths through remote farms and in the deeper reaches of the bush, lines of dark-clad figures carrying packs and weapons moved silently toward the east, converging in a slow tide upon Kinnube.

At the top of a rise where the trail passed between grassy hillocks dotted with tangles of trees standing out stark in the night whenever the moonlight broke through the clouds, Sam Letumbai stopped and turned with the butt of his rifle resting on his hip. He tipped his Australian slouch hat to the back of his head, hooked a thumb through the strap of his pack to rest his shoulders from the weight, and ran his eye back over the line of guerrillas extending in strung-out single file back into the darkness.

A youth carrying an AK47 with one arm, three grenades on each webbing strap, and a box of two-inch mortar shells slung on top of his pack, caught Letumbai's eye as he passed. His teeth flashed white in a grin, and he made an exaggerated show of puffing to get his breath back. Letumbai grinned back at him.

"Where you goin', boy?"

"Goin' to Kinnube."

"What y'gonna do there?"

"Gonna blow them comrades all to hell."

Letumbai straightened himself up to call back down the line. "Keep it moving, guys. Gonna be in Kinnube before you know it. An' we're goin' there to stay, right?"

"Yeah!" someone responded.

"You all comin' there with me?"

"*Yeah!*" several more voices answered.

"Well, I'm a-tellin' ya, I ain't no brother. I ain't no comrade. I'm the *chief!*"

"YEAH!"

Chapter Forty-four

FALLON HAD BARELY HAD TIME TO RINSE HIS FACE
the next morning when a series of sharp raps on the door
announced the arrival of the police. Minutes later, he was
hustled outside, past the inevitable gaggle of onlookers, to
where a jeep was waiting to take him in for "routine
questioning."

Julius Embatto was not looking pleased when Fallon
was brought into an office inside Kinnube Central Police
Headquarters fifteen minutes later. Sitting beside Embatto,
Makon Ngoyba wore a matching expression of solemnity.
Apparently the geniality that he had shown when Fallon
met him in London wasn't appropriate to occasions when
the chief was present. Sullivan, as usual, sat by the door,
glowering.

"Tumratta was a valuable resource to us," Embatto
said. "Was it necessary to go to such an extreme? Did you
have to kill him?"

Fallon had been expecting the question and answered
matter-of-factly but firmly. He still felt a warm glow inside
at the turn which that particular event had taken; an
attempt at faking any great regret would have been impossible. "He walked in at the wrong time. There was no way
I could know whether he was in on the plan or if he would
have blown it. Shutting him up was the only way to be
certain that Trojan Horse wouldn't be wrecked before it
had even begun." Fallon shrugged. "And it presented an
added opportunity to convince the girl. Which was more
important? I had less than two seconds to decide. What
would you have done?"

He got the feeling that Embatto could already see this
and was going through the motions of protest mainly as a
matter of form. Embatto looked at Ngoyba for an opinion.
"If he hadn't seen it that way, he'd hardly be the right man

for the job," Ngoyba offered. "Ruthlessness is what we're paying for."

Embatto appeared to consider the statement, finally signaling his acceptance with a curt nod. He waved a hand to indicate the tape recorder standing on the desk. "Let us get to the rest of it. . . . Well, Mr. Fugleman, what is your overall conclusion from the mission? Is Trojan Horse practicable in your opinion?"

"Yes, I reckon so." Fallon produced the notes that he had prepared before leaving Tenyasha. Before launching into them, he expressed surprise that Thombert wasn't to be present at the debriefing. It was the general, after all, who had outlined the plan to Fallon and given him the list of targets.

"General Thombert was not a party to our, ah, understanding concerning the two people who escaped from the jail," Embatto informed him. "President Molokutu asked that knowledge of the affair be kept to the absolute minimum. Consider this a preliminary session. Thombert will be joining us formally for a more complete covering either tomorrow or the day after. He is otherwise engaged today. The army units for the Scabbard operation are already being moved out."

"Yes, I saw some of them on my way here," Fallon said. "Why the haste? You didn't even know what my answer on Trojan Horse would be until just now."

"We are anxious to move as soon as possible. Anticipating a favorable answer from you avoided alerting the enemy by a lot of rushed troop movements at the last moment. The orders could always be canceled if it turned out to be negative."

Fallon nodded. Ngoyba leaned forward and pressed the "record" button on the tape unit.

For the next hour, Fallon went through his notes with them and presented his version of the things that had happened since his departure from Kinnube. The other two listened carefully, interrupting only now and again with questions or requests for him to elaborate on some point.

"We've received indications from certain sources that the ZRF are moving their headquarters north to a place called Boake Rift," Embatto said at one point. "What do you know of that?"

"That's a decoy operation," Fallon told him. "The real place is the caves at Tenyasha, farther up above Owanden. They have a large base there. Barindas, Letumbai, and Guridan are already there. Yolatta and the rest will be joining them. False rumors are being put out about Boake Rift for the benefit of any informers you've got operating there." He noticed Embatto and Ngoyba exchanging faint nods, and added, after a short pause, "I get the feeling that you already know that."

"It confirms our other intelligence," Embatto said. "Thombert is concentrating his force in that direction. I have ordered our own SS Second and Third Battalions to proceed there also as a reserve, designated Cobra Force." Embatto didn't press Fallon for further details of the ZRF strength and installation at Tenyasha, thus tacitly admitting that he possessed the information already.

This was confirmed a few minutes later when Embatto said, "One of the people there is a German by the name of Tannerling. You met him." Fallon had been wondering when this would come up. Clearly, if Tannerling had been caught and executed as a spy—which was the official story—Fallon would know about it. It wouldn't have taken Fallon long to guess whom Tannerling had been a spy for, and Embatto wasn't bothering to try and deny it. By the same token, he was also telling Fallon that that was how he had known about Tenyasha already.

"He's dead," Fallon replied. Embatto's eyebrows rose, indicating surprise—which Fallon doubted very much to be genuine. It was simply Embatto's way of not revealing whether he had other sources operating. Fallon went on, "He was caught radioing coded signals out and got shot trying to make a break for it." He paused for a moment to inject an appropriate note of speculation. "I, ah, assumed he was probably yours."

Embatto shrugged. "I'm sure that you understand the necessity of being doubly cautious in this kind of business, Mr. Fugleman."

They moved on and came to the time of Fallon's departure for Kinnube. Ngoyba asked, "Who was this old man that you collected on your travels?"

"Just an old man. He offered to help with chores in return for a ride back to Kinnube. There didn't seem any point in refusing. In fact it seemed a good idea, since there was no way the girl was going to come back here. Hannegen had left with a guide. It would have looked odd if he came back without one at all." Fallon shrugged. "And I needed one, anyway. I wasn't sure of the right road."

"Why did he want to come into Kinnube?" Embatto asked.

"He didn't talk much ... not about anything that made sense, anyhow." Fallon tapped his temple. "I think he was going a bit soft up here."

"Where did you leave him?"

"He got out suddenly somewhere on the south side of the city—it was in a market of some kind."

"You don't know where he went then?"

"No. I was glad to get rid of him. He smelled like a goat."

That seemed to cover all the major points, with one exception: the timetable for the whole operation.

"The news from our London embassy is that the people Stroller has recruited are assembled there and ready to move," Embatto said. Stroller was the code name for Henri Monaux that Fallon had given to Ngoyba. "You'll need to remain in Kinnube for a couple more days until we have agreed the final details. Then Konrad Hannegen's work in Zugenda will be finished and he can leave the country. I would allow two days, say, for you to return and brief the others on the operation, another two for you to enter Zugenda via your various routes, and a further five beyond that for you and the primary squad to renew contact with Barindas, by which time the support group should have infiltrated separately. Therefore, we should be talking about a jump-off date around eleven days from now. Do I take it that I have your agreement to notify General Thombert and the president accordingly?"

Fallon sat back and stared into the distance as he thought through everything one last time. At last he focused back on the two men watching him. "Yes, I think that would work out just fine," he told them.

"Very good." Embatto nodded and seemed satisfied. "Then there is just one other thing. We shall be flying helicopter operations in support of Cobra Force. There will be a preliminary briefing for pilots and gunners at HQ tomorrow morning, which I'd like you to attend, Mr.

Fugleman. Your observations of the ZRF dispositions around Owanden and Tenyasha would make a valuable contribution."

"Okay..." Fallon looked puzzled. "What do you want me to do—just walk into SSHQ?"

"You will be contacted at Tobins."

So, somewhat to his surprise, Fallon found himself walking back out onto the street again less than an hour later. Following the instructions that Xavier had given him, he made a detour on his way back to Tobins, which took him through an area of litter-strewn streets populated by the destitute and the derelict, hungry-looking dogs, and poorly clad children. Along one of the streets was a boarded-up shop with a sign overhead written in Indian, next to a rickety wooden apartment house with a balcony looking down over the street. The balcony was bare. It meant that no meeting with Yolatta and Barindas could yet be fixed.

He spent the early part of the afternoon sauntering around to familiarize himself more with the layout of the city. It would be good, too, for the Zugendan security men who had been tailing him ever since he left the police headquarters, some of whom looked as if they could use the exercise, he thought. Then he spent a few hours relaxing in his room back at Tobins to let them cool off.

But at the same time, the outcome of the morning's events had left him feeling uneasy. He'd seen enough Embattos to know how their minds worked. They trusted no one, suspected everything, and took no chances, which said that by all the rules, Fallon should have been kept safely out of the way until the time came for him to leave Zugenda, and not left free to walk the streets.

Was Embatto worried, perhaps, that detaining Hannegen for collusion with the rebels would give away the existence of his other sources in Tenyasha? Fallon couldn't see it. For one thing, the source of that information could just as easily have been Tannerling, who was dead, and now known to the ZRF to have been an SS agent anyway. And for another, governments in countries like this didn't need reasons for arresting people, so it wouldn't have aroused undue suspicions in any case.

The whole business didn't feel right. He lay for a long time staring up at the ceiling, going over everything that

had happened and searching for other oddities to see if any
pattern emerged.

Since Embatto was planning a coup, the exclusion of
Thombert from the proceedings had been not unexpected—
Fallon had expressed surprise for appearance' sake. The
preliminary session had been to allow Embatto to reassure
himself that Fallon would say nothing out of place at the
formal debriefing. So everything seemed straightforward
there.

The movements of the army at such an early date did
seem strange, however. It was true, as Embatto had said,
that staggering them over a period would attract less
attention than leaving everything till the last moment. But
eleven days seemed an unduly generous allowance to
make—especially before Fallon's verdict on Trojan Horse
was even in.

All in all, there wasn't a lot, he had to admit when he
analyzed the facts. But nevertheless, some deeper part of
his mind had sensed something that was causing a tingling
along his spine and up the back of his neck, giving him the
uncomfortable feeling of a fly just beginning to realize that
its surroundings had a distinctly parlorlike look about
them. He wondered where the hell Marlow was and how
long it would take him to get in touch.

Early in the evening, Fallon left the hotel again to eat
at a greasy curry shop on the corner. Afterward, he walked
a few blocks farther, following a route that took him along
the same street that he had checked earlier in the day. A
line of washing had appeared on the balcony of the wooden
apartment house, and the items hanging on it included a
red headscarf between two white handkerchiefs. Fallon
continued for another couple of streets, then went into a
bar and sat down after ordering a cigar and a beer.

The security man entered a minute or so later, ordered a bourbon, and took up position at a table in the
corner, making himself about as inconspicuous as a bishop
in a chorus line. When Fallon got up a short while later
and went out through the rear entrance, the security man
knew that he was just visiting the urinal shack outside and
would be back shortly, because he had left his glass
two-thirds full and his cigar burning in the ashtray beside
it.

Five minutes later, he was becoming less certain.

His apprehension was substantiated when he went out to check and found the shack empty, with the Dane nowhere in sight. But at the briefing earlier, the target had been described as possibly slippery, and both the front and rear of the premises would have been watched by other members of the surveillance team that had been deployed.

"Blue Three to Control, come in," he said into the two-way pocket radio that he was carrying.

"Reading you, Three."

"Contact lost at Kelozi's bar on Forge Street. Evasion was deliberate."

"It's okay. Subject has been picked up by Blue Five, heading north."

"Want me to head up that way and take another sector?"

"No, I guess you're blown now. Better report back."

"Roger."

"Out."

Within minutes, a transcript of the exchange had been passed to Embatto in his office on the top floor of state-security headquarters. "Hmm, interesting." He handed the sheet to Ngoyba and exhaled from one of his monogrammed cigarettes. "What should Mr. Fugleman have to hide from us that makes him want to lose them?"

Ngoyba read rapidly. "Already...? Do you think it could be what we're hoping for?"

"We'll soon find out."

Fallon crossed the street, entered the lobby of the Independence Hotel, and without giving anyone at the desk time to object, went straight on past the cane-screened coffee shop to the bar at the rear, which was already busy with the evening's trade. He paused at the door and ran an eye over the room. Stan and Pete, the sallow, blond-haired youth and the lanky, bearded one who had been here the evening when Fallon first came to Kinnube, were sitting on stools at one end. Fallon edged his way through and found himself a place between them and a slim, midtwentyish white girl in safari suit with name tag and armband, who was expounding ardently to a male companion on why the Africans simply *had* to be made to see that the answer was to stop cutting down the trees.

Fallon ordered a drink and sipped intermittently at it for a few minutes, all the time casting uneasy glances around the room, particularly toward the far end, where a number of girls in colorful, glittery dresses were chattering. Finally he leaned forward and tapped the youth called Pete on the shoulder.

"Hello again. Do you remember me?"

"Should we?" Pete wore the same expression of cunning and suspicion, tempered by an ever-present alertness to grab any chances that might be going. Stan, as before, remained vacant-eyed and listless.

"I arrived a couple of weeks ago. We spoke here at the bar."

"Oh, yeah ... from Holland or someplace, right?"

"Denmark."

"Was it ... ? Okay."

"You, er... you mentioned at the time that you have many kinds of, I think you called them 'connections.'" Fallon glanced around furtively and drew closer. "I wonder if I might ask you a question. You see, it's like this. ..."

He talked intently in lowered voice with the two youths for a few minutes, ending with a series of rapid nods and slipping Pete a folded bill. Then he finished his drink quickly and left. Stan and Pete watched him go, then looked at each other and shrugged. Pete waved the bill in his hand and called to the bartender for refills. The Zugendan security man who had followed the exchange from a booth near the door came over to them.

"That man who was talking to you just now, what did he want?"

Pete turned on his stool and looked the questioner up and down. "What the fuck's it to you, man?"

The security man pushed an ID card in front of his face with one hand and seized the front of his shirt roughly with the other. His voice was low but menacing. "Listen, you streak of white shit, when *I* do the askin', *you* answer." He twisted the material of the shirt, screwing the knuckle of his fist into Pete's throat. "Now, who was the dude and what did he want?"

"Jesus! Arghh ... Okay, back off. I dunno who he is. A prick who was in here a couple weeks back, into some kinda shit to do with animals. We talked to him at the bar. That's all I know."

"What did he want tonight?"

"Piece of ass. Says he's been out in the boonies for weeks and needs to get his rocks off. . . . We sent him to Sadie's. Anything wrong with that?"

Back out on the street a minute later, the security man radioed HQ. "Blue Four to Control, subject has left the Independence."

"Roger, Four. We have him. Move east on Central and take up position at the intersection with Bank. Over."

"Wilco, Control, but I think the heat's off. We can all save a lotta time on this."

"What do you mean, Four?"

"He's feelin' horny, that's all. Headin' for Sadie's place. Someone's gonna have a long wait outside there for nuthin', and I hope it ain't me."

"You sure about that?"

"Sure I'm sure."

"Then why's he being to secretive about it?"

"How do I know? You've only gotta be white to be crazy."

Embatto handed the sheet to Ngoyba with a resigned look a few minutes later. "It appears that our hopes were a little premature," he said. "Mr. Fugleman evidently has a more human side to him than we'd appreciated." He studied the sheet again and shook his head. "I must say that I applaud his professionalism—playing out the pompous Konrad Hannegen to the end. But he will lead us to Barindas eventually."

"Shall I call off the blue team?" Ngoyba asked.

"Mmm . . . better keep a couple on standby to make sure that he gets back to Tobins without trouble. I'd hate anything to happen to him at this late stage. And then there's the risk that he might be stopped by a patrol and need to be extricated. . . . But have them out again at full strength first thing tomorrow morning."

Chapter Forty-five

THE FRONT DOOR OF SADIE'S WAS OF HEAVY, polished wood with an inlaid pattern of colored glass, standing atop a short run of steps. Fallon pressed the bell push and was greeted by a curvy, long-haired girl with heavy makeup and a skimpy dress that left nothing to be imagined about her ample, coffee-colored breasts and not much more about her shapely legs underneath. She treated him to a pout and a sultry smile. "Hi. Looking for some company?"

"I was told that Dora would look after me personally. The name is Hannegen."

"Oh. Wait here, I'll see." The girl disappeared through a curtained archway at the back of the room. She returned a minute or two later with a fuller-bodied, older woman, generously adorned with jewelry and wearing a dark, satiny dress with silver embellishment.

"Good evening, Mr. Hannegen. Yes, we were expecting you. I think you will find the arrangements satisfactory. Follow me, please. Thank you, Lila. That will be all."

Dora led the way through some interconnecting rooms with chairs and sofas and up a series of stairways and landings to the top floor. From there, a twisting corridor divided by doors took them to the rear of the building, where more stairs brought them back down to ground level in a part that Fallon guessed to be off limits to normal visitors and probably accessible only by the tortuous route they had taken. A cupboard built into an alcove at a bend in the stairs turned out to be a concealed door. Beyond it was a short passage containing several more doors. After closing the false cupboard behind them, Dora tapped on one of the doors and murmured in a low voice, "It's Dora. He's here."

The sound of a bolt being drawn came from the far

side; then the door opened to reveal the face of Dr. Felix
Velker. Barindas was at a table in the room behind him,
and with him was the huge, ebony, solid-jawed figure of
Haile Yolatta, clad in a drab brown peasant's robe, shawl,
and sandals.

"Good to see you again," Velker greeted, shaking
Fallon's hand warmly and ushering him in. "Did you have
any problems?"

"It looks as if it all went okay."

"Splendid. Now, you haven't met Haile yet, have you?
This is Boris, at last. You've both been hearing a lot about
each other."

"I'd better get back front," Dora said. She pointed
across the room. "The button's there if you need anything." Then she left, closing the door. Her footsteps
receded and silence fell. Velker and Fallon sat down with
the others.

"How safe is this place?" Fallon asked.

"How safe is anywhere?" Velker answered. "The quick
way out is the window in the room opposite. We've got
ZRF watching the streets from some of the houses
around."

Fallon nodded. "I presume Sam made it okay," he
said, looking at Yolatta.

"He got the decoy group away to Boake Rift ahead of
schedule, and should be on his way to Kinnube by now,"
Yolatta confirmed. "We should see him tomorrow, maybe
even sometime tonight."

"Good." Fallon nodded again. "So . . . by now you
should be fairly up to date on what's been going on. What
do you think of the plan in general?"

Yolatta bunched his mouth and nodded his head slowly.
"Obviously there have to be risks. But I can't see how
you'd improve on it much."

"How did the debriefing with Embatto go?" Barindas
asked.

"Well, he was a bit upset about us croaking his
interrogator, but we expected that."

"What about the timetable? Did you get anywhere
with that?" Yolatta asked.

Fallon nodded. "I leave probably two days from now,"
he replied. Barindas began writing in a notepad. "A couple
of days to get to London and clue the team up, a week

more to get everyone back here and into position, and
he'll be expecting a signal around then."

"Let's see, eleven days." Barindas pored over some
notes lying on the table between him and Yolatta, along
with a diary crammed with scribblings. He flipped a page.
"I make that the twenty-second." He looked up.

"Right," Fallon confirmed. "The army have already
begun moving out, and they're going the right way."

"We know," Yolatta said. "There's an SS force concentrating down toward Glimayel too."

"Embatto says it's a reserve for Thombert," Fallon
said. "But I think it's more likely to be on hand to take
over after the army and the ZRF have fought it out."

Yolatta nodded. "That's what we figured."

"Austin is arranging the defenses there," Barindas put
in.

"How does it seem?" Velker asked anxiously, looking
from one to another.

"I think we're in business," Yolatta said. "Our units
have begun moving in. Some of them ran into trouble, but
we've got a few in the city or pretty close to it already. We
should have a good enough buildup in that time, even
allowing for wastage."

"How far did you and Sam get with the operation
here in the city?" Fallon asked Yolatta. "Did the outline
that we worked out seem on the right track?"

In answer, Yolatta reached inside his robe and produced a flat leather purse, tied with a thong. He took out a
wad of folded sheets and spread them on the table. "A lot
depends on exactly how the fight goes between the army
forces and the SS, but these are the objectives that we see
as minimum. It's pretty much on the lines that you and
Sam proposed. The main change we made was assigning
more rocket units to Mordun."

Fallon scanned the sheets quickly while Yolatta sum-
marized. They contained details of key points to be seized—
police and military headquarters, the Radio Building, presidential palace, Mordun air base, and several others that
Fallon hadn't listed—with estimates of manpower and
special weaponry required, notes on tactics and timing,
guesses of casualties.

Despite his garb, Yolatta's proud-set features and
upright bearing stamped him as every inch the warrior. Yet

he spoke, curiously, in a firm but quiet, softly resonant voice, using few words and coming directly to the point. His very lack of forcefulness underscored a natural authority that didn't need overt displays of assertiveness to carry itself. Fallon recalled again the complementarity that he had sensed earlier between the personalities of Yolatta and Barindas, and how effective such a combination might prove. To Fallon's relief, he didn't seem to have any hang-ups about losing face or having his authority undermined at the idea of using outsiders. As long as they were competent, he would use all the help he could get. Fallon was satisfied that he was dealing with a professional.

"It's changed a bit from the original idea, I know," Fallon said when they had finished. "I only wish that my team could take out the general management for you the way we first planned. But we can't be in two places at once. We'll make sure that the guys coming over the border down south bring plenty of stuff with them to help out, though." He spread his hands in a way that said the situation was beyond his control, but then he noticed that Yolatta was giving Barindas a questioning look. Barindas returned a faint nod.

"There is something more that you can do for us," Yolatta said. He got up and went over to a closet in the corner of the room. When he opened it, Fallon saw a small cache of automatic weapons and pistols inside, hanging ready for instant use. From the shelf above, Yolatta took a brown cardboard carton about the size of two paperback books stacked together, closed the closet door, and came back to the table.

Inside the package was a notepad, about the size of those used by newspaper reporters, held shut by two stout rubber bands. There was a ballpoint pen pushed underneath one of them. Fallon looked at Yolatta oddly, and Yolatta nodded for him to go ahead. Fallon picked up the book, removed the bands, and set the pen aside. The book turned out to be considerably thicker than a typical reporter's pad, however. It was bound by glued tape along the top, with a paper cover carrying a commercial design and logo, and a cardboard backing sheet. When he flicked curiously through the sheets, he found them to be of uncommonly heavy-gauge paper. They were unruled and blank.

"A present from your colonel," Yolatta said.

"You can talk about him here," Barindas threw in.

Fallon examined the book again, then weighed it experimentally in one hand. Suddenly a light of comprehension dawned in his eyes. "RDX?" he queried. Yolatta nodded. Fallon picked up the pen and turned it over between his fingers. "Detonator."

"You've got it."

RDX was an extremely versatile explosive, generally obtained by extraction from C4 "plastique." A chunk of it the size of a potato would level a bungalow. RDX could be moistened and used like a plastic explosive, or mixed with flour and stored without arousing suspicion. In fact, the combination of RDX and flour could be mixed with eggs and milk and made into such things as pancakes and biscuits, innocent in appearance yet fully retaining the substance's lethal properties. In the version that Yolatta had produced, the sheets were a soluble paper base filled with a compound of RDX and a binding agent.

"You're familiar with this stuff?" Yolatta said, cocking an eye. To one side, Velker made a distasteful face but said nothing.

Fallon nodded. "Sure." The package would simply need to be moistened into a solid mass before use to remove the air pockets, and the detonator pushed into it. In the meantime it was quite safe.

Yolatta took another, smaller box from the wrappings, showed it for a moment, and then put it inside his pocket. "The detonator is radio-triggered. You arm it by rotating the clip through three-sixty degrees twice, like this, like this, then pressing the retractor button." Yolatta demonstrated by turning the clip through a full circle once about its attachment point to the top, which turned out to be pivoted. Then he turned it back again. "When the action starts here in Kinnube, you'll be down in Glimayel. But for the next couple of days right now, you're going to be around Embatto most of the time. There's a chance that you might get taken inside SS headquarters. Down underneath it there's a bomb-proof command bunker which is where Embatto will most likely be when things start to happen. If it all goes the way he plans, we'll end up with Thombert and Molokutu out of the way, the army and SS mauling each other all over the city, and only Embatto and his crew down in the bunker holding everything together." Yolatta gestured at the device in Fallon's hand. "If you can get that inside there somehow before you go, and we pick that moment to press the button..." Yolatta shrugged and left the sentence unfinished.

"Down in a bunker?" Fallon looked doubtful. "What kind of range are we talking about? Can you be sure that a signal would penetrate?"

"We'll worry about that. The signal is relayed through some powerful stuff we got hidden in this city, and the detonator only needs a whisper. Your colonel has some interesting friends."

"I can't guarantee anything," Fallon cautioned.

"We understand that," Barindas said. "But you appreciate the difference that it could make. Let us know over the link when you get to London if you had any success."

Fallon nodded. "I'll do my best."

"That's all we ask."

Fallon opened the notebook, took a regular pen from his pocket, and began scribbling some notes and reminders on the first few pages to make it look more legitimate. "So what's the news with the colonel?" he asked, glancing up at Barindas as he wrote.

"He's been very busy. Your friend from the U.S. arrived safely."

"Tam?"

"Yes."

"Great."

"There's quite a story coming together."

"Did they manage to get anywhere with Bouabbas's notes?"

"I think it would be best if the colonel told you that story himself," Barindas said.

"He's still here, then?"

"Oh, yes, at a safe place. He'll be in touch when we can find a way to lose your tail for a while. It would be too conspicuous to try bringing him here."

"Is Lichuru still around?" Fallon asked.

"Apparently he's out of the country again at the moment," Velker said. "We believe, in the States."

"That's interesting, anyway. . . ." Fallon looked around the table.

"That's about as much as we can say for now," Yolatta said. "Is everyone happy?"

"What if the army and state security bury their differences and close ranks against us when we move?" Velker asked.

"Well, half the army's already on its way to Owanden," Fallon replied. "And I think that a big chunk of the rest will defect if things start to go our way."

"You think?" Velker repeated uneasily. "That's nice, I agree, but all our necks happen to be depending on this. How do you *know*?"

Fallon stared down at the table. It was a valid question. But there were some things that it was pointless to dwell on beyond the limit of one's ability to alter. That was how demoralization always set in.

"There's only so much that you can do, Felix," he said, looking up. "My neck depends on this too, don't forget. We'll be in the way of the half that's heading south. There are some questions you have to have answers to; with others you just hope you're right. And that's one that we just have to leave to the historians to worry about after it's all over."

It was after midnight when Dora led Fallon back up and through the roundabout route down to the front lounge again. There was music playing from a tape deck, and lots of noise and laughter. Two blacks in shirtsleeves and unfastened ties were swaying and whooping with their arms around a pair of girls each, while another was sprawled back on one of the sofas, clutching a bottle and looking very much the worse for wear. Lila was slapping his cheek lightly and trying to rouse him. More laughing and screaming was coming from a door at the rear.

"Hey, whitey, come an' join the party," one of the men yelled. "Jus' t'prove that *we* ain't prej'diced."

"Hey, why not?" one of the girls invited.

"They're just having a good time, don't worry about them," Dora said, steering Fallon to the door. "We'll soon get them quietened down. It's part of the trade." Then, in a louder voice, "Good night, Mr. Hannegen. I hope we see you again."

Fallon descended the four or five wooden steps outside the door and turned to head back toward Tobins. On a far corner, a figure in a dark windbreaker detached itself from a lamppost and began moving in the same direction. Fallon tightened his grip on the jacket that he was holding slung over one shoulder with the RDX notebook stuffed into one of the side pockets.

He walked briskly, going over in his mind one more time all the things that had now been set in motion, searching for the flaws and the weaknesses—in anything that connected with the real world, there were always some. The premonition that something, somewhere was wrong was still sending up currents of uneasiness from deep below the level of thought, like some subconscious process of convection, but he was unable to bring the cause to the surface. But with everything set in motion he could hardly call a halt now purely because of a vague misgiving that he was unable to substantiate—a normal enough reaction in circumstances like this, even at the best of times. There was nothing for it now but for them to press on and hope that the momentum they had built up would carry them through, one way or another.

Back at Sadie's, Dora closed the door to the private lounge behind her and rested her back against it with a sigh. From the other side of it, the roaring and screaming continued unabated. Three more financial advisers from the ministry had arrived, and she'd had to send upstairs for more reinforcements of girls. "You're just gonna have to take care of 'em," she told Lila, who was opening another carton of Scotch. "I hate to leave you holding it all, honey, but I've got to get away early tonight."

Lila smiled. "Don't you worry about me. I've handled worse. You get along. We'll see you tomorrow."

"You're a doll."

"You'd do the same."

"'Night, then."

Dora crossed the room and walked along a passage and down the stairs that led to her private office. She opened the door with the key that she kept on a chain inside her dress, let herself in, and slipped the bolt behind her. Then she opened a glass-fronted cabinet opposite the desk, which contained drinks, glasses, and a few orna-

ments, and released a hidden catch that enabled it to
swing away from the wall. The recess behind contained a
panel with sockets connected to wires coming from rooms
all over the building. The tape recorder that was plugged
into one of the sockets was still turning, its take-up reel
only two-thirds full.

Dora stopped the machine, changed the tape for a
clean one, and set it running again. She placed the used
tape in a package with the others she had been collecting
throughout the afternoon and evening, and sealed it shut.
Then she closed the cabinet again, put on her coat and
hat, locked the office behind her, and left the building
inconspicuously through a side entrance, clutching the
package and her purse. An unmarked car with a driver in
plain clothes was waiting for her in the shadows at the far
end of the alley. Only when they were out of the city
center and sure that nothing was following did they turn in
the direction of General Thombert's residence on the
outskirts of town.

A little over an hour later, Thombert called the presidential palace on a secure phone from an armchair in the
master bedroom suite of his former colonial villa and was
put through to a sleepy-sounding Molokutu.

"Embatto has set everyone up," he told the president. "He's fixing up to take over, and he's about ready to
move."

"*What?*"

"That's not all. Fugleman is screwing all of us. He's
working for the ZRF."

The sleepiness went out of Molokutu's voice. "You're
certain?"

"And Barindas and Yolatta aren't at Tenyasha. They're
right here, in the city."

"That's impossible."

"You can hear it all for yourself. I've got it on
tape."

"Shit . . . You'd better get over here."

Dora, propped against silken pillows in the bed on
the far side of the room, looked up from the magazine she
had been flicking through. "Don't tell me. Business
calls."

"Get some rest," Thombert said, replacing the phone

and rising from the chair. "I reckon this might take a while."

"Will you be back by morning?"

"Can't say. Probably not."

"Maybe I should just go home."

Thombert frowned and shook his head as he reached for his tie. "I wouldn't do that. Better stay here." He pressed a bell push to summon his valet. "In fact, don't go out on the streets at all until I get back or until you hear from me, okay. I've got a feeling that all hell's gonna be breaking loose by morning."

Chapter Forty-six

THE EASTERN SKY WAS JUST BEGINNING TO BRIGHT-
en when three army trucks drew up in the streets around
Sadie's. Shouted orders and the clatter of boots on cobbles
broke the dawn silence as steel-helmeted regular troops
threw a cordon around the sides and rear of the building,
while more trucks, a staff car, and several armored vehicles
deployed in front. The colonel who was in command rapped
loudly on the door with his baton.

"Open up. C'mon, move it in there."

"What the hell is it?" Lila's voice shouted from a
window above.

"This is official. You've got one minute to open up.
Else we're coming in."

Faces peered out of windows along the street. A man
in white undershorts, clutching a bundle of clothing, tried
to bolt from the side door in the alley and was stopped by
troops.

Then Lila opened the door, wide-eyed and confused,
still pulling on a silk robe. "What is this? What's going
on?"

"Where's Dora?" the colonel demanded.

"She ain't here. She left last night. What the hell—"

Another officer pushed her aside and the colonel
waved his men through. The crash of breaking doors
reverberated through the building, intermingled with shrill
screams and deeper shouts of indignation. The colonel's
orders were to make the search look authentic, but without overdoing damage to the property. To protect his
source, Thombert had not given the exact location of the
room hiding Barindas and the others.

Struggling, spitting, and shrieking obscenities, the
girls were hauled out of the rooms in whatever clothes
they were found in, which in many cases meant none at

all, with a lot of groping and pawing that the soldiers seemed to enjoy. The guests who were still on the premises, sleepy-eyed and hung over, were brought down to the ground-floor lounge. A fat man with a bald head, his face contorted in fury, tried futilely to preserve a shred of dignity while struggling to pull on his pants.

"It'll be your fuckin' ass for this," he bellowed at the colonel as a trooper prodded him back against the wall with the muzzle of a rifle. "Have you any idea who I am?"

"Orders come down from the president personally. I don't give a rat shit who you are," the colonel retorted.

Another important-looking personage was pushed into the room wearing makeup on his face and clad in female underwear. "Oh, boy," a sergeant muttered, turning his face away to smirk out of a window.

Consternation had broken out in the secret rooms at the rear, where the occupants could hear the banging and commotion through the structure of the building.

"Will they find us back here?" Velker gasped as he sat on the edge of the cot he had slept in, fighting to lace his canvas shoes.

Yolatta listened tensely. "They're searching for something," he said.

"You mean they know we're here?" Barindas said, horrified.

"Maybe."

Yolatta looked out of the door, then crossed the passage outside to the room opposite, where the escape window was located. He moved the drapes a fraction and looked through the chink. "The street's sealed off," he hissed to Velker, who had followed him.

"What is it?" Barindas whispered anxiously from the doorway behind them.

"Soldiers out there," Yolatta answered. He turned from the window and strode back past the other two. They followed, and by the time they came back into the other room he was opening the closet in the far corner. He took out various automatic weapons and sidearms and handed them out. Velker accepted a Sterling submachine gun and stared at it uncomfortably.

Out on the street at the front, the sound came of approaching sirens, and moments later several cars of the city police pulled up among the clutter of khaki-clad figures and army vehicles. An angry-looking deputy police chief strode up the steps and was challenged by the guards at the door. He pushed them aside and went in to seek the commanding officer. On the street, the soldiers and policemen eyed each other warily.

"This is inside city limits," the deputy police chief told the colonel. "You got no authority here. Jesus! Do you know what you're gettin' yourself into, bustin' into this place like that? What in hell's goin' on?"

"Orders from the president personally. That's my authority. So you can just get your ass out."

"I ain't heard nothin' about no orders."

"Then go check it with army HQ."

Sounds of breaking glass came from a corridor. A voice screamed somewhere upstairs: "Get your hands off me, you apes!"

The deputy police chief shook his head. "I'm tellin' ya, there's a lotta people in this town who ain't gonna like this. . . ."

While the argument developed inside, figures were slipping forward from house to house along the surrounding alleyways. Hands pushed magazines quietly into place and disengaged safety catches. . . .

The first bursts of automatic fire raked the street from different angles, causing instant pandemonium among the soldiers and policemen caught out in the open in the cross fire. A number panicked and began running about in confusion amidst those falling and writhing on the ground, while others ran to the vehicles for cover. Then a series of rocket-propelled grenades hit the vehicles when the targets were tightly bunched together, sending a truck and one of the police cars up in flames simultaneously. Most of the remainder fell back toward Sadie's . . . and converged into the line of fire from the machine gun that had been trained on the entrance from a roof across the street. The soldiers inside and out returned fire indiscriminately at every window and doorway in sight, while officers shouted frantically for them to reposition and regroup. ZRF projectiles hit the ground-floor windows, setting the front of the building alight. Then the sounds of explosions and more firing came from inside.

The officer leading the search of the back rooms had

been told to look behind an alcove at the bottom of some stairs and had just found a suspicious-looking cupboard when he heard the noise of the action out front. Deciding that this was no time for playing games, he rolled a grenade at the base of the cupboard, flattened himself behind an angle in the wall, and called his men down from above. The explosion blew the cupboard to pieces, revealing a passageway beyond. As the soldiers moved forward to investigate, another grenade came through from the opposite direction. It detonated as they scattered, sending fragments ricocheting off the walls and gouging into the woodwork, and blowing out the stairwell window. One man went down and was still; another reeled back, hit in the face and chest. The private behind them turned to run back up the stairs, but the officer clubbed him with his rifle and ordered him back down. Other soldiers poured fire into the passageway and approached it cautiously.

At the rear of the building, meanwhile, the soldiers forming the cordon had retreated behind cover upon hearing the firing. The ZRF watching them waited until the diversion at the front had erupted into a full firefight before opening up to keep them pinned down. Then they ignited drums packed with gasoline-soaked rags and shredded rubber and rolled them out into the street, which was soon blanketed in a pall of black, oily smoke. Under cover of the smoke, a detachment ran forward as a window at the back of Sadie's was broken open from the inside and a huge, bearded figure brandishing a submachine gun loomed for an instant in the opening.

Yolatta turned from the window and shouted back toward the doorway: "Quick! They're outside now!"

But the other two were still in the room across the passage, and bullets were raking it from one end. "We can't get across," Velker's voice called back desperately.

Tugging the pin from another grenade, Yolatta went back across the room and curled an arm around the side of the door frame to lob the grenade at the soldiers. As it detonated, he leaned around and poured a burst into the opening where the back of the cupboard had been. At the same time, Velker, crouching and holding the Sterling, came out of the doorway opposite. Barindas was close behind him ... too close. They bumped against each other and became entangled in the narrow doorway. Barindas caught a foot on the bottom of the jamb and fell.

"Get up, man!" Yolatta shouted. He leaned out and grasped Barindas's collar, but two soldiers appeared through the smoke at the end of the passageway. Yolatta, his back half-turned to them as he stooped to lift Barindas, was caught fully exposed. Then Velker stepped forward into the center of the passage to cover them, facing the soldiers squarely and firing from the hip while splinters and fragments flew off the walls on both sides of him. One of the soldiers let out a cry and crumpled. . . . And then Velker was hurled backward, cannoning into Barindas just as Yolatta was getting him to his feet. Blood poured over them and over Yolatta's hand, causing his grip to slip. Barindas went down again with Velker's body on top of him. Figures appeared in the window behind Yolatta, framed against the smoke outside.

"Come on!" a voice called frantically. "There's a way through across the street."

Soldiers were advancing into the passage. Yolatta seized Barindas's arm, heaved him clear, and practically hurled him across the room, where the waiting guerrillas bundled him unceremoniously over the sill. Yolatta backed after him, shredding the doorway with sustained fire to keep the soldiers back.

"Get out!" the voice shouted again.

Yolatta turned and vaulted through after Barindas while the guerrilla who had waited there fired past him. Ducking low, he zigzagged through the smoke to the far side of the street, where more shadowy figures sped him on into a doorway.

The army was active all over the city that morning, with firing breaking out in a number of places. Not far from military headquarters, an inexperienced tank driver had turned his vehicle across a narrow street, blocking the thoroughfare and stopping a troop carrier that was trying to go the other way, much to the annoyance of its commander. It was important, he had been told, that the arrest of the Dane, Hannegen, at Tobins Hotel, should coincide precisely with the raid on Sadie's.

*   *   *

Fallon awoke to the distant sounds of gunfire and explosions coming from several directions. He dressed quickly and met Xavier in the corridor outside, evidently on his way to Fallon's room.

"I don' know what in hell's goin' on," Xavier said, looking worried. "News over de phone says dere's tanks out all over. Shootin' around the west side o' downtown, where de gov'ment offices are."

One certain thing, however, was that if the action was about to involve Fallon, his staying at Tobins would merely increase the risk of the hotel's other secrets being discovered. "I'm getting out," he told Xavier. "If anyone's coming to get me, at least it'll draw them away from this place."

Fallon checked the streets at front and back from windows. He couldn't see any sign of Embatto's surveillance watchers, but what that might mean in relation to all the shooting, he didn't know. "When I'm sure I'm clean, I'll head back to Sadie's," he said. "I'll wait there with Barindas and the others until I hear from Marlow."

"Sounds good to me."

Fallon slipped out the back door into a cobblestoned yard flanked by cracking walls of sunbaked brick and littered with trash. He crossed it to emerge into a back street of shuttered stalls and dilapidated frontages, empty but for a burned settee and the stripped carcass of an automobile.

The sun had barely begun rising. Although gunfire was sounding clearly, farther on he found the town stirring with signs of life. Frightened people were scurrying about getting ready for a siege: moving into basements, collecting supplies, and boarding up windows. Shutters remained in place, and no children appeared on the streets. The soldiers that had been in evidence everywhere the day previously were gone, presumably recalled to barracks and strong points.

Ominous.

The white Fiat had been following him for a couple of blocks, keeping about fifty yards back. He had registered it automatically, presuming that the Zugendan surveillance team was on the job after all. It was only when he turned into a long stretch of unbroken street, with walls and closed doors flanking the roadway on both sides and no way to escape before the next corner, that the car began to speed up noticeably. But it closed on him only gradually, causing him to increase his pace until he was almost running and thinking that he might make it.

Given the time to look at it another way, he would probably have realized that the stratagem also put more distance between him and anyone else who might have been tailing him on foot.

When the car accelerated to draw alongside him with the door opening, he turned and flattened himself against the wall, gun already in hand. But instead of the strong-arm men that he had expected to come tumbling out, the black driver leaned across, holding the door, and hissed urgently, "Get in! It's okay: ZRF."

To stand any chance of finding out what was going on, he would have to take someone's word. He slipped the gun back under his jacket and climbed in. The car accelerated with a screech of rubber before he had closed the door. It turned at the first intersection, then immediately again, heading toward the maze of the inner city. Fallon looked across quizzically, but the driver kept his eyes fastened ahead. Then a voice spoke from the rear seat.

"Sadie's got hit first thing this morning. We don't know the score there yet, but it looks bad. First we'll get you to the base where Marlow is. Then we'll try and figure out what the hell we do now."

The voice was American, with a firm but worried drawl. Fallon's face creased with disbelief even before he turned.

It was Leroy Wylen.

So *that* was who the colonel's source in Kinnube had been!

Chapter Forty-seven

THE ACTIVITY AROUND THE PRESIDENTIAL PALACE resembled an army's deploying for battle. The tanks that had arrived soon after dawn from the main depot on the outskirts of Kinnube had taken up positions covering the approaches, and reinforcements to the regular palace guard were busy laying mines, erecting wire, and sandbagging extra defenses. President Molokutu watched through the armored glass of his upstairs study. His initial dazedness at hearing General Thombert's revelations in the middle of the night was giving way to deep, slow-burning rage at the way he had been duped from both directions.

It was bad enough to have been told that Embatto was on the verge of launching a coup and that Lichuru was behind him with foreign support—Thombert hadn't been able to confirm precisely where from, but Molokutu had the discomforting certainty that after his deals with Moscow it could only be the Western side of the consortium. All along, Embatto had intended Trojan Horse and Scabbard not simply as a way to defeat the ZRF, but as a means of paralyzing them while at the same time drawing the army's strength away from Kinnube when he made his move.

And then listening to the Englishman's own voice describe how he was in reality working for the ZRF and double-crossing both Molokutu and Embatto had stunned him with the realization of how close they had been to disaster. For the ZRF clearly knew Embatto's entire plan, which Molokutu and Thombert had only that night got their first inkling of. Far from bringing in assassins to eliminate the ZRF's leaders, Fugleman was mounting an elaborate deception to mislead Embatto into attacking the army while the rebels concentrated in the city to take on the remnants of both sides when they were at their weakest.

Molokutu had immediately ordered Fugleman and the ZRF ringleaders at Sadie's to be rounded up at dawn, which would constitute a major setback to the rebels for the time being. Tenyasha was therefore no longer a pressing issue, and Thombert had issued orders to recall the forces that he had begun moving southward for Scabbard. That would leave Embatto's "Cobra Force" of mobile Special Action detachments facing the ZRF alone down there—which was so much the better. If a fight developed between them, then both forces would be easier to deal with after the situation in the capital was stabilized.

The first priority after that was to forestall Embatto while they held the initiative. Accordingly, the army units in the area had been directed to neutralize all state-security forces and to take over state-security headquarters, using whatever force was necessary. With half the army strung out between Kinnube and Glimayel, the situation was, admittedly, far from what Thombert would have preferred; but the general had judged it better to move now and go for total surprise rather than embark on more elaborate preparations that would have tipped Embatto off that his plans were uncovered. A bounty had been offered to the officer who took Embatto, and double the amount if alive. Molokutu wanted to deal with *him* personally.

A knock sounded on the door. A guard outside opened it, and one of Molokutu's presidential aides came in. He didn't look happy.

"We have the report from army headquarters, Excellency. Barindas and Yolatta managed to escape. The Englishman, Velker, was killed resisting arrest."

Molokutu's face throbbed with anger. "What! Half his army there, and he let them get away? That's not possible."

"Apparently the entire vicinity is a nest of ZRF supporters. They were attacked from all sides."

"Tell them to take hostages!" Molokutu shouted. "Shoot fifty every hour until they are found. Tear the whole area down street by street if you have to, but I want them found!"

"I'm told that the area has been sealed off. General Thombert has ordered reprisals."

"Was Fugleman picked up?"

"The unit sent to arrest him was delayed. He had disappeared from the hotel by the time they got there."

"Have the commanding officer stripped of rank and arrested. And I want to talk to Thombert."

"He's holding for you now, Excellency."

Grim-faced and trembling, Molokutu strode from the room.

He should have guessed earlier, Fallon told himself. Who better to monitor development in a city like Kinnube than a journalist, whose business was to cultivate contacts—and especially one with something of a disreputable image, who, with Zugenda being the place it was, would be more likely to attract those who had fingers in the things that mattered.

"That wasn't just an accident that Jonas happened to be hanging around when I needed a place to go, was it?" Fallon said over his shoulder as the Fiat twisted and turned through the back streets of Kinnube. "Jonas is your helper."

"Had to keep an eye on you," Leroy replied.

"And it was Jonas who took Parnum to Tobins. You set that up too."

"Right."

Fallon half turned in his seat as a new thought crossed his mind. "And what about that first night in the Independence? Were you really that drunk . . . or was that part of the act too?"

Leroy shrugged. "I knew your aim was to get arrested, and it looked as if that was what you were trying to do. So I figured I'd oblige."

"Oh-oh," the driver muttered.

Ahead of them, two stationary tanks were blocking the street, their guns pointed the other way. Soldiers were taking cover in doorways on either side. As the Fiat crashed to a halt, one of the tanks fired and demolished a house at the far end. The driver reversed the Fiat into the mouth of an alley, stopped, and came out again with tires screeching to roar back the way it had come.

"Reckon we try de udder way," he announced sagely.

"A squad of army showed up for you at Tobins just

after you left," Leroy said. "It seemed time to get you off the streets."

"Did they find anything else?" Fallon asked.

"No. They came right out again and went away when they found you'd blown."

Fallon turned back in his seat and sat in silence for a while, forcing his mind to function coherently. They had gone straight to Sadie's... the very morning after the meeting. It could only mean that there was an informer there.

He looked back again at Leroy. "You said it was the *army* that came to Tobins?" he checked.

"Right."

"Not regular police or state security?"

"No."

And it was the army that had raided Sadie's. So the informer was somebody who worked for them, in which case they would have passed the information on to Molokutu— or the informer could have been one of Molokutu's to begin with. Either way, it added up to the same thing.... And suddenly the reason for the fighting that morning became clear.

"Molokutu has found out about Embatto's plan and preempted it," Fallon said. "We'd expected Embatto to move first. Well, it isn't going to happen that way. That's what's going on. They're at each other's throats already."

"Could be," Leroy said from the back after a pause. "I don't know. Let's hope that the others have gotten a fuller picture.... But it could be, all right."

They came finally to a run-down industrial quarter by the river in the northeast quarter of the city. The Fiat turned off the road and crossed a paved lot with weeds growing through the cracked concrete, and rusting metal castings scattered about in disorder. There was an opening on the far side, between a high breeze-block wall and a disused foundry building. Across the gap was an improvised barrier of concrete blocks and a section of telephone pole, manned by rebels sporting an assortment of automatic weapons, sidearms, bandoliers, caps, flak jackets, and camouflage gear. The driver exchanged some words in a native dialect with the leader, in which Fallon managed to pick out the words "English," "Barindas," and "Yolatta." Leroy, presumably, didn't make a habit of coming here.

After some curious looks at its passengers, the car was waved through. Only then did Fallon see the machine gun that had been covering them from a doorway to one side.

At the rear of the building, a large corrugated steel door with flaking, black paint was opened from the inside and closed again as soon as the car had passed through. The noise and activity that they found themselves in contrasted sharply with the desolation and apparent absence of human presence outside. Beside where the Fiat had stopped, two mechanics were working on a jeep mounting a .50-caliber machine gun, which was riddled with bullet holes that looked fresh and still carried army markings. Behind it, a human chain was passing mortar rounds and antitank projectiles out to a ramshackle green truck. Boxes of grenades and small-arms ammunition were being broken open and distributed, a casualty on a stretcher was being carried inside, and in the background a white-skinned figure in a dark blue shirt and jeans was supervising the assembly of a rocket launcher. Despite the strain of the moment, Fallon managed a grin as he stepped out of the Fiat and recognized the sandy hair, tanned, wiry figure, and twangy Arizona drawl.

"Hello, mate. I should have known you were here as soon as the trouble broke out. It follows you around."

Tam Czaryski looked around, grinned, and came over. "Me? Hell, it wasn't too bad until you showed up." They clasped hands firmly. "Good to see you again, buddy. Sometimes we'll do this over a beer or something, the same way as everybody else does. . . ." His manner became more grave. "What's happening in town? The news we're getting is pretty garbled."

Sam Letumbai had emerged through the throng and was talking with Leroy. When he saw Fallon with Tam, he turned and came across. "Well, we made it this far, eh? Only trouble is, I ain't too sure where it all leads next. Colonel Marlow and George are upstairs."

They moved to an inner part of the building, through a ferment of guerrilla squads preparing to depart for various destinations, and matériel being unpacked and issued. From the general haste and disorder, Fallon got the impression that the place was being evacuated. Through a door in one corner they came to a stairwell and began ascending. On the way Sam gave Fallon as much as he knew of other developments that morning: army tanks and artillery were attacking state-security headquarters, where a heavy fight was in progress; in the area around Sadie's, the army was reported to be running wild in an orgy of killing and burning after the surprise ZRF attack, and Letumbai was sending in what units he could to try and draw them off. As yet there was no firm news of whether the attempt to get Barindas and the others out had succeeded. A rumor held that they had all been killed.

At the top of the stairs was a room containing radio equipment manned by a couple of operators and a map table with several ZRF gathered around. Colonel Marlow and George were there with a wild-looking, colorfully bedecked ZRF commander whom the colonel introduced as Crosby. Other ZRF were cramming papers into bags and boxes and feeding more into a woodstove by one of the walls.

"There seems to be a bit of bother, all right," Fallon agreed, taking in the fragments of the situation that had been pieced together on the map. "It's all just blown up. Everything seemed fine when I left Sadie's last night."

"I'd 'ave thought yer'd be makin' the most o' things an' samplin' t'merchandise in a place like that, not startin' a bloody war," George said. "Anyroad, glad yer still in one piece fer a bit longer."

"Make anything of it?" the colonel asked Fallon.

"I think Thombert's gone for Embatto first," Fallon answered. Letumbai would have given the colonel an account of what had been happening in Tenyasha, including Fallon's conclusions about Embatto's real intentions.

The colonel confirmed it with a nod. "Hmm, that's about the way we saw it too."

Fallon looked around. "So what's the score here?"

"It's all a mess. Nothing was supposed to happen for another ten days, so nothing's ready. Only dribs and drabs of the ZRF have arrived, and we've lost Barindas and Yolatta." The colonel gestured in the direction of Letumbai, who had gone over to talk to Crosby and his staff. "On top of that, Sam says that Tannerling knew about this place. That means Embatto knows about it—he was probably biding his time and intending to take it out as part of the action. Embatto may have his hands full just at this moment, but obviously we're not secure here." He shrugged disconsolately. "So we're pulling out to salvage what we can for better days. What else is there to do?"

For once, the colonel's genial, self-assured, imperturbability, his characteristically English inability to conceive of things not working out somehow in the end, however bad the odds, was gone. The china-blue eyes were heavy and solemn.

George had gone to where some cots were standing along the far wall and resumed packing items into bags. Leroy folded his arms and leaned against one of the roof-support pillars. Crosby and his staff were preoccupied, and for the moment there didn't seem a lot that Fallon could do. "How long have we got?" he asked, turning back to look at the colonel.

"Oh, probably a while yet. Why?"

"Time to tell me about what's been going on at this end? Those notes of Elizabeth Bouabbas's that I gave you—did you get anywhere with them?"

The question brought some life back into the colonel's features. "Oh yes, indeed. They were the beginnings of a very interesting story."

Fallon waited a few seconds. "Well . . . ?"

The colonel paused to gather his thoughts, which just at the moment were scattered. It wasn't a time to be going off into details of how George and Tam had got inside the state-security helicopter base and what they had found there. He nodded, and against a background of messengers coming and going and radio operators cupping phones to their ears and scribbling on pads in front of them, began to summarize what he had learned from Simon in England of Infinity Limited's further delvings since Fallon left Kinnube.

"It turns out that Platinum Group Metals is the name of this game. A little under twelve years ago, a consortium of American and European financial and industrial interests found indications of deposits that could make this place the Rand north of the Congo."

"Twelve years? We're talking about before Molokutu's time, then?"

"Correct. Molokutu was installed as a stooge. The Marxist posturing was just a front to stake out the claim. You can't just march an army in and grab the goodies these days. It's gone out of fashion."

Fallon nodded. "Barindas explained that angle."

The colonel went on: "The money crowd didn't have the stomach to get involved in the messy side of the business directly, however, so they got an Iranian faction to stage-manage the actual coup d'état which brought down Chrensy—he was Molokutu's predecessor. The deal was that the financial side of the consortium would provide the backing in return for extraction-and-processing concessions afterward. Barindas saw what was happening and tried to organize an opposition party, but without the pull and the influence he didn't stand a chance. They drove him into the bush and told the world he was a terrorist."

Tam had moved over to join Crosby, who was trying to interpret a garbled message that had come in about a building on fire somewhere.

"But Molokutu got too serious about Moscow and started doing arms deals," Fallon guessed.

The colonel nodded. "While at the same time milking the U.S. for all the dollars he could get. That put the investment in jeopardy. So now Molokutu has to go, and Embatto is to be put in as the new caretaker, with the whole thing being passed off as just another Third World domestic takeover."

Fallon took a few seconds to digest this. "So is there an Iranian side to this group backing Embatto, as well as Lichuru's Western connection?" he asked.

"Apparently not. Things in Iran have changed since Molokutu's revolution was engineered ten years ago, and what few are left there today of the original consortium are out of favor. Embatto is purely the Western side of the family's man."

"You mean they've decided to monopolize the assets and cut the Iranian side out?"

"So it would seem."

"And that's Pyramid," Fallon concluded.

"Correct."

"All good pals together."

"The way of the world, regrettably. Perhaps they consider the present regime in Iran to be founded on spurious claims to office, and therefore without legitimate title as successors to the deal."

Fallon mulled for a few seconds over the ramifications. "Would I be wrong in guessing that the Iranians are pushing someone of their own too, with the same idea in mind?" he asked. "Or is that being too cynical?"

"If they are, it's a side that we haven't uncovered," the colonel replied.

"Hell, isn't it tangled enough already?" Leroy asked, from where he was still leaning against the pillar and listening.

Images flashed through Fallon's mind of the scenes he had witnessed since entering Zugenda: Elinvoro, the refugees, the wounded at Tenyasha, Candy in the prison cell, the thousand similar things that happened every day. "Do we know who the actual people are yet who make up Pyramid—the ones behind it all?"

"There was one U.S. lead to them, but they shut him up permanently." The colonel shook his head wearily. "Right now, the trail's at a dead end." He raised a hand to indicate the scene around them generally, the base outside the confines of the room, Kinnube, Zugenda. "Barindas, the ZRF, the rebellion, everything—all in shambles."

Distant gunfire sounded somewhere outside. The colonel cocked an inquiring eyebrow at Fallon. "I can't help thinking it was all too neatly set up. You at Tobins, the others inside Sadie's, us sitting in this trap here . . . All just waiting to be picked off. Could it have been accidental, do you think?"

Fallon frowned as he thought it over, then shook his head. "I can't see how it could have been set up," he said finally. "It was *our* idea to move everything and everyone into the city like that. It wasn't something that came from Embatto at all, or from Thombert."

Leroy said from where he was standing, "That was what Sam told us too. You're sure? That's really the way it was?"

Fallon nodded. "I was there—at the briefings in Kinnube, and at the talks in Tenyasha. And yes, that's the way it was."

Chapter Forty-eight

ARMY HEADQUARTERS WAS A CHEERLESS, GRAY, concrete building behind a wire-topped wall, situated between the Ministry of Defense and the Foreign Office on the west side of Kinnube center. The dawn swoop by the army against the state-security forces positioned in the vicinity had resulted in an hour of confused but fierce fighting that had left the streets hazy with smoke from burning vehicles and littered with bodies, rubble, and broken glass. Now the roadway in front was secure, with tanks posted solidly at both ends, while inside, shaken ministers and officials in pinstripe suits emerged from underneath desks and out of basement stairways.

In the situation room, General Thombert stood in front of the large-scale wall map of the city, trying to gauge the progress of the operation. In view of the way everything had been so hastily improvised, the news could have been a lot worse, he thought. Inevitably, there had been mix-ups and delays—B Company of the Parachute Brigade was at the wrong bridge; two units from the Ninth Infantry had arrived at Mordun instead of one; the force sent to invest Djamvelling had been turned around and brought back again without his orders—but at last he was beginning to feel some relief from the misgivings that had been assailing him since the decision he had reached at his all-night conference with Molokutu.

The only major setback had been at SSHQ itself, where an overconfident commander had driven his tanks straight up to the front gates and had half of them wiped out by missiles that Thombert had had no idea state security even possessed. Presumably they had been supplied by whoever had been aiding Embatto. But the suddenness of the army's attack had prevented the weapons from being deployed as effectively as intended, and the attacking force had fallen back to regroup in a ring around the complex and await reinforcement by the units returning to the city. Elsewhere, some SS units were holding out and scraping together retaliatory attacks with armored cars, but in general the initial surprise had enabled Thombert's forces to retain the initiative.

Thombert was still smoldering from Molokutu's tirade over Barindas and Yolatta's escape. From the days when he had risen out of the ranks during the British era, Thombert had earned his pips as a qualified general officer. Molokutu was an incompetent who had come from nowhere, levered into power by foreign interests precisely because he *was* stupid and manipulatable. A janitor—literally—in a gold-braided cap. But orders were orders, and Thombert had tolerated the situation like a dutiful officer. Now, as the reports accumulated and the situation became clearer as more markers were added to the map, the feeling grew within him that the time to settle up a long list of grievances might be approaching.

An aide came over from a communications desk. "We've taken the SS post on St. Paul, sir. The commanding officer reports moderate casualties, twenty-three prisoners captured."

"Do we know yet where those Panhards are and which way they're heading?" Thombert asked a major who was standing on his other side.

"The patrol we sent out across Central to check has tangled with ZRF. But I've pulled two tanks back from the Thirteenth."

"How's the ZRF action generally?"

"It's mainly concentrated around Sadie's. Otherwise, pretty scattered. We obviously took them by surprise. They don't have any coordination."

Thombert stared at the map and interpreted the pattern of movements and positions. With its strength dissipated, its leaders dispersed, and its timetable disrupted, the ZRF wouldn't be a major problem for a while. And if Embatto was already reeling, it would take just one act of nerve and decisiveness now to eliminate all the obstacles that had stood in the way of Thombert's own goals. He thought of Napoleon, Bismarck, Hitler, Patton. . . . It was a time for resoluteness and boldness, he told himself. Such times didn't repeat themselves often.

"Get General Waroon at Mordun on a secure line," he instructed the colonel. "And find Colonel Sahle at once. I'll be in there."

He went into a small office separated from the situation room by a partition wall with a glass window and stood running his fingers impatiently on the narrow desk facing the wall. Sahle joined him a minute or so later and closed the door. "You wanted to see me?" Sahle said.

"I say we go now," Thombert said. "The time's right, the situation's right. We've got Embatto in a bottle and the ZRF don't know what day it is. Why wait?"

"Don't you think you'd better let Ziggurat know?" Sahle queried in a worried voice.

Thombert nodded. "That's what I want you to do. Get a message off to Tehran summarizing the position. Tell them that I propose bringing everything forward for execution immediately, and I'm proceeding accordingly on the assumption of their agreement."

"Wouldn't it be an idea to get Tehran's agreement first?"

"The chance is here now. We can't risk losing it while politicians talk."

"But all the—"

The red scrambler phone on the desk sounded. Thombert picked it up. "Yes?"

"General Waroon on the line."

Thombert covered the mouthpiece. "Just do it. Tomorrow I'll make you a general." He raised the phone to his mouth. Sahle nodded and left. "Thombert here."

"Waroon."

"What's your condition?"

"Standing by."

"Be prepared to execute Lizard, phase one. I'm notifying Ziggurat."

"Will do. Are we going with Mustard too?"

"Hold back on it for now," Thombert instructed.

"Understood."

Mustard was the code name for an air strike at Djamvelling. Somewhat to his surprise, Thombert had received no news of reaction from that direction. He didn't were only equipped for counterinsurgency work against comparatively lightly equipped rebels. That would make them more useful for Thombert to retain intact, if he could, for his own use later—when the time came to finish off the ZRF.

It was the weapons that Lichuru had procured from Western sources via Pyramid that had saved Embatto that morning—in particular the Dragon and Stinger anti-tank missiles. The army's attack on SSHQ had been hastily organized and carried out, with perhaps an overreliance on surprise. Even so, it might well have succeeded if it hadn't been attended by a lot of initial confusion in the streets, which along with the shooting already going on elsewhere had caused an alert duty officer to call a general standstill on his own initiative and have the weapons issued in time. As a result, the first assault by the army had been solidly checked, then repulsed, and the situation—for the time being—was a stalemate. Smoke shrouded the surrounding area from at least a dozen tanks still burning where they had been stopped and from several fires inside the complex. Since the initial clash, the army had fallen back to more protected positions, from where they and the SS troops in the fortified base were keeping up a steady exchange of mortar, artillery, and small-arms fire, which had already reduced parts of the barracks and much of the nearby streets to rubble. One end of the headquarters building itself was also in flames.

In a blast-proof bunker to the rear of the main building, Julius Embatto sucked anxiously at a cigarette as he watched over the shoulder of a telex operator to read an incoming message. Thuds and concussions from the bombardment above shook the structure continuously; from the direction of the doorway came the intermittent rattling of a heavy machine gun firing from somewhere nearby. Sullivan, grim-faced beneath a steel helmet and nursing an automatic rifle under one arm, had posted himself a short distance inside the entrance, from where he could scrutinize everyone coming in as they were stopped by the guards.

The main thing that Embatto didn't understand was how Molokutu, who had to be behind Thombert's move, had found out about the intended coup—for what other reason could there be for the morning's attack everywhere? Embatto had kept advance knowledge of it to the absolute minimum number of people, and his security precautions had been intensive. The explanation could only be treachery. He wondered if Fugleman might somehow have been onto him after all in the strange game of cross and double cross that they had both been enacting.

A captain at a table to one side looked up from a telephone. "Koleba has got to the Jardanier Bridge. They're setting charges. Looks like we've bought some time."

Embatto nodded. It meant that the army column that had left the city in the direction of Djamvelling and then turned about would be halted at the bridge, where another force of Embatto's armored cars and antitank guns was heading to try and hold it. From other quarters the news was not good. The counterattack against army HQ that Embatto had hoped to scrape together was not materializing, and the relief force of state-security commandos that had set out for Embatto's HQ was bogged down in clashes with the ZRF, who seemed to be all over the city—the shooting that had broken out around Sadie's at first light was spreading and escalating into a three-cornered fight.

Embatto wasn't sure what had drawn Thombert to Sadie's, but it seemed likely that it had some connection to Fugleman's visit there the night before. He wondered bitterly if that had been where Barindas and Yolatta had been all the time; and Fugleman had led him straight to them, exactly as Embatto has intended! But Embatto hadn't known.... How, then, had Thombert and Molokutu known? Had Fugleman been not just smarter, but a *lot* smarter than he'd ever suspected, and been secretly working for them all along? Had the strangers who had got inside Djamvelling been associates of Fugleman and hence another part of it?

And to think that as recently as the night before, he'd imagined that it was *he* who had outsmarted Fugleman!

A dull *crump* sounded above the rattle of small arms and bangs of grenades coming from a few blocks away. A ZRF guerrilla peered upward, picked out the mortar bomb against the sky, and shouted a warning. The detonation came from nearby a second or two later in a solid wave of pressure that numbed the ears and stunned the senses. Debris showered down around Barindas as he lay with his arms covering his head.

He looked up again from the hole beneath a tilted slab of wall in the partly demolished house. A few yards in front of him in the rubble was an arm in a red shirtsleeve, still clutching an AK47. Just an arm. A guerrilla crouching behind the wall beyond ducked low as he retreated to the cover of the house. "Are you okay?" Yolatta's voice called from nearby.

"Yes."

Another house farther along the street was burning. Through the smoke they could see soldiers running about frenziedly and hear them shouting and screeching. The shock of the ZRF attack in front of Sadie's and the ensuing panic seemed to have roused them to a blood lust, which they were directing against anyone they came across not in uniform. Barindas could see people from the surrounding houses, male and female, including even children, being dragged out amid wailing and screaming to be pushed up against a wall. There were some shots, and some of the figures fell. Another was being bayoneted on the ground. The soldiers were setting up a machine gun facing the wall. Barindas watched in horror.

A short burst of fire sounded from somewhere nearby, and one of the soldiers with the machine gun collapsed. The other soldiers turned and began raking the area. Barindas ducked his head again as bullets exploded fragments off the masonry around him. But then more figures rushed out into the street, hurling bottles and other missiles and assailing the soldiers with axes, knives, clubs, garden tools, iron bars, anything that came to hand. Some had guns and were shooting. Some of those who had been lined up against the wall picked up rocks and stones and joined in. The soldiers who hadn't gone down under the onslaught fell back in disarray. Two of the civilians got to the machine gun and turned it on them. From another doorway, several soldiers emerged and began tearing off their uniforms, while guerrillas were rising from the positions around where Barindas was, and running forward.

Yolatta came over as Barindas stood up. "Those aren't

ZRF, Haile," Barindas gasped, wiping dust from his mouth. "Do you see what this means? The *people* are fighting! All of them. They think this is the rebellion. All they need is for us to lead them. It doesn't matter how many of our units haven't reached the city yet. We've got our army here already!"

"Maybe," Yolatta said. "But we ain't gonna do too much of it from a hole in the ground here. Let's move while we've got the chance."

Chapter Forty-nine

NORTHEAST OF THE CITY, THE GUERRILLAS THAT
had begun collecting at the foundry base as part of the
ZRF's intended buildup were continuing to disperse,
departing in groups as the weapons and supplies were
distributed. In the upper room, Fallon stared down at the
map table and listened as Crosby described as much of the
situation as could be pieced together. It was a confused
picture. With everything happening ten days ahead of
schedule, the command structure that Yolatta and Letumbai
had laboriously planned to be in place by the time of
Embatto's move hadn't even begun to come together. And
with Yolatta and Barindas gone, there was no coordinated
plan for it to convey, anyway. Everything was too soon;
nothing was ready.

"One report we've got says that the army has taken
the SS depot at Ashangi. Another says the fighting's still
going on." Crosby pointed in turn to several places where
lines and symbols were penciled on the map. "There are
tanks here and here... and SS holed up in some houses
by the river there. There doesn't seem to be any question
that SS is getting the worst of it. The only place where the
army ran into any real trouble was at SSHQ."

"Aye, that were where Embatto 'ad them missiles
'idden," George said.

Crosby nodded. "It was probably Thombert's main
objective, but he got stopped dead. It sounds as if there's a
siege around the place."

"What about air action?" Leroy asked.

"Waroon seems to be holding back for now. The
situation in the city's probably too mixed up for planes to
do much good, anyhow."

"How are your lot doing?" Fallon asked Crosby.

"It's all independent actions. But there's more of it

going on than we can account for. Half the city's coming out. . . . They think the ZRF started it. They think it's us, official."

Colonel Marlow rubbed his mustache apprehensively with a knuckle. "If things run their course, it will all be over too soon, with Molokutu in full control. Then he'll turn everything on them. It'll be a massacre. Aside from what happened at SSHQ, Thombert's forces have barely been scratched."

Then Tam Czaryski, who had been staring at the map with a thoughtful expression, looked around at the others and said abruptly, as if suddenly seeing something that should have been obvious long before now, "Doesn't something strike you as just a little strange about all this?" They returned puzzled looks. Tam waved a hand. "What's happened to Embatto's choppers from Djamvelling?" He looked across at Crosby. "Djamvelling hasn't been attacked by the army so far, right?"

"That's right. But it's fifteen miles out. The army's strung out enough as it is. They're probably waiting for more of their guys to get back."

"See what I mean?" Tam said. "Okay, maybe Thombert doesn't know about the antiarmor capability that SS has got down there, and he's given it low priority. But Embatto knows. . . . So why isn't he using it?" There was an exchange of curious looks. "He's got all kinds of ground-attack and fire-suppression hardware, and from what we're hearing, his side's in trouble. So how come he isn't using one of the best weapons he's got?"

"That's a good question," Letumbai said.

"A *very* good question," the colonel agreed.

There was a short silence. Then Fallon said, "I think I know." All eyes turned toward him. "There was supposed to be a briefing at SSHQ this morning to initiate more of the people who'd be involved in the coup. I was supposed to attend it before I left for England. All his chopper pilots were due to be there too. My guess is they're stuck there. That's why Julius isn't flying today."

There was another silence while everyone wondered what difference that could make to anything. "Well, there's nowt much we can do ter change that," George said finally, voicing the thought for them.

"I'm not so sure. . . ." Tam said distantly. "I think

there might be. You see, we've still got that chopper. If we could get to it, we might be able to get Embatto his air force back...."

"*What?*" Leroy straightened up abruptly from where he had been lounging against the pillar. "Give Embatto a hand? But he's the guy that all this is supposed to be against."

"Just for a little while, to even things up a bit."

Fallon was looking nonplussed. "What chopper?" he asked, blinking.

"Just believe that we've got one of Embatto's choppers stashed away outside the city," Tam said. "We had to...kinda, make an emergency getaway from Djamvelling."

"*You* were inside Djamvelling?"

"Me and George, with a couple of Crosby's guys. Look, it's a long story. You really don't wanna hear it right now."

Fallon stared at him, perplexed. "Well, okay, so we've got a chopper. What do you propose doing with it? Are you saying we just land it on the roof and ferry Embatto's pilots over to Djamvelling for him?"

"Why not?"

Fallon waved a hand exasperatedly at the map. "He's surrounded by tanks and under fire in there, for Christ's sake."

"Sure, but they're not our tanks. His fight's with Molokutu right now. So how about this: we know he's got friends out west, right? Well, that's where a couple of us here happen to be from. Also, we know that Lichuru is out of the country." Tam shrugged. "So we invent an arm of the organization that Lichuru didn't know about—people like these are all paranoids. They watch each other all the time. If we can find a way to get in touch with Embatto, we might swing it." He looked at Fallon. "Embatto still thinks you're on his side. We have to be able to use that somehow."

The old light had reappeared in Colonel Marlow's eyes as he saw the straw of a possibility bobbing amid the flood tide of the morning's disasters. One glance told Fallon that the sheer audacity of the idea was going to be irresistible. Sam Letumbai was massaging his forehead again as if searching for the flaw that he knew had to be there, but not quite being able to find it.

"What d'yer reckon?" George asked, watching Marlow's face. There was an urgent undertone to his voice, saying in effect that they had to give it a try: what alternative was there?

The colonel was nodding his head slowly, a distant expression on his face. Fallon could see a strange, excited light starting to animate the porcelain eyes that only moments ago had been dull and despairing. "That's what we need," the colonel murmured, half to himself. "A way to restore the balance somehow, temporarily. Our whole strategy was based on letting the army and SS wear each other down before we came into the open. But as things are, everything's tilted in Thombert's favor."

"Hell, it's the only thing that anyone's been able to come up with," Tam pressed. "If Embatto won't buy it, then all you can do is let him and Thombert slug it out and get as many of your guys out as you can before the heat turns this way. But that's what you're doing, anyhow. So there's nothing to lose."

Just then, two of the guards appeared from downstairs. With them was a guerrilla in torn combat dress, discolored by smoke. One leg of his camouflage pants was ripped to the thigh, and he had a rough bandage showing bloodstains tied around his head beneath a navy watchcap. "Only the English doctor was killed at Sadie's," he announced, directing his words at Crosby. "Barindas and Yolatta got away. They're with Bruno's squad between Forge and Central. . . . Wanted to know the situation here before they move anywhere."

Everyone in the room straightened up, electrified by the news.

"Why didn't Bruno radio us?" Crosby demanded.

"Lost his operator. Whole backup section wiped out. It's all shit everywhere back there."

Letumbai looked instinctively toward Marlow. With the ZRF's two top leaders out of action, it was evident that the colonel had become the de facto focal point whom everyone was expecting to hold things together. As Fallon knew and the others sensed, it was a role that came naturally to him.

The colonel thought rapidly. "The first thing is to get that chopper. Tam has to go, obviously. . . and you'd better go with him, Boris, since you're the one that Embatto trusts." He looked at Tam. "Are you going to be able to get in if the place is still under fire?"

"There's smoke all over the area, which'll help," Tam said. "I've scouted that part of town when I was blacked up. We'd have a pretty well-covered run in from the northwest if we stay low. And the roof of the main building is wide enough to be blind from the ground."

"Very well. We'd better get you two on your way as quickly as possible. Crosby, can you organize a couple of jeeps or something and an escort of, say, ten for them? Mounting cannon or machine guns if possible. And include a radioman and backup, as well as two sets. We'll need to let them know how things with Embatto work out."

"Will do," Crosby affirmed.

"And if you're pulling the troops out of here, it might be an idea to send some of them to Djamvelling with as many ground-to-air missiles as you can find. I wouldn't want to risk shifting things too much in Embatto's favor."

"Will do," Crosby said again. While he turned away and began amplifying the orders to two of this staff, the colonel looked at George and Leroy.

"Which leaves you two. And the next thing we have to do right away is establish contact with Barindas and Yolatta." Marlow glanced across at the ZRF messenger who had brought the news from the city. "Your name is what?"

"Frano, sir."

The colonel turned his head back to the other two. "You can leave with Frano right away... although I'd get kitted up into something a little more suitable than that, Roy." Leroy was still wearing the tan suit he'd had on when he intercepted Fallon. "And you'd better stay with me, Sam. We'll keep a skeleton crew here for as long as possible so that at least there'll be one place to try and coordinate things from."

Fallon could only shake his head dazedly. "I've heard some crazy ideas from you, Tam, but this has got to be the most insane of the lot. What's happened? Has the Bible Belt over there got to you at last? Do you believe in miracles now, or something?"

The sandy-haired American shrugged and raised his eyebrows in the kind of grin that said it was all out of everyone's hands anyway, so they might as well go with it. "Believe in 'em?" he said. "Hell, you know me. I *rely* on 'em."

Leroy and George left shortly afterward with an armed party of ZRF, using a sandbagged flatbed truck for the first leg of the journey into the city center. Fallon and Tam departed northward with another group in three vehicles a little over half an hour later.

By early afternoon Thombert was satisfied that the SS forces were being contained. The situation at SSHQ was unchanged and would resolve itself when the reserves got back. More drastic action was therefore uncalled for at that stage—which Thombert was hesitant to resort to in any case without express confirmation of support from Tehran. In the meantime he should be on his way, he decided. The aides and officers from HQ who were to accompany him were already assembled, and he had contacted the ones from other locations and arranged for them to meet his party at his residence on the city's outskirts. They would all proceed together from there.

He gave orders for his personal armored staff car to be brought to a side entrance and an escort assembled, and for the president to be notified that he was on his way to the palace to report. While that was being attended to, he joined Sahle in the situation room.

"How is everything?" he inquired.

"Messy but not dangerous. The fire from Sadie's is spreading."

"I'm going now. I'll leave you to take care of things here, okay?"

Sahle nodded. "Good luck."

Thombert lowered his voice. "Anything from Ziggurat?"

"Not yet. If something comes in, I'll let you know."

Thombert nodded curtly, turned to go through to where the rest of his party were waiting, and then as an afterthought changed his mind and stepped into the small office adjoining the situation room. He picked up the yellow phone and punched the code for his own residence. The officer in command of the guard detachment posted there answered. "What's the situation?" Thombert asked him.

"Some SS showed up in the area about an hour ago, but they've been pushed back. There's intermittent firing, some damage to the roof and windows. Patrols engaging ZRF a half a mile north."

"How's the woman there?"

"She's okay."

"Put her on for a minute."

There was a short delay, then Dora's voice came on the line. "Hello, this is Dora."

"Everything okay?"

"A bit better than it has been. The place was hit."

"Are you all right?"

"I guess so . . . but jumpy. Bullets scare me."

"I'll be back there in about half an hour to an hour." He paused and thought for a second. "Maybe you'd better come on with us."

"Who's us? Where to?"

"Don't worry about it. Let's just say I've got a surprise for you. You did a good job last night. It did a lot more for us than you think. I told you once you'd be the richest lady in the country, remember? I never break promises to people who play things straight with me. Now it's your turn to collect."

The crash of collapsing masonry sounded, and Embatto felt the floor shudder. A cloud of dust spewed from a fresh crack in the roof. Through the haze, the shape of Makon Ngoyba materialized from an inner door leading through to the communications room. On top of the strain that was showing on every face, his expression was confused.

"A message has come through to you from Tenyasha," he said. "It's being decoded."

Embatto frowned. "Tenyasha? Nothing's happening there."

"The message is kind of strange. . . . It's from the Englishman there, Reid."

"But you said it was in code."

"He's using Drummer's code." Embatto's frown changed to complete bemusement—that had been Tannerling's code name. Ngoyba went on: "The message appears to have originated from Skater."

"Skater?" Embatto repeated. That was Fugleman. The last they'd heard of him was that he had returned to Tobins the night before after visiting Sadie's. With everything else that had been happening since dawn, nobody had given any thought to renewing the surveillance on him.

"Where is he?" Embatto asked.

"Still in Kinnube, I guess. The message doesn't say."

"Let me see this." Embatto walked into the communications room, where a half-dozen-or-so operators were working in a cramped environment of consoles, electronics racks, cables, and clattering printers. Ngoyba followed and indicated a girl seated at one of the stations, laboriously converting code groups from a handwritten sheet, while the supervisor watched alongside. Embatto waited impatiently, his face showing tension from the explosions above. Finally the supervisor took the sheet and handed it to him.

```
TO: KING RED
FROM: REID, TENYASHA
FOLLOWING RELAYED FROM SKATER/KINNUBE.
UNABLE TO REACH HQ DUE TO CURRENT ACTION.
APPEARS YOUR SITUATION SERIOUS. HAVE BEEN
CONTACTED BY PERSON WHO CLAIMS TO BE
ASSOCIATE OF LICHURU AND REFERS TO PYRAMID.
MEANS NOTHING TO ME, BUT HE SAYS YOU WILL
UNDERSTAND. HAS POSSIBLE PLAN TO EXTRICATE
YOU AND REGAIN INITIATIVE.
CONFIRM AGREEMENT. ALSO BELIEVE YOUR PILOTS
TO BE AT HQ. CONF REQUESTED.
ENDS
OUT
```

Embatto frowned, read the message again, and passed the sheet to Ngoyba. Ngoyba studied it, then looked up with a baffled expression. "What does it mean?"

"I don't know. I can't make any sense of it."

"I've always said there was more to him than meets the eye."

"The consortium must have set up a channel for emergencies. But how could it connect with Fugleman?"

The lights flickered as an incoming shell from a tank

cannon shook the room again. "It might be as well for us that they did," Ngoyba muttered. "Let's worry about the details later."

"We're holding the channel to Tenyasha open for a reply," the supervisor told Embatto. The operator was looking up, pen poised, waiting.

Embatto lit another cigarette shakily. He didn't understand what it meant, but even if it was a trap, he would rather be taken or die cleanly than wait to be incinerated or blown to shreds here.

He instructed, "Reply as follows: 'Situation here critical. Hemmed in all sides, tanks and artillery. Risk of air strike anytime. Agree your proposal. . . .'"

Chapter Fifty

HOLDING HIS ASSAULT RIFLE AT READY, GEORGE flattened himself into a doorway and scanned the surrounding windows and rooftops while Leroy ran to the gap in the low mud-brick wall enclosing one of the yards behind the row of houses. Leroy ducked into the cover of the gap, paused to check that the ZRF guerrilla was covering from the door into the building ahead, and then sprinted across the yard to join him. George went next and followed on into the house while Leroy and the guerrilla continued to cover for the two more ZRF who had been behind George.

"I can see yer've done a bit o' this in yer time," George commented as they came through and Leroy retreated from the doorway.

"You'd be amazed at some of the things I've done," Leroy muttered.

They passed through a dingy room with old boxes for furniture and piles of dirty straw on the floor, which from the look of the clothes and belongings scattered around them were used for sleeping. Several wide-eyed children watched them fearfully from the far side. In the next room three women were unpacking boxes of cartridges and loading them into magazines and drums for automatic weapons while a youth in a far corner was priming grenades. None of them paid any attention to the procession of heavily armed figures moving through to the front of the building.

Frano was waiting by the door. "Two more blocks," he told them. "We can use this street. It was impassable earlier."

They emerged through a boarded-up shop front onto a street in which a burned army truck was still smoldering. There were a lot of bodies, both civilian and uniformed, some still lying in the positions that they had fallen in, while others had been moved to one side. Figures were moving out in the open roadway in both directions, some running quickly with weapons, others carrying sacks and ammunition boxes on their heads, although the sounds of firing and explosions were now quite close. Several doors farther along, they passed a shop that was being used as a casualty clearing station, where a Land Rover was unloading stretcher cases. Past it was a group of bodies in SS uniforms that looked as if they had been beaten and hacked to death. The building on the corner was in flames, and the ZRF had established a strong point beside it. George noticed that some of the men digging and erecting barricades were wearing army-issue pants and boots.

A gap torn through a wire-link fence brought them to an asphalted yard that had been cratered in several places by mortar bombs and was strewn with rubble, shell fragments, and spent cartridge cases. A minibus lay on its side, burning, and a few other vehicles stood scattered untidily at odd angles. The building ahead of them had a set of corrugated steel double doors on the ground floor and windows of what looked like offices above, most of them broken. Frano led the way through a side door into a storage warehouse or supply depot of some kind. There were two desert-painted Land Rovers bearing yellow and blue United Nations insignia, stacks of crates and sacks at the far end, and an assortment of tools and agricultural appliances. In a smaller room beyond, a group of youngish Europeans in bush shirts were huddled nervously against what promised to be the strongest wall of the building. One of the girls was jabbering compulsively and continuously in a high-pitched wail and sounded as if she was bordering on hysteria. Leroy recognized some of the faces as aid workers that he had seen at the Independence. From the surprised looks on their faces, one or two of them evidently recognized him too.

"Coom on, what's the matter wi' you lot?" George growled as the squad of guerrillas filed through. "You coom 'ere to 'elp these boogers, din't yer? Well, get up off yer arses, then, an' get a bloody gun in yer 'and."

"It's not our bloody war," one of them mumbled back surlily.

"Chuckin' Molokutu out's the only kind of 'elp that's

goin' ter do any good around 'ere," George retorted.
"There's an 'ospital back down the street. Why not go an'
see what yer can do there, then?"

A couple of them looked at each other, nodded, and
moved off toward the door through which the guerrillas
had entered.

"Were you really in the paras, or a recruiting sergeant?" Leroy asked him.

"Oh, yer'd be amazed at some o' the things I've
done," George replied.

A number of the buildings on the far side of the street
they came out onto had been more badly damaged, and a
couple were demolished with wreckage spilling across the
full width. A tank, its turret dislodged by a direct hit and
its gun hanging downward, stood partly buried by one of
them. Stray shots from somewhere were passing over, but
high. Again, the squad covered each other across in turn.
Bruno, the commander of the ZRF section holding the
area, met them at the end of a passage that had been
cleared between two of the piles of rubble.

"I thought it'd be tougher getting through on this
side," Frano said as the group re-formed around them.

"We pushed 'em back. Yolatta organized it. You should
have seen it. When the guys realized it was him, there was
no stopping 'em." Bruno waved a hand. "He took out that
tank himself."

"Is Barindas okay? Are they still here?"

"Through this way."

They found Barindas exhorting a group of ZRF in a
boiler room. Yolatta was supervising the emplacement of a
couple of antitank guns somewhere nearby. The morning's
action had stirred Barindas's fighting side, and he was
furious when he heard what was happening at the foundry.
"They should be ashamed!" he railed, meaning Colonel
Marlow and Sam. "All over Kinnube the people are coming out and fighting with their bare hands... and our
soldiers are pulling out! What kind of army is this? What
kind of rebellion? Today I have seen boys attacking tanks
with bottles of gasoline... women taking up shovels against
SS troops. Why, right here in this street—"

"I know, and it's great," Leroy said, raising a hand to
stem the harangue. "But nobody at the foundry knew any
of that. All they knew was that the army was attacking,

nothing was ready, and you and Yolatta were out of it. They were trying to save the revolution for when the time's right, not run out on it."

Barindas waved a hand. "Well, we're not out of it, and the right time is right now. We need them here."

"But we came to get you out," Leroy protested.

Barindas dismissed the suggestion with a scornful gesture. "The word has spread that we're here. Look for yourselves at the effect it's having. We have to let the whole city know that same message . . . the whole country! The people are turning. The army is ready to come over. All they need now is one clear voice to lead them. We *must* go all the way now! We won't see a day like this again."

There would be no stopping the outpouring of words, Leroy could see. Barindas's voice rose and carried as he spoke, evoking cheers and shouts of encouragement from all of the guerrillas within earshot. Then the bearded, ferocious-looking figure of Yolatta appeared, changed now into combat clothing from the peasant's garb he had worn that morning and holding a light machine gun one-handed like a rifle, as if it were a toy.

"All the way?" Leroy looked uncertain. "What are you talking about?"

"The revolution is now!" Barindas exclaimed. "We are only blocks from the Radio Building. We have to get in there and tell the nation. All they need is to hear. The rest is done for us now."

Leroy looked around at the faces of the guerrillas who were listening. They were all eager, intoxicated with the vision, ready to go. He looked at Bruno. "Is it possible?"

"It'll be tough," Bruno said candidly. "It was one of the first places that the army secured when they moved this morning. They've got it pretty solidly buttoned up."

Leroy looked at Yolatta.

"We're moving all our strength into this sector. We can do it," Yolatta said decisively.

Leroy looked at him for a second or two longer, then shifted his gaze again. "What do you think, George?"

George too looked around at the faces watching, and suddenly his own words of a few minutes earlier came back to him. There was only one answer he could give.

"Aye, well, we did come 'ere to 'elp these boogers," he said resignedly. "I suppose we'd better gerron with it."

The Land Rover bringing up the rear signaled with several blasts of its horn that it was in trouble. The three-vehicle convoy came to a halt, and Homassu, the same driver who had driven the BRDM for Tam, went back to investigate, and returned less than half a minute later to report that its motor was overheating from a holed radiator. A brief conference by the side of the track ensued. It was unlikely that the stricken vehicle would make the remaining distance to Lommerzo—the village near the quarry where the Mi-4 was hidden. But with a top-up of water from the jerry cans strapped to the side, it could get to Zedekiah's place, which was only a couple more kilometers. The other two vehicles would escort it that far and then leave it and its crew at least in friendly hands.

"What's Zedekiah's place?" Fallon asked as Homassu climbed back in and they began moving again.

"Just a farm. But he's reliable. We use it as a kind of staging post."

It turned out to be a shanty house surrounded by a clutter of chicken coops and fencing thrown together from baling wire and assorted junk, some rickety tin sheds, several gutted automobile carcasses, and a pile of scrap metal and old tires. There were a number of people about, most of them armed and looking wary with the trouble afoot that day, although little of it appeared to have arrived here.

The three vehicles drew up, and there was another conference with a knot of people who came out of the house, centered around a heavily built, white-haired man with a black hat, whom Fallon guessed to be Zedekiah. Fallon and Tam remained in their own vehicle, disinterested in gossip and impatient to be on their way. Then two men opened the door to one of the sheds, and Zedekiah waved at the driver of the defective Land Rover to drive it inside. There was a pickup and several motorcycles inside already, Fallon saw, and a couple of large drums supported on bricks that looked as if they contained oil or fuel. A little more than just a staging post, he decided. Tannerling had probably known about every location like this that the

ZRF used. Fallon found himself wondering just what they might have been letting themselves in for if they had waited for Embatto to move first. He took a long swig from his water bottle to wash the dust from the trail out of his mouth, screwed back the top, and then paused in the act of clipping it back on his belt as a new thought suddenly struck him: ironically, Thombert might well have saved the ZRF from being smashed.

Homassu came back to the car and jumped in. "They say the way to Lommerzo is clear all the way through," he reported. "So we should make up for the lost time. There's a telephone line open to it from a pumping station near here. They're going to call ahead and have the helicopter brought out ready for us."

"God! Don't tell me something's actually worked out right," Fallon said as they followed the other Land Rover back out onto the track.

"You see, you never can tell whose side He's on from one day to the next," Tam told him. They held on tight as the vehicle ahead swerved this way and that amid its cloud of dust, and Homassu gunned them back up to the usual lunatic Zugendan pace.

"But seriously, Tam, why does it always end up like this?" Fallon tossed out a hand in exasperation. "I mean, we had it all set. Weeks of plans, timetables, schedules, preparations—all of it worked out and ready to go like clockwork. And then suddenly it all blows up in your face, everything's a mess, and you're left to sort out what you can by the seat of your pants. So why do we bother? What's the point of all the planning? Why even waste time thinking about it? You know it isn't going to happen. It never does."

"Aw, that's just you limeys," Tam replied. "Too rigid. That's why you need Americans around. It's what we call 'flexible response.'"

"So, tell me about this chopper you've got."

"The colonel wanted to check out what SS had inside Djamvelling. They use Russian techs there, and me and George got ourselves inside dressed as two of them, okay?"

"Right. And?"

"The missiles at SSHQ aren't the only new toys that Embatto's been bringing in. He's turned his chopper fleet into tank busters—and we're talking about sophisticated stuff: smart ATMs, thirty-millimeter API Gatlings—"

"All from Lichuru's connection in the West?" Fallon checked.

"Seems like it. Marlow can give you the line on that. . . . A guy that we bumped into there sounded American. That was what blew it. George had to KO him. The Russian techs must only look after the regular stuff. All the secret stuff's inside a place they keep locked up next door." Fallon nodded slowly. It fitted. Embatto hadn't wanted word of the intended coup to get back to Moscow. The secret work would have been done by technicians supplied by Pyramid. Tam shrugged and concluded, "So, when the fireworks went up, we grabbed a machine that had just come back from an operation, and got out."

"Quick thinking," Fallon complimented.

"It was George's idea."

"Flexibility of response: British, you know."

"Never miss a trick, huh?"

"You led with your chin. All I had to do was stick a fist up."

"Okay, let's run through it again. What's the drill when we've got the chopper? First we—"

"*Jesus!*" Homassu yelled and hit the brakes as they rounded a curve behind the vehicle ahead and found it skidding about all over the track and themselves closing on it fast. Ahead, the road was blocked by a barricade with uniformed figures manning weapons positions, and several state-security armored cars stationed farther back, in front of a cluster of shacks and trees.

The ground on either side of the tracks was flat for some distance back, and dotted sparsely with scrub and thornbushes. The lead driver, in the split second that he had to decide in, veered off into a wide turn, intending to complete a circle that would rejoin the track in the opposite direction. But there was a tremendous detonation as the vehicle struck a mine and disintegrated in an orange flash and a cartwheeling mass of exploding pieces that was carried at least twenty feet into the air.

"*Stay on the track!*" Fallon shouted.

Homassu crashed the vehicle to a halt, slammed into reverse, and shot backward into the curve that they had emerged from, just as one of the armored cars fired its cannon and a shell erupted slightly wide of where they had been. In the shelter of the dead ground around the bend they turned off to the side, stopped, came out forward to complete the turn, and sped back the way they had come.

"I thought the road was supposed to be clear," Tam yelled.

"I said it was one of those fucking days!" Fallon told him savagely through clenched teeth.

"What do we do now?" Behind them, the two ZRF manning the .50-caliber machine gun were swiveling it around and moving themselves forward to train it on the road behind.

"Is there another way to get to Lommerzo?" Tam shouted at Homassu.

Homassu shook his head. "Not that won't take us all day. . . except if you went cross-country. But you won't do it in this. Too steep and narrow—too rocky."

They came to the end of a long, straightish stretch, which afforded a view for a considerable distance back. "Are they coming after us?" Homassu shouted back over his shoulder. The gunners peered into the pall of red dust hanging over the trail behind them.

"Ain't sure," one of them yelled back.

They came to Zedekiah's again and stopped in the yard in front of the sheds, while surprised figures were already hurrying out to see what the problem was. Homassu rattled out a hasty explanation. Weapons started to appear, including an old bazooka of what looked like World War II vintage. Somebody was directing the others to take up defensive positions. There was a lot of yelling and running about. Then Fallon remembered the motorcycles that he had glimpsed inside one of the sheds.

"Could we get there on bikes?" he shouted, grabbing Homassu by a shoulder and jabbing a finger in the direction of the shed. Homassu stared at him in confusion. "Motorbikes! They've got motorbikes in that shed!"

"What de problem here?" Zedekiah demanded, coming over to them.

"He wants to go cross-country," Homassu said.

"Those motorbikes you've got in the shed. Are they working?" Fallon asked.

"Everythin' we got's workin'. What d'you think this is, some kind o' junkyard? How many you need?"

Fallon looked at Tam. Only the two of them had been due to fly the helicopter out. But they'd need Homassu to get them to Lommerzo, since he knew the way. "Just three of us," he said. "Two machines'll do."

"I see dust," a lookout called from a perch on one of the sheds. "I think they're coming."

"How far?" Zedekiah snapped.

"Half mile, maybe."

"Hurry it up wit' dem bombs." The old African waved at another of the men. "Get two dem mo'cycles out. We geddem dere 'nother way instead."

"You mean they're going cross-country?"

"Wadda hell d'yo think I mean? They gonna fly or sump'n? Move it."

The shed yielded a Yamaha, surprisingly new-looking, and a respectably battered British Norton, 500cc, painted khaki and probably a relic from colonial times. Homassu took the Yamaha, slinging his rifle across his back, and Tam the Norton with Fallon on the pillion seat behind with both their weapons. The motors kicked into life after some unnerving coughs and splutters.

"Looks like maybe they're stopping," the lookout called down. "Could be they're turning back."

"I hope he's right," Fallon said to Zedekiah as Tam tried the clutch.

"What de hell for? We could use our piece o' action too. You jus' get on your way an' help Barindas win de war. We'll take care o' dem if they come this way. Don't you worry none 'bout dat."

Homassu pulled away, with Tam and Fallon following. They bumped across some uneven ground on the side of the house away from the track and began angling down the curve of a hill. Past a shallow creek crossing, the ground became more open, and they speeded up. A flock of birds rose, screeching in alarm from a clump of acacias.

Fallon leaned forward to shout into Tam's ear above the noise of the motor. "Do you know, I think maybe this lunatic idea of yours might come to something after all."

"You mean you ever doubted it?" Tam shouted back over his shoulder.

"Although I suppose you realize that we don't have a

radio now. So we won't know what's happened with Embatto—
if anything's happened at all."

"Then I guess we just show up and hope something
has."

"You mean we just put down on top of SS headquarters roof in the middle of a bloody war and hope we're
expected?"

"Got any better ideas?"

"Well, in view of the somewhat shitty day it's been up
to now, what happens if we're not?"

"Flexible response, buddy. Flexible response."

Chapter Fifty-one

ESCORTED BY ARMORED CARS AND A FULL TRUCK of combat troops before and behind, the two staff cars, one of them flying General Thombert's personal pennant, slowed as they approached the outer roadblock on the avenue leading to the presidential palace. While the driver of the first exchanged formalities with the guard commander, a radio call came through for Thombert from Colonel Sahle at army HQ.

"A signal just came in from Ziggurat," Sahle advised. "Message reads, 'In view of situation, approve immediate action. Total control essential now. Extreme measures permissible.' Message ends."

Jubilation shone in Thombert's eyes. He licked his lips and replied, "Acknowledge as follows: 'Received and clear. Concur fully. Anticipate complete resolution today.' End."

Thombert cleared the call and sat for a moment, savoring the feeling. Then he leaned forward to punch a code for a scrambler channel into the console facing the rear seats. General Waroon acknowledged from Mordun.

"We have Tehran's all-clear to proceed," Thombert said. "Execute plan Lizard, phase one, immediately. I'm arriving at the palace now."

"Understood," Waroon replied, and cleared down.

As the vehicles moved forward through the palace defenses, Thombert leaned back in his seat and patted Dora's thigh. "It's going to be okay," he reassured her. "It's one down, one about to go down, and one on the run. Just stick with it."

Dora smiled but looked uneasy. "Should I be coming here like this?"

Thombert laughed. "Why not? The president's not going to object."

She glanced at him uncertainly. "Who do you mean, 'president'?"

Thombert laughed again. "Who do you think, baby. Who do you think?"

At the Radio Building, things were not going well. A state-security attack had materialized in the afternoon from the direction opposite from that in which the ZRF were grouping, and was driven back by the army defenders. Since then, the ZRF had begun attacking also, and a fierce, three-cornered fight had developed, with the army still in possession. The ZRF and SS were entrenched at opposite ends of the main street at the front, and a confused situation had developed in the streets behind, with houses and yards changing hands constantly.

George peered out from the wreckage of what had once been a family's living room—there was a trunk that had contained linen and lady's dresses, all since torn up to make bandages, and some homemade children's toys, carefully nailed together from pieces of wood and painted. The firing from the SS positions seemed to be slackening off, and for a while now there had been no more of the incoming mortar shells that had been leveling this and the adjacent block.

The Radio Building lay halfway along the street on the far side, and beyond it the city prison, which the army had also occupied to extend their cover in that direction after the fighting began, its outer wall breached in two places by missiles. The defenders of the Radio Building were concentrated in the ground floor, which was a mess, as was much of the floor above, where the army had been placing snipers and machine guns. Above that, everything was fairly intact apart from the windows, those which had escaped being hit having been knocked out by the people inside to avoid flying glass. The object of both the sides besieging the place was to acquire it, not destroy it, and miraculously it was still operating. Several bulletins had been broadcast in the last few hours, relayed by land line from army HQ, telling people to stay off the streets and explaining the day's troubles as an attempted mutiny by some units of the SS forces, which was now contained with the authorities in full control.

Barindas had dismissed the claim as propaganda. George was less certain, since the news coming in via runners and garbled radio signals was fragmentary, and often contradictory. If there was some truth to it, then half the opposition was out of the running. On the other hand, the army would also be free to focus on the ZRF, which was not such good news. And if that meant they could now disengage their tank forces and move them to begin clearing the area around the Radio Building, it wasn't very good news at all.

George couldn't fault the guerrillas for not trying, nor did he question their bravery: the street was littered with their dead. As for the wounded, whom no one had been able to get to, they were still moving and calling out for aid, and the snipers were leaving them deliberately, to try and entice others to risk making a dash for them. But bravery and effort didn't stop bullets. Yolatta, crouching behind a pile of rubble and fallen roof timbers, studied the face of the building through glasses. "If we're going to do it, this is the time, before the army gets here in force," he said.

"Yer'll be stopped dead, same as last time," George said. "The street's too wide. There's no cover."

"If we quit now, then what was the use of any of it?" Yolatta asked.

Bruno appeared in the opening from a passageway leading back through the block. He looked drawn. "They're moving up behind us," he announced. "There are tanks less than four blocks away. They're going to clear this whole area. Leroy thinks we may have to pull out."

"Where are the tanks?" Yolatta demanded.

"There's two across Bank, one coming east along Bridge, and another the other side of the intersection where the agricultural depot is. You'd better get over and take a look."

Yolatta cursed and thought furiously. An explosion tore up the rubble nearby, showering them with debris. "You stay and hold things together here," he instructed Bruno. "Get some marksmen forward to take on those snipers." He looked at George and jerked his head. "Let's go."

George followed Yolatta back through the ruins of the block and across a side street into the next, where the boiler room was located. Barindas was still there, looking more shaken than earlier but still determined to see it through or perish trying. They moved on through and came to the warehouse where they had passed the European volunteers, but there was no longer any sign of them. Instead, they found the front wall blown in and the large corrugated steel door buckled and off its hinges, while ZRF worked frantically to prepare positions amid the wreckage. An antitank gun was pointing from one of the craters in the asphalted yard beyond, and a machine gun was firing nearby. The scene had changed a lot from when they had came through before. It seemed that the area that had been won earlier was about to be contested again.

"Where's Leroy?" Yolatta asked the ZRF officer in charge.

"One block farther, with Frano. There are a couple of tanks moving this way. They're trying to set up a gun in the way of 'em."

George and Yolatta hurried on, keeping low and making use of cover with bullets whining intermittently about them. They found Leroy in a forward post dug out of a crater, with a ZRF called Komil and two others manning a machine gun, while more were in slit trenches scattered ahead and on both sides. Another group in a concealed redoubt set farther back were positioning an antitank gun to command an area of open ground and sandy mounds lying in front of a jumble of storehouses and commercial buildings.

"'Ow is it?" George asked as they crawled up beside Leroy.

Leroy pointed. "There's a tank back around that corner. It got to there, but backed off when we fired a couple of RPs at it. One missed and the other bounced off, and we don't have any more. . . . They've got an infantry support section moving up on that side, so it's only a matter of time before it comes around again."

"Where's our blokes?"

"LMGs there and there, and another gun on that corner. There was an automatic cannon crew over on the left, but it got hit by the tank. That's them splattered all over the sidewalk."

Yolatta looked grim and said nothing. George stared

out over the scene, assessing fields of fire and registering the dead ground. If they lost this block, they might as well abandon any thought of getting into the Radio Building. They'd be trapped between two forces in a strip that was too narrow. He thought back to the situation as it had been there, in his mind gauging distances and the layout along the street, with ZRF and SS stalemating each other from opposite ends while the army held the objective of both securely in the middle. "There's only one way anyone's goin' ter get into that bloody place," he growled, almost to himself.

Yolatta turned his head to look at George, saw the strange expression on his face, and watched silently. In the end Leroy asked, "What are you thinking?"

George didn't reply for several seconds longer. Then he said, "Could you get a coverin' group up behind those 'umps an' as far as that wall to make that lot over there keep their 'eads down?"

"Maybe," Komil answered. "Why?"

"So a couple of us can get to that 'ole, up past where them posts are, an' wait for that tank when it cooms. . . . And can we move that gun back and over that way?"

Komil looked dubiously in the direction that George indicated. "Not the best place," he said. "You'd be lengthening the range and asking to get outflanked."

"That's what I want," George said. "I want to tempt the booger to coom farther on."

"You won't stand as good a chance of taking it out that way," Komil insisted.

"I don't want that, either."

Leroy frowned beneath the steel helmet he was wearing. "What are you aiming at, then, George?"

George emitted a sigh. "Well, it seems as if everyone else 'as decided ter play silly boogers today, so I thought I might as well join in." He turned to look back at Yolatta. "All right, then. If yer want to 'ave another go at radio station, I'll come back wi' yer as far as that ware'ouse place—there's some things there that I want. An' on yer way through t'boiler 'ouse, tell Barindas to coom out 'ere. 'E wants to be a ruddy 'ero does 'e? All right, then. Get 'im oop 'ere, an' we'll see what kind o' stuff 'e's made of."

*   *   *

Fallon folded the map and tucked it back into the pouch between the forward seats of the Hound. He didn't need it anymore. The plume of smoke rising above the city marked the location of SSHQ clearly enough. He returned his grip to the M16 propped upright between his knees and looked back from little more than rooftop level at the fleeting montage of Kinnube rushing by below.

Two children out in a yard at the rear of a house ran, terrified, back inside.... Armed figures on some roofs looked up as the helicopter passed over; several of them aimed at it, but if they fired, scored no hits. ... An overturned car was burning, and soldiers were running along a street.... Bodies were scattered like rag dolls across an open square.... Figures that looked like guerrillas were taking shelter among some walls.

"That's it, right?" Tam yelled over the roar of the 1,700-horsepower engine.

"It's got to be."

They had been veering south from a westerly course and were now to the northwest of the compound. "Okay, hang on to your ass. We're going in."

The helicopter banked to port and dropped even lower as Tam hugged the ground to gain maximum cover and minimum exposure until the last moment. Fallon winced inwardly as they flew between two buildings, through a gap that he wouldn't have thought wide enough for the rotor. He saw a woman's frightened face staring out of one of the windows, seeming almost close enough to touch.... Now they were skimming along a street, with figures scattering below, some throwing themselves to the ground. And then an office building was rushing at them, its face scarred by broken windows, and a sudden, lurching lift to snatch height for the final run in. Fallon braced a leg along the side of the open doorway and raised the M16.

Over the first smoke, troops below, looking up, startled, from positions among heaps of rubble and vehicles parked haphazardly behind the buildings.... Tanks, fires, demolished buildings. They were crossing the army positions encircling Embatto's HQ. As the machine climbed and broke cover, Tam threw it into a series of gut-wrenching twists. Fallon felt bullets hitting the structure now, but he could identify no worthwhile target to fire back at.

The headquarters and barracks compound, together

with the surrounding streets, looked like part of the bombed city from a World War II news clip. The perimeter walls and buildings of the complex had been reduced to rubble, and fires were burning in a dozen places. Flames poured out of the windows along half the length of the five-story main building, one end of which had collapsed. Tam headed up into the smoke, holding maximum climb rate until they were just clearing the parapet, and then losing speed abruptly to drop the machine into a hovering attitude in the dead zone immediately past the edge.

One end of the roof had caved in and was gushing flames and smoke. As the downdraft from the rotor cleared the immediate surroundings, Fallon made out a ramped enclosure housing a roof door, from which figures were already emerging. Some ran to the helicopter, while others seemed to be struggling with each other. One went down, another was flailing his arms wildly at another.

"Seems they got a call," Tam decided.

The first two, wearing combat smocks and carrying weapons, reached the door behind Tam and scrambled in. Behind them was Embatto, tense-faced and moving jerkily, with three others in a protective cluster around him, and carrying several bags and satchels bulging with documents. In the middle was Sullivan, easily recognizable from his size. They hauled themselves in, piling the bags behind the pilot's and co-pilot's seats. Then came Makon Ngoyba with two more. That made nine already, and another was squeezing into the door behind Fallon while more milled about. And others were still coming out onto the roof.

Somebody tried to pull Ngoyba back as he stepped up. "Why's he goin'? He ain't no pilot," a voice shouted.

"Get them back!" Embatto shouted from inside.

"Lemme in! Lemme in!" Scuffling broke out around the door. A face crazed with fear appeared, hands clawing inside, trying to tear at anyone to make room. Sullivan shot the head point-blank with a pistol. On the other side, Ngoyba threw himself through into the crush behind the cockpit.

"That's it. That's enough!" Tam yelled above the roar of the motor. If the ones outside started shooting in, everyone would be lost.

"*Go!*" Embatto cried out.

The machine started to rise. Fallon saw one of the figures still on the roof taking aim through the smoke. He fired reflexively, and the figure buckled. A bullet shattered the Plexiglas by Tam's head. That seemed to trigger the others behind, and they began shooting indiscriminately in all directions as the helicopter lifted away. Some of the figures below fell while others retreated, and then the smoke closed in, blotting out the scene.

Fallon looked back to find Embatto peering forward between his and Tam's shoulders. "Bad?" he asked needlessly.

"Terrible. The army attacked without warning at dawn . . . with tanks."

"Molokutu found out about you and moved first," Fallon said bluntly.

Embatto's head snapped around in surprise. "You know about *that*?"

Fallon waved a hand to indicate Tam. Their roles were planned and rehearsed. "That's what he tells me. You weren't on the level. There was a lot more going on than I was ever told about."

"One must take precautions, Mr. Fugleman," Embatto said vaguely, seeming at that moment to be mystified for some reason. "You are the one who initiated the message?" he said, addressing Tam. "Who are you?"

"Let's just stay that Lichuru and I talk to the same people," Tam replied.

"You are with them?"

"People who put up that kind of money like to have some insurance in situations like this."

"Lichuru never mentioned it to me," Embatto said after a few seconds of silence.

"Lichuru wasn't told," Tam said. Embatto sat back and fell silent, as if he were pondering some profound problem.

The Hound climbed sluggishly with its load, and the houses fell away at last. "Green fields ahead," Tam shouted across the cockpit. "We're clearing the city. Just a few minutes more now."

Back at what was left of state-security headquarters, the army force had pulled its forward troops back behind the bomb lines. As the sound of the departing helicopter faded to the west, the whine of approaching jets came from the opposite direction. Moments later, the first formation of General Waroon's MiG-19s came in on a shallow dive across the city and completed the demolition of the main building with salvos of high-explosive rockets. The next wave blasted the compound from end to end with general-purpose bombs, after which the last wave unloaded napalm.

Soon thereafter, all further resistance by the defenders ceased.

Chapter Fifty-two

PRESIDENT MOLOKUTU PUT DOWN THE PHONE IN his study and turned with a bewildered expression on his face toward General Thombert, who was standing behind him. "What's happening?" Molokutu demanded. "Waroon's planes have just bombed Embatto's HQ. I never authorized that. Who—"

Shots sounded outside the study. The confusion on Molokutu's face increased. He came out of the room to find two of his bodyguards lying dead on the landing and soldiers holding the guards who had been posted there at gunpoint. A group of General Thombert's staff officers were striding up the palace's red-carpeted stairway from the mezzanine floor below.

"*I* ordered it," Thombert said.

"What . . . ?" Molokutu faltered, glancing uncertainly from side to side.

"Your time's up. The political puppet is finished. This country's going to be run a soldier's way now."

Molokutu gestured wildly at the nearest officer. "This is mutiny. Arrest him. *I*, the president, order you."

"You don't give the orders anymore," the officer said, drawing his pistol. Footsteps sounded below, and more soldiers came into view in the hallway, marshaling bewildered members of Molokutu's staff. A door opened on the landing, and more frightened faces peered out.

Thombert nodded to one of the colonels, who had been briefed. "Okay, let's not waste any time about it. Take 'em out back. . . . Take all of 'em. We're going to have a clean sweep around here."

Thombert went back into the private suite and study, followed by his entourage. From the window, he could see the tanks drawn up around the palace and the defense preparations still in progress.

All his, now.

"Get me a line to Mordun and put Waroon through," he instructed the aides through the doorway behind. The order was relayed to somebody downstairs.

Immediately below, the two staff cars were parked before the main entrance. He moved over to Molokutu's desk, sat down at it, and tried the voluminous, leather-upholstered chair for size. It felt comfortable.

The call came through. An aide answered it and passed the handset over. "General Waroon for you, sir."

"The term, now, is 'Excellency,'" Thombert corrected.

"My apologies. . . . Excellency."

Thombert spoke into the phone. "This is the first order from your new president."

"My congratulations," Waroon's voice replied.

"Execute Lizard, phase two." Lizard Two called for an ultimatum to the commander of Cobra Force, which Embatto had stationed near Owanden, followed by a second air strike if he failed to comply. Either way, it spelled an end to any further trouble from state security.

"Understood." Waroon cleared down.

Which left the way open, now, to deal finally with the ZRF. The trouble with politicians was that they got too clever for their own good, Thombert reflected as he took a gold pen from its holder and examined it. All that most situations required was a little straightforward military logic and directness. And the way to start with the ZRF was by demoralizing them.

"I want an immediate announcement put out that the regime has changed," he said. "Broadcast that an attempt by Molokutu to subordinate the Army of the People to his own private force has been crushed, and that Barindas has fled after an abortive attempt to show himself in the city. The army is now in complete control."

"At once, Excellency." The aide began moving back to the door.

"And another thing," Thombert called after him. "Bring the lady up from the car down there. She might as well start getting used to this place right away."

There were many reasons for Embatto to be more than curious, but at the same time he was conscious of an overriding need for caution until he could form an idea of what was going on. He knew that Fugleman was lying, which made the Englishman's motives far from clear. As for the American, his claim to be a hitherto unsuspected, additional agent of Pyramid might, or might not, have some truth to it. But this was certainly the helicopter that had been stolen from Djamvelling. If that had been Pyramid's doing, Embatto could make no sense of it.

"So, how long have you been in the country, Mr. Czaryski?" Embatto asked. "I presume your entry was illegal. Otherwise my department would have been aware of it. If I had seen the name, I would recall it."

"Awhile," Tam answered. "They wanted us to stay invisible from everybody. I didn't ask questions."

"Us?" Embatto repeated.

"Like I said, it's a pretty substantial investment to protect."

"And you approached Mr. Fugleman to arrange this operation."

"Those were my orders."

"Were you aware that he was working for me?"

"I didn't ask. It seemed pretty obvious."

"I see." Embatto didn't. The remark was reflexive. He took a long breath and extended a half-open hand. "Let's deal with an obvious point. This aircraft. You know, of course, that it was taken from Djamvelling—in irregular circumstances, to say the least. Do I take it that you were among the party that infiltrated the base?"

Tam and Fallon had, of course, been expecting the question. "No," Tam replied. "They were from the Iranian side. They suspected that they were being dealt out of the original arrangement. How we got our hands on it is another story."

Embatto wiped a hand over his brow. Still leaning forward behind their seats, he turned his head toward Fallon. "When did Mr. Czaryski approach you?"

"This morning—I guess, after he realized you were in trouble."

"Where?"

"At Tobins, where I was staying. . . . I went straight back there from Sadie's." Fallon shrugged. "I assume I was being watched."

"Why did Thombert raid it first thing this morning?"

"You tell me. I've been out of town."

"Tannerling told us that Barindas and Yolatta were coming to the city," Embatto said. "Is that where they were hiding?"

For a second Fallon was taken aback. "If they were, I don't know anything about it," he replied after a short hesitation.

"Why did you go there?" Embatto asked.

"Not to sing hymns... Christ, I'd been out in the bush for weeks. Why does anyone go to a place like that?"

"Hold tight, we're coming in," Tam called out. The helicopter banked and began descending toward the base.

Embatto had radioed ahead after receiving the message via Reid, and since then, mechanics and armorers had been working furiously to bring the number of machines fitted to take the newer weapons systems up to a dozen. Besides Embatto, Sullivan, Ngoyba, and two other senior state-security officials, the Hound had lifted out twelve pilots. During the flight, they had been arguing in the seats behind to decide target priorities. Some feared an air strike and wanted to concentrate everything on Mordun. Others were for a counterattack to relieve the situation around state-security headquarters. Another proposal was to take out Thombert's HQ in retaliation. As the machine steadied into its approach, one of the officers called for Embatto's ruling.

Embatto, however, now they were in safe surroundings, could feel a cold anger rising at the calamity that had been inflicted on him, and he was thirsty for more personal revenge. He moved back and turned toward the rear of the cabin. "Let us not forget the original objective. Our intention was to bring Molokutu down, not fence with him. Why destroy assets that we might possess?"

In the co-pilot's seat in front, Fallon had gone very quiet. As the helicopter continued descending, he checked his pockets for something to write on... and his fingers found the explosive notebook that Yolatta had given him. He took it out and rested it on his knee, then felt inside the pouch between his seat and Tam's. There was a regular pad there, with a pen attached to it by a cord. Fallon eased it out, checked quickly over his shoulder that Embatto was still looking the other way, and then scrawled hurriedly:

Stay ready for immediate takeoff!

Tam caught the movement and flashed him a puzzled look. Fallon shoved the pad across into his lap. Tam glanced down, took in the message, and nodded. Fallon unclipped the canteen from his belt, took off the cap, and surreptitiously trickled water in between the leaves of the RDX compound. He pressed the mass together, set the detonator pencil, and pushed it into the center. Below, more machines were waiting in readiness, dispersed among the banks in front of the apron, a couple by the hangar, as the Hound hovered above. There were a dozen or so figures on the apron, most of them in mechanics' coveralls. The perimeter defenses were manned and at readiness, which was to be expected. Slowly and carefully, Fallon reached a hand around between his seat and the door, and found one of the satchels of books and documents that Embatto and his aides had brought with them. It was crammed full and hadn't been closed. He slid the RDX pack in among the contents and withdrew his hand just as the helicopter was touching down.

At once, the passengers began grabbing the weapons and other things that they had brought and tumbling out. Tam kept the rotor turning and made as if he were checking something in the controls. Fallon pretended to be searching for something in the map pouch. Sullivan heaved himself out of the door behind Tam. Only Embatto was left, half-standing, half-crouching behind Fallon's seat.

Fallon whipped around as Embatto was drawing a pistol from inside his jacket. He grabbed Embatto by the lapel, drew him across the doorway with a heave, and in the same motion delivered a powerful kick that sent Embatto flying headlong to sprawl full length on the concrete. Without waiting for him to hit the ground, Fallon seized his M16 and leveled it at Sullivan, who had turned and begun raising his own rifle to aim back in. Sullivan saw the muzzle of Fallon's gun coming to bear on him and hurled himself aside.

"*Go, Tam!*" Fallon shouted.

Tam banged open the throttle and the Hound, shed of its load now, leaped away, and cleared the hangar roofs before the rest of those on the apron below had realized what was happening. The attention of the defenses was all directed outward, not inward—and in any case nobody had alerted them to fire on one of their own machines. Nothing opened fire in the few seconds it took them to be over the boundary fence and away.

"This is getting to be a habit," Tam shouted as the ravines and hillsides sped by below. "Now, would you mind telling me just what the hell that was all about?"

"He knew," Fallon said. "He knew that what we told him was bullshit. He knows we're with the ZRF."

"How'd you figure?"

Fallon's brow knitted into a frown for a few seconds before he answered. "Tannerling wasn't the spy.... He was just small potatoes. There's another one."

Tam flashed a surprised look across. "Who?"

"I'm not sure yet."

They flew on, gaining height. "Where to?" Tam asked.

They hadn't thought ahead this far, Fallon realized. He wondered if it could be because subconsciously they hadn't expected to pull it off. "Back to the foundry," he said. "Let's find out what's been happening... if there's anybody left there by now to tell us."

Former General, now Acting President Naguib Thombert pushed open the ivory-handled doors of the presidential private suite and walked through. Behind him, Dora stopped in the doorway, momentarily awed by the splendor of the black-lacquer-and-gilt Regency furnishings, intermingled with pieces of chinoiserie, silk Persian carpets, Chinese wallpaper, and a massively ornate crystal chandelier.

"This is the life." Thombert turned and spread his arms wide, showman style. "You could open up a whole new operation in a place like this. Maybe that's what the business needs: a touch of class. What do you think?"

A sustained burst of automatic-rifle fire sounded from the rear of the house. Dora flinched, then closed the door and moved into the center of the room. She tested the carpet wonderingly with her foot.

"You should do something, after the mess your people made of my old place," she said.

Thombert laughed, involuntarily, elated now that the danger was past and enemies vanquished, and at the prospect of power unlimited.

"You're out of that business now, so it don't matter. Gonna have to learn to be a president's lady from now on."

"That's probably just as well," Dora said. "I don't know if the government would have gone much for the idea, anyhow."

The sound of pistol shots came from outside.

Thombert waved a hand toward the window. "Did you hear that? Know what it means?" He jabbed at his own chest several times with a finger. "It means I *am* the government. And there's nobody left anywhere who can do a damn thing about it."

He went into the bedroom suite and ran an admiring finger down the mahogany carving of the huge four-poster bed, decked with a scarlet canopy and hung with silken drapes. "Now that's what I call room. We could get a dozen of your girls on this thing and have a real good time."

"Whatever the president wants," Dora said.

Another round of gunfire came from outside.

Dora turned away to inspect the bathroom, which lay through another doorway. Thombert moved close behind her, slipped his hands around her to fondle her breasts. She looked back over a shoulder but held still. He dropped his hands to her hips, drawing her back and pushing himself against the curve of her behind. "All this excitement makes a man horny. We'll have to celebrate in a big way when it's over."

"Of course . . . But that's later. Right now, is there any chance of something to drink around this place?"

Thombert released her and looked around. "There has to be. What's in there?" He walked over to a black-lacquer cabinet with inlaid doors. "Look at this. We've got enough to open our own bar here. Cold-shelf too. Let's see now . . . how about champagne? It's a celebration, right?"

He uncorked a bottle with a loud *pop.* Dora took out two glasses. "Aren't there things you should be taking care of?" she asked

Thombert looked questioningly at her as he poured. "What is there left to take care of? Embatto's wiped out. Barindas's rebels are strewn all over the country, and he's gone down a hole. All that's left is a rabble on the streets. It's as good as all over already."

Chapter Fifty-three

THE IDEA HADN'T COME TO GEORGE OUT OF nowhere—in situations of acute danger, men's instincts revert to their most primitive; innovation doesn't thrive. But something that he had seen on the the way through the storage depot reminded him of it: something he'd heard that the rebels in Afghanistan had tried against the Soviets. For them, it hadn't worked. Indeed, against a professionally trained and disciplined army, it shouldn't have worked. But the Zugendan soldiers were inexperienced and jumpy, and the majority of them frightened conscripts who felt ill at ease in their unfamiliar mechanized environment. As George had said to Leroy, everybody else seemed to be playing silly buggers that day; they had nothing to lose but their necks.

He lay in a hollow well forward of the ZRF positions, clutching the steel nozzle and trigger connected by a flexible tube to the twin metal cylinders slung in the harness on his back. The weight and ungainliness of the contrivance did nothing to ease his feeling of vulnerability and exposure as he watched the tank clanking and grinding toward him over earth mounds and rubble, now no more than fifty feet away. On one flank, the rebels had fallen back very visibly to lure the tank forward, while on the other side, Frano's section had squirmed their way forward to the positions George had indicated. Leroy, cradling an FN assault rifle, was lying in a crater close to George. From over to the right, the antitank gun that George had repositioned flashed, firing a low-power round which bounced harmlessly off the tank's side. The tank's turret turned, seeking the source, and the tank halted.

"Coom on, let's 'ave yer," George growled under his breath. Leroy glanced at him questioningly. George measured distances and angles with his eye and shook his head. Leroy looked toward the position that Frano was watching them from and raised an arm, signaling for them to wait. The tank's secondary turret-mounted armament sent a long burst into the area where the gun had fired from. The commander was trying to entice it to reveal itself again before committing a shell. Its motor roared, and it began moving forward again, twisting around onto a course that would take it close to where George and Leroy were concealed.

Good enough.

Thirty feet... The distance and timing would have to be just right: enough to make sure he was visible to the tank crew, but at same time giving them minimum opportunity to bring any weapons to bear on him. Leroy would stay close by him as cover, and Frano's section would pin down the tank's supporting infantry for the few crucial seconds that he would need.

He cocked an eye at Leroy. Leroy glanced across at Frano's waiting group again and nodded. "Ready."

Twenty feet... The noise of the tank's motor was right on top of them. Suddenly the looming steel bulk of it seemed immense and impregnable, like a castle on the move.

"Now!" George shouted above the din. Leroy's arm fell.

There was a short delay while somebody behind relayed the order and then they heard the rapid series of reports as the mortars farther back behind the block fired. One second... two... three... Then the bombs began landing among the Zugendan support infantry. At the same moment the covering group opened up with machine guns while Frano's section broke from cover and ran forward, firing and throwing grenades. Leroy was on his feet, stooping to help George up, then moving forward, slowing to let George catch up. The din all around was deafening. It seemed impossible for them not to be hit.... Straight toward the front of the tank as it ground forward... ZRF closing from the side... The turret was starting to swing back. Still too far away, not enough time! The heavy machine gun alongside the cannon was depressing.

And then, as George and Leroy continued to close, Frano and Komil were running up to the tank. Without checking their stride, Komil stooped to form a stirrup with his hands, Frano stepped into it, and Komil hurled him up onto the hull, where he kicked the protruding muzzle of the machine gun high just as it fired.

But by now George was within a few feet. He lumbered up in full view of the commander's observation periscope, and with Leroy and Komil lifting, and Frano hauling from above, scrambled up onto the front armor glacis and jammed the nozzle through the driver's observation slit. Leroy swung up next to him and pushed George down as the main cannon lowered and the turret rotated in an attempt to knock them off. The gun brushed harmlessly over the metal cylinders on George's back, but caught Frano and swept him off. George squeezed the trigger below the nozzle and could hear the screams from inside, even through the armor and above the noise of the engine.

"*Flamethrower!*"

"Shit, it's all over me!"

The tank stopped, and the turret hatch flew open. The commander and gunner tumbled out, and the driver appeared from between the tracks via the underneath escape hatch. He was hysterical, his coveralls soaking. Komil and several other ZRF grabbed the two crewmen, while George yanked the commander around to the covered side of the tank, thrust him back against the hull, and thrust the muzzle of a pistol up under his chin.

"Right, we'll 'ave no bloody nonsense from you. As of now, yer workin' for us. Oonderstand?"

The tank commander, still shaking from the fright, was already tearing off his insignia. "Yes, sir! Anythin' you say! You got it."

"Then tell 'im ter stop screamin' an' get back inside. We've got things ter do."

The covering group intensified their fire while George booted the terrified driver back under the tank, then lifted the commander off his feet and stuffed him into the turret. "We'll see yer back at t'ranch," he yelled to Leroy as he tore the apparatus and harness off his back 'and threw it away. Then he drew his pistol from his belt and climbed up to follow. "See 'ow bad Frano is. 'E did a right good job, that un."

The liquid that he had squirted through the visor was in fact water, and the equipment a portable pesticide sprayer from one of the UN health programs, which he had spotted in the storage depot. Maybe he should try his luck on the horses one day, he told himself as he slammed the hatch shut.

Barindas was waiting with a covering party farther back. As the tank moved forward and shielded them, they rose and hurried out to it. The escape hatch below opened again, and hands urged Barindas forward and helped him crawl down between the tracks. A runner left to take the news to Yolatta at the Radio Building. "Coom on, get a move on, you lot out there," a strange voice said through the tank's loud hailer. "We 'aven't got all bloody day."

Barindas climbed up into a cramped, noisy vault of machinery that smelt of cordite, oil, and the peculiar odor of human fear. The driver was lower down and to the front, and another crewman helped Barindas up into the turret space, where he wedged himself next to George. The engine roared and the tank began bumping and crashing its way forward over debris.

"A bit cramped in 'ere, is this," George bellowed above the din, in what Barindas supposed was some kind of British dialect. "It's only supposed to 'ave three, really. But it's only a short ride. Not exactly what yer'd call the last word in luxury, these things, are they?"

There were army vehicles below, stopped along the approach roads to the derelict industrial quarter where the foundry was situated. As the helicopter lost height, Fallon could see figures crouched behind walls and moving between doorways. The ZRF's comings and goings had probably attracted the attention of the military's spotter planes, he reflected.

Shells were falling around the foundry when they touched down among the rusty castings littering the forecourt. Colonel Marlow came hurrying across, accompanied by Sam Letumbai. As promised, he had stayed until the last. Crosby was still inside, throwing together a defense. They had established intermittent radio contact with Barindas since Fallon and Tam's departure for Lommerzo, and their whole spirit had changed. Units that had left earlier were either returning and pitching in or moving to block the army columns on their way back to the city.

"Barindas thinks that the whole city is on the verge of rising and that the army will desert," the colonel told

Fallon and Tam through the door, while outside, Letumbai waved a squad of heavily armed ZRF forward from the foundry door. "He's going to try and take the Radio Building. He's convinced that if he and Yolatta can go public now, that's all the spark it will take."

"What do you think?" Fallon asked him.

"Lord, I don't know. He knows these people best, I suppose."

"So what's the idea right now?" Tam gestured with a thumb to the guerrillas clambering aboard behind.

"Apparently the situation down in the street there is touch and go," the colonel answered. "So we're going to try getting in from the roof to have Sam there as a standby in case they don't make it. Extra insurance, as it were. Barindas thought we were deserting the ship, and Sam was a bit upset about it. He's determined to contribute something."

"And you went along with this crazy idea?" Tam said.

"Everybody seems to be having insane ideas today, Tam," the colonel returned evenly, stepping up into the doorway behind.

"You're coming too?"

"Naturally."

"Got your speech all worked out?" Fallon said to Sam as Sam hauled himself up behind the last of the guerrillas.

Before Sam could answer, a shell burst nearby and something hard struck behind and above, in the area of the engine mounting where the tail boom joined the fuselage. The helicopter lurched violently. For an instant Fallon thought it was going to overturn, but Tam fought at the controls and righted it. The note sounded different now: screechier, with an intermittent juddering. Three more shells burst in rapid succession across the lot, and another hit the foundry building.

"Could we get a move on, please?" the colonel suggested.

Tam opened the throttle carefully. The rotor kept turning. With Fallon convinced that the fragile capsule they were in was about to fall apart at any moment and Tam yelling encouragement and praises to Russian engineering, the machine clawed its way back into the air.

* * *

The bathroom was like a sultan's palace, with a sunken Jacuzzi in marble and ornamented with onyx, gold faucets set with pearls, and built-in TV, all surrounded by mirrors.

"If you don't like the decor, we'll tear it all out and have it changed," Thombert declared. "You just have to say the word. You know, I like owning my own country. There's four million people out there, and they're all going to be working for me. *I* own them. I sort of like that. . . ."

While Thombert was speaking, four Mi-4 Hound attack helicopters had cleared the treetops and were swooping toward the air base at Mordun. The defending garrison had not been warned about the possibility of an aerial assault and had barely begun registering the situation when the leader fired the first rocket salvo and opened up with Gatlings.

The attack caught General Waroon's MiGs out in the open, lined up wing tip to wing tip while they were being refueled and rearmed for Lizard Two, the intended attack on the SS Cobra Force near Owanden. The defenders woke up in time to down one of the helicopters with gunfire as it was leaving.

But by that time—as an operational entity, at least—the Zugendan air force had ceased to exist.

The street a block from the Radio Building was a shambles, with bodies sprawled among smoldering ruins, and wounded being carried back to a dressing station that had been set up in a bakery. The tank rumbled to a halt as a ZRF soldier ran forward, waving his hands in a crossing motion in front of his face. George opened the commander's hatch atop the turret and looked out.

"You won't get through ahead. There are SS dug in at the end of the street. They're still shooting."

Barindas craned his head through to peer out from beside George. His jaw tightened at the scene around them. "We can't give up now, not after all this," he insisted. "Not when we are this close."

"We'll roon right over 'em in this," George shouted down at the ZRF soldier. "Gerrout me bloody way."

"They have TOWs. They knocked out two of the tanks on Main Street. It's not possible."

George glowered toward the shooting, and then at the side of the street, in the direction where the Radio Building was located just one block away. "Oh, in't it? We'll see about that." He leaned down, tapped the driver's shoulder with a foot, and shouted into the intercom mike, "Okay, Geronimo. 'Ard left, right 'ere."

Confused, the driver looked back up into the turret. "There isn't a way left here, sir."

"So bloody what? Fook 'em, we'll make our own. . . ." George closed the hatch and squeezed back down beside Barindas. "Coom on, then," he yelled at the driver. "Let's gerron with it."

Chapter Fifty-four

THE MOTOR WAS COUGHING FITFULLY AND SHAK-
ing the entire air frame as the Hound came down over the
Radio Building roof, making the descent more of a
semicontrolled crash than a landing. The port-rear wheel
mounting of the tricycle undercart gave way, causing the
machine to keel halfway over, and the still-spinning rotor
smashed into the concrete base of the radio mast and
disintegrated. Fallon had no idea what to expect as he and
Sam Letumbai climbed from the upward-facing starboard
side of the craft, followed by three ZRF. The port side was
impassable, and Tam and the colonel had to clamber across
to follow them. The rest followed, leaving two who had
been hurt in the impact.

Nobody had been expecting an assault from that
direction. The roof was occupied only by a four-man
observation team with a telephone, who had been too
astonished by the helicopter's sudden appearance to summon the presence of mind to use it. When they saw the
attackers emerging with assault rifles and holding grenades, they threw up their hands and sat back against the
parapet wall. Fallon and the leaders reached the roof
access door in a few seconds. Sam kicked it open. Fallon
checked, then moved through to cover as Tam and the
assault team stormed in.

Colonel Marlow went to the front parapet and looked
down over the main street to see what was happening
below. The fighting had obviously been severe. Just at that
moment, a force he presumed to be Yolatta's was mounting
an attack along the street from the direction opposite to
the prison, but it seemed to be bogging down. The colonel
turned and went inside after the others. The sounds of
firing and a grenade exploding came up from below—and

not especially close. Fallon was a floor down into the building already.

This time they were so close. A spearhead of ZRF had actually made it into the side of the Radio Building and seemed to be still holding out there . . . but then a machine gun in one of the windows above had cut off the supporting section. Oblivious to the bullets and splinters zipping around him, Yolatta stooped to help Bruno, leader of the ZRF squad that had got Yolatta and Barindas away from Sadie's.

"Get up! You can't stay out here. How bad is it?"

Bruno was down on one knee. He struggled up and steadied himself. There was blood on his shirt, but it seemed to be just around the shoulder. "Not too bad."

"That chopper could mean anything. We have to go on."

"It's no good. Look, we're being cut to shreds."

"There's still—" Yolatta broke off as a rumbling, crashing noise became audible behind them, muted at first, but growing louder. "What in hell . . . ?"

"It's coming from inside there. It—"

As they stared, a jagged section of the wall of the building across the street from the Radio Building collapsed onto the pavement in a cloud of rubble and dust, and a tank burst out of the hole, its tracks churning and crushing. It rose over the heap of debris, then plunged down into the roadway with masonry and bricks pouring off its sides. It emerged fully onto the street, corrected course, and without slowing, headed straight for the front of the Radio Building. The stunned soldiers manning the positions around the entrance and inside the lobby came to their senses just in time to hurl themselves aside as forty tons of armor and steel plowed in through doors, walls, lobby, and stairs like a cannonball hitting a crate of eggs, demolishing most of the front of the building's lower two floors. For a moment Yolatta could only stand transfixed, wondering how it hadn't brought the whole structure down. And then he shook himself back to life.

"It's Barindas!" he roared at the ZRF along the street, turning his head one way, then the other. "He's made it!

diers inside were still too dazed to react. With a cheer that spread like fire through dry brush, they swarmed forward across the street, over the wreckage, around the tank, and onward into the building.

Fallon ran along a yellow-walled corridor with bodies on the floor and bullet scars in the paintwork, with several ZRF behind him to hold the stairway leading down. Behind, Tam ducked in through the doorway where Letumbai and ZRF were waving a terrified announcer and two engineers away from a booth. Back in the corridor, two Zugendan soldiers came out of a doorway and approached stealthily. Colonel Marlow appeared at the end of the corridor behind them and calmly shot them with a pistol. He walked on and entered the green room to find Letumbai in the booth and Tam standing over a technician at the engineer's panel.

"That's quite all right. You needn't have waited," the colonel informed them.

A red light illuminated. The technician nodded at Letumbai.

He stared at the microphone for a moment. Explosions from the ground floor shook the building. He took a deep breath. "Citizens and soldiers of Zugenda, this is Sam Letumbai talkin', second-in-command of the military forces o' the Zugendan Republican Front.... They told you we were on the run, miles away out in the bush. They said we'd been driven up into the hills. They said this was their city.... Well, we're not runnin' through any bush, and we're not up in any hills. I'm talkin' to you from right here in Kinnube. This is *your* city.

"All day we've been seein' security soldiers killin' army soldiers, army soldiers killin' security soldiers.... What for? You're all just the same kind o' guys, grew up on the same streets. Lot o' poor boys killin' each other because rich men tell 'em to. But none of you's gonna get rich. You don't see any rich men killin' each other...."

Downstairs, the tank was practically buried in concrete and rubble blocking the topside hatch. The driver opened the floor hatch, and a cloud of dust billowed up inside. George grabbed a rifle and wormed his way down through the machinery. Barindas followed.

They crawled forward between the tracks and came

up into what looked like the aftermath of an air raid, with collapsed masonry, buckled girders, concrete beams propped at crazy angles, and dust and smoke everywhere. Scattered shooting was still going on. Shadowy figures materialized and turned out to be ZRF. One of them clambered over a mound of bricks to take Barindas's elbow. It was Haile Yolatta.

"This way. There are stairs in front. Who was in the chopper?"

"What chopper?" George asked.

"A chopper hit the roof a couple minutes ago."

"It couldn't be who I think, could it?" George said.

They moved forward cautiously toward a main stairway overlooking the lobby. Soldiers from the far end of the building were coming forward to try to block the way. Yolatta fired at them, calling to other ZRF for support. Bruno and several others came forward. George waved at Barindas. "Coom on. We'll 'ave ter make a dash fer it. Foller me."

He ran forward at a crouch, just as more figures appeared, gesturing, at the top of an open steel stairway overlooking the lobby area. George recognized Fallon, with a couple of ZRF. "They're oop there!" he shouted exuberantly. "Look, it's Bern. They're bloody well 'ere!"

The party rushed forward toward the stairs, George leading, while Fallon's group fired to cover them from above. A burst of fire from the soldiers hit a couple of the ZRF. Barindas ducked back to shelter behind a pillar. A moment later, a grenade clanked onto the floor, rolled, and stopped just a few feet from him.

Barindas stared at it, paralyzed, his eyes wide. George turned his head to look back, but he was already on the stairs and moving the wrong way, unable to check himself.

And then Bruno, who had been behind Barindas, instead of taking cover, threw himself on top of the grenade and smothered the blast with his body as it exploded. It lifted him into the air like a piece of rag caught in a gale and dropped him ten feet away. Barindas stared, horrified, and then Yolatta grabbed his arm and yanked him on up the stairway behind George. All the way up, he kept turning his head to look back at the crumpled shape, moments ago a human being, now a discarded piece of waste. . . .

Fallon watched grimly from above as the group came hurrying up the stairs toward him. . . . It had happened in the final seconds. The tank had knocked the remaining fight out of the defenders. Down below, the shooting was dying away as dusty shapes began emerging from cover with their hands raised.

"What's the matter with you?" Thombert demanded angrily at the aide outside the doors of the suite. "Didn't you hear me giving orders not to be disturbed?"

"My apologies, Excellency, but there is something on the radio that you should hear yourself. If it weren't of the utmost seriousness, naturally I would never have—"

"All right, all right." Thombert came out and walked toward the study. The aide accompanied him.

"What is it?" Dora inquired, appearing with her glass still in her hand at the doors from the presidential suite behind.

"Some kind of emergency. I don't know. . . ." Thombert marched in to the study and found an officer standing by the radio on a side table. "Well?" Then Thombert stopped in his tracks as he recognized the voice coming from the speaker. It sounded frail, shaky, but more determined than he had ever heard it. His eyes widened disbelievingly. "This isn't possible. . . ."

"Yolatta is there too," the officer told him somberly. "So is Letumbai."

The voice of Jovay Barindas was saying, ". . . that you were told I had run away like a rabbit. Well, my friends, as you can judge for yourselves, that report had been somewhat exaggerated. . . ." The voice caught, and Barindas swallowed audibly. The emotion that he felt seemed to issue tangibly out into the room. "I want to tell you about some of the things that I have seen with my own eyes here in Kinnube today. . . ."

"Where did he come from?" Thombert growled as he began losing his calm. "I was told that we were in control of the city. Get me Colonel Sahle immediately."

At that instant another officer came running up the stairs and burst in without preliminaries. "Excellency, Mordun has been bombed!"

Thombert stood stock still, stunned.

"How bad is the damage?" the aide snapped.

"I don't know. Sahle is on the line."

"Put him through up here," Thombert instructed numbly. Then, when the call was transferred: "What's happened? How bad is it?"

Sahle sounded bewildered. "The first report is garbled. But it sounds as if the whole base is in flames. At least—"

"Hello...? Hello...? What the hell?" Thombert jiggled the cradle impatiently. Dora, who had stopped in the doorway, came into the room, looking worried.

"Palace main office," a different voice said in Thombert's ear.

"I was talking to Colonel Sahle at army HQ. I've been cut off. What's going on?"

"One second. I'll check."

"Bombed?" Thombert muttered as he waited. "Who by? What with?"

"Excellency?" The voice from the palace office came back on the line.

"Well?"

"I don't understand it. All our lines to army headquarters appear to have gone dead."

"What? Every one? How could...?"

Thombert's words trailed away as the sound of engines growing louder came from beyond the window, accompanied by the *crump-crump* of the palace defenses opening up. The officer rushed across to the study's picture window, overlooking the front drive. Thombert, grim-faced, strode over behind him. Dora and the aide followed.

They found themselves staring out at the chilling silhouettes of three attack helicopters, bristling with weapons pods, rocket pylons, and gun racks, coming straight at them in line abreast....

And the office of the Zugendan presidency became vacant once more, less than five seconds later.

Embatto heard the broadcast from the treatment room in the infirmary of the barracks section of the Djamvelling base, where he had been taken with a badly strained shoulder after Fallon kicked him out of the helicopter door. While the remaining attack helicopters that he had despatched wrought havoc on the tank forces withdrawing from the ruin that had been SS headquarters, others closing belatedly around the Radio Building, and the column approaching Kinnube from the south, he listened to Barindas telling the nation how evil had at last preyed upon evil, with the two repressive organs of state power destroying each other, along with the men who had controlled them. For once, Embatto lost his grip of the self-control that he had always taken such pains to cultivate.

"Get them!" he screamed at Ngoyba, who had driven him across to the infirmary. "While they're all together: Barindas, Letumbai, that ape Yolatta. Fugleman was behind it—he'll be there as well. Flatten the Radio Building! I don't want two bricks of it left standing! Arggh!" He winced as the doctor wound a bandage tightly around his shoulder.

"Have to keep it still for a few days," the doctor said. "You'll need a sling."

"All the machines are out," Ngoyba said. "They'll all be empty now, on their way back." Ten of the original twelve remained operational: one had been shot down at Mordun, and another had returned from the strike on the palace too damaged to go back into action.

"Reload them and turn them around," Embatto ranted. "Right away, while those peasants are still in there. Get over to the hangars and give them the order right now."

Ngoyba nodded and strode quickly out the door, past Sullivan. He reappeared outside the window, jumped into a jeep, and roared away across the parade ground toward the helicopter area on the far side of the base. Two machines came in low over the perimeter fence and landed out of sight behind the hangars.

Embatto continued to watch, chafing, while the doctor finished securing the bandage. Another two machines came into sight as he reached for Embatto's shirt. Gunfire sounded from somewhere in that direction, coming from the ground. Embatto jumped up and rushed to the window. Somebody—army or ZRF—was trying to pick the returning helicopters off as they came in. Then something small and flaming shot up from behind a ridge. It struck one of the incoming machines, exploding rearward of the fuselage. The helicopter's tail boom separated, and the machine plunged out of sight. Moments later the sound of an explosion reached the room, and a plume of smoke rose up into the sky.

"Get them! Kill them! Kill them all!" Embatto shrieked, shaking his fist demoniacally as more machines came in and touched down.

On the far side of the hangars, the helicopters were waved down onto the apron immediately outside the doors, where Makon Ngoyba was frantically directing armorers and technicians as they wheeled new loads of bombs, rockets, and ammunition outside. A fuel tanker had been brought up, also. Time was at a premium, and everything was grouped in a cluster: helicopters, munitions, fuel truck—with pilots, gunners, and ground crew all milling about together in their haste. . . . And almost in the middle of it all, piled outside the hangar doors where they had been dumped for the time being by the party that Fallon and Tam had ferried in earlier, were the bags of documents and other valuables that they had brought with them from SSHQ.

That was when the radio operator with the ZRF force that Crosby had sent overland to Djamvelling reported to Sam Letumbai in the Radio Building that all of the surviving machines had been counted back in.

And Yolatta closed the switch on the triggering device, which he still had with him, for the radio-detonated bomb.

Some said later that the shooting across the city started to slacken even before the broadcast had finished.

When Fallon went back downstairs afterward, the battle in the street outside was certainly over. He walked silently through the wreckage of the building and stopped to look at the grim line of mangled, blood-covered shapes being laid out and covered alongside the wall. Weary, disheveled figures were coming out of the ruined buildings, some of them dazed and shocked, moving in a strange, dreamlike way. At one end of the street, a group of SS prisoners were being brought out, their hands clasped on top of their heads. Thick smoke was curling up above the smashed building opposite from tanks burning a couple of blocks away after helicopter attacks.

He shouldered his M16, turned away, and walked slowly through the aftermath of the fighting to the prison. Soldiers were coming out through the gate and the breaches in the wall, and ZRF were entering to take over. Fallon went past them and made his way through the bare, forbidding corridors that he had seen before, and into the high-security wing. He found the steel stairs that led up to the landing where he had made his entry from the roof, climbed them, and came to the guardroom where Candy had killed Tumratta. The guards had fled, leaving the keys. Fallon picked them up and opened the barred gate leading to the first corridor. He let himself through it and began unlocking the cells, one by one. His only regret was that Candy couldn't be there to help him.

Chapter Fifty-five

WIND WAS LIFTING FLURRIES OF DUST OFF THE crags and ledges of the old cliffs overlooking the valley of Tenyasha. Low and heavy clouds were forming overhead. The rains would begin any time now.

On a steep path that led up the minor gorge above the rear entrance to the restricted-access quarters, Candy climbed with a smooth, silent effortlessness that derived both from the lessons in stealth that she had learned in her years with the ZRF and the natural litheness of her body. She was wearing a camouflage smock, which with her natural coloring blended into the surroundings of rock and thornbushes; the Uzi submachine gun that she carried was wrapped in dull tape at the places that might clink against a stone or reflect a glint of light. She moved intermittently, timing her shifts from one place of cover to another for the moments when, her instincts and her experience told her, the figure of Marie Guridan that she was following would be too attentive to the ground ahead to look back.

The slope eased for a short distance at the head of the minor gorge, and then the path doubled back and ascended again, winding around the massif above the cliff faces containing the main caves, to lose itself among the jumble of shattered boulders forming the humped crown, among which Jimmy Reid had placed the antenna to the secret radio facility that he had set up with Hardy Coal. But instead of continuing the turn in that direction, which would have led rightward, away from the main cliff line, Guridan continued clambering over some rocks and then dropped into a hollow backed by a low scarp and screened from the principal valley below by a horizontal slab. Candy hung back and waited, watching through the chink between two boulders while Guridan turned to check back along the path one last time, then disappeared down out of sight.

Candy decided that the direct approach would be too exposed and risky. So instead of following by the same route, she slung the Uzi across her back and picked her way up and to the right, climbing a vertical corner and moving over the top of the rock hump topping the scarp at the rear. She could see Guridan about ten feet below her, crouched in a natural aerie behind the horizontal slab, lifting a metal box with carrying straps out from a recess behind a flat rock. From where Candy was, a steep fissure led down to the depression from the right, away from the direct approach up from the path. Candy unslung the Uzi again and, moving slowly and quietly, began easing herself down.

After the bomb went off at Djamvelling the previous evening, more ZRF forces had arrived, stiffened by army units that had already started to come over to Barindas, making it only a matter of time before the base either surrendered or was overrun. Although all of the remaining combat-readied helicopters were out of action, a few other machines farther away in the dispersal area had escaped damage. As night came, Embatto, along with Sullivan and several of the topmost SS officers, had got away in two machines: an Mi-4 that had not been adapted for the high-performance role, and a smaller Mi-1 trainer. They had flown south and joined the state-security mobile force of guns and wheeled armor, which by that time was at Owanden. It wasn't clear whether Embatto's motive was purely revenge or an attempt to secure a defensible position for what was left of his forces, but after a predawn start, the morning found them advancing up toward the valley of Tenyasha.

Marie Guridan opened the hinged lid of the radio pack to uncover the operator's panel and extended the antenna. She put on a headset, switched on, adjusted the frequency, and spoke into a mike on an extending coil of cord. "Kestrel to Cobra Force, come in."

She'd had to move quickly. Until now, the assumption had been that if anyone attacked Tenyasha, it would be the army—Cobra Force had been positioned nearby in order to move in after the fighting between Thombert's force and the ZRF, when Embatto launched the coup in Kinnube.

Hence she hadn't made any great effort to ascertain the details of Austin and Sung Feng's defense preparations. But after yesterday's catastrophe everything had changed, and the first thing she had learned that morning was that Cobra Force was above Owanden and approaching. Austin had seemed delighted. When Guridan quizzed him on why, his revelations had horrified her.

"Kestrel to Cobra Force, this is urgent. Are you—" A hand tore the headset from her ears, and a sharp kick in the ribs sent her crashing off balance into the dust. She whirled about and sat up to find Candy looking down at her coldly over the barrel of an Uzi. Candy motioned her back until she was at a safe distance with her back to a rock and then, keeping the gun trained with one hand, squatted for a second to flip the radio off. Then Candy straightened up, pointed at the sidearm that Guridan was carrying, and snapped her fingers. Guridan put her hand to her belt but shook her head. A bullet hit the ground between her thighs as she sprawled, half-sitting, half-lying, inches from her crotch. She hastily took out the pistol and threw it over.

"No, I don't think we tell your friends where the ambush places are," Candy said. "We let them come. They find out for themselves.... Besides, I do a lot of work there, digging. I never see you doing very much digging. But then you are the intelligence expert, yes? You work with your brain. Well, I do a little work with my brain too. You see, there are two people who know that it is not me who kills Tannerling: me, and whoever did kill him. And I think I know then that it must be you.... But I can't tell anyone, because if they do something and I'm wrong, then it will tip off the real one. So I have to make sure myself."

Malice glittered in the eyes behind the large, round spectacle lenses. But Guridan had to know where she'd gone wrong. "What told you?" she breathed.

"Because there is only one reason for killing him that makes sense: to stop him from talking before Fugleman has a chance to ask him questions about how Victor and me were betrayed in London." Candy shrugged. "Why mustn't he be allowed to talk? Because he doesn't know anything. It wasn't Tannerling that did it. If Fugleman realizes this, then Fugleman knows there is somebody else. Tannerling is just the small-time spy, making extra money. So Embatto lets him go to save the big fish. . . . Yes, it was so, right? Do I make the good intelligence expert also?"

Guridan moistened her lips and glared back malevolently, but said nothing.

Candy went on: "It must be someone who knows the plans for London, which you do, naturally. . . but others do too. But then I remember how Fugleman tells me that you ask if I might do something foolish because Tannerling still walks around free . . . that maybe I might try to kill him, yes? You tell him how I behave strangely. But I am doing nothing strange at all. It is something that you try to suggest, so that when he is killed, the first person they all think about is me. And you asked Fugleman just before Tannerling is shot, where I am gone. I talk to Imo, and I find you are nowhere that anyone can see you, either. You went across to give Imo the information for Tannerling to send to Embatto. Then you leave, and it is sometime later that you meet Austin—enough time to go back inside the battery room from the outside, shoot Tannerling when you know he will be inside the radio room alone, and get back to the others. And that's how it was, yes?"

The look on Guridan's face was answer enough, making further discussion pointless. "He was no loss to either side," she said, her voice coming as more of a hiss now that her initial shock was wearing off and giving way to anger.

For the first time, curiosity showed on Candy's face. "What I don't see is why. You are not a fat official in Kinnube who thinks only of his cattle ranches or how to get more of the foreigners' money. You have lived here with ZRF. You see the way things are with the people. Why do you work for a man like Embatto?"

Guridan looked back disdainfully. She shifted herself to a more upright posture against the rock. "Why? Because of things that people like you, with your misguided ideas of freedom and independence, could never comprehend or grasp. Because he represents what countries like this need if they are to be anything in the world: order, authority, discipline. And yes, it may necessitate some harsh measures at times. But the powers that grew rich off this country didn't become what they did by worrying about rights of individuals; they did it through *strength*. That was what made them the rulers and us the ruled."

Candy regarded her without surprise or any special show of emotion, more still with curiosity, like a collector of insects studying a new specimen. "So all the time you are living the lie while you travel with Barindas, yes?"

Guridan's mouth curled into a sneer. "He has nothing to offer but a fool's dreams. Independence? Independence from what? For what? Yes, he would make Zugenda independent—a hermit among nations. Embatto will bring us friends who have the power to make us strong and the wealth to invest that will make us rich. That is what we need."

"We? Who is this 'we'? I am not the politician, you understand. I have just the simple mind. It is not the Zugendan people who will be protected and grow wealthy. They will be the slaves in their own country. You don't care about this?"

"The people!" Guridan spat. "For ten thousand years they have scratched in the dirt with wooden plows. They have always been slaves, and they always will be. Their nature is to be ruled. Barindas might as well try to teach the cattle to stand up and walk on their hind legs if he thinks it can ever be otherwise. There are—"

At that moment a series of powerful explosions sounded from the direction of the lower valley, muted somewhat by the intervening ground, but not so far away—just a few miles. The sharper barking of gunfire commenced immediately afterward.

"Ah, so the party is starting already, it seems." Candy stood up and peered into the distance as if hoping to see some sign of the combat, but never letting Guridan out of the corner of her eye. Guridan turned her head to look apprehensively over her shoulder. "I think maybe your Embatto doesn't have the same ideas as you about who is so powerful now," Candy said.

"Go ahead, crow and enjoy it while you've got the chance," Guridan grated. "How long do you think the spineless country that Barindas will create for you is going to last?"

"Well, maybe so, maybe not," Candy said carelessly. "But since you are not going to be around to watch it happen, you don't have to worry yourself."

Guridan looked back at her sharply. "Why?" she asked uncertainly. "What do you mean? What are you going to do?"

Candy looked surprised, as if the answer should have been too obvious to need voicing. "I am going to kill you, of course. After Victor and what happened in London, the fun your nice friends had with me in Kinnube, and then you try to frame me with a murder, you think I let you walk away?"

Fear was showing on Guridan's face for the first time now. "But I didn't do any of those things. I have my beliefs, like you. We're not really so different."

Candy appeared not to hear, but went on, speaking absently, as if the matter were of mild interest, without particular bearing: "In some ways I agree, Barindas can be too soft. There is too much chance that he would let you live because of his principles, and what he sees as needless killing is not his way. . . . Oh, but before I shoot you, I must thank you for taking care of Tannerling when I cannot do it, because of the orders from Barindas. But this time, the war is over. I don't think I give Barindas the chance to make another order."

Guridan shook her head. "No. You can't!" Her eyes darted about desperately. "They'll want to talk. They'll want information that only I can tell them. For *your* cause!"

Candy made as if she were considering the suggestion, then dismissed it with a light toss of her head. "No. Your information isn't important anymore. Who cares what you know about yesterday? Today everything is different." The noise of the distant gunfire continued unabated.

"I can give you names of others—others who betrayed the ZRF."

"I don't care about any others. I'm only interested in putting things straight for *me*."

Beads of perspiration were appearing on Guridan's forehead. "I was paid well. Embatto had good sources. I'll split it with you. You can be comfortable for life. Why waste it on these people? You could live in luxury in Europe, America. . . ."

Candy let her eyes roam casually over Guridan's body, allowing them to rest pointedly for a few seconds on her stomach, her knees, her feet. "I'm not sure if I make it fast and kind, or slow," she murmured.

Guridan was almost gibbering incoherently in fear. "Live among different people, people who have influence. They could make you anything you want."

"In Kinnube jail, for me, it was very slow. . . ."

"*No!*" Guridan shrieked. She leaped up from the ground and onto the rock slab forming the wall between the depression and the top of the cliff face. "*I won't let you! Never!*" She ran two paces to the edge and hurled herself off. Her voice turned into a scream that came floating up, growing fainter. Then it ceased abruptly.

Candy stepped up onto the slab and moved to the edge. Far below, Guridan was lying twisted like a broken doll on the rocky slope not far from the path that ran past the mouths of the main caves. Several figures ran out to check the body, then stepped back and peered up. Candy stood looking down at them impassively.

"Stupid bitch," she muttered. "I only wanted to see you sweat a little, that's all."

But she wasn't going to shed that many tears over it.

Shouldering the Uzi, she turned away and stepped over the rocks to the path leading down.

Chapter Fifty-six

THE ACTION BELOW TENYASHA WAS SWIFT AND decisive. With its head and tail pinned in narrow defiles and the body between them exposed below commanding positions, the SS column was cut to pieces. By midday, the ZRF were moving down to mop up the last pockets of resistance scattered along the trail. A few individuals and small groups managed to slip out of the trap to disappear into the surrounding hills or make for the border, but most of the survivors were captured. Embatto, in his third narrow escape within twenty-four hours, was among them.

Fallon, along with George and Tam, arrived from Kinnube with Sam Letumbai and several ZRF officers in a light airplane, late of the Zugendan army, early in the afternoon. Fallon had, of course, contacted Jimmy Reid by radio the previous evening to warn that there was still a high-level spy at large in the organization. Beyond that, Fallon hadn't been able to offer a lot of help. Then Reid had radioed Fallon late that morning, shortly after the plane took off from Kinnube, to advise simply that the spy had been dealt with, and who it had been.

They landed on a flat, stony expanse in the higher reaches of the valley, and by the time they had trekked down to the caves, victorious guerrillas were appearing from lower down, some on foot, others piled into the vehicles, all of them dusty, battle-grimed, and weary, but jubilant—all the more so when they learned for sure that the war was over.

Fallon found Parnum below the main caves, taking photographs of grinning ZRF poising singly and in groups, weapons slung jauntily across shoulders and with great exhibitions of camaraderie for the record. Not far away, Mamu had become a celebrity in his own right and was answering questions in the middle of an incredulous crowd.

He had maintained his impersonation successfully until the end, and been revealed only when the real Barindas began speaking suddenly and unexpectedly on Kinnube radio late the previous afternoon. Sam Letumbai went on ahead to join Austin, who was conferring nearby with a group of his lieutenants. Jimmy Reid was with them, and so was Sung Feng. Seeing Reid, George ambled over to him, and Tam tagged along.

Marie Guridan had known Mamu's true identity all along, and hence Embatto had known. Therefore Embatto had not only known who the old man was whom Fallon had driven with to Kinnube, but also that their first move after arriving there would be to rendezvous with Haile Yolatta. And *that* seemed to Fallon to be the explanation of why he had been left free to roam the streets after his arrival: to lead Zugendan intelligence to the safe house that Velker had arranged—not only to locate Yolatta, but to find Barindas again as well after his vanishing act in the market-place. But only interrogation of Embatto after he was taken back to Kinnube would confirm it.

"So what was the story with Marie Guridan?" Fallon asked Parnum as they trudged to the top of the rocky slope outside the main caves. "Were you mixed up in it?"

Parnum shook his head. "Candy got her. That's really all I know, mate."

"Candy? How?"

"Honest, I don't know any more than you—it only happened this morning, and I've been up to my neck. We'll both have to get the story from Austin and Jimmy."

Fallon nodded. "How's it going in Kinnube?" Parnum asked.

"There are still people settling up scores and grudges," Fallon replied. "It'll be a few days before everything calms down." They turned and looked back over the valley. "So you finally got your scoop," Fallon went on. "What you always said you wanted to write: the Zugendan story from the inside, the way it really was. And none of the competition had any coverage. It all happened too fast."

Parnum stood taking in the scene as the news spread from the returning troops, tensions evaporated, and people scrambled out of the caves and down from the overlooking slopes to join in the spontaneous expression of relief and elation. "There's only one thing you never told me to complete the picture," he said. "When you organized the jail break back in Kinnube—who *was* the inside man?"

Fallon told him. It couldn't make any difference to anything that mattered, now that everything had worked out.

Parnum turned his head back and stared in astonishment. "You're joking!"

"Strange world, isn't it?" Fallon said.

Parnum shook his head incredulously as he absorbed the implications. "You, ah . . . you seem to believe in balancing on pretty thin edges," he said finally.

Fallon shrugged. "It wasn't so bad really. With the situation that developed, there was no way of telling from my behavior which side I was on. Anything I did was compatible with either possibility. So everyone saw what they wanted to."

Austin saw them together and came across, with the group he had been talking to gravitating behind. He seized one of Fallon's hands and clapped him on the shoulder, still high on the adrenaline charge from the fighting. "We did it, eh? I'm hearing all kinds of bits and pieces about you getting Embatto off the roof and stealing helicopters. Later you have to tell me the whole story."

"Make it when you've got plenty of time. It's a bit involved," Fallon said. "Things went okay down the valley?"

"Goddamn fuckin' light!" Sung Feng answered. "We fix 'em. Embatto mo'fuckahs brown to pieces aw over prace down veah. We fix 'em pletty damn good."

"I can't see 'ow anyone oonderstands a bloody word 'e says," Fallon overheard George muttering to Jimmy Reid.

"Embatto and the rest of the prisoners are being brought up," Austin said to Fallon. "Will you want to see him?"

Fallon shook his head. "Not really. There isn't anything to say. It's your country now, and he's your prisoner. My job's finished."

"I'd sure as hell like to see him," Parnum said. "The only journalist on the spot, with the prospect of an exclusive. What d'you reckon the chances are?"

"Well, he wasn't being too talkative the last time I saw him," Austin said. "But I guess it wouldn't hurt to give it a try. Let's see what we can do." He saw Fallon trying to catch his eye.

"Where's Candy?" Fallon inquired.

Austin inclined his head in the direction of the rear of the cave to indicate the chambers above the rockfall. "Up back."

"Is she okay?"

"She's fine. Go on through. I'll catch up in a few minutes."

While Austin was organizing a group to go with Parnum, Fallon and Reid began walking past the rows of hammocks, blanket rolls, and general accoutrements of billeted troops. Sam Letumbai went with them. On the way Jimmy Reid gave a brief account of what had happened. Not knowing whom he could trust after he received Fallon's message the previous evening, he had confided finally in Candy as the only person he was sure that the spy couldn't be—she would hardly have ended up as she had in Kinnube if she were. Candy had played it from there.

They found Candy with Imo in the quarters above the rockfall. She was in a calmly exhilarated mood, obviously freed from what had been a greater personal burden than anyone had realized. While the inevitable pot of water was being boiled for tea, she told her story again, in more detail.

"I should have guessed it long ago," Fallon said when she was through. "I thought it through on the flight down from Kinnube. It was staring us in the face all the time."

"How is that?" Candy asked.

"Guridan let it slip once when we were talking alone," Fallon said. "It was right outside here, down by the middle bridge across the gorge. She asked how anyone could betray the ZRF cause to a man like Embatto. But there was nothing then, as far as we knew, to single Embatto out, rather than Thombert, say, or Molokutu." Fallon snorted lightly. "I even picked her up on it at the time. . . . She came up with some answer or other, and I never thought any more of it."

Reid looked dubious. "That sounds a bit slim to me," he remarked.

"Oh, that wasn't the only thing, Jimmy. Much later than that—yesterday morning, in fact, after everything blew up in Kinnube—it seemed uncanny how perfectly everything seemed to have been set up. We asked ourselves if Thombert couldn't have been behind it. I couldn't see how. But we were right: it was set up. Only not by Thombert."

"Set up, how?" Candy asked. "How do you mean?"

"We were all like sitting ducks: me at a hotel; Sam and the ZRF's main base in Kinnube at an old foundry that Tannerling knew about; and Barindas and Yolatta in a place that the army went straight to as soon as they were both installed there. You were with us yesterday, Sam. You know how it all seemed just too quick and deliberate to be all coincidence."

Sam nodded, but at the same time he was looking puzzled. "Yeah, I hear. But it was Thombert who hit Sadie's. Now you seem like you're sayin' it was Embatto that tried to set it up. I'm not followin'."

"And how does it connect with Guridan?" Jimmy Reid asked, equally mystified.

"Think about it," Fallon said. "We all went into the city like rats walking into a trap. And that was exactly what we were supposed to do."

There was a strained silence for a few seconds. "You mean . . . Embatto *wanted* us to go to them places?" Sam Letumbai said uncertainly.

"Yes!" Fallon told them. "And he'd have mopped them all up in one swoop."

Candy shook her head. "You mean . . . ? Are you saying this was his whole plan all the way along, even from the time in London? That the talk about sending assassins into the ZRF was never serious? I can't believe that."

"Oh yes, that was serious to begin with," Fallon replied. "But as soon as I got involved with uncovering Tannerling—which Marie Guridan would obviously have reported back—Embatto knew that things weren't going to work out that way."

"That's right." Sam's eyes widened as the full realization dawned on him of just how far back they had been blown. "You musta been a marked man right then."

"I probably was," Fallon agreed. "But I don't make a habit of being as careless as brother Gustav was. . . . And then something else happened that forced Embatto to change his ideas: I figured out the side of it that we weren't supposed to know."

"You mean about him planning the coup?" Jimmy Reid said.

Fallon nodded. "And the first person I mentioned it to was Marie Guridan—in fact at the same time I mentioned a minute ago, when we were talking alone in the gorge. I didn't see it at the time, but it's clear now that she was stunned. But she reacted noncommittally."

"She would, until she'd reported back," Reid said.

"Right. And the reaction came a couple of days later, after we'd nailed Tannerling." Fallon looked around, inviting the others to recall the sequence of events at that time. He reminded them. "That was when Barindas called the council of war on where to go next, now that we thought we had the spy."

"That's right. When we came up with the idea of movin' everybody into Kinnube an' going for broke, while the army was movin' out," Sam Letumbai said, nodding as he remembered.

"Yes," Fallon said. "But not quite 'we.' *Who* was it that came up with that proposal?" He nodded to confirm the looks on their faces. "Marie Guridan! And we bought it. . . . Embatto knew that Trojan Horse wasn't going to happen, so he came up with an alternative plan which Guridan initiated for him: the ZRF and its leaders would go to him instead. With the ZRF compromised and my cover blown, the only thing he needed to know was the safe house where Velker had stashed Barindas and Yolatta, and he'd have cleaned the whole lot up on the first morning of the coup. The rest would have been a cinch."

Parnum was looking aghast. "The only thing that saved it for us was that Thombert had his own spies too, found the place first, and the whole thing exploded ten days earlier than Embatto meant it to," he said weakly.

"I'm not even sure he was going to give it ten days, Roger," Fallon said. "He had Thombert moving the army out already. Cobra Force was already down here."

"Christ . . . !" Reid breathed.

Sam Letumbai put a hand to his brow, still grappling to come to terms with it. "But the decoy operation at Boake Rift . . . Embatto went with it. He sent in that ground team up there, flew photo missions. . . . You mean he already knew we weren't settin' up any HQ here at Tenyasha? Why would he bother with all that?"

"Not *his* ground team," Fallon reminded him. "Thombert's. It was to fool Thombert and Molokutu. He had to play along with them too. I mean, let's give credit where it's due. Embatto had it all pretty well worked out. He came close... real close."

There was a long silence while the others sat back looking at each other. Gradually, each of them became aware of the full enormity of just how close a thing it had been. "Jesus...!" Sam exhaled shakily at last. It was enough to express the feelings of all of them.

Then Jimmy Reid said, addressing Fallon, "Okay, I think I can see what you're saying now. But there's just one more thing I'm curious about. That radio call of yours last night, when you told us it wasn't Tannerling; that there was another spy somewhere. What told you?"

"Embatto did," Fallon replied. "You see, when we picked him up off the SSHQ roof, he knew I wasn't with him, yet I was getting him out. He couldn't figure it—but in the mess he was in, he wasn't going to argue."

"SSHQ musta been bombed minutes after you got him out," Sam threw in.

Fallon nodded. "So he was curious, and he kept fishing. There's a whorehouse in Kinnube called Sadie's. Thombert's troops raided it at dawn, and Embatto guessed that had to be where Velker had hidden Barindas and Yolatta."

"And was it?" Candy asked.

"Yes. But Embatto had to know for sure—he realized that was where he'd come unstuck. So he tried to get it from me. He said Tannerling had told him that Barindas and Yolatta would be coming to Kinnube, and he asked me if Thombert had gone to Sadie's because that was where they were hiding." Fallon paused and cast an eye around the listening faces invitingly. But they were all too saturated with new revelations just at that moment to work out any more. "You see, sending Barindas and Yolatta into Kinnube was part of the *new* plan that Marie Guridan came up with.... But that was *after* we'd uncovered Tannerling. Tannerling couldn't have told Embatto anything about it. We were controlling everything that he sent."

By nightfall, the valley had become a scene of festivities. Bonfires burned on both sides of the gorge outside the main caves, turning the cliffs and rock buttresses into walls of flickering orange against the night; extra food was broken out from stockpiles; there was music and dancing, modern and traditional. After staying for a meal and the beginnings of the celebrations, Fallon, George, and Tam made the walk back to the upper valley to return to Kinnube that night. Since Sam and the ZRF officers who had accompanied them earlier would be staying at Tenyasha, there were some spare seats, which Parnum and Mamu, anxious to return to the city to complete the story, decided to take advantage of. Reid came too, along with Austin, who, now that Sam was on hand to take charge of things in Tenyasha, would be reporting to Barindas and Yolatta. Candy was with the group that came up to the landing strip to see them off.

They stood, looking at each other in the light from two lines of torch holders shuffling into position to illuminate the takeoff path, while behind them figures milled around the plane, exchanging last-minute words and instructions and heaving bags and packages on board. The motor was idling, drowning out the sounds from lower down the gorge.

"We have much to thank you for, Mr. Fugleman," she said.

"You never did get the hang of 'Boris,' did you?"

Candy's teeth flashed in a smile. "Suddenly there is no time, and there are so many things ... there is too much to say."

"Don't worry too much about it. It'll teach me not to talk to strange women in pubs. Look at the kind of trouble it gets you into."

"Oh, you will be talking to many strange people in different places, no doubt many women, and getting into lots more trouble before very much longer, I think," she replied. "You are not a kind of person who stays out of it for very long."

"Maybe. It seems to stick, all right.... What about you? It looks as if you're pretty well out of a job now. Had a chance to make any plans yet?"

"Oh, I don't know. There should be many opportunities in Kinnube. I think I like the city, maybe.... Who knows? Maybe if I get bored, I come to London and help you find some more trouble. The world has enough for two of us, yes?"

Fallon eyed her warily. "That might not be something

to joke about. But if you do show up there again, I'll buy you something better than a sandwich in a pub. I'll promise you that."

"And maybe I take you back to somewhere better after, too."

Fallon raised his eyebrows. "Is that a promise?"

Candy's eyes glittered impishly. "Fishing again? Always fishing, Mr. Fugleman."

George's voice bellowed from the open door of the aircraft. "Coom on. We're all waitin' ter be off in 'ere. A fine time ter pick for chattin' up t'bloody women is this. 'Ow long were you two 'ere before?"

Fallon shrugged. "I guess that's it." Candy held out a hand. He took it and gave it a squeeze. She leaned forward quickly and kissed him on both cheeks, then let go and stepped back to join the others gathered behind. Fallon stepped up into the doorway, turned to raise a hand, and somebody pulled the door shut behind him.

The plane turned to line up between the rows of torches, then halted for a moment. Its engine noise rose to a roar, and as the pilot released the brakes it began bumping away and gathering speed amid a ghostly cloud of dust. Moments later it lifted off, cleared the sides of the gorge, then climbed away, banking and turning onto a northerly course for Kinnube.

Chapter Fifty-seven

"LOOK, BERNIE, I KNOW THAT WRITERS HAVE TO
be allowed their bit of eccentricity—and especially British
writers," Jerry Doyland, literary agent for the author John
Clyde, said over the phone from New York. "But how
about trying to play the game a little, eh? I mean, all this
disappearing without a trace or a number where we could
get ahold of you.... Tom's really waiting for this book.
He's been getting worried."

"Oh, come on, Jerry," Fallon replied. "You also know
that inspiration requires some peace and quiet every now
and again, and a respite from people—especially Americans. Anyhow, I took it with me. Didn't Julia tell you?"

"Yes... What would we have done without Julia?
Sometimes I get the feeling that she knows more about the
book than you do."

Fallon winked across the office at Julia, who was
sitting in an easy chair just inside the steps leading down
from the library. The phone was on an amplifier so they
could both hear. "She does like to get involved," he agreed.

"Okay. So how much longer d'you figure we're talking
about?" Jerry asked.

Fallon looked inquiringly at Julia. She held up a
finger and silently mouthed, "One month."

"Could Tom live without it for another month?" Fallon
asked into the phone.

"I guess he'd go for that okay. Can I tell him it's
definite?"

Fallon looked at Julia. Julia nodded. "It's definite," he
said.

"Great. Well, I've got another call on hold, here. I'll
talk to you again when things ease up. Glad you're
back... And take care, eh?"

"You too, Jerry. We'll be in touch."

"'Bye."

Fallon hung up and lounged back in his chair. "I'll have to make some time today to find out what I've been up to," he said, noting the growing stack of manuscript pages on the shelf beside Julia's desk.

His stay in Kinnube had not been long. By the time he returned from Tenyasha, Colonel Marlow had vanished, erasing himself and the shadowy background involvement of Infinity Limited from the scene before the final picture that the world would see could stabilize. Taking his cue accordingly, Fallon had spent the following day concluding his farewells and tying up loose ends in Kinnube, and left Zugenda the day after, just behind George and Jimmy, who managed to get the last two seats of a flight out of Zaire, connecting via Cairo. Tam Czaryski left at about the same time to return directly to the States.

Fallon had arrived back in England the previous evening, exhausted not only by the journey but also by the pent-up effect of all that had happened. Nevertheless, he had kept Julia up until the early hours with his story over a bottle of cognac, and dawn had been showing when he finally crawled away to catch up on his sleep. Julia stayed in the guest suite, as she often did, rather than return to her own flat in Belgravia. Exhaustion finally caught up with him then, and he had only just got up.

"And the only other immediate thing," Julia said, checking her notes. "George called about two hours ago. He's with Jimmy and they're on their way ... but they're in Frankfurt."

"Frankfurt? What the hell are they doing in Frankfurt?"

"Oh, there was some kind of mix-up with the flights. He's not even sure yet what time they'll get in."

"What about Henri and his casting agency?"

"We think that Zugendan intelligence did get onto them—probably because of loose tongues at the European end somewhere. The Zugendans picked up the leads that somebody was putting together a hit team for something special and managed to track them back to Henri. He's back in France right now, but should be over again tomorrow or the next day. He's paying off the team."

"Hmmph. I bet that's some of the easiest money they've earned in a long time." Fallon stretched and stifled a yawn. "Okay, so what's Oscar been up to? I assume things are getting exciting."

"Of course. An honest politician surfaced who was going to blow the whole scam—"

"A what? Come on! I don't write science fiction."

"—but he got bumped off, naturally, so now we're into political assassination, blackmail, and mass brainwashing of the public."

Fallon rubbed his chin and nodded. "It sounds a promising mixture. Ah, does John Clyde have any plans on doing anything set in Africa, by any chance?"

"Strangely, I . . . do get the feeling that something like that might be on his list to do one day, yes."

Fallon grinned. He took a wad of pages off the pile and began turning through them curiously. "Hello, what's this? A kinky lesbian movie producer with a penchant for young starlets?"

Julia didn't respond, but continued staring at him, her chin resting lightly on a knuckle.

"Is this where the sex and violence comes in? I didn't know I had this in me."

"The parallel is quite uncanny when you think about it," Julia murmured absently.

Fallon realized that they were on different wavelengths. "What is?" he asked.

"The premise of the book, and what's happening in Africa . . . When you stand back and look at it from a distance."

Julia had become serious all of a sudden, Fallon saw. He set the pages aside. "How do you mean?"

"Well, in the book, there's a conspiracy between development interests and local government to create impoverished areas in the city, precisely so that they can be bought cheaply and exploited."

"Right. And Oscar discovers that . . ." Fallon's voice trailed away. He thought for a moment, then looked back at her. "There is, isn't there?"

Julia nodded. "And not just with Zugenda, but what's been happening to almost all of Africa for the last thirty years. We keep hearing the same lines over and over about how concerned everybody is, and all the public expressions of grief. But verbiage aside, what's the reality?" She tossed out a hand lightly. "You talked about it yourself last night. Financial policies imposed from the outside after the country has been reduced to total dependency by ruinous debts, which stifle investment and destroy initiative; obsessive state intervention in the economy to a degree that even the brain-dead could see has proved disastrous wherever it's been tried; government-to-government aid programs which subsidize incompetent regimes that would have fallen apart long ago if the needs of the people had anything to do with it. . . . And yet, as Barindas told you himself, Africa could be a net exporter of food on a huge scale. And it's got the potential to earn the capital to invest—I checked some figures this morning. Over half the world's gold used to come from there; forty-six percent of its chromium; sixty percent of its manganese and diamonds . . . all with just eight percent of the population. What does all that say to you?"

"It *is* like the book," Fallon agreed in a distant voice. "The city is where the money's made."

"In the quarter century after 1950, the average world food production went up by over twenty percent," Julia said. "And that's per head: in other words, allowing for the population increase, so forget about all the Malthusian nonsense that the media pump out. But there was one glaring exception, where output and incomes actually declined."

"Africa?"

Julia nodded again. "Africa . . . where the political systems just about everywhere seem designed to make things worse and not better."

Fallon sat back as he registered fully what Julia was saying. "It's like in the book. Everything's being devalued. Economies are in shambles. Entire areas are being depopulated."

"Well, you can't send in the cavalry to exterminate the Indians these days. So you get their own governments to do it for you. . . . It would be an explanation that's consistent with their actions, wouldn't it?" Julia swiveled her chair back toward the keyboard and resumed tapping in an aide-mémoire that she had been working on.

"They've been staking out their property rights for the big carve-up," Fallon mused finally. "Both sides playing the same game . . ." He stood up and walked over to the window to stare out at the hodgepodge of piled-up architecture, spreading trees, and overgrown shrubbery that formed the vista of Kelso Close.

"That's what it's all about, isn't it?" he said. "Infinity Limited. Marlow said that it's international . . . beyond ideologies and creeds." He turned from the window to find Julia watching him, as if she had been waiting for him to reach that conclusion.

"It's you," she said simply. "It's what you've been trying to do all the time, in your own way. That's why they approached you. I've a suspicion that we might be dealing in a different league before very much longer, Bernard. You said a moment ago, Infinity Limited doesn't waste its time on the errand boys who can be replaced. It goes for the instigators behind it all."

Fallon gave a resigned snort. "Well, I don't know what they're going to do about them in this instance. From what the colonel said, Lichuru's vanished, and the line they were following got cut dead in Florida."

"Not quite," Julia said after a moment's thought.

"What do you mean?"

"There's still one person who can lead them back to Pyramid."

"Who?"

"Embatto himself."

Fallon frowned. "But he's . . ." His voice trailed off as he saw what she was getting at. "They wouldn't."

Julia shrugged. "It would be a return for a price. . . . And when you think about it, what would the price be, really? Embatto's more use to Infinity Limited now than he is to the consortium. In fact, as far as the consortium's concerned, he's more of a liability. He knows too much. So the only price would be to miss delivering a little justice where it's due. . . . But then, revenge isn't really Barindas's style. I don't think it's Infinity Limited's either." Julia turned back to her keyboard.

Fallon came back across the room and stood watching over her shoulder. Whatever happened, it was out of their hands now. "So, do you think we'll be saying good-bye to our old clientele?" he said in a tone of mock disappointment. "No more Aniello Franginis?"

"There are enough pest exterminators in the business to take care of them."

"Maybe I'd better order some new suits."

"They'd probably be more appropriate than jungle camouflage," Julia said.

Fallon went over to the doorway. "Fancy a cup of tea?"

"Mmm, please."

"I'll put on the kettle." He turned away and disappeared through the library toward the stairs leading down at the back of the house.

"What are your plans for today?" Julia called after him.

"I'm not sure yet. I think for a start I might go for a stroll and eat breakfast out. It'll be nice to walk down the street without having to worry about being followed or shot at for a change. I think I'll just be Bernard Fallon again for a while."

In the office, Julia closed the folder containing the documentation on the now defunct identity of Konrad Hannegen and put it in a tray for filing later.

"'Allo, Mr. Fallon. 'Aven't seen yer fer a while."

"Hello, Bob. No, I was abroad for a bit. Just got back last night."

"Business, was it, or takin' it easy for a spell?"

"In my line you can't tell the difference.... Just the paper today, please." Fallon took a copy of the *Times* from a rack.

"Book goin' all right, is it?"

"Oh, give it about another month."

"Thirty pence, please... Thank you. Don't let it get you down too much."

"I only believe the ads."

"Ar, I remember. A good un, that. Good day, Mr. Fallon."

"See you, Bob."

Outside the shop, Fallon stopped and unfolded the paper to scan the front page. For months there had been nothing to report from Zugenda except routine military operations and human tragedies of the kind that readers and viewers had long grown bored with. So when something did finally happen, suddenly and unexpectedly, most of the media had been caught with nobody on the spot, and the initial stories flashed around the world had been garbled mixtures of rumor, speculation, and second- or thirdhand accounts picked up in the capitals of adjoining nations. In the last few days, press and TV correspondents had been flooding into the country and the stories being sent out were beginning to show a closer connection to reality. In the process, the headlines had shrunk, and the subject had been relegated to the lower right-hand side. BARINDAS ASSUMES POWER IN BOMB-TORN KINNUBE was the head. Below it, Fallon read:

Following the elimination of the nation's president and other political rivals in an outbreak of violence that included tank battles and bombing attacks on the city center by Soviet-supplied MiG-19 jets, Jovay Barindas, leader of the Zugendan Republican Front guerrillas, was proclaimed head of state in a communiqué issued from Kinnube today. According to a spokesman for the new regime, the position is provisional, pending the result of elections to be held within a month. Although willing to go through the motions, the new strongman in Zugenda is openly sceptical of the democratic process. "Votes should be weighed, not counted," sixty-year-old, gray-bearded Barindas remarked at a press conference yesterday. "The problem is deciding who should do the weighing."

As the dust settles after a short but fierce period of fighting that involved units of the Zugendan army and state-security forces engaging each other as well as the ZRF, analysts are divided in their opinions on the kind of regime that should be expected to emerge, and its likely political leanings. Barindas has been a persistent critic of the doctrinaire Marxist policies of his predecessor, Aloysius Molokutu. At the same time, he spurns Western aid programs for economically devastated and drought-plagued Zugenda as "irrelevant." In the eight-year campaign which has brought it from bush guerrilla warfare to the new ruling force in Zugenda, the ZRF has been accused of employing terrorist methods in a systematic policy of political intimidation. So far, official recognition of the Barindas regime has not been forthcoming.

To be expected, Fallon supposed, sighing to himself. He read on.

It is also confirmed that along with former President Molokutu, General Naguib Thombert, commander-in-chief of the Zugendan armed forces, was also killed in the early days of the fighting. Julius Embatto, former head of the state-security apparatus, is reported to have been captured in further fighting south of the capital and imprisoned along with numerous other officials of the previous regime.

[The full text of Barindas's proclamation is given with a special report on Page 6.]

Just another takeover by terrorist-gangsters in a place few people had heard of, where things like that were accepted as the everyday norm, was Fallon's reading of what the public would see. The conditioning for the next attempt—against Barindas this time—was beginning already. One of the errand boys was gone; the instigators were still in business. He stuffed the newspaper into his pocket and stalked away, so disgruntled just for the moment that he failed to notice Audrey starting to smile in recognition as she approached on the far side of the street.

He headed north toward the High Street and then east in the direction of Kensington Road, stopping for a coffee at an Italian restaurant and spending a quarter of an hour relaxing with the crossword. By the time he came back out he was feeling more resigned to the situation. He continued eastward, enjoying the sights of people, the traffic, and the greenery beyond the Royal Garden Hotel. It was always good to be back.

He crossed the main road at Hyde Park Gate and continued along it until he was opposite the squat, red-stone rotundity of the Albert Hall, where he entered Kensington Gardens. Some boys were playing a noisy game of soccer; couples strolled arm in arm; a businessman taking time out lay on the grass, soaking up the sun, his face hidden under a folded newspaper. Overhead, a jet descended westward on its approach to Heathrow. Zugenda was suddenly far, far away.

At the Serpentine lake he followed the bank left toward Bayswater, slowing his pace to watch the ducks bobbing and dipping in the shallows and two swans gliding like windjammers farther out near the center. He came to the Peter Pan statue and sat down on an empty bench facing the water. A woman at another bench farther along was tossing bread to the ducks and talking to her spaniel, which sat humoring her obligingly. Farther along, a nanny cautioned a toddler against going too close to the edge. A pigeon strutted past Fallon's feet, pouting self-importantly. It was all part of a scene that he had known since his childhood days, but he never grew tired of it. There was no reason that he could think of why a Londoner would want to live anywhere else. He wondered if the people of places like Zugenda would one day be able to sit in parks in the centers of their own cities with the same feeling of security and contentment. Wasn't that what Barindas's revolution was all about?

He opened the newspaper to the crossword again and studied it idly. "Mainly fearless?" was the clue for 10 Across. Starting with a "D," and then an "N" about halfway along. "Main" could be a hint of a maritime connection, Fallon thought.... "Dreadnought" perhaps? He decided it was, and took his pen from his pocket. As he began entering the letters, a shadow fell across the bench from behind him.

"Out for a breath of air, I see, Bernard. A splendid day for it too. I'm glad to see that you made it back in one piece." Fallon looked up over his shoulder. Colonel Marlow came around the bench and sat down next to him. He was back in his bowler and, despite the weather, still carrying a rolled umbrella.

"I was wondering when you'd turn up," Fallon said.

"Well, time and tide, and all that ... I must congratulate you on an excellent show of initiative in very trying circumstances. The organization was very impressed."

"I'm glad to hear it." Fallon glanced sideways. "And did everything else work out ... satisfactorily?"

"Yes, pretty much," the colonel replied breezily. "Zugenda is in better hands now, and on its way to a brighter future. The press allowed its prejudices to get a bit tangled up with the facts, but that's to be expected, of course."

Fallon nodded and stared back across the lake. "You know, the part where you really had me fooled was having Leroy there all the time like that. He played it perfectly."

The colonel sighed. "It's a shame to have to deceive one's own side sometimes. But routine security ... I know that you appreciate the necessity of these things. He's a good man."

"I suppose he's back in the States by now?"

"He will be very soon, anyway. He had to stay on for a few days. There was one last job we needed him for."

" 'We'—meaning the new firm?"

"Of course."

Fallon thought back over what Julia had said that morning. "Corrupt governments aren't the real targets in all this, are they?" he said. "You're aiming at something behind them."

Marlow nodded. "We suspect that most government in the world today is merely a tool that controls people on behalf of less visible interests, yes. And ultimately, those are what we are concerned with. One of their primary aims at the present time is to reduce global competition by retarding the industrialization of the Third World—which is the only thing that can ultimately help places like Zugenda. Imagine the effects of another ten Japans on the planet. But in the long run they won't prevail."

"You never did explain why it's called Infinity Limited," Fallon said. "Is that what we're getting to now?"

The colonel nodded again. "Mankind is essentially a creative, productive being. That's what has elevated us from the level of the animal to where we are now. But that's only the start of it." He made a sweeping motion in the air. "Our scientist friends tell us that matter and energy are the same thing, and there's a universe out there that goes on forever. There's no end to how far we can go when we get off this planet, to how much we can accomplish, or to what we can become. But only a society of individuals who are free to create and discover will be able to unlock that potential. Any other course will lead to self-fulfillment of the doom prophecies that you hear every day. But we believe it can, and will, be done. Our species has a glorious future someday... I don't know, somewhere out there among the stars, which very probably neither you nor I are capable of imagining. But *all* repression of human freedom, whether to impose a god, preserve a social order, advance an ideology, or monopolize a market, is ultimately an impediment to realizing that destiny.... And *that* is why we oppose it."

The colonel gave Fallon a keen look. "Why are you interested? Should I take it that you've had a chance to consider our proposition?" He looked across, then realized that Fallon had been staring fixedly at him while he was speaking. Fallon had suddenly realized what the colonel's earlier remark had meant.

"When you were talking about Leroy... What kind of 'one last job' did you need him for?" he asked suspiciously. The colonel said nothing, but sat staring back with an expression that said Fallon should be capable of working it out for himself. "It's Embatto, isn't it?" Fallon said. "You're going to spring him."

Marlow didn't insult his intelligence by denying it. "He's the only link to Pyramid that we've got left. If we want this whole thing to have been for anything at all and not to end with the small fry, we have to give it a try."

"Is Barindas in on it?"

"Of course... And he agrees."

"So what happens if you do get to them?"

"I'm not sure yet. I suppose it depends on exactly who they turn out to be and what the options are. One thing at a time."

Fallon stared hard for a few seconds, then exhaled sharply with a grin. "Does that mean I might get another crack at him one day, then?"

"Aha! Does that mean that you accept?"

"I think you already know the answer to that."

"Splendid, my dear chap! I'm delighted to hear it. As to your question, we can only wait to see what the future brings. But either way, I can guarantee plenty to keep you busy." The colonel consulted his watch. "But as for now, I must be on my way. Welcome to the club, and all that. You'll be hearing from us shortly." He stood up. Fallon did likewise, pocketing his newspaper. They shook hands. Then the colonel turned and marched briskly away in the direction of Lancaster Gate, tapping the ground with his umbrella in time with his stride.

Fallon stood and watched until the figure vanished among the strollers and office workers taking their lunch-time break beneath the trees by the fountains at the end of the lake. Then he turned and began walking slowly back the way he had come.

He would eat breakfast, he decided, in the Royal Garden coffee shop. And tonight, maybe take Julia out for a good dinner somewhere in town.

There would be a lot for them to talk about.

Epilogue

JULIUS EMBATTO HELD A MATCH TO THE CIGA-
rette, drew it to a glow, and exhaled the smoke distastefully.
There was no supply of his personalized brand with the
gold monogram. He had been left a couple of packs of a
cheap French brand to go with the coarse coffee and plain
food. When he complained about the soup, the guard had
spat in it and said it was better than anything that anyone
here had ever seen when Embatto was it charge of things.
Nobody would have dared speak to him like that when
Sullivan was around. The feeling of vulnerability that came
from not having a protector constantly at hand was difficult
to get used to.

He got up from the chair and paced across to the
window of the cell. It was late into the evening already,
and rain was falling steadily. As he stared up into the dark
sky above Kinnube's jail, his mind went back bitterly again
to the final events of those dreadful two days, more than a
week ago now. He had been informed of Molokutu's and
Thombert's deaths, but what satisfaction he derived from
the knowledge was overwhelmed by the realization of how
completely Fugleman had anticipated his actions. For the
crowning irony was that it had been the rising en masse of
the people and the army's defection to Barindas that had
proved decisive, rather than any military prowess on the
part of the ZRF; and it had been Embatto himself—in
ordering the helicopter strikes—who had brought those
things about.

He had been lured into creating the vacuum for
Barindas to step into. As for the events that had led up to
that, he was still unable to account for the surprise attack
by Molokutu and the army. Clearly they had been forewarned
of his intended coup. The only explanation was treachery,
but exactly who had betrayed what to whom, Embatto

hadn't been able to unravel. All Barindas had needed to do was sit back and allow the two major focuses of power in the state to neutralize each other. After that, everything had fallen into his lap.

Embatto could see now how he had been tricked into complicity in the jail break. Was it possible, he asked himself, that Fugleman had been working all along for some organization that Embatto had never suspected, who had engineered precisely the situation that had now come to pass? But try as he would, he couldn't see how. The entire plan had been revised when Marie Guridan—otherwise known as Kestrel—reported from Tenyasha that Fugleman had deduced his true intentions. It was inconceivable that anyone before then could have predicted the course that events would follow. But then he remembered the intruders who had gotten inside Djamvelling and the mysterious American helicopter pilot that Fugleman had appeared with—all pointing to connections that Embatto's intelligence operation had never even suspected. He didn't know who or what might have been behind it all. Now he probably never would.

Keys rattled in the lock. Embatto turned and looked at the door. A guard opened it, and Barindas came in. He was wearing the plain and comfortable native style of baggy trousers with loose shirt and jacket—more African than European, but at the same time without the ostentatiousness that would have made a political message out of it. The guard remained outside and pushed the door to without locking it.

Embatto sat back down on the wooden chair rather than be seen to concede anything by remaining standing. Barindas didn't look very conscious of any role as the triumphant conqueror. All the same, Embatto said sourly, "I assume you've come to gloat over your imagined achievement. Go ahead if it pleases you. But the pleasure will be short-lived. That rabble will turn on you as they turned on me, like the idiot children that they are—as soon as you fail to satisfy their whim of the moment. But *you* will never have the strength to resist them or the will to control them. So you will be swept away." Embatto made a throwing-away motion in the air. "*Poof!* Nothing . . . A piece of chaff in the wind."

Barindas looked back at him with an expression that

contained no reaction to the provocation; rather, it seemed to express resignation to a gulf that was unbridgeable. "That's the way you think of the people, isn't it?" he said. "A rabble, without rights, or dignity, or feelings . . . Just a resource to be exploited. To be bled dry."

Embatto raised his chin defiantly. "And that's what they are: the source of wealth and power for those who possess the wit and the ability to channel that potential to a worthwhile end."

"You consider *that* a worthwhile end?"

Embatto pulled the face of someone whose patience is being strained. "What other end is there? Life is too short and brutal not to look out for oneself. If you've come here to lecture me on the errors of my ways, save your breath."

Barindas sat down on the edge of the cot. "No, I accept that we speak different languages. And what you choose to believe isn't of as much concern to me as you seem to think."

Embatto cupped an elbow in the other hand, rested his chin on his fingers, and looked across the room with a different expression on his face. "You know, Barindas, I could almost admire you for being what you have become: the winner, who holds what we all played for. But now you'll throw it all away because of your daydreams. How can such ability coexist with such foolishness? It mystifies me."

"You don't seem to realize, we're not playing the same game."

"Aren't we? Don't tell me that you don't want anything for yourself out of all this."

"Of course I do. All human actions are motivated ultimately by selfishness. I want to see the kind of society that I believe in, and to derive enjoyment and comfort from it. I agree that our goals are the same. I simply have different notions about how best to achieve them."

"You'll find that nothing you try to impose will suit everyone," Embatto retorted. "And then the only way to achieve conformity will be through force. Once that happens, all the apparatus necessary to compel cooperation and suppress dissent will follow." He laughed humorlessly. "Don't get rid of me too hastily. You mightn't find a qualified replacement so soon."

Barindas was already shaking his head. "That's what

you can't comprehend: the notion of not *imposing* anything. Why insist on conformity to anybody's way? Let people *choose* their own, as individuals. A system that protects their right to determine their own lives will get more support than one which denies them any. Isn't that obvious?"

Embatto looked at him contemptuously. "And what kind of society will emerge from that?"

"I have no idea. Let it evolve, and we'll see."

"And if the people choose to remove you, you would let them?"

Barindas shrugged. "If that became the case, I don't think anything I did would make much difference in the long run. You tried stopping them with tanks and bombs, and look where it got you. Violence and deceit are self-defeating in the end. The aggressors always end up being buried by their intended victims. The Nazis are history, but the Jewish people are still with us. The British and the French are gone, and we have prevailed. . . . Molokutu and Thombert are dead and you are in here, while outside the Zugendan people are about to rebuild their country. Western Christian culture declined because its morality was based on myth. . . . And the new socialist religions will fail because they depend on force. In the end the only workable kind of system is one that recognizes freedom and builds its ethic on the sovereignty of the individual."

Embatto looked away. "Don't weary me with academic speculations. I only understand practicalities."

"Of course," Barindas agreed. He thought for a moment, then sat forward on the cot, his hands planted palms-downward on his thighs. "But it wasn't just an attempt to satisfy your own personal ambitions, was it?" he said. "We know that you were financed and backed by powerful and remote interests." Embatto shifted his weight uncomfortably, but said nothing. Barindas went on: "Lichuru was your link to them. Who were they?"

Embatto snorted. "Why should I help you?"

Barindas sat, staring at him in silence for a while. Finally he slapped his thighs lightly in a gesture of futility and stood up. "You are right. Perhaps in some ways I am naive. I was naive enough to hope that maybe something of what I said might have got through . . . but of course, that cannot be."

"Aren't you going to try the rubber truncheons and the electric shock treatment?" Embatto asked in a tone that was openly taunting.

Ignoring the remark, Barindas walked over to the door and tapped lightly. The guard opened it from outside. As he was leaving, Barindas turned in the doorway and gestured widely, indicating the prison in general. "Oh, by the way, we shall be dispensing with this establishment. You will be transferred to another facility later on tonight. Collect together anything that you wish to take."

"Don't you think you'll have any criminals to worry about in this utopia of yours?" Embatto asked derisively.

"Oh, of course there will be delinquents. And they will be dealt with appropriately," Barindas said. "But this place has too many undesirable associations to remain as a place of detention. One suggestion is that it be converted into an orphanage. Some would demolish it completely. But it isn't the kind of monument that we would wish to preserve."

Barindas left the cell, and the door clanged shut behind him.

A lieutenant, now of the army commanded by Haile Yolatta, arrived a little over an hour later, accompanied by six guards. One of them picked up Embatto's bag, and the party proceeded down to the main yard of the prison, where a staff car and jeep were waiting. Nothing was said. Embatto was ushered into the rear seat of the car, the lieutenant climbed into the jeep, and the guards distributed themselves between both. The two vehicles moved out into the main street of Kinnube. Although scarred from the fighting, the city was still permeated by an atmosphere of celebration made all the more intense by the coming of the rains that had coincided with its liberation. There were many people about, laughing and smiling despite the downpour, a lot of music coming from the houses.

The two vehicles drove north, out of the city, past several villages already asleep, and on to where there was only hills and the night. For the first time, Embatto grew apprehensive. "How far are we going?" he asked uneasily. The guards didn't answer.

And then the car slowed into a bend dark in the shadow of a grove of trees. Suddenly headlights came on from a stationary vehicle that had been waiting there, blocking the road. The staff car and its escort stopped, and another vehicle swung into the road behind them. Dazzled, Embatto made out the shapes of armed figures coming forward on both sides, silhouetted in the rain against the glare.

The door opened and he was forced out. While several men in dark hoods held the lieutenant and the soldiers back at gunpoint, others steered Embatto to another car parked in the shadows. Four men got in with him, two in the front and one either side of him. They seemed sinister, all in dark clothing and with hats pulled low. "Who are you?" Embatto demanded. They didn't answer. The car moved off into the night.

Beside Embatto, Leroy had decided that the best way to be sure of not saying the wrong thing was to say nothing. The day after Embatto's capture at Tenyasha, a ZRF patrol to the south had observed his former bodyguard, making his way in the direction of the border. It had been Marlow's idea for Leroy to fly down there and intercept him—Leroy had operated successfully under cover in Kinnube all the way through, and there was nothing to connect him with Fugleman, Barindas, the ZRF, or anything else. In other words, he could have been an undercover agent for anybody.

After about twenty minutes, the car pulled off the road. The going became bumpy for some distance, then the car halted. Only then did Leroy speak. "All right. This is as far as we go." Turning his head toward Embatto a fraction, he murmured, "I'm from Pyramid. They had an additional cover on their investment. We're getting you away." Then before Embatto could reply, the two with him in the back got out, as did the one beside the driver. Embatto followed. The driver remained seated.

They were on a gravelly shoulder by a muddy track. One of the three turned and led the way down through some bush and thorn, indistinct in the rain and the darkness. Embatto stumbled behind, slipping into puddles and a small torrent flowing down the rutted center of the track, and the other two followed. Then the American said, "Okay, this'll do," and reached into his pocket. Sudden doubts assailed Embatto, and he found himself shaking uncontrollably.

But what the American drew out was a flashlight. He

aimed it back in the direction where the car was parked, and sent three quick flashes. The car's headlights came on, illuminating flat, open ground. Moments later, the roar of an engine starting up came from nearby, and a light, single-engine airplane taxied into the beams with the rain slicing through them, and turned about. Someone inside threw the door open. Embatto stared uncertainly at the three men. One of them handed him his bag from the prison and waved curtly in the direction of the aircraft. Embatto turned away from them and walked woodenly forward across the sodden grass, with fear surging inside him again now and half expecting to feel bullets thudding into his back. But nothing happened, and within minutes he was airborne and climbing into the African night.

Only when they broke out through the cloud cover and into the moonlight above did he recognize the immense, square-shouldered form squeezed in the seat in front next to the pilot. Relief surged through him finally, then. He looked out at the silver tops of the clouds falling farther below in the night and tried to puzzle out in his mind what it all meant. Slowly it registered on him that for escorts, the soldiers from the jail had shown remarkably little inclination to resist.... And there had been something phony about the act in the car too. Then the pieces came together, and he laughed out loud in the shadows at the back of the cabin.

"I think I can guess what happened," he said to Sullivan. "Somebody approached you with an offer to get me out. Am I right? He claimed he was from Pyramid.... Do you know what it means? It means that they hope I'll lead them back.... Ha-ha-ha! The fools! You think they'd be able to come up with something original, wouldn't you? That's twice now that they've tried that ruse. The American helicopter pilot gave me the same story. He tried to tell me that Pyramid had somebody else here all the time that I didn't know about. Can you imagine anything—" Embatto stopped abruptly as Sullivan turned in his seat, and moonlight glinted off the barrel of the automatic in his hand.

"They did," Sullivan said, and shot Embatto through the middle of the forehead.

Sullivan turned the gun in toward the pilot. "Never

mind the directions you were given. Just do what I tell you."

The pilot raised a hand briefly and forced a tone of matter-of-fact acquiescence. "Sure thing, boss. Whatever you say. I just fly the plane."

"Come 'round onto course three-three-zero. Stay at eight thousand feet. Set your nav to twenty point six. We rendezvous with another plane at a strip about two hours from here. There'll be a top-up of gas waiting for you there, and then you'll be free to go...."

ABOUT THE AUTHOR

Born in London in 1941, James P. Hogan worked as an aeronautical engineer specializing in electronics and for several major computer firms before turning to writing full-time in 1979. Winner of the Prometheus Award, he has won wide popularity and high praise for his novels with their blend of gripping storytelling, intriguing scientific concepts, and convincing speculation. Mr. Hogan currently makes his home with his family in Ireland, where he is finishing his latest novel.

THRILLERS

Gripping suspense...explosive action...dynamic characters...international settings...these are the elements that make for great thrillers. Books guaranteed to keep you riveted to your seat.

Robert Ludlum:

☐	26256	THE AQUITAINE PROGRESSION	$5.95
☐	26011	THE BOURNE IDENTITY	$5.95
☐	26322	THE BOURNE SUPREMACY	$5.95
☐	26094	THE CHANCELLOR MANUSCRIPT	$5.95
☐	28209	THE GEMINI CONTENDERS	$5.95
☐	26019	THE HOLCROFT COVENANT	$5.95
☐	27800	THE ICARUS AGENDA	$5.95
☐	25899	THE MATERESE CIRCLE	$5.95
☐	27960	THE MATLOCK PAPER	$5.95
☐	26430	THE OSTERMAN WEEKEND	$5.95
☐	25270	THE PARSIFAL MOSAIC	$5.95
☐	28063	THE RHINEMANN EXCHANGE	$5.95
☐	27109	THE ROAD TO GANDOLOFO	$5.95
☐	27146	THE SCARLATTI INHERITANCE	$5.95
☐	28179	TREVAYNE	$5.95

Frederick Forsyth:

☐	28393	THE NEGOTIATOR	$5.95
☐	26630	DAY OF THE JACKAL	$5.95
☐	26490	THE DEVIL'S ALTERNATIE	$5.95
☐	26846	THE DOGS OF WAR	$5.95
☐	25113	THE FOURTH PROTOCOL	$5.95
☐	27673	NO COMEBACKS	$5.95
☐	27198	THE ODESSA FILE	$5.95

Buy them at your local bookstore or use this page to order.

Bantam Books, Dept. TH, 414 East Golf Road, Des Plaines, IL 60016

Please send me the items I have checked above. I am enclosing $_____ (please add $2.00 to cover postage and handling). Send check or money order, no cash or C.O.D.s please.

Mr/Ms _____

Address _____

City/State _____ Zip _____

TH–11/90

Please allow four to six weeks for delivery.
Prices and availability subject to change without notice.